ALICE C

DEATH FRAN

ALICE Campbell (1887-1955) came originally from Atlanta, Georgia, where she was part of the socially prominent Ormond family. She moved to New York City at the age of nineteen and quickly became a socialist and women's suffragist. Later she moved to Paris, marrying the American-born artist and writer James Lawrence Campbell, with whom she had a son in 1914.

Just before World War One, the family left France for England, where the couple had two more children, a son and a daughter. Campbell wrote crime fiction until 1950, though many of her novels continued to have French settings. She published her first work (*Juggernaut*) in 1928. She wrote nineteen detective novels during her career.

MYSTERIES BY ALICE CAMPBELL

ALICE CAMPBELL

DEATH FRAMED IN SILVER

With an introduction
by Curtis Evans

DEAN STREET PRESS

Published by Dean Street Press 2022

Copyright © 1937 Alice Campbell

Introduction copyright © 2022 Curtis Evans

First published in 1937 by W. Collins & Sons

Cover by DSP

ISBN 978 1 915393 00 5

www.deanstreetpress.co.uk

ALICE IN MURDERLAND

CRIME WRITER ALICE CAMPBELL, THE OTHER "AC"

IN 1927 Alice Dorothy Ormond Campbell—a thirty-nine-year-old native of Atlanta, Georgia who for the last fifteen years had lived successively in New York, Paris and London, never once returning to the so-called Empire City of the South, published her first novel, an unstoppable crime thriller called *Juggernaut*, selling the serialization rights to the *Chicago Tribune* for $4000 ($60,000 today), a tremendous sum for a brand new author. On its publication in January 1928, both the book and its author caught the keen eye of Bessie S. Stafford, society page editor of the *Atlanta Constitution*. Back when Alice Ormond, as she was then known, lived in Atlanta, Miss Bessie breathlessly informed her readers, she had been "an ethereal blonde-like type of beauty, extremely popular, and always thought she was in love with somebody. She took high honors in school; and her gentleness of manner and breeding bespoke an aristocratic lineage. She grew to a charming womanhood—"

Let us stop Miss Bessie right there, because there is rather more to the story of Alice Campbell, the mystery genre's other "AC," who published nineteen crime novels between 1928 and 1950. Allow me to plunge boldly forward with the tale of Atlanta's great Golden Age crime writer, who as an American expatriate in England, went on to achieve fame and fortune as an atmospheric writer of murder and mystery and become one of the early members of the Detection Club.

Alice Campbell's lineage was distinguished. Alice was born in Atlanta on November 29, 1887, the youngest of the four surviving children of prominent Atlantans James Ormond IV and Florence Root. Both of Alice's grandfathers had been wealthy Atlanta merchants who settled in the city in the years before the American Civil War. Alice's uncles, John Wellborn Root and Walter Clark Root, were noted architects, while her brothers, Sidney James and Walter Emanuel Ormond, were respectively a drama critic and political writer for the *Atlanta Constitution* and an attorney and justice of the peace. Both brothers died untimely deaths before Alice had even turned thirty, as did her uncle John Wellborn Root and her father.

Alice precociously published her first piece of fiction, a fairy story, in the *Atlanta Constitution* in 1897, when she was nine years old. Four years later, the ambitious child was said to be in the final stage of completing a two-volume novel. In 1907, by which time she was nineteen, Alice relocated to New York City, chaperoned by Florence.

In New York Alice became friends with writers Inez Haynes Irwin, a prominent feminist, and Jacques Futrelle, the creator of "The Thinking Machine" detective who was soon to go down with the ship on RMS *Titanic,* and scored her first published short story in *Ladies Home Journal* in 1911. Simultaneously she threw herself pell-mell into the causes of women's suffrage and equal pay for equal work. The same year she herself became engaged, but this was soon broken off and in February 1913 Alice sailed to Paris with her mother to further her cultural education.

Three months later in Paris, on May 22, 1913, twenty-five-year-old Alice married James Lawrence Campbell, a twenty-four-year-old theatrical agent of good looks and good family from Virginia. Jamie, as he was known, had arrived in Paris a couple of years earlier, after a failed stint in New York City as an actor. In Paris he served, more successfully, as an agent for prominent New York play brokers Arch and Edgar Selwyn.

After the wedding Alice Ormond Campbell, as she now was known, remained in Paris with her husband Jamie until hostilities between France and Germany loomed the next year. At this point the couple prudently relocated to England, along with their newborn son, James Lawrence Campbell, Jr., a future artist and critic. After the war the Campbells, living in London, bought an attractive house in St. John's Wood, London, where they established a literary and theatrical salon. There Alice oversaw the raising of the couple's two sons, Lawrence and Robert, and their daughter, named Chita Florence Ormond ("Ormond" for short), while Jamie spent much of his time abroad, brokering play productions in Paris, New York and other cities.

Like Alice, Jamie harbored dreams of personal literary accomplishment; and in 1927 he published a novel entitled *Face Value,* which for a brief time became that much-prized thing by publishers, a putatively "scandalous" novel that gets Talked About. The story of a gentle orphan boy named Serge, the son an emigre Russian prostitute, who grows up in a Parisian "disorderly house," as reviews often blushingly put it, *Face Value* divided critics, but ended up on American bestseller lists. The success of his first novel led to the author being invited out to Hollywood to work as a scriptwriter, and his name appears on credits to a trio of films in 1927-28, including *French Dressing,* a "gay" divorce comedy set among sexually scatterbrained Americans in Paris. One wonders whether in Hollywood Jamie ever came across future crime writer Cornell Woolrich, who was scripting there too at the time.

Alice remained in England with the children, enjoying her own literary splash with her debut thriller *Juggernaut*, which concerned the murderous machinations of an inexorably ruthless French Riviera society doctor, opposed by a valiant young nurse. The novel racked up rave reviews and sales in the UK and US, in the latter country spurred on by its nationwide newspaper serialization, which promised readers

> . . . the open door to adventure! *Juggernaut* by Alice Campbell will sweep you out of the humdrum of everyday life into the gay, swift-moving Arabian-nights existence of the Riviera!

London's *Daily Mail* declared that the irresistible *Juggernaut* "should rank among the 'best sellers' of the year"; and, sure enough, *Juggernaut*'s English publisher, Hodder & Stoughton, boasted, several months after the novel's English publication in July 1928, that they already had run through six printings in an attempt to satisfy customer demand. In 1936 *Juggernaut* was adapted in England as a film vehicle for horror great Boris Karloff, making it the only Alice Campbell novel filmed to date. The film was remade in England under the title *The Temptress* in 1949.

Water Weed (1929) and *Spiderweb* (1930) (*Murder in Paris* in the US), the immediate successors, held up well to their predecessor's performance. Alice chose this moment to return for a fortnight to Atlanta, ostensibly to visit her sister, but doubtlessly in part to parade through her hometown as a conquering, albeit commercial, literary hero. And who was there to welcome Alice in the pages of the *Constitution* but Bessie S. Stafford, who pronounced Alice's hair still looked like spun gold while her eyes remarkably had turned an even deeper shade of blue. To Miss Bessie, Alice imparted enchanting tales of salon chats with such personages as George Bernard Shaw, Lady Asquith, H. G. Wells and (his lover) Rebecca West, the latter of whom a simpatico Alice met and conversed with frequently. Admitting that her political sympathies in England "inclined toward the conservatives," Alice yet urged "the absolute necessity of having two strong parties." English women, she had been pleased to see, evinced more informed interest in politics than their American sisters.

Alice, Miss Bessie declared, diligently devoted every afternoon to her writing, shutting her study door behind her "as a sign that she is not to be interrupted." This commitment to her craft enabled Alice to produce an additional sixteen crime novels between 1932 and 1950, beginning with *The Click of the Gate* and ending with *The Corpse Had Red Hair*.

Altogether nearly half of Alice's crime novels were standalones, in contravention of convention at this time, when series sleuths were so popular. In *The Click of the Gate* the author introduced one of her main recurring characters, intrepid Paris journalist Tommy Rostetter, who appears in three additional novels: *Desire to Kill* (1934), *Flying Blind* (1938) and *The Bloodstained Toy* (1948). In the two latter novels, Tommy appears with Alice's other major recurring character, dauntless Inspector Headcorn of Scotland Yard, who also pursues murderers and other malefactors in *Death Framed in Silver* (1937), *They Hunted a Fox* (1940), *No Murder of Mine* (1941) and *The Cockroach Sings* (1946) (*With Bated Breath* in the US).

Additional recurring characters in Alice's books are Geoffrey Macadam and Catherine West, who appear in *Spiderweb* and *No Light Came On* (1942), and Colin Ladbrooke, who appears in *Death Framed in Silver*, *A Door Closed Softly* (1939) and *They Hunted a Fox*. In the latter two books Colin with his romantic interest Alison Young and in the first and third book with Inspector Headcorn, who also appears, as mentioned, in *Flying Blind* and *The Bloodstained Toy* with Tommy Rosstetter, making Headcorn the connecting link in this universe of sleuths, although the inspector does not appear with Geoffrey Macadam and Catherine West. It is all a rather complicated state of criminal affairs; and this lack of a consistent and enduring central sleuth character in Alice's crime fiction may help explain why her work faded in the Fifties, after the author retired from writing.

Be that as it may, Alice Campbell is a figure of significance in the history of crime fiction. In a 1946 review of *The Cockroach Sings* in the London *Observer*, crime fiction critic Maurice Richardson asserted that "[s]he belongs to the atmospheric school, of which one of the outstanding exponents was the late Ethel Lina White," the author of *The Wheel Spins* (1936), famously filmed in 1938, under the title *The Lady Vanishes*, by director Alfred Hitchcock. This "atmospheric school," as Richardson termed it, had more students in the demonstrative United States than in the decorous United Kingdom, to be sure, the United States being the home of such hugely popular suspense writers as Mary Roberts Rinehart and Mignon Eberhart, to name but a couple of the most prominent examples.

Like the novels of the American Eber-Rinehart school and English authors Ethel Lina White and Marie Belloc Lowndes, the latter the author of the acknowledged landmark 1911 thriller *The Lodger*, Alice Campbell's books are not pure puzzle detective tales, but rather broader mysteries which put a premium on the storytelling imperatives of atmosphere and suspense. "She could not be unexciting if she tried," raved the *Times Literary Supplement* of Alice, stressing the author's remoteness from the so-called "Humdrum" school of detective fiction headed by British authors Freeman Wills Crofts, John Street and J. J. Connington. However, as Maurice Richardson, a great fan of Alice's crime writing, put it, "she generally binds her homework together with a reasonable plot," so the "Humdrum" fans out there need not be put off by what American detective novelist S. S. Van Dine, creator of Philo Vance, dogmatically dismissed as "literary dallying." In her novels Alice Campbell offered people bone-rattling good reads, which explains their popularity in the past and their revival today. Lines from a review of her 1941 crime novel *No Murder of Mine* by "H.V.A." in the *Hartford Courant* suggests the general nature of her work's appeal: "The excitement and mystery of this Class A shocker start on page 1 and continue right to the end of the book. You won't put it down, once you've begun it. And if you like romance mixed with your thrills, you'll find it here."

The protagonist of *No Murder of Mine* is Rowan Wilde, "an attractive young American girl studying in England." Frequently in her books Alice, like the great Anglo-American author Henry James, pits ingenuous but goodhearted Americans, male or female, up against dangerously sophisticated Europeans, drawing on autobiographical details from her and Jamie's own lives. Many of her crime novels, which often lengthier than the norm for the period, recall, in terms of their length and content, the Victorian sensation novel, which seemingly had been in its dying throes when the author was a precocious child; yet, in their emphasis on morbid psychology and their sexual frankness, they also anticipate the modern crime novel. One can discern this tendency most dramatically, perhaps, in the engrossing *Water Weed*, concerning a sexual affair between a middle-aged Englishwoman and a young American man that has dreadful consequences, and *Desire to Kill*, about murder among a clique of decadent bohemians in Paris. In both of these mysteries the exploration of aberrant sexuality is striking. Indeed, in its depiction of sexual psychosis *Water Weed* bears rather more resemblance to, say, the crime novels of Patricia Highsmith than it does to the cozy mysteries of Patricia Wentworth. One might well term it Alice Campbell's *Deep Water*.

In this context it should be noted that in 1935 Alice Campbell authored a sexual problem play, *Two Share a Dwelling*, which the *New York*

Times described as a "grim, vivid, psychological treatment of dual person-ality." Although it ran for only twenty-two performances during October 8-26 at the West End's celebrated St. James' Theatre, the play had done well on its provincial tour and it received a standing ovation from the audience on opening night at the West End, primarily on account of the compelling performance of the half-Jewish German stage actress Grete Mosheim, who had fled Germany two years earlier and was making her English stage debut in the play's lead role of a schizophrenic, sexually compulsive woman. Mosheim was described as young and "blondely beautiful," bringing to mind the author herself.

Unfortunately priggish London critics were put off by the play's morbid sexual subject, which put Alice in an impossible position. One reviewer scathingly observed that "Miss Alice Campbell . . . has chosen to give her audience a study in pathology as a pleasant method of spending the evening. . . . one leaves the theatre rather wishing that playwrights would leave medical books on their shelves." Another sniffed that "it is to be hoped that the fashion of plumbing the depths of Freudian theory for dramatic fare will not spread. It is so much more easy to be inter-ested in the doings of the sane." The play died a quick death in London and its author went back, for another fifteen years, to "plumbing the depths" in her crime fiction.

What impelled Alice Campbell, like her husband, to avidly explore human sexuality in her work? Doubtless their writing reflected the temper of modern times, but it also likely was driven by personal impera-tives. The child of an unhappy marriage who at a young age had been deprived of a father figure, Alice appears to have wanted to use her crime fiction to explore the human devastation wrought by disordered lives. Sadly, evidence suggests that discord had entered the lives of Alice and Jamie by the 1930s, as they reached middle age and their children entered adulthood. In 1939, as the Second World War loomed, Alice was residing in rural southwestern England with her daughter Ormond at a cottage—the inspiration for her murder setting in *No Murder of Mine*, one guesses—near the bucolic town of Beaminster, Dorset, known for its medieval Anglican church and its charming reference in a poem by English dialect poet William Barnes:

> Sweet Be'mi'ster, that bist a-bound
> By green and woody hills all round,
> Wi'hedges, reachen up between
> A thousand vields o' zummer green.

Alice's elder son Lawrence was living, unemployed, in New York City at this time and he would enlist in the US Army when the country entered the war a couple of years later, serving as a master sergeant throughout the conflict. In December 1939, twenty-three-year-old Ormond, who seems to have herself preferred going by the name Chita, wed the prominent antiques dealer, interior decorator, home restorer and racehorse owner Ernest Thornton-Smith, who at the age of fifty-eight was fully thirty-five years older than she. Antiques would play a crucial role in Alice's 1944 wartime crime novel *Travelling Butcher*, which blogger Kate Jackson at *Cross Examining Crime* deemed "a thrilling read." The author's most comprehensive wartime novel, however, was the highly-praised *Ringed with Fire* (1943). Native Englishman S. Morgan-Powell, the dean of Canadian drama critics, in the *Montreal Star* pronounced *Ringed with Fire* one of the "best spy stories the war has produced," adding, in one of Alice's best notices:

> "Ringed with Fire" begins with mystery and exudes mystery from every chapter. Its clues are most ingeniously developed, and keep the reader guessing in all directions. For once there is a mystery which will, I think, mislead the most adroit and experienced of amateur sleuths. Some time ago there used to be a practice of sealing up the final section of mystery stores with the object of stirring up curiosity and developing the detective instinct among readers. If you sealed up the last forty-two pages of "Ringed with Fire" and then offered a prize of $250 to the person who guessed the mystery correctly, I think that money would be as safe as if you put it in victory bonds.

A few years later, on the back of the dust jacket to the American edition of Alice's *The Cockroach Sings* (1946), which Random House, her new American publisher, less queasily titled *With Bated Breath*, readers learned a little about what the author had been up to during the late war and its recent aftermath: "I got used to oil lamps. . . . and also to riding nine miles in a crowded bus once a week to do the shopping—if there was anything to buy. We thought it rather a lark then, but as a matter of fact we are still suffering from all sorts of shortages and restrictions." Jamie Campbell, on the other hand, spent his war years in Santa Barbara, California. It is unclear whether he and Alice ever lived together again.

Alice remained domiciled for the rest of her life in Dorset, although she returned to London in 1946, when she was inducted into the Detection Club. A number of her novels from this period, all of which were published in England by the Collins Crime Club, more resemble, in tone and form, classic detective fiction, such as *They Hunted a Fox* (1940). This event may have been a moment of triumph for the author, but it was also something of a last hurrah. After 1946 she published only three more crime novels, including the entertaining Tommy Rostetter-Inspector Headcorn mashup *The Bloodstained Toy*, before retiring in 1950. She lived out the remaining five years of her life quietly at her home in the coastal city of Bridport, Dorset, expiring "suddenly" on November 27, 1955, two days before her sixty-eighth birthday. Her brief death notice in the *Daily Telegraph* refers to her only as the "very dear mother of Lawrence, Chita and Robert."

Jamie Campbell had died in 1954 aged sixty-five. Earlier in the year his play *The Praying Mantis*, billed as a "naughty comedy by James Lawrence Campbell," scored hits at the Q Theatre in London and at the Dolphin Theatre in Brighton. (A very young Joan Collins played the eponymous man-eating leading role at the latter venue.) In spite of this, Jamie near the end of the year checked into a hotel in Cannes and fatally imbibed poison. The American consulate sent the report on Jamie's death to Chita in Maida Vale, London, and to Jamie's brother Colonel George Campbell in Washington, D. C., though not to Alice. This was far from the Riviera romance that the publishers of *Juggernaut* had long ago promised. Perhaps the "humdrum of everyday life" had been too much with him.

Alice Campbell own work fell into obscurity after her death, with not one of her novels being reprinted in English for more than seven decades. Happily the ongoing revival of vintage English and American mystery fiction from the twentieth century is rectifying such cases of criminal neglect. It may well be true that it "is impossible not to be thrilled by Edgar Wallace," as the great thriller writer's publishers pronounced, but let us not forget that, as Maurice Richardson put it: "We can always do with Mrs. Alice Campbell." Mystery fans will now have nineteen of them from which to choose—a veritable embarrassment of felonious riches, all from the hand of the other AC.

Curtis Evans

CHAPTER ONE

DIANA Lake pressed her small watch against her ear to make sure it was going. Even so it was impossible to catch the faint tick above the surrounding clamour.

What a hullaballoo these creatures made! Every table but hers swarmed with young Indians—students, she gathered, from the near-by School of Economics. She sighed to think that overnight, as it were, her serene Daffodil Tea-Room had turned itself into a social club for failed B.A.'s—with their frequent glances in her direction.

Here was another, who, taking advantage of her gesture, had thrust his own wrist-watch under her nose. He had two gold teeth, and, worse horror, a girl's bangle studded with turquoises.

"He is very late, what?" His grin was gleamingly facetious. "It is now five-fifteen. You see?"

She must make short work of him.

"Thank you," she said coldly. "But I have the right time." And with an aloofness which froze—or should have done—she fixed an expressionless gaze on the door through which Adrian, at any moment, might come.

But would he? Most likely he still had his eye firmly glued to a microscope, calmly oblivious to the passage of time. It was too bad of him, considering he had wired her to meet him, and she, instead of going home after her long train journey, had come straight here. He had news for her—and she had already guessed what the news would be. Indeed, she was secretly hurt that Adrian, oddly dense in some ways, should be rushing to her with the very tidings she least wanted to hear. He had been offered a post. That meant he would be sailing at once back to America. In other words, it was all over save for registering a wholly spurious delight, and composing a nice, sisterly letter for him to read on the boat.

"Oh, well"—and Diana squared her young shoulders philosophically—"since it had to be, how much better now than in another six months! Nothing could come of it for years, even assuming—which I certainly don't—that Adrian felt differently about me. If we don't see each other again till we're middle-aged people, why, there's no harm done."

If her reflections were tinged with regret, no one, watching her, would have suspected it. Tranquil and steady, she drank the tea she had very wisely ordered, lit a cigarette, and rather than waste time on sentimental fancies unfolded a letter she had meant to reread, and gave it—to the outward eye at least—undivided attention.

Diana's type was Irish. Her grey eyes under slender black brows and her dark hair, smooth and with a natural wave in it, she had inherited from her handsome actor-father, Herbert Lake; her milky-pearl skin, humorous mouth and general look of capability came from her little actress-mother, Margaret Fairlamb, now playing in London. In dress she inclined to the unembellished—and this fact contributed largely to her air of restful poise. Dark blue suited her best, and, as a rule, she stuck to it. Her dress now was blue, glove-fitting, without pleat or frill. She had pressed it last night, in Leeds, with her small electric iron, while she was packing up. Blue also was her straight-brimmed little hat, perched at an angle; and the heavy grey gauntlets—she had worn dark ones in the train—lying with her bag beside her cup were stitched in navy. Two-and-twenty she was. She had looked that since eighteen, and she would go on looking it till well past thirty.

The letter she was reading was from her mother, who last week had been in Liverpool. Delayed by tardy forwarding, it had only just reached her, and having glanced at it hastily, she wanted to reassure herself about certain passages. Aunt Rose Somervell—Rose Walsh to the theatre public, and not a real aunt, but only a godmother—had recently died of a stroke. Diana's mother seemed badly upset over it, though why she wrote as she did . . . was this the bit?

"Only sixty-five, and such a splendidly fit person always! I really can't take it in." Diana skimmed. "I suppose, strictly speaking, she and I never had a great deal in common, but after all these years . . . the good times we had together. . . . I keep thinking how kind she was to me when I had my first speaking part in her company and dried up on the opening night. One doesn't forget these things."

"Precious Mummy! She doesn't," mused Diana, thinking of all her warm-hearted little mother must have endured from the ex-star's variable moods, and of the good deeds in the stage-world doomed to speedy oblivion. "No, that wasn't it. Funeral at Marraford—Uncle Nick did everything. He would, of course. Memorial service at St. Martin's—saw that on the news-reel. Oh, here we are."

"Most odd she should have suffered from high blood-pressure and not suspect it. I, personally, should never have guessed. People with that complaint are so energetic, and, as you know, poor, dear Rose never exerted herself if she could help it. What I did notice was her increasing forgetfulness. Only lately, though, and I put it down to the constant little nips of brandy she was so fond of taking, or else to her fearfully strong cigarettes . . .

"It's strange to think that almost certainly I was the last person she spoke to. Just as I was getting off for my tour she rang up. When we'd talked for ten minutes, I heard a crash, and then no more. I tried to get through to her again, but her receiver was still off—and I was obliged to fly for my train not knowing what had happened. Seeing her death notice in the *Manchester Guardian*, I wrote at once to Nick, and his reply furnished the explanation. It seems old Petty smelled something burning. It was Rose's cigarette, fallen on the rug—and Rose herself lay unconscious, her head having struck the fender. She revived a little, but could not clearly articulate, and though a doctor was fetched, she died in only a few hours' time. I've been a wee bit troubled, because of something she said which made me wonder if it really was stroke. I have not written about it to Nick, not wanting to add to his distress, but I shall be seeing him next week, and shall learn all about it, just to set my own mind at rest."

Of course it was stroke. What else could it have been? Besides, the doctor would have known. Diana was about to tuck the letter into her bag when on the back sheet she noticed one of her mother's inevitable postscripts.

"Apart from the hints she dropped, I've no notion how her little fortune was left. We may take it for granted, though, that it will not go to any one who has real need of it. Please don't think this a harsh criticism! I mention the matter only because I should have liked so much to see Adrian get something. It would be common justice, in a way; but, of course, such a possibility is out of the question. You know how hard I've tried ever since Adrian came over to get her to see him. After all, his sole offence, when she and Joe parted, was to stick by his own father; but it was no use, she refused to be interested. Strange that any one so charming should possess this rather hard streak!"

Strange? Not in the least. Rose Somervell had been a thoroughly selfish old woman, as all but Margaret would admit. It was her greed over alimony at the time of the American slump which had helped ruin her divorced husband. Oh, Rose knew that—and she also knew how Adrian's struggle to complete first his Harvard medical and later his studies in brain surgery had been rendered ten times harder through her rapacity. Here Adrian had been since last April, living in a cheap boarding-house, hardly able to buy shoes, his one idea to crowd a year's work, under the celebrated Gordon, into six months—yet not once had Rose asked him to a meal or troubled to inquire how he was doing. That was Rose all over.

"Just as it's Mummy all over to want things for Adrian instead of for herself." Diana's thoughts ran on. "Mummy's right, though. Petty will be left some miserable little legacy. Mummy will get that hideous diamond sunburst and maybe a fur coat, and everything else will go to—"

She looked again at the door. A tall, absent-looking young man in a somewhat battered Burberry had entered the shop, and through horn-rimmed spectacles was scanning the crowded tables. He had the air of trying to recollect just why he had come, and yet he seemed eager, keyed-up with a sort of apprehensive expectancy. Diana sprang up, wormed her way through the throng, and before he had seen her touched his arm.

Adrian Somervell jumped. His near-sighted brown eyes lit with a glad, nervous brightness, but he did not speak, only gripped her hand, let it fall, and swallowed hard.

"You have kept me hanging about!" she chid him. "Look, there's our table, at the back—and, by the way, I shan't come here again. This place is spoiled. What are you having? Poached eggs, I suppose?"

He had stripped off his Burberry and dumped it on the floor by the wall. Now he was seated opposite her, regarding her with a fixed gaze till the hovering waitress caused him to start.

"Eggs? Good Lord, no! I'm not hungry. Tea—coffee—oh, anything!"

"Tea and crumpets," Diana ordered briskly. She was used to attending to such matters, but she wondered why, for once, Adrian was less famished than a sandwich-lunch usually left him. Altogether he was not himself. He was staring at her still in a shy, speculative way that for the first time in their renewed acquaintance made her self-conscious. She put up a barrage of light chatter between herself and the new awkwardness which for some obscure reason had descended on them both.

"The family doesn't know yet about our company going on the rocks. I didn't want to worry Mummy till she'd got her first night over. Did you see the notices of her new play?"

"Notices? Your mother's, did you say?"

"Adrian!" She gave him up in despair. "Don't you ever know what's going on outside your hospital? Last night. The Trafalgar. Went over with a bang. Here, wake up!"

"That's great," he murmured, contrite and vague. "No, I thought both your parents were out of town. I've not been round since you left. And you? Planning to stick here for a bit?"

"If I'm lucky enough to land a part. I'm a makeweight actress, Adrian. I ought to be behind a typewriter, not footlights. Funny, isn't it? There's Mummy, practical as they make them, but able to do whatever she likes with an audience; and there's Daddy, brimming over with temperament, but can't act for nuts. I must have drawn the wrong combination, that's all. Between ourselves, I'm ready to chuck it."

"Chuck the stage? You mean you wouldn't mind?" He was playing for time. How irritating of him!

"Mind? Don't be silly! Here, look to your crumpets. Do eat them while they're hot."

She dropped three lumps of sugar in his cup and handed him the fork he was vaguely seeking. Round and round he stirred his tea, no longer looking at her; and now it struck her that his brown hair was very sprucely brushed, and that the flecks of red in his lean cheeks added enormously to his appearance. Why, he was definitely good-looking! Or was it some change in herself which made her see a greater attraction in him than ever before? Her eyes dwelt on his mouth. It was a reticent, stubborn mouth, somehow curiously defenceless. The sight of it brought a sudden lump into her throat. At no time had Adrian attempted to kiss her—a thing she could not have said about her other men friends; and now she felt a pang to think that he would soon be going away without leaving her the knowledge of what it was like to—to—

"Adrian!" she cried. "Don't tell me that's a new suit!"

He was blushing.

"I slipped round to my digs to put it on," he said simply. "It made me late. Do you like it?"

"Do I! Immensely! A new tie, too. Dark red suits you. But why all this grandeur just for me? Go on, out with it. Is it a job?"

"A job? Oh, no, not at all. I say, you did get my wire, didn't you? Yes, naturally. Well, then, I rather wanted you to be the first to know. That is, I—" He stammered, confused, and disjointedly mumbled: "Most stupefying luck. Knocked me endways, it has. Altered my whole outlook. Can you guess what's happened to me since I saw you?"

Now she understood—and the certainty stabbed her to the quick. Adrian, her comrade, had got himself engaged. He was head over heels in love—and shy about telling her. Swiftly she tried to imagine who the girl could be. The woman at his boarding-house—Uncle Nick Blundell's secretary—was out of the question, therefore it was—oh, of course!—the American heiress to Tobacco Combine millions, she who had trailed him across the Atlantic to dangle her plutocratic invitations before his study-fogged eyes. Avid little huntress! So she had won out after all. . . .

"Well?" Diana smiled encouragement. "I'm listening."

"Changes everything," he muttered. "From my viewpoint, that is. Here—read this letter." He pulled a long, folded sheet from his pocket and shoved it across to her. "That'll tell you."

Uncomprehendingly she stared at the heading. This was no love-letter. Nicholas G. Blundell? Why, he was a solicitor, her godfather, as it happened, and Aunt Rose Somervell's close friend! She glanced at the communication and uttered a gasp.

"But, Adrian!" she whispered. "Is this true?"

"Oh, yes. Blundell himself drew it up. It is pretty astounding, isn't it?"

"Astounding! Why, Adrian, I . . . but wait, let me read it through."

With knit brows she pored over the letter—and as she read her bewilderment grew. In dry, legal language, as though stating the most ordinary fact, it announced that Mrs. Rose Somervell, by her last will and testament, had bequeathed the bulk of her property to her divorced husband's only son, Adrian Somervell.

CHAPTER TWO

SHE roused to find Adrian watching her with a curious anxiety. So engrossed had she been in her own amazement she had momentarily forgotten what was expected of her.

"Oh, my dear, how pleased I am!" she cried wholeheartedly, seizing his two hands and giving them a hard squeeze. "It does seem quite too good to be true, doesn't it?"

"I was struck dumb," he returned candidly, but his eyes still searched hers in a way she found faintly puzzling.

"How do you explain her doing a thing like this?" she continued. "Was it a sort of death-bed repentance, or what?"

"Don't ask me. Of course, when a thing's happened, one generally manages to rationalise it. I suppose I must have impressed her more favourably than I thought these last few weeks."

Diana stared at him.

"You mean you've actually been seeing Aunt Rose?" she demanded in still greater astonishment. "When? How? You never wrote me about it."

"Perhaps I didn't. It never seemed important enough to mention." He hesitated, and added thoughtfully, "I'll tell you how it came about. It was through old Blundell, as a matter of fact. You may recall I met him at your mother's sherry-party just before you left town?"

"Yes, I remember." Diana still stared, thinking what a tremendous lot seemed to have happened since she had last sat at this table with Adrian. "It was the time Aunt Rose didn't turn up, and Mummy was so relieved, because—well, because she was afraid Aunt Rose might have been rude to you. Go on."

"I didn't recognise him at first. We'd been talking several minutes before I realised he was the chap who used to let me fish for newts at his place in Berkshire, and gave me whole quid tips. He seems a generous old duffer—very friendly and so on. My father always said he was."

"Oh, certainly!" Diana agreed without any marked warmth. "He's my godfather, you know. That was because when my brother who died was first born he was so frightfully decent to Mummy and Daddy. You see, Daddy couldn't get a part, and Mummy couldn't act on account of having a baby. Uncle Nick lent them money and forever won their hearts. It is queer to think he was the one to bring you and Aunt Rose together again—and yet, I don't know. It is rather like him."

She mused a moment, brightened, and bade him continue.

"Well, what then?"

"He took down my address, and an evening or two later he looked me up and drove me back to his flat for dinner. You know, he's got a rather posh outfit over by Albert Hall. Owns the whole house. Her flat was above his."

"Yes, they've had that arrangement for quite ten years. They were the greatest cronies, of course. Oh, nothing romantic. Just friends. She was a good bit older than he."

"I gathered they sort of lived in each other's pockets, but that it was entirely platonic. Naturally, we got talking of her. Blundell told me confidentially that she was feeling slightly hurt over my being in London for months and never coming to call."

"Hurt! Don't make me laugh."

"Well, all considered, I did think it a bit thick. But from my recollections of her she was never exactly a reasonable woman, and certainly when I was a kid she was good to me in a way." Adrian paused, examining his spoon. "Anyhow, Blundell pointed out that she was old now and feeling rather lonely with no relations she hadn't quarrelled with—apt, in fact, to imagine she was being slighted. He said it was her pride that had kept her from making any advances, but that if I could bring myself to take the first step it would do me no harm and give her a lot of pleasure. He suggested we go up together and take her by surprise. It was a matter of complete indifference to me, so up we went—and that began it."

"And she was glad to see you?"

"I don't quite know." Adrian studied the morsel of crumpet impaled on his fork. "I thought her a spot stiffish just at first. Later it wore off. I see now she must have liked my coming. Blundell said she could never let me see how bucked she was, because that would have been admitting she'd been in the wrong. I expect she knew my father had behaved with extraordinary decency over that divorce."

"And the alimony," Diana added dryly. "Undoubtedly she was flattered. She was vain as a peacock, even at sixty-five. What on earth did you three find to talk about?"

"Oh, this and that. Blundell soon got her in a good humour, pulling her leg and being a bit of a clown. It seemed to go down with her extremely well."

"It did." Diana nodded. "They were an odd sort of couple, all full of mutual appreciation. I've often wondered they didn't marry each other, but I dare say they were happier having their separate establishments, and just hobnobbing like two old women. Do you imagine Uncle Nick put her up to leaving you her money?"

"It seems possible." Adrian spoke slowly, as though he had weighed this idea before. "He tells me he thought the world of my father, and he's shown a decided interest in my future career. Of course, he's never said anything. Well, to cut it short, I went there a fair amount. It wasn't thrilling, but with you away it was somewhere to go. It certainly never crossed my mind she hadn't a good twenty years to live, even less that I'd gone over strong enough to warrant her doing this incredible thing; but there it is, she did do it, and that's that. I can't quarrel with it, can I?"

"Quarrel! I should say not. It may upset all our previous views of Aunt Rose's character, but that's a mere detail. When did you last see her?"

Her question woke him from a reverie.

"When? Oh, the very day she died. Sunday, a fortnight ago. Blundell and I lunched with her. She seemed perfectly well, ate a hearty meal. We left directly afterwards, because Blundell was golfing, and I had a job to finish off. He dropped me at the hospital, and I had no idea anything had happened till the following day. It seems when he got to his clubhouse there was a telephone message waiting for him. She'd been taken ill soon after we left—and she died about five-thirty that same afternoon. It appears she'd made this will only two days before."

"Two days!" Diana gasped. "What miraculous luck!"

"I'll say it was," he said frankly. "Blundell now tells me she seemed in a perfect fever to get it done—as though she had some sort of premonition. I don't know anything about that. It's a complete mystery to me."

"Never mind about mysteries. Oh, Adrian, I am so pleased! It will mean no more pinching and scraping, won't it? You can wait and choose exactly the right post. Isn't that so?"

She had impulsively taken his hand again to give it another quick little squeeze. He retained her fingers a second, then released them. All at once she felt he had not told her all, and that in a few minutes he might be wanting a different kind of felicitations. If not, why this embarrassment?

"It does mean all that," he said in a low voice. "I've got down to my last hundred pounds, as it happens, and would have had to snatch up anything that came along; but—it means something more."

He paused, reddening till his very eyes seemed suffused.

Now it was coming. Diana sat tense, steeling herself for the confession.

"Suppose," he went on awkwardly, "I were to tell you that this sort of thing can't go on?" His voice had suddenly gone dry. "You and I meeting like this, without any possibility of—" Again he floundered, mopping his brow angrily. "It's got to end," he blurted out. "You see that. Or don't you?"

She met his gaze, understanding.

"Quite, Adrian, dear. Now this has happened, you'll be wanting to get married. I quite expected it."

"Married! That's it."

He caught her up with an energy which startled her. Oblivious of the surrounding company he leant forward to pour out a flood of words.

"I can't go on. It's got to end one way or the other. Get me? I've not the slightest reason to suppose that you—but I can't bother about that now. It all shakes down to this: Are you going to have me? Are you? Tell me, quick!"

All the breath in her seemed suspended. The yellow-walled room, Indians and all, swam in a roseate haze.

"Me?" she whispered incredulously. "Oh, Adrian! Is it me you want?"

"Who in hell did you think it was?" he fired back at her. "My God, what other girl have I looked at but you?"

"I don't know." She laughed, dazed by the onslaught. "I thought—"

"Don't think, answer me! Will you, or have I drawn a blank?"

"I . . . oh, Adrian, yes!"

Flame seemed to leap up and devour her.

"You mean it? You will? Diana! Oh, blast this place!"

He dragged his chair round to her side, seized her two hands in a grip of steel. No embarrassment now. Above the beating of her own heart Diana believed she could hear the clamour of his. He was a new Adrian—one she had never really known existed. She still saw him glorified, through a mist in which all her senses quivered. It was a full minute before the wonder of it subsided to the point where speech was possible.

"But I never guessed!" she whispered at last. "Tell me, when did you begin wanting me?"

"When?" He brushed the question aside as of no consequence. "How do I know? Directly I came over—or maybe before, when we were kids. Anyhow, I've died a thousand deaths."

"But why, darling?" she reproached him. "You could so easily have found out if I cared. I could never have been sure till I knew how you felt, but the money part wouldn't have mattered."

"Oh, wouldn't it?" he muttered.

"Certainly not," she retorted warmly. "We might have got married long before you were able to keep us both. I'm working. I like having a job. Mummy's always done her share. Why shouldn't I?"

He shook his head.

"I couldn't have let you. Not possibly. No use arguing. Don't you understand? It's exactly because you are strong and independent that I couldn't let you slave for me. I'd have sunk in my own esteem. No, as things were, it was simply no good. I'd never have told you." There was no denying the fact that this obstinate pride of his delighted her, for all she must protest against it.

"You mean you'd have gone back to America without ever saying a word? Oh, Adrian, you couldn't!"

"Why not? It would have been a cad's trick to expect you to wait for me indefinitely—and with the ocean between us. For one thing, you might have fallen for some one else and felt bound to me."

"So might you have done," she reminded him.

"Maybe. I don't think so, though." He viewed the possibility dispassionately. "You see, much as I want certain things, my job comes first, and always will. It's only fair to tell you that, so you'll appreciate what you're letting yourself in for. Women as women don't interest me enough to make me go chasing after them."

Diana laughed.

"No, it's they who do the chasing," she said tenderly. "And I like having you as you are. I shan't mind if your job comes first. I'll be perfectly happy just looking after you. You'll never be able to do that for yourself, will you?"

He gazed at her, too fascinated to summon more than a faint smile.

"You think me pretty darned impractical, don't you?" he returned. "You would. Well, I may be, though left on my own I seem to muddle along all right. Anyhow, get this. I'm not marrying you to turn you into a drudge. There's no need now, thank God!"

Her eyes, dove-grey, caressed his ardent ones. With a proprietary touch she straightened his new tie.

"I know one girl who'll be tearing her hair over this," she remarked irrelevantly. "Now, tell me the truth. Hasn't Bobbie Ackland been begging you to marry her?"

"Rot!" He reddened, annoyed. "What gave you that notion?"

"Oh, I guessed! It's so, isn't it?"

"Supposing it is," he muttered, "why bring it up now?"

"Oh, darling, how transparent you are! And how about Uncle Nick's secretary, Elsie Dilworth? Is she another victim?"

She had meant this as the wildest jest. The sudden frown contracting his brow proved it had been no random shot.

"That poor nut!" he exclaimed under his breath. "Now, who's been gassing to you about her?"

"Why, no one! Don't you remember? We sent you to that boarding place because we knew about it from Elsie—and because it was close to your hospital. Months ago you told me she'd been extremely nice to you. I was teasing you, that's all."

"Well, she's gone now." He spoke shortly, running a lean brown finger inside his collar. "And a good job, too. Bit wrong in the top story, if you ask me. Oh, she may be okay as a secretary, but—she was getting a confounded nuisance in some ways."

"Oh, was she?" Diana watched him with demure amusement. "Oh, dear," she sighed, "what heaps we'll have to talk over, shan't we? How I wish I hadn't to go home!"

"Go home? Why? I thought we'd have dinner together."

"I'd love it, only you see I've not yet seen Mummy, and if I'm to catch her before she leaves for her theatre I must fly this instant. I'll tell you, suppose you come with me, and we'll break our news to her. How enchanted she'll be when she hears!"

"Will she?" She fancied he was showing a slight return of diffidence and hesitation. "I hope so—but, no, I won't come with you. I ought by rights to put in another stretch at the hospital. Couldn't we get together later, say about ten?"

"Of course! We might fetch Mummy after the show, and hold a little celebration at the flat. Daddy'll be home by then, and it'll buck him up. Poor lamb, he's a bit side-tracked these days. Now, let's hunt a taxi. No 'buses for me this night!"

As they paused by the cash-desk, the dark-skinned owner of the bangle turned and stared at them with singular pointedness.

"Look," whispered Diana, "I do believe everyone here's been taking in every word we've said!"

Adrian hardly troubled to glance back as he pocketed his change. "Oh, I expect they've noticed me in here fairly often—and they're an inquisitive crowd. Shall we go?"

In the cold, misty darkness they drifted, pressed close together, till, within sight of the thoroughfare, they reached the entrance to a mews. With one accord they halted, looking at each other. Then Adrian drew Diana into the sheltered opening, set down her suitcase, and crushed her in his arms. How strong he was—and how starved! It now seemed incredible that hunger like this could have been hidden so completely, the more so since the need Diana sensed in him was peculiarly and definitely for her. Other women had wanted him, but there had been nothing for them. With the realisation of this her joy in his kisses took a quickened thrill. Long moments passed before either could tear away. When they did, both were trembling.

There was another, final embrace when they parted at the taxi-rank.

"Darling—darling! You will ring up the instant you're finished?"

"I wish it was now. Diana! You do—?"

"Oh, so much, so much, Adrian! I never knew I could feel like—oh, there! Do be careful!" she admonished, as, stepping back, he narrowly missed an oncoming car. "What did I tell you?" she laughed happily. "Can you look after yourself?"

He gazed raptly at her, a man in a dream. For half a minute she saw him, marooned on an island in the Kingsway traffic, then he was blotted from view, and she sank back in the taxi to savour, in solitude, her newfound rapture.

How was it, she marvelled, that till now she had never dimly suspected the depth of her own feelings? A miracle had happened. Looking back, she saw her twenty-two years of existence as a calm, land-locked lagoon, from which, by the touch of one pair of lips, she had set sail on the open sea. Adrian—hers!

"And to think," she murmured into the darkness of the cab, "I owe it all—everything—to Aunt Rose Somervell, whom I never really liked! I want to apologise to her. I do wonder how on earth she came to do it?"

It occurred to her that her mother—yes, even tolerant little Margaret— would be more astounded than any one else over Rose's action.

"She was mistaken, that's all. I think I see how it was. When Aunt Rose met Adrian again and actually realised the struggle he'd been having she got an attack of conscience. Still, for her to pop off like that, directly afterwards! A shame to say it, but how awfully well-timed!"

It tempted one to believe in guardian angels—but come to think of it, might not Nicholas Blundell have played just that role? He could scarcely have foreseen Rose's decision, but at least he had paved the way for it, and at the critical moment had not interfered. For once, where her godfather was concerned, Diana's gratitude was spontaneous and untempered by criticism. Officious, bull-in-a-china-shop Uncle Nick, wanting every one to be happy, but usually so clumsy in his efforts! This time he had wrought better than he knew.

The taxi stopped in a little, retired square close to the Marble Arch, where, in the upper part of a converted house, the Lakes had their abode. As Diana sprang out she noticed a large Sunbeam car drawn up at the entrance. It seemed familiar, but before she had bestowed a second glance on it the man of whom she had been thinking came out of the house door.

Uncle Nick himself—but what had happened to him? He was not smiling. Indeed, as he came towards her, squat, rugged, powerful, the strange, set gravity of a face habitually humorous gave her a curious shock. Then she remembered what Aunt Rose's death must have meant to him. How stupid of her to forget it! She touched his arm.

"Why, Uncle Nick!" she cried. "Aren't you going to speak to me?"

He turned, startled, and for a second his yellowish-grey eyes met hers without recognition. She saw, then, that although his tremendous dynamic force seemed unimpaired, he had quite definitely aged. Nicholas Blundell, bursting with health and vigour, had become an old man.

CHAPTER THREE

THERE was an instantaneous alteration as the solicitor took in his goddaughter's identity. His smile returned, forlornly bringing into play the deep, semi-circular grooves which in gravity had seemed so unfamiliar.

"Well, well, well! So it's little Didi! Home again?"

"Just. Have you been calling on the family?"

He had laid one good-humoured hand on her arm to stop her fumbling in her purse, but she did not realise his intention till she saw his other hand reach into his change-pocket and bringing out a couple of silver coins hand them to her taxi-driver.

"Oh, you mustn't!" she begged, trying to stop him. "Really, Uncle Nick! You make me feel so silly when you will do things like that."

"Nonsense, nonsense! Don't often get the chance, do I?"

Though he detained her, patting her arm, she sensed his preoccupation. He seemed to hesitate, baulked of his immediate purpose, and only tardily to realise he had not answered her question.

"The family?" he repeated absently. "Oh, I brought your mother home—from my place, you know. I'd a word with your father, too, but he was just buzzing off to Wimbledon. I suppose you've not seen either of 'em yet?"

"No, it was so hurried. I just thought I'd take them by surprise."

She supposed she ought to offer him sympathy, or at least make some reference to Aunt Rose's death, but it was difficult, for the awkwardness she invariably felt in his presence had descended on her, and besides, though he still stood there holding on to her arm, he seemed oddly shy of conversation. For a second, she fancied he was about to ask her some question. She glanced at him expectantly, saw he had apparently changed his mind, and got out her latch-key. He released her with a final pat.

"That's right, best get inside out of this raw night," he mumbled hastily. "You'll lunch with me one day soon, eh? That's right," and with a wave of his gloved hand he got into the Sunbeam, which, as often happened, he was driving himself.

Diana gazed after him, thinking that a moment ago, before he had seen her, his battered old features had seemed less sorrowful than angry. Furious, she would have said, only the change had come so swiftly she could not be sure. Whatever his emotion, the bluff kindliness replacing it had been forced. Altogether she had the feeling of having seen for an instant beneath the surface something vaguely disturbing. She thought of her mother's letter, and a tiny query re-entered her brain.

"Rubbish!" She pushed the wall-button which flooded the green-carpeted interior with light. "It can't be. Adrian would have been sure to suspect. No, there's nothing in it—but Mummy, of course, will have heard about this extraordinary will, so part of my thunder has been stolen. Not the best part, though . . ." and with this happy reflection she raced, fleet-footed, up the three flights of stairs.

A brilliant radiance greeted her when she let herself into the small, tidy hall with its Bokhara rug and its prim row of old woodcuts. That meant Mummy's play was a hit—and another sign was the big bowl of orange marigolds on the dark oak chest, for Margaret Fairlamb, so canny in most respects, ran riot with lights and flowers the moment she was in funds. Home again, after seven weeks of fusty, provincial lodgings—and with news like hers to impart! Light-headed with joy, Diana tore off her hat, and gave an echoing shout.

Far down a passage a crimped grey head thrust itself turtle-wise from a door whence were wafted warm cooking odours. Stern eyes surveyed her from over steel-rimmed spectacles, then the owner bore down on her staidly, dusting floury hands on a spotless apron.

"You, Miss Di?" It was almost an accusation. "What's brought you back so unexpected? And what's that red in your cheeks? Fever?"

"Not rouge, anyhow, Mrs. Todd," the returned wanderer laughed. "Where's Mummy?"

"She's having a bit of a wash. Just got in, she has. There, give me that bag! In you go. She can do with a treat, hard-worked as she's bin, poor little lady!"

So saying, the factotum who for ten years had ordered the Lake household with Spartan rigour gave Diana a push which sent her into a bedroom gay with starched chintz and glowing with a bright gas-fire. It was an empty room at the moment, but it bore the usual comforting signs of its little owner's cosy, utilitarian personality. Here were her new press-cuttings, jumbled helter-skelter with her husband's unmended socks; there, over a Sheraton chair, hung an absurdly small brown taffeta blouse, waiting to be put on; midway the smooth, mauve surface of the bed sprawled a shabby handbag, burst open, like an over-ripe pod, and spilling its contents in varied confusion. A card-table, drawn near the fire and covered with a snowy cloth, was laid for the high-tea most stage people were having at this hour, while on a brass trivet below stood the silver tea-pot and muffin-dish presented to Herbert and Margaret on their twenty-fifth anniversary, just past.

Diana called, "Mums! Are you there?"

Water in the adjacent bath ceased to splash. The communicating doorway framed a diminutive, half-clad figure from whose dripping face an eye bright as a robin's cocked an inquiring glance. The next instant Margaret Fairlamb uttered a small shriek of delight, and with arms widespread rushed to enfold her tall daughter.

"Darling! What fun! How did it happen?"

Diana explained, they laughed in unison, and hugged again. What, so old Tom Chetwynd—*Sir* Thomas, indeed!—had come another cropper and thrown all those poor young things out of work? Just what one might expect if he would keep casting that great meal-sack of a wife for Rosalind and Juliet. Diana need not mind, though. Things here were simply booming, and it would be lovely to have her at home.

"Then your show has clicked?"

"Too wonderfully! Oh, Gwen's raging, of course, because Hal's up to his old trick of backing upstage—the joke being that the scene he really ruins isn't hers but mine, only she doesn't know it." The robin's eye twinkled merrily. "As though it mattered! With a marvellous press and a huge library deal, what more can one ask?"

What, indeed? That was Mummy, thought Diana, never troubling if her scenes were pinched, content to be earning regular money, so cheerfully ready to tackle all the most thankless tasks that in the theatre she was called "Little Red Hen." A brisk, apple-cheeked little creature she was, with round brown eyes wholly innocent of make-up, quite the wrong shade of powder—if any!—and thick, russet hair, just tinged with grey, braided unfashionably over her small ears. Here she was already prattling about the new clothes her daughter must have when her own wardrobe was in its usual hopeless state of neglect. Diana, eyeing with disfavour the shapeless tweed skirt just being wriggled into, formed firm resolutions to take her mother in hand.

"And Daddy?" she asked, deliberately postponing her great news. "Stand still while I brush you. Why, you're all over fluff!"

"Daddy?" The small face puckered with regret. "Poor darling, I'm not at all happy about him. He closes this week, and really there does seem so little for him these days. I can't think why. There's not the slightest reason for his going on tour. Not now—but you do know how absurd he is, don't you?"

"Absurd? Not a bit! Do you honestly expect Daddy and me to toast our toes by your nice warm fire while you do the work?"

"Baby! Don't be a beast." Margaret looked hurt. "What possible difference can it make which of us happens to be earning? I'm sure there have been times . . ."

If so, Diana did not remember them; but the glance she directed at the silver-framed photograph of her father, prominent on the mantel, was full of affectionate sympathy. What she saw was a singularly handsome face, rather like her own, only more dreamy and wistful. It was a sad irony that a face like this, so admirably suited for Hamlet and Lear, should inevitably be cast for nondescript uncles and make-weight friends-of-the-family in plays which expired after a fortnight. Mummy had plans. She always had, but they would come to nothing.

"I'm going round to Felix to-morrow," she was confiding, hairpins in mouth. "He does owe me something, for, after all, didn't I go on half salary all during the last general election when things were so bad? He simply must find Herbert a part—but not a word, mind! We must never let Daddy think I'm pulling wires for him." Margaret emerged from the temporary eclipse of her blouse with a queer, excited gleam in her eye.

"And now," she whispered, "what do you suppose I've just heard from Nick about my poor, precious Rose? Quite staggering! She—"

"I know," Diana interrupted. "She left all her money to Adrian. But wait. That's nothing. Adrian and I—well, we're getting married. We fixed it up an hour ago. There! Aren't you pleased?"

There was a flutter and a squeak—as though a robin had been trodden upon. Comb in hand Margaret twisted round on the stool before the dressing-table and stared at Diana in a strange, pained fashion.

"Baby! You're joking. Adrian and you—?"

"Well, why not? Is it so astonishing?"

Her mother was surveying her with hard, bright attentiveness. One would say she was trying to fit together bits and pieces and finding the result not wholly satisfactory. Diana felt slightly damped. She had been so sure!

"Oh, darling, do be glad!" she begged. "Only think that but for this marvellous thing happening he'd never have dared ask me. I'd have lost him. Oh, don't you see what that would have meant?"

Margaret melted utterly, kissed her.

"Sweet! Of course, I'm glad. You took my breath away, that's all. I've been an owl, I suppose, not to have seen this coming; but there, it's all perfectly heavenly, and just what I could have wished—since you're happy. You do love Adrian?"

"Terribly!"

"I see—and Rose's money will make everything so comfortable. What a blessing! Early struggles are all very well and so good for the character, but I confess I'd rather hate seeing you go through the mill like—like some we've known."

Margaret was gagging. Oh, very cleverly, but Diana was not to be fooled.

"You like Adrian, don't you?" she demanded anxiously. "On his own account, not just because I'm marrying him?"

"Like him? Why, Didi, how can you ask? You know quite well that both your father and I are extremely fond of Adrian—and we have such a high opinion of his ability. I'm sure we've often said that with that one-track mind of his he'll get just whatever he sets out for. In his profession, I mean," Margaret hastened to add. "No, it would not surprise me if he became a very famous brain-surgeon. I expect Rose thought that, too, or else . . . but no, I mustn't be small-minded! You knew, of course, that they'd got quite intimate?"

"I'm certain they weren't at all intimate. Adrian was just as bowled over as we are; but what did Uncle Nick say on the subject?"

"Not a great deal." Margaret sounded oddly distrait. "I hadn't long with him, and there was so much to talk over. You see, I'd snatched my first free moment to run over for a word with old Petty, who I'd heard was still at the flat. I was chatting with her when Nick came in to give some instructions; I had only about ten minutes' conversation with him and then he drove me home. When we got here, your father was just leaving, so I'd no chance to tell him about Rose's will. How astonished he'll be!"

"I understood Uncle Nick drew up this will. Did he approve?"

"I—I think so." Margaret was fastening her collar with unwonted care and did not look round. "Oh, yes, to be sure, he must have approved! He brought them together, after Adrian had rather sounded him on the subject of Rose's attitude towards him. Adrian wanted to see her, and wasn't sure how she'd take it. Well, you know how Nick likes to have every one on good terms. It seems he had a bit of an argument with Rose, who let him bring Adrian to call. One can only suppose her old fondness revived, for suddenly, in a rather shame-faced way, she consulted Nick about making a will in the boy's favour. Naturally Nick insisted on making certain inquiries, just as a wise precaution, you understand; but he declares Rose was most determined—impatient, even—to have her way. Odd, wasn't it, after never seeming to bother about him?"

"Very odd!"

An awkward silence fell. Diana was thinking that this version differed a little from the one Adrian had given her, but that it was easy to see why Nicholas Blundell, a vain man, liked altering facts to suit his own book. Knowing Adrian, she could not believe the initial move had come from him. He had cared nothing whatever for the woman who for six years of his early boyhood had been his stepmother. Even now, he was not pretending the least sorrow over her death.

"Mummy," she said abruptly, "how did we get the idea that Aunt Rose intended leaving her property to Uncle Nick?"

Margaret made embarrassed murmurs. Had they thought this? Well, perhaps they had.

"I—I must have got a wrong impression from some remark Rose made oh, quite a long time ago! She had certainly made no such will, any will at all, in fact. As so often happens, she'd put it off—and as for Nick's inheriting anything—well, didn't we always say how ridiculous that would have been? I'm positive such a notion never entered his head. He doesn't want money, least of all hers. Coals to Newcastle it would have been."

"But has Uncle Nick always been so prosperous?"

"I see what you mean. No, certainly not; but for some years everything he's touched seems to have turned up trumps. Rose knew that. Indeed, she was always boasting to me about his wonderful business ability. Above all things, she admired success. As I may have said, that would have been her reason for making him her heir—that, and her gratitude to him for so cleverly handling her own investments. Still, I now question she ever seriously meant to do so. She was a bit fond, you know, of weaving romances."

At this juncture the housekeeper stuck a disapproving face in at the door to remind them of the time. Margaret sprang up, guilty as a schoolchild caught whispering in class.

"So sorry, Toddie! We'll eat now—but it's all right, I'm not on till the middle of the act."

As they sat down at the small table, Diana noticed that her mother's expression was troubled and evasive. Again she experienced the dim sense of disturbance which the sight of Nicholas Blundell's face had given her.

"It was stroke, I suppose?" she asked tentatively. Wariness leaped into the brown eyes. Margaret was alert, on guard.

"Why do you ask that? Oh, I see, it was the letter I wrote you. Yes, it was stroke. At least—well, Nick does seem to be brooding a trifle, but—"

"Brooding! Why?"

"Because—and I was struck by this, too—Rose's own doctor, Sir Eustace Milford, never saw her at all. He was in Bournemouth, nursing a septic throat. It was his partner, Dr. Cross, who came. Oh, a good man, undoubtedly, but—well, the end came so quickly, and her tongue being paralysed she was never able to tell them just how she felt. It may have made no difference to the diagnosis, and then again—"

Why did Margaret falter, only to dart off at a seemingly irrelevant tangent? Diana herself was beginning to feel vaguely curious about what, when all was said, could not be very important. Rose Somervell was dead, laid to rest in a quiet Berkshire churchyard. Discussion now would not make the cause of her death one whit the clearer, nor was it likely that Sir Eustace Milford—favourite with the aristocracy, but a joke amongst his medical confrères—would have seen what his partner missed.

The gas fire shone red on teapot and muffin-dish, coaxed burnished gleams from her mother's plump braids. At peace again, Diana gave absent attention to her companion's rambling discourse, while her inner consciousness strayed ecstatically in a region wherein illness and death played negligible parts. Presently a name caught her ear. She roused lazily.

"Petty?" she repeated. "What were you saying about her?"

CHAPTER FOUR

"I was just wondering," continued Margaret, drinking her tea in little, bird-like sips, "if Petty was telling me the truth when she declared no one was with her in the kitchen? I could have sworn there was, but why should she lie about it?"

"I can't imagine. What happened?"

"It was like this: The flat door was open, so, thinking Petty had just slipped downstairs for a moment, I walked straight in. I was in the drawing-room, looking down at a scorched spot on the rug and realising that here was where poor Rose must have dropped her cigarette when she fell, when all at once I heard Petty speaking, quite agitatedly—or so I thought. All I caught was something about Mr. Blundell's wanting a consultation, only there hadn't been time; but I certainly got the impression she was protesting or arguing. Not wanting to be found eavesdropping, I called out that it was me, Mrs. Lake, and then I marched through to the kitchen."

"And—?" prompted Diana, as her mother paused abstractedly and toyed with a fish-cake.

"Oh, Petty was quite alone! Swore she was talking to herself—but she seemed so hot and flustered when she saw me that . . . she was ironing, of course. Yes, it was the pink crêpe suzette nightdress Rose had worn when she died. To be sure, the person with her could have stepped quickly into the passage; still, I dare say I was wrong."

"What time was it?"

Diana hardly knew why she asked this question, the answer to which stuck in her memory.

"Exactly six, by the clock on the dresser. I hadn't much time, so I looked to see. By the way," meditatively, "did your Aunt Rose ever use chypre?"

"Chypre?" echoed Diana with scorn. "Catch her! No, Soir de Venise, at two guineas a bottle. Why?"

"Oh, it's of no consequence. . . . You've heard, of course, that Adrian lunched there the Sunday she died?"

"Certainly. Did Petty mention it?"

"In passing. She described how she found Rose, lying semi-conscious on the floor of the drawing-room, not half an hour after the guests had gone. She got her to bed, tried sal volatile and brandy—which Rose couldn't swallow—and then got horribly frightened. Nick's cook, Mrs. Ransome, rang up the golf club for her, then they got hold of this Dr. Cross. That was about all I learned from Petty, because when she'd reached this point Nick popped his head in on us. How we both jumped! Petty's all nerves, poor old thing; and I jumped because—well, silly as it sounds, I still felt there might be some one hiding in the passage. Nick was the last person I expected to see. We must have looked idiots, both of us."

"I suppose Uncle Nick was pleased to see you."

"He was, pathetically. Did you notice how aged he's grown? Until I actually saw him I don't think I'd fully realised how this would break him up. He told me all about the funeral—and here's a bit that will amuse you. It seems that, me being gone, he called on Charlotte Moon to engineer the arrangements—which she did, memorial service and all, in the best possible style."

"Dame Charlotte!" Diana laughed. "What a grim joke!"

"Yes, wouldn't Rose have hated it?" Margaret gave an answering twinkle. "And yet, Rose herself would have admitted that Lottie does lend the impressive touch, now she moves in almost royal circles. Poor Nick, he did so want everything done as Rose would have liked it!" After a moment's musing the little actress resumed, again with hesitation.

"Striking her head against the fender gave her a slight concussion, which no doubt hastened her end. I say that because as a general thing people don't die from a first stroke. I little thought, hearing that crash . . . and yet, it did give me the weirdest feeling! Like that horrid play, *Le Téléphone*, which your father and I once saw in Paris—you know, when the husband hears his wife being murdered, and—"

Margaret broke off, her face comic with dismay.

"Oh, dear, you'll think me an absolute dunce! There was no one there but Petty, who was washing up in the kitchen. I know that now."

"Did you tell Uncle Nick all about your telephone conversation?" Diana inquired thoughtfully.

"Well—not quite all, though naturally he wanted to hear about it. You see, she had talked almost entirely about him, which made it so awkward. I had to hedge a bit. You'll hardly believe what she was grumbling about. It was Nick's secretary—you know, Miss Dilworth, that plain, quiet girl! Rose was saying that Miss Dilworth was setting her cap at Nick in quite a shameless way."

"Elsie Dilworth? Nonsense!"

"Possibly it's true," declared Margaret defensively. "Nick's well-to-do, not above fifty-five. Many women would consider him quite a catch. Anyhow, Rose believed it. She was most incensed over what she called Miss Dilworth's kittenish behaviour, and the gay, unsuitable clothes she'd taken to wearing."

"Why did she assume all this was for Uncle Nick's benefit?" asked Diana, recalling Adrian's annoyance when the secretary was mentioned.

"Oh, she had her reasons! It seems Miss Dilworth had followed Nick upstairs that very day while they were at lunch, on what Rose declared was a trumped-up excuse; and she was wearing a pair of long green ear-rings, which Rose was rather cruel about. Rose said Miss Dilworth was trying hard to undermine her influence with Nick, and that she intended to put a stop to it. Well, it's all very trivial, but you can see how impossible it was to repeat such things to Nick. He's a shy man where women are concerned. It would have embarrassed him most painfully."

Diana's eyes danced. With Adrian present at that lunch table, why look farther afield for Miss Dilworth's motives?

"Poor dear Rose was always rather jealous," Margaret went on. "And with so little cause! Nick's not at all the marrying sort, and I doubt if any woman, old or young, could have taken him from her. I've even thought that in some ways he was far more dependent on her than she on him.

That was because of her superior social poise. When she first took her affairs to him he was, one must admit, rather a rough diamond."

"He still is, if you ask me," said Diana bluntly. "Whatever did she see in him?"

"I've told you," retorted her mother with warmth. "She admired his intellect."

"Intellect! Oh, darling!"

"Well, then, his financial sense." The Red Hen's feathers were ruffling, as they always did if the faintest slur were cast on one of her friends. "Let me tell you, Nicholas Blundell now occupies quite an important position. He has the handling of some of the biggest estates, and only lately Rose was enumerating, with pride, the distinguished men who were not only his clients but his personal associates."

"Any titles among them?"

"Diana, don't be horrid! Haven't we all our little weaknesses? There were titles—big ones. She mentioned Lord Limpsfield, and this new baronet who's been made a minister—Sir Norbury Penge. You see, two of the most prominent people in England. Oh, Rose knew! She'd been keeping private tab on his visitors."

"I'll bet she had!"

"And why not? Remember what little interest there was in her life these latter days. Naturally she liked feeling she had a finger in the various big pies—and as you well know it was Nick's great delight to talk it all over with her. What he'll do now without her companionship I can't think. If ever he imagined—"

Margaret's voice trailed off. "Goodness!" she exclaimed, "what drivel I'm talking!"

Diana sat very still.

"Mummy," she said, "you're keeping something back. Oh, yes, you are! You think Petty was, too. Now own up: Exactly what did Aunt Rose say to you on the telephone which you've failed to speak of?"

A hunted look sprang into her mother's eyes.

"How ever did you guess? It was nothing, really. I shouldn't have told Nick. I didn't dream it would upset him to that extent." Margaret moistened dry lips. "It was just her complaining—oh, not seriously—of the odd feeling in her tummy."

"Feeling! Was it a pain?"

"No, she described it as a tingling sensation, first in her tongue, then inside. Several times she spoke of it, then went on to other things. I told you, didn't I, how she'd taken to repeating herself? At the last she said she was feeling a bit sick."

"Was that all? I dare say she'd overeaten—as usual."

Diana could have laughed with relief. Well she knew the sort of meals Rose Somervell had partaken of, not wisely but too well.

"Oh, she didn't seem bothered about it," her mother hastily rejoined. "It was only the thought of her being unable, afterwards, to explain anything. It did seem just possible that . . . Heavens! Eight o'clock! I must fly."

In a flurry she sprang up, brushing crumbs from her mouth, and, having jammed on a disreputable old felt hat, began gathering up her jumbled belongings from the bed. Suddenly she paused and held out two small jewel-boxes for Diana to inspect.

"Rose left me these," she said in a hushed voice. "Nick being the executor, there was no reason, as he said, why I shouldn't have them at once. The diamond sunburst, you see, and the big emerald ring I always admired. Adrian's father gave it to her. It must be yours, I think."

"Mine? Not much!" Diana slipped the square, green stone on her finger, let the light play on it, then handed it back. "It's yours, and you must wear it—with a really good, new frock, which I shall make you buy. Mummy!" she cried sternly, seeing the jewel-boxes and a fat roll of banknotes being shovelled casually into the handbag. "Do you mean you're actually going to cart all that wealth about with you? How can you be such an idiot?"

"Don't worry, pet. Now, where are my gloves?" Margaret made a frantic search. "I've been too rushed to bank my fortnight's salary—got home on Sunday, you know—but it's much safer having it with me than leaving it in an empty flat. You did say you and Adrian were coming to fetch me?"

"If he finishes in time, but don't wait for us. Hold on, you've got to have a taxi. I'm coming down to see you do."

There was a stand in the Edgware Road. The front taxi veered towards them and Margaret got inside.

"Wait, darling!" Diana kept her hand on the door. "Why do you suppose Aunt Rose said nothing to you about this will?"

Was there a momentary confusion in Margaret's eyes? If so, it vanished quickly as she made glib reply. She had not seen Rose at all during the three weeks of rehearsals. Rose, after the stubborn stand she had taken over Adrian, must have felt a hesitancy about "climbing down."

She would, most understandably, have wanted to prepare Margaret for an admission of this kind.

"She did mean to tell me," added Margaret, with suspicious brightness, "because when we were speaking on the telephone she said twice over that the moment I was back in town she might have some surprising news for me about a matter we'd touched on not long ago. There! Do you see?"

"Oh!" Diana nodded to herself. "And you'll promise to be sweet to Adrian? Very nice indeed?"

"Precious lamb! What a silly you are! Toodle-oo!"

The taxi made off, and Diana, hatless on the foggy street corner, eyed the ruby glow of a chestnut-vendor's barrow and tried to analyse the vague misgivings the past hour had engendered, Mummy was not altogether happy over her news. Was she afraid her daughter might not receive quite the same whole-hearted devotion Herbert Lake had lavished on herself? Surely it was not that. Mummy was too sensible. Then what was it? It occurred to Diana that Uncle Nick Blundell might have let fall some slightly disparaging remark concerning Adrian.

"That's unlikely, too," she mused. "He of all people must know that Adrian can't have schemed to bring about this will. Why, he was in London six whole months without making a single move to—"

What was that news-seller shouting? The words "Kensington" and "actress" reached her above the blare of a hurdy-gurdy. No one she had ever heard of obviously. It never was on these occasions; but she might as well see, since there was a penny loose in her pocket. Moist paper in hand, she moved towards the brilliance of a radio shop the better to make out the headlines—and gave a shrug. The usual sell. The front page was plastered with football news and some incredibly dull stuff about arterial highways.

But look! Here was the item, lonely in the blankness of the "Stop Press" column. Five lines of blurred print:

"Following information received, the Home Secretary has ordered the body of Mrs. Rose Somervell, better known as Rose Walsh, the celebrated comedy-actress, to be exhumed for medical examination. No details are yet known."

CHAPTER FIVE

WITHOUT noise, Diana let herself into the flat and stood listening. Mrs. Todd was still pottering about in the kitchen, and the telephone was in the passage where every word would be audible. Slipping into her small blue and white bedroom she sank on the couch-bed to wait. Though she was still breathless, like a diver just emerged from Arctic waters, her deep-rooted sense of security was asserting itself. A false alarm, this. It could be nothing else, for all her mother must have had some unformulated dread lurking in her mind.

"She was trying so hard not to let me guess. I'd have got it out of her if I hadn't blurted out my engagement right at the start. Oh, God, does that mean she was afraid that Adrian, my Adrian—"

Even to herself she could not finish the sentence, but she knew quite well the meaning of her mother's dim fear, and that Nicholas Blundell must share that fear, at least since learning about Rose's peculiar sensations. No telling what the two old friends had said to each other. Supposing her mother had mentioned the fact that Adrian was down to his last hundred pounds and bitterly lamenting his inability to continue his research into obscure brain-tumours?

"But wait! This paper went to press long before Mummy and Uncle Nick had their talk. That means the information, whatever it was, was handed in days ago. By whom? Not Uncle Nick. He'd have said something about it just now."

At long last she heard the staid steps of Mrs. Todd creak down the passage. The instant the front door closed she sprang for the telephone.

"Prince Regent's Hospital? Dr. Somervell, please . . .. Oh, Adrian, is it you?"

He had answered with astonishing quickness. Even under her present stress of emotion she wondered how he came to be so close to the instrument, and why his "Hallo" sounded so sharp and brusque. Two mighty efforts she made, one to speak naturally, the other to detect from his voice the information it was vital for her to learn. She had concocted a ruse, but would it conceal her anxiety?

"Dear, I've got a small errand, down near the hospital. Shall I call for you? That is, if you're finishing soon."

His answer was slightly delayed, and when it did come sounded oddly restrained.

"Good. Fine," he said, and then, after a second pause, guardedly, "How long will you be?"

"Oh, twenty minutes. That all right?"

"Perfectly. I'll be seeing you."

He hung up so abruptly that she was still straining her ears when "Number, please," struck a jarring note. She realised then that she had discovered just nothing. Adrian's wariness—if it was that—could mean he had seen the news about Rose, or equally that some third person was standing close by. His telephone manner was always laconic, like his letters. All she had gathered was his eagerness to see her, which had come through somehow, though whether it was a lover's impatience or something different it was impossible to say. At all events, she would soon know.

At nine o'clock she alighted from a taxi before the main entrance of a huge, dark block of buildings near the British Museum. She paid her fare, and turned so quickly that she ran bolt into a tall, ungainly woman who at that precise moment blundered headlong, blindly down the hospital steps. Diana murmured an apology. The other said nothing, but with one distraught and unseeing look from eyes swollen with weeping gulped down a sob and tore off in the direction of Bloomsbury Square.

Diana stared after her. The features just seen were vaguely familiar, yet so distorted it was hard to connect them with the drab, circumspect female hitherto regarded as a mere adjunct to office furniture. And those clothes! Juvenile, vivid green, absurd, a grotesque caricature, in fact, to say nothing of the mouth crudely smeared with scarlet lipstick. . . . It could not be! Then, in the distance, she noticed, pendent from the crea- ture's ears by silver chains, two blobs of jade which quivered and bobbed wildly as their owner's long strides bore them away.

"It is—Elsie Dilworth, whom we were talking about; and those are the ear-rings Aunt Rose . . . but what's wrong with her? Some one she's fond of desperately ill?" It took a full half-minute for the alternative explanation to dawn. Adrian—of course! She had been to see him. But why? Her presence here at this particular time seemed faintly ominous, still more her distraught condition. A bird of ill-omen. . . .

The door was opened by a young man, stocky and blond, whose tentative smile Diana did not interpret till later, when she remembered having been introduced to him by Adrian, some months before.

"Dr. Somervell? He was here a second ago. Oh, there he is! Somervell!"

Adrian came towards her, his Burberry over his arm. His air was hesitant and awkward, his face bore a flush from recent anger or morti- fication, which Diana was quick to connect with the visitor just seen to depart. Breathing hard, he waited till the blond colleague had withdrawn, leaving them alone in the high-vaulted lobby. Then he put an arm round her, dropped it on noticing her expression, but not before she had felt its tense rigidity.

"What's up?" he inquired. "Anything happened?"

"No—yes. That is—" She reconnoitred and took an oblique tack. "Wasn't that Elsie Dilworth who just went out?" she asked.

"Oh! So you ran into her, did you?"

"She seemed frightfully upset. Why did she come?" His jaw set hard. Brown eyes smouldering wrathfully, he muttered:

"You can search me. She was here when you rang up. I was doing my best to get rid of her. Plain loony, that's what it is. Well," more moderately in answer to her astonished gaze, "call her a hopeless hysteric, if that sounds any better. Let's wash her out. Shall we push off?"

"Wait, Adrian." She was speaking as casually as she could manage. "I rather wanted to ask you if by any chance you've had a look at the *Evening Banner*?"

"The which? Oh, the newspaper! No—that is—I do seem to recall buying some paper, this afternoon, on my way to meet you. Though what I did with it, I—"

"There!" She swooped down on his Burberry. "Isn't that it?"

A dazzling recollection had flooded her brain. She had noticed this self-same paper, folded as now, protruding from his side-pocket when he dumped the Burberry on the tea-shop floor. How like Adrian to buy a paper and not read it! If any doubt had remained, the very way in which he drew the journal forth and abstractedly looked at it would have reassured her. *He hadn't known!*

She began to laugh shakily. He lowered the sheet and gazed at her with dismay hard bordering on exasperation. Surfeited with feminine emotion, that was plain.

"Di! What *is* it?"

"I'm all right. Look, dear, can't you find it? Here!"

He stared at the item blankly, then with fixed attention. Now she was perfectly sure. He was seeing this news for the first and only time.

"Holy Christmas!" he made slow ejaculation. "What the hell does this mean?"

"How do I know?" She fumbled for her handkerchief. "Somebody's kicking up a row. Who do you suppose?"

Still staring, he frowned, and scratched his chin. The sight of his brown, sensitive fingers, with the surgeon's scrupulously clean nails, moved her poignantly. She caught his hand, to find her pressure but half returned.

"Somebody else is crazy," he muttered. "That's certain."

"I think," she said, "we ought to find out who it is. Is there any person connected with this who—who might bear you a grudge?"

"Bear me a grudge? Why me?" His eyes, meeting hers, narrowed in tardy comprehension. "Good Lord!" He drew in a whistling breath. "So that's your notion. Here, look at me, Di!"

He wheeled her about so that the overhead light shone down on her face. A searching scrutiny, then his mouth gave a wry twist.

"Crying," he stated. "That's funny, too. . . . For the moment I'd clean forgotten I was the lucky heir. Matter of fact, I was too darned mad just now to be wide awake to anything. You, I can see, tumbled to this straight off. You're thinking, I suppose," he went on in a formal tone, "what's fairly obvious—that if there's been any dirty business over this death, my connection with Mrs. Somervell will come in for some close examination. Is that it?"

His detachment cut her to the quick. Oh, what a fool she'd been, to give way like this!

"Darling, don't!" she begged. "It was a jar, naturally. And your voice over the telephone—so short, so . . . I understand it now, with that girl bothering you, but when I saw her come out in such a state, can't you see how worried I was? Do let's go where we can talk it over quietly. Shall we try Joe's?"

He looked steadily at her, but did not speak. Instantly she could have bitten her tongue for having made matters worse in her stupid attempt to better them, and her misery increased when, on the silent walk to Southampton Row, she felt his arm stiff as wood within her own. She would put things right between them—oh, very quickly! Still, to have doubted him and to have admitted that doubt was a serious matter.

Joe's sandwich bar was empty but for a garrulous bagman at the counter. Joe, always genial, placed two anaemic coffees on the far table they chose, offered a few opinions on the next flat-race season, and tactfully lounged away.

"First of all," said Diana, "can there be anything in this?"

"Why ask me?" was the brief reply. "If I knew, is it likely I'd admit it?"

"Adrian!" she reproached him, and more silence fell.

Presently he said:

"Sorry. No, as I told you before, all I know about the affair is what I was told."

"Naturally! But you see, I've been talking with my mother, who'd just been seeing Uncle Nick. She—well, she was evidently just a little uncomfortable over something Aunt Rose said to her on the telephone. It was about a queer feeling she had, directly after that last meal. While they were speaking, Aunt Rose collapsed. Quite suddenly. I didn't tell you, but Mummy wrote me about it."

All he said was "Oh?" in a tone betraying little or nothing; but a moment later he inquired exactly when it was her mother had seen Blundell.

"I know what you're thinking," she made quick reply, "but it's quite impossible for him to have done this. I don't imagine he had suspected anything out of the way; and yet," she mused, "he can't have been so entirely ignorant. Now I think of it, the Home Office people must have been making inquiries of him—and of Petty."

"Who?"

"Aunt Rose's housekeeper. Oh—here's a bit more my mother told me. What do you make of it?" and she repeated what Margaret had said on the subject of the unseen visitor in the kitchen. "It was certainly not Uncle Nick," she reasoned, "because Petty was talking about him. If the exhumation order had already been issued, it can't well have been a detective. So who was it?"

He shook his head so faintly that she thought he had scarcely been listening. His eyes had not once met hers, and he was stirring the contents of his cup round and round just as he had done that afternoon. It startled her, therefore, when, quite suddenly, he fixed a frowning gaze on her face and put an abrupt question.

"Your mother," he said. "Exactly what did she overhear?"

CHAPTER SIX

HATING herself, Diana made swift calculations. No, if Petty's clock was right, the visitor could not have been Adrian. She gave her answer, adding that according to her mother Petty had been very nervous.

"As she would have been if she was lying—though, as Mummy said, why should she lie?" Another thought struck her. "Adrian, you are sure it wasn't you who first suggested calling on Aunt Rose?"

"Of course, I'm sure. I didn't want to see her."

Believing him, she felt comforted. How often, she asked, had he seen Rose Somervell, and were they at any time alone together? Adrian leant his head on his hand and rumpled his hair.

"Let's see," he said slowly. "There was the first time, with Blundell. Then, maybe a week later, he and I were invited to tea, and he was called away, so I stayed on alone. Next—oh, yes!—she'd a box to some theatre, asked Blundell and me to come along. I remember I had to borrow a clean evening-shirt from Ladbroke—that's our house-surgeon—because I've got down to one decent one. Soon after this the three of us spent a week-end at Blundell's cottage. She drank a fair amount of brandy, and got quite expansive. That sums it up, I think, except—oh, yes—I had tea again at the flat, by myself, and, of course, there was the Sunday lunch."

"Did you drop in for tea?"

"She wrote me a note, asking me to come, and not being able to work that afternoon—they were doing a repair job in the research room—I went along. That was the time I noticed how hopeless her memory was getting. I could have sworn she'd forgotten I was coming, though she covered it up pretty well."

"But did you answer her note?"

"No. She said she'd expect me unless I rang up to the contrary, so I left it at that. Still, I rather imagined her extreme cordiality on that occasion came from believing I'd come off my own bat. It's an odd thing," he remarked dispassionately, "how even at that age personal vanity is still the main drive. As Adler put it—"

"She usedn't to be so woolly-minded," Diana pinned him down. "Mummy spoke of it, too. How, on the whole, did she strike you?"

"Physically, remarkably fit," he replied, weighing the question. "Mentally slack, very slow on the uptake. She'd stare at you, ask you to repeat a thing, and then like as not come back with something totally irrelevant. She'd a bad trick of talking in circles, if you get me. And that wasn't all. Once she started pouring tea into a full cup. Made the hell of a mess, and never noticed it. Oh, quite a few things of that sort!"

"Did you think of drugs?"

"Drugs?" Again he considered. "Well, a person dependent on morphia does tend to be absent and vague when a dose is overdue. I've seen them get drowsy. She did that. She'd yawn a lot, and at the theatre that evening she dozed right off. Still, she didn't fidget or grow irritable, and she hadn't the look of a morphia-addict, none of the sparkle that follows an injection. On the contrary, I found her always rather dull; but to tell the truth, I didn't study her very closely. I wasn't interested."

"What did you and she talk about?" asked Diana curiously. "Your work, your plans?"

"Hardly mentioned them—which you may think surprising, in view of that will. Neural pathology meant just nothing to her. She did once ask me, jokingly, if Blundell was right about my having a big future in front of me, but straight away she side-tracked on to Blundell's financial cleverness, and rambled off on a long yarn about things and people I'd never heard of. It was the same when I spoke of operating for five months in Madrid, under Mendoza. Her sole reaction was to reminisce about a bull-fighter who'd thrown her a rose. And yet"—Adrian wrinkled his brow—"after the first time or two she always kissed me most affectionately. I supposed she did that to almost anybody; but Blundell assured me I'd scored a hit."

"It's quite evident you did," agreed Diana briskly. "Now, about that Sunday meal. It's probably unnecessary to go into it, but what did you have to eat? Were you at all upset?"

His searching glance told her he had caught her meaning.

"Not me," he answered curtly. "It was better food than I'd been having, and I enjoyed it. What was it, now?" He made an effort to recall. "We started with alligator pear—first I've seen in England—and then there was roast beef, Yorkshire pudding, and so on. After that, some kind of tart with cream, and toasted cheese wafers for a finish. Coffee and port— good stuff. I remember all four of us did full justice to it."

"Four!" Diana grew alert. "Why, who else was there?"

"Didn't I say? Some old theatrical manager. Bald, thin, fiery beak of a nose. Great pal of hers."

"Felix Arenson," murmured Diana promptly. She pondered the information and shook a doubtful head. "Did he leave when you did?"

"Practically, because while I waited for Blundell outside his door I saw this what's-his-name bird going out."

"I see." Diana paused. "And Elsie Dilworth? When was she there?"

Adrian started, winced, and backed into his shell.

"Who told you she was there at all? I'd almost forgotten it."

Diana explained. He listened with a set expression, nodded, and reconsidered her question.

"We were at the table. She wanted to consult Blundell about some shorthand notes. I'd say she hung about a good five minutes. I noticed Mrs. Somervell turned decidedly snappish. You see, Blundell was carving, and had to leave off."

"I suppose," said Diana calmly, "Elsie wanted a glimpse of you and made the notes her excuse. Am I right?"

"Ask me another," he muttered, and was silent, only to strike the table softly with his clenched fist and exclaim under his breath, "God, I'm a prize ass!"

A poisoned dart of suspicion stabbed Diana's mind. After all, why not? Adrian was human, lonely. This woman had thrown herself at him. . . .

"Adrian," she said gently; "you weren't engaged to me then. If you've been making love to Elsie Dilworth, don't be afraid to tell me. Was it that?"

He glared at her.

"Me make love to that neurotic female? Not a chance! Here, if you're taking that tack, I'd better cough up the whole story—such as it is."

He hesitated, then with a cold and dogged reluctance set forth details every word of which, to Diana's thinking, rang true. Elsie Dilworth, well over thirty, plain, and fairly intelligent, had sat next him at table in Bloomsbury Street, and had been exceedingly pleasant. From displaying a keen interest in neurology and brain-surgery she had taken to inviting him up to her comfortable bed-sitting-room in the evenings to partake of cocoa and biscuits. She was company, Diana was away, and fast-dwindling finances permitted him few outside diversions. Now and then, by way of return, he had taken Miss Dilworth to a cinema—and there, for him, the thing ended.

Not so with Elsie, who after a bit began making heavy claims on his sympathy. She would pour out the woes of her starved existence, lamenting the fact that life was passing her by and giving her none of the things she craved.

"Women of all ages talk like that to a doctor," said Adrian bitterly. "Even if we're only students, they seem to look on us as their legitimate prey and turn themselves inside out. I blame myself for not putting a stop to this at the start, but I was in the thick of it before I saw where it was leading. When I did try to side-step, it only made matters worse. At last I had to tell her quite baldly just how impossible it was for me to think of marrying. It seemed more tactful to put it like that," he explained apologetically.

"So you gave her lack of money as an excuse!" Diana hid a pitying smile. "Poor darling! Did it work?"

"Like hell, it did!" he exploded. "Wait till you hear."

Simply to avoid her, he had taken to staying out at night, but whatever time he returned there was Elsie, waiting up in the vain hope of consolation. Never had she been attractive—and since she had begun making herself up and losing every vestige of good sense and reticence the very sight of her was loathsome. Finally, she cornered him and adroitly managed to put him in the wrong. Why couldn't they still be friends? It was all she asked. It was a fine, warm Sunday. Wouldn't he show she was forgiven by taking her into the country?

"Well—I did. God, what a day! She commenced by being coy, and finished by—no, it makes me sweat to think about it!"

"Floods of tears, I suppose?"

"Yes—and worse. She threatened suicide if I kept turning her down. We were in a punt at Richmond," added Adrian between his teeth. "I'm sorry now I didn't let her jump overboard."

"Instead of which you kissed her," Diana murmured, but he was in no mood to respond.

"I had to do what I could to smooth her down. I tell you, I was desperate. I got her home—and went out for a drink. Stayed out till one in the morning—and then, when I did sneak up to my room, dog-tired and disgusted, I give you two guesses as to what I found. Elsie, draped on my bed, in some vile sort of négligée, literally saturated with scent! That put the lid on it. I picked her up bodily and carted her across the hall—yes, kicking and screaming with hysterics. The whole house must have thought I was murdering her. I decided right then to hunt another boarding-place, but she forestalled me by clearing off herself, early next morning. And that's that."

"And you didn't see her again until the Sunday Aunt Rose died?"

"Not once."

"But to-night—what possessed her to come?"

"I've told you, I haven't the foggiest notion. She barged in, wild-eyed, talking the most incomprehensible rot. To get rid of her I told her I was engaged to be married. She turned a sort of pasty-green, gave one gulp, and bolted."

Diana laid her hand on his clenched one.

"Had her coming anything at all to do with—this affair?"

He frowned and hesitated, still showing the same strong repugnance to the topic.

"If it had, she was talking in riddles," he answered. "She babbled something about making mistakes and wanting to atone. There was some bilge about—about being willing to be my slave if only I'd chuck everything and come away with her, out of England."

"Come away with her! Oh, what nonsense!" gasped Diana. "She must be mad."

"She had it all mapped out," he continued grimly. "Some friend in a shipping office had got her two passages on a fruit boat bound for God knows where. She offered to pay for them—oh, yes, I'm telling you. And now, let's drop it. I promise you it won't get us anywhere."

"One thing more, and we'll not mention Elsie again. She knew, of course, that you were friendly with Aunt Rose. Did she ever say anything about Aunt Rose's money?"

"She may have done." He did not look up. "She used to go on a bit about Mrs. Somervell's selfishness. Declared she'd never been known to give a penny to any one who needed it. Once, if I remember rightly, she called her a grasping, nosey old fool."

"Elsie said that? I'd never have thought it—but then, she does seem so utterly different from what I supposed. Oh, well," sighed Diana despondently. "How futile all this is! The worst of it is we'll have to wait days before we know what did happen to Aunt Rose. I rather hate having to go home and hear the family talk about it." Adrian looked at her, then stared woodenly at the floor. Every word she uttered seemed a more ghastly blunder. The hand she had hoped he would take in his remained untouched on the seat between them, mute symbol of the breach no present effort of hers could heal. Joe's customers drifted in and out. For a long interval neither she nor Adrian spoke. She could bear it no longer.

"Adrian!" she pleaded. "What's come over you?" He started to speak, closed his lips and glanced away. "I can't think why I was so stupid," she whispered. "Oh, Adrian, we do love each other! Can't we be ourselves again?"

"I don't quite see how," he said; "until this rotten business is cleared up—if then." The final words came as by after-thought, slowly. "It's not your fault," he added. "So don't think it. Here, it's past eleven. Shall I take you home?"

"No, please. We'll walk to the Strand, and I'll get a bus. In the morning I mean to see Uncle Nick and find out—what I can. What will you do?"

"Me? Oh, carry on as usual." He fumbled with small coins. "I've plenty to do."

She told herself he could not fail to be anxious, but be that as it might she felt certain he would, as he said, continue to dissect brain-tumours, classify them, make careful notes for the treatise he was preparing. The desire seized her to shake him violently, force him to some display of emotion; but the feeling passed, leaving her limp. In a small voice she asked if he would ring her up.

"Of course," he promised, but his tone lacked all warmth.

She knew, then, that in one thoughtless moment at the hospital she had wrought damage far beyond her ability to repair; and yet, even so, could she wholly regret having taken the sole means at her disposal towards banishing her doubt? Wretched though she now was, she had a blessed conviction which nothing could shake. A little suffering, and all would come right. It must. Rose Somervell, when all was said, could have had no real enemies. . . .

When she alighted at the Marble Arch, the two big cinemas were closed and darkened, but a stream of home-goers poured from the Tube exit. She felt a touch on her arm, and, turning, saw her father, tall, vague, distinguished, close at her side.

"Why, Didi! This is a surprise!"

He fell into step with her, the mild pleasure in his eyes giving place to indignation, also mild—for Herbert Lake, at his most vehement, remained a gentle soul. What was the meaning of this inquiry into Rose's death? Disgraceful! The Home Secretary must be out of his senses. Did Pegs know? Oh, to be sure, Diana had not been to the theatre! Well, Pegs would be at home now, waiting to talk matters over. They must hurry along out of this beastly mist, so bad for the throat.

The park, an etching of dark trees and blurred lights, was shut from view. They reached their sheltered square, now deserted, and mounted their own steps. Herbert removed his hogskin glove, took out his key. Then, in a pitch-black hall, he stumbled and mildly swore.

"I've trodden on something. Great carelessness, leaving parcels on the floor. Didi, the light."

Vivid glare, two smothered cries, and father and daughter knelt beside the huddled body which formed the obstruction. It was Margaret Fairlamb—still warm, but stone-dead.

CHAPTER SEVEN

WHAT followed was a period too agonising to be dealt with more than briefly. Margaret Fairlamb had been genuinely loved; her death at the hands of an unknown, brutal assailant was a calamity fraught with horror not only to her family and friends but to a wide public as well. Let us hurry past the interval between the discovery of the body and the memorial service arranged by sorrowing colleagues, and confine ourselves for the moment to the conclusions drawn by the police.

Every known fact pointed to robbery as the motive. What other belief was possible when the victim had not an ill-wisher in the world, and when the handbag taken from her had contained close on a hundred pounds in addition to valuable jewels? It was assumed that the thief had meant to overpower, not kill. Two savage blows had been inflicted, one at the base of the skull, the other on the left temple; and as these had produced fractures and cerebral haemorrhage with little external injury they argued the sort of weapon—sandbag or piece of lead pipe wrapped in a sock—likely to be used by a professional thug. The first blow must have been given as the actress reached for the light-button, the second after she had been felled into the position in which she was found, face upturned, head against the bottom tread of the stairs. There seemed little doubt that the assassin had lain in wait at the foot of the stairs, most likely wearing gloves, since no fingerprints were left behind. The deed accomplished, he had gone quietly out, closing the door, a quarter of an hour, at most, before the husband's and daughter's arrival. The caretakers in the basement had heard nothing.

The question now arose of how the assassin had got in. The street door was opened by latchkeys belonging to the landlord and tenants, or, in the case of visitors, by the instrument of automatic buttons operated from within the various flats. Unless, therefore, the person who entered possessed a duplicate key, he must perforce have rung one of the four bells and been admitted by some one from inside. This, it would appear, was precisely what did happen, as will be seen from the following facts:

The house contained four flats, including the basement premises of the caretakers. The landlord, occupying the ground floor, was a nervous old gentleman who insisted that the street door be kept closed both day and night as a precaution against chance invaders. On this occasion, the Lakes' flat, at the top, was empty, for Mrs. Todd did not live in, but the two floors which remained belonged to a youngish widow, a Mrs. Cathcart, who kept two maids, and both of these, at about eleven-twenty, were roused from sleep by a ring at the street door. Their mistress was dining out. Thinking she had forgotten her keys, they argued a little, after which the cook got up, pressed the automatic button outside the kitchen, and waited in readiness to open the private flat-door the moment the second bell should sound. No further ring occurred, whereupon the cook returned to bed, grumbling, satisfied that the wrong bell had been rung, or else that some idler had been having a game. Not till she learned of the murder did she realise what must have happened. The latch below had yielded when she pressed the button, the thief had come in and hidden himself on the basement flight till assured no investigation was being made.

As some of the newspapers remarked, the ruse was so simple the sole wonder was it had not been employed more often. Simple and safe—for the intruder, if discovered, had only to pretend he had come to the wrong house, and go out again.

The timing of the attack seemed to indicate that the assassin was some one well acquainted with his victim's habits, even with the contents of her bag on this particular evening. Strong in this belief, the inspector in charge of the case interrogated each and every person with whom Miss Fairlamb had spoken during the two days prior to her death. With the fellow-members of her company she had travelled down from Liverpool to London on Sunday, being met by her husband at Euston Station. On Monday and Tuesday she had gone direct to the theatre and rehearsed steadily till after three o'clock, a fact for which all the company could vouch. In other words, at least a score of people—including the stage-hands—might have assumed that she had been unable to bank her two weeks' salary, although whether any of these knew she was actually carrying the money about with her was not discoverable.

Two, however—they were Miss Mears, the star, and Florence Baillie, a dresser—had seen the jewels, for in the second interval Miss Fairlamb unlocked her wardrobe, displayed the sunburst and ring and locked them up again. As neither of these two could say positively if the door had been closed at the time, it seemed possible that a third person had glanced in, while it was equally possible that some one from the unsavoury neighbourhood on which the Trafalgar Theatre backed had looked in at the window from the fire-escape. Children frequently did this, while Miss Fairlamb was dressing. During previous runs they had proved a pest to all the company but Margaret, who had encouraged them by handing out sweets. As a result, she was a great favourite, with a crowd of juvenile admirers to cheer her when she emerged, unimpressive in her street clothes, to hurry to her bus.

This latter fact was considered significant. Who was to say that before now some Luigi or Tonio, whose offspring had Margaret Fairlamb's picture pinned to the kitchen walls, had not tracked the actress to her home in anticipation of a future theft? Or that, having sighted the present rich haul, the same scoundrel had not watched her leave the theatre and forestalled her homecoming by car or a taxi? It was a theory to work on, but nothing came of it. Similarly, every other line of inquiry fizzled out. Fully thirty persons were shadowed to no purpose. Days were spent in ransacking Soho and Paddington, questioning taxi-drivers, checking the movements of servants, caretakers, electricians, stage hands. Two hawkers were detained and released for want of evidence. A careful watch was being kept on pawnshops, which so far revealed no sign of the jewels. An ugly rumour cropped up in connection with the heavy indebtedness of the leading man, Henry Bantock—but it died down again. Lastly, it was conjectured that the intended victim was not Margaret at all but the occupant of the bigger flat—Mrs. Cathcart, who wore real pearls and quite an astonishing number of diamond bracelets, and was apt to come home decidedly the worse for her nocturnal indulgences.

And there, for the present, the matter rested. Already the sensation was simmering down, the theatre ball, which never had ceased to roll, was spinning as busily as before. In another week the affair would be ancient history. Poor, darling little Pegs! One of the best. Was her death to be just one more unsolved atrocity, like that of the young schoolgirl strangled under West Kensington laurel bushes? So it appeared. . . . And now, what about this new comedy Peter's bought? Any good part for a strong character-actor? Oh, he's got his eye on Bob Ainslee! Well, if crystallised mannerisms are what he wants . . .

Alone in the room which had been her mother's, Diana spurred herself on to some further task which, by sheer exhaustion, might ease the sick misery within. There were belongings to sort and put in order, things no hands but hers must be allowed to touch; yet how to begin, when every object she saw reminded her of her loss?

She still wore her dark-blue frock. It would have been cruel to put on mourning when the Red Hen had so hated it. "No black, please!" she could hear her mother saying, as plainly as she could see the bright brown eye cocked at her from the bathroom door, or the same, strangely clouded, stealing glances at her from across the tea-table. That eye had not wished to meet hers. Why? And again, Why?

Throughout these ghastly days of funeral preparations and sessions with the police the Why had thudded ceaselessly inside her brain. It had rendered her almost dumb in the presence of solicitous friends—what hosts there had been!—most of all with her godfather, Nicholas Blundell, for all the latter's great kindness and unprecedented tact. She could not meet him with any frankness, and she fancied he noticed the strangeness of her manner; but how could she ask him any details of his last talk with her mother when to do so would have been equal to admitting an anxiety she must, at this uncertain stage, conceal? She had spoken not one word about her engagement to him, or to her father. Even that, she felt, would be an error. At moments she struggled hard to recapture her confidence that Rose Somervell's death had been from purely natural causes, but that confidence had been shattered irremediably by her mother's sudden end. To be sure, if nothing came of this pending inquiry into old Rose's illness, then the lurking instinct which sought to weave a connection between the two deaths could be dismissed on the instant, and life would go on again.

What did that instinct say? It all grew out of her mother's idea of some person having been with Aunt Rose's servant on Tuesday afternoon. That person, granting he or she existed, could easily have lingered in some part of the flat and thus overheard what Margaret Fairlamb said to her friend, Nick Blundell—yes, not only the discussion of Rose's attack and the telephone conversation preceding it, but Blundell's suggestion that Margaret take her small legacy home with her. What Margaret declared or hinted might have been too veiled to reveal her whole meaning to the solicitor, but the listener, completely understanding, might have been terrified of what this one witness stood ready to disclose in a court of law. Needless to say the listener would have had to be some one who knew Margaret's domestic arrangements, the hour of her return from the theatre. Not Adrian! Thank God that was settled; but Margaret most certainly had Adrian in her thoughts—Adrian, grown worried because the Home Office had been to him with awkward questions; Adrian desperately trying to learn from Petty the full extent of what might have to be faced. . . .

"Oh, too horrible!" groaned Diana. "That she should have had such a suspicion in her mind—that she should have died, still thinking it! Or, if she hadn't died, to have gone on, maybe for ever, with a hideous doubt about—her own son-in-law!"

Adrian had been with her every day, but ill at ease, mute as herself. She had accepted his silent sympathy, seen the shut-in suffering of his eyes, but all her faculties had been deadened, damped down. This state could not last. At any moment she would be stung alive again, but for the present all she had power to do was to perform an endless round of mechanical tasks and wait—wait, for the result of the autopsy.

Now she bestirred herself and stretched out her hand for the packets of letters it was her duty to run through and destroy. Should she just burn the lot? It would be easier; but no, here at the very top were two letters in Aunt Rose's handwriting. Postmarked Vichy—so they were quite recent, written in September, while Rose was taking her cure. Better read them over, just to make sure. . . .

Her father's voice in the passage. Some one with him, too. She would be wanted. More strain. This job must wait.

"Yes, Daddy? I'm here. Have you just come in?"

Her father! Another, separate problem for her to solve—and how? She did not know. Her mother had always thought and planned for him. She must do the same—but what could be done? Herbert Lake was crushed. After two nights' absence from his company he had striven to carry on, with disastrous results. No more acting for perhaps an indefinite time, and meanwhile he could not live long on the modest sums tucked away in War Loan, or on her own debatable earnings. If she and Adrian . . . but the future once so solid, was melting into mist. She and Adrian might never be married.

"Diana?"

The door cracked open, and Herbert's face, stricken and drawn, looked in. The sight of it smote her; and yet was it fancy, or did she detect a faint gleam of something like hope in the sunken eyes?

"Diana, Nick is with me. I—that is, he—has a matter to discuss. May he come in?"

Her thoughts flew to her mother's murderer.

She sprang up, white-faced, scattering the letters.

"Not—? Do they know who—?"

Her father winced painfully.

"No—not that. It's—quite different. I'll let Nick explain."

The dragging step receded down the passage. The door opened wider to frame the broad, deep-chested figure of Nicholas Blundell. Diana murmured, "Come in, Uncle Nick." And partly to hide her face from him, stooped to gather up her mother's letters. Now she would have to nerve herself once more for one of those encounters which she found supremely trying. She would be conscious of sparring, of keeping her own features like a mask and, at the same time, trying in every way possible to get out of her godfather just what he knew or suspected concerning his old friend's death.

CHAPTER EIGHT

SHORT, deep-chested, and with an immense span of shoulder, Blundell seemed, as always, to fill the room, and to overcharge the atmosphere with his superabundant vitality. His head, with its back-sweeping mane of coarse, iron-grey hair, had a crude, compelling magnificence only partly offset by the comedy lines of a battered nose and mobile muscles ever ready, it seemed, to convert his leathery face into a mask of quizzical humour. There was, as Diana had often thought, more than a touch of the lion about him—a caged lion, pacing restlessly behind bars of his own making; and now for the first time in her life she wondered what would happen if those bars were smashed and the passions pent behind them let loose to rampage. The idea sent a stab of fear through her. She glanced at his eyes. They were compassionate, reassuring; but they were also light-coloured and flickering, their lids wrinkled less from age than from exposure; and they were three-cornered in shape.

Where had she heard it said that three-cornered eyes denoted recklessness? Solicitors as a rule were cautious folk—and yet, Nicholas Blundell, late of Johannesburg, was no cut-and-dried representative of his profession. Always there had been something adventurous and expansive about him. Too expansive for her liking, that was the trouble. Even his open-handedness irritated her. It struck her as too—flamboyant? Exuberant? Perhaps overpowering best described his manner of lavishing gifts and so plainly deriving pleasure therefrom. It had the effect of driving her into a shell; but it was petty now to cavil at a quality which had smoothed rough places for her parents in time past and at the present moment was trying to find means of bringing comfort in her sorrow. She made fresh resolutions to keep watch over her feelings, meet any exasperating witticisms with the amiable tolerance her mother would have shown.

"Well, Didi! Hard at it, eh? Quite right to keep busy. Here, let me pick those up." And with one hand resting with clumsy playfulness on her shoulder, Blundell stooped towards the scattered letters. "Hers, I take it? Going to keep 'em?"

"Don't trouble, Uncle Nick." She tried not to stiffen under his touch. "I'll burn them, I think. What was it you wanted to say to me?"

He was squeezing his big body into her mother's small arm-chair—a close fit, as his squirming showed. Diana tore several letters across and dropped them into the waste-paper basket. Then she looked at the two from Vichy, hesitated, and slipped them into the back-flap of her bag. Blundell was eyeing her, apologetically, and with a half-hearted smile. Now he rested his hairy hands on his knees and leant forward.

"It's Herbert. He's in a bad way, but you know that as well as I do, don't you? Well! One thing's obvious. He's got, somehow, to be shaken out of himself. Make a clean break. Otherwise, we can't answer for him, eh? I see you agree. Right! Then here's a scheme—mine—cropped up in the nick of time. Nick! Not bad, what?"

It was the typical Blundell pun, which, for all her good intentions, found no response. She waited, stony-faced, for him to continue. He changed his tone to one of business-like shrewdness.

"Now, then! Ever heard of Boris Weingartner?"

"The Hollywood film director? Yes. He's in London now."

"Quite so—and I've had the luck to run into him, at Lord Limpsfield's, the other evening. He's doing a big historical film and he wants to get hold of an English actor who's well educated and a gentleman to vet his effects and steer him clear of—of—what's the word I want?"

"Anachronisms?"

"You've said it. Well, I told him Herbert was his man. I've just come from having the two of 'em meet, and Weingartner's made an offer. Everything's on velvet, only Herbert has to have his mind made up for him. Quick, too, because the *Gigantic*'s sailing on Wednesday, and if Herbert don't go on it, some other chap will. How about it? Think you can manage it?"

Diana gasped. Hollywood—her father's dream! Now it would mean to him infinitely more than the realisation of a pathetic ambition. To go completely away from all that reminded him of her mother, to be deferred to, made to feel important. . . . It was the one perfect solution. . . .

"Weingartner wants to take him for a bit to a big ranch he's got and let him pull himself together. Work won't start till January, and meantime Herbert can ride, bathe in a super-swimming pool, browse in an A-one reference library. He'll get a retaining fee, understand; and if you hate the idea of separation, why, I might arrange for him to take you along. You may even get a part in the next production. It's a chance worth considering. Does it appeal to you?"

Diana stared, dazed by the rapidity with which things were moving. She shook her head.

"Not for me—thanks tremendously, Uncle Nick. Daddy must go, of course. We can't let him refuse." Her godfather looked ludicrously downcast.

"You won't go? I rather hoped you would. There'd be more opportunities. Look!" He lowered his voice. "If it's this business you're thinking of, your being on the spot won't get the inquiry one bit forwarder. I'll guarantee the police don't lie down on their job. Besides, where so much public feeling's been roused—"

"I—I'd rather stay in London, I think."

He watched her kindly, but asked no questions.

"Well," he said with regret, "you know best; but if you think better of it, just say the word and I'll see what can be done. You will tackle Herbert?"

"Leave him to me. It's terribly good of you, Uncle Nick."

"No, no!" He waved an expansive hand. "I was in luck, that's all."

She wished she had been able to make her thanks sound less formal. The truth was, in spite of her vast relief, she was thinking how irksome it was to accept so much at Uncle Nick's hands, even for her father, for whatever Uncle Nick might say, she felt certain it was he who was paying this retaining fee, perhaps offering the hard-boiled Weingartner other inducements to choose, from a great army of eligibles, her own not-very-competent father. Then she recalled what her mother had said about Lord Limpsfield's being on such friendly terms with the solicitor who managed his affairs. The Limpsfield Press was a mighty power which no film magnate, however successful, could afford to antagonise. No doubt influence had been at work. Limpsfield probably had shares in Weingartner's company. Maybe Uncle Nick had some interests there as well.

The tick of the little gilt clock became audible above the purring of the gas fire. Blundell, his eye beginning to rove, stirred restlessly in his tight-fitting chair, and from an alligator cigar-case drew forth a fat Corona.

"Uncle Nick." Diana spoke in a dry voice, not raising her eyes from the letters in her lap. "Have you had any news at all about—Aunt Rose?"

He paused, looked at her. His face hardened.

"Not yet," he replied grimly. "It seems the chap who does these things is down with 'flu. Why?"

"I was wondering, that's all. It struck me they were taking a long time over it."

Blundell slowly ripped the band from his cigar.

"You'd a talk with your mother that evening I saw you. That right?" As she nodded, he went on, "Did she tell you what she told me?"

"You mean about her telephone conversation with Aunt Rose? She did. Up till that time, I suppose, it hadn't ever occurred to you her death mightn't be—natural?"

"I don't believe it now," he said shortly. "At least—well, that feeling she mentioned may not have meant anything except what the doctor said. Some lunatic's been starting a rumour, of course. I hoped it might come to nothing. That's why I didn't want to distress your mother—in case it petered out, you know. I didn't know myself till I saw the evening papers, just after I left her. Do you think she ever saw that notice?"

"She did. One of the cast showed it to her in her dressing-room. She—wouldn't make any comment on it." Diana gripped her two hands tightly together, thinking what that silence must have meant. "You say some lunatic . . . Have you the least idea who it was?"

"Not the ghost of one. I've done my damnedest to find out, but the Home Office people won't give me any clue."

From the mortified chagrin in his voice she knew he was speaking truth. It must, she thought, be intensely humiliating to him that some person had been sharper-eyed than himself where his beloved Rose was concerned. His peace of mind, like hers, had been shattered. If she was apprehensive, so was he, if for a different reason. Adrian Somervell could not fail to be uppermost in his thoughts, no whit less than in her own. That his name had been mentioned by neither of them seemed ominous.

"I'll speak to my father," she said, getting up and going into the passage. "As you say, there's no time to lose."

As she reached her father's door she heard Blundell behind her, at the telephone, dialling a number. She stopped to listen, holding her breath.

"Blundell speaking," she heard the gruff voice saying. "Sir Bruce able to carry on? Oh, he has! Well, what's he found?"

Sir Bruce! That meant Sir Bruce Baynes, the analyst, whose decisions figured in all cases of suspected poisoning. Her heart beat suffocatingly. A smothered "Good God!" reached her ears, then after an interval, "H'm—I see. What did you say it was? . . . Spell it. . . . Ah-h-h! Yes, I've got it. Aconite. What does it do? . . . You say it paralyses the lips and tongue? . . . That's enough! I'm coming round."

Diana's bag, clutched in her hand, clattered to the floor. She turned to confront a being she scarcely recognised. Blood had surged into Nicholas Blundell's three-cornered eyes, knotted veins bulged forth from his temples. As she saw his powerful hands clinching and unclinching and heard his laboured breathing wheeze through his nostrils all she could think of was the enraged man-killer—old, wounded, revengeful.

If only she could calm him down—for one instant claim his attention! She laid her hand on an arm unyielding as the limb of an oak and vibrating with fury; but before she could speak her father, come out from his room, spoke for her.

"They've made the examination? Nick, old man! You can't mean they've—that Rosie Walsh was poisoned?"

"Poisoned! Murdered's the word. Don't stop me!" Blundell glared at the father and daughter, seeing neither; then with a savage violence which left them speechless, he caught up his overcoat and hat from the hall-chest and charged from the flat. All the way down the three flights they heard him thundering. The banging of the street door shook the house, and following hard upon it the Sunbeam's engine whirred raucously.

Gone—to the Home Office. For what purpose? Diana could conceive of but one. He had formed his conclusion, could envisage no alternative possibility. Before an opportunity of making him see reason presented itself, who could say what damage might be done? She must act—now, at once. Even so, it might be too late. . . .

Herbert Lake drew his hand over his eyes. It was a fine, shapely hand, but ineffectual, like the rest of his handsome person.

"Rosie meant so much to him," he murmured. "We always knew she did. He'll leave no stone unturned to . . . Why, Diana, I thought you were with me?"

The passage was empty save for himself. Diana too, had flown.

CHAPTER NINE

IN FIVE minutes' time a taxi was whirling Diana across the park. Through one window rose the new, monumental buildings of Park Lane, out the other stretched green, damp flats with acres of upturned iron chairs and a mist of bare trees beyond. All she saw was a squat, lion-like figure, its face swollen, distorted with rage. It followed her like a menace.

Soon, however, she recalled two facts which steadied her. First, Nicholas Blundell was a solicitor, therefore unlikely to let his anger lead him into any indiscretion. Second, he could have no reason, beyond the obvious incident of the will, for suspecting Adrian over and above another person. Money offered only one of several possible motives; and as Diana arrived at this point her thoughts gravitated to the fourth guest at Rose's luncheon table—old Felix Arenson.

The actress had not been on speaking terms with her former manager for a period of years, till recently, when a truce had resulted in a sort of armed neutrality and the interchange of many honeyed pleasantries. This was not strange. Rose Somervell had quarrelled with most of her associates at one time or another. Diana could not remember the cause of this particular rupture, though it was probably due to some defamatory statement, true or false, which Aunt Rose had made concerning Felix's honesty. How she regretted paying so scant attention to the tittle-tattle her mother had with amused indulgence retailed! It was simply that the petty jealousies, tale-bearing, and weather-cock emotions of the world in which she had grown up were to her a distasteful, boring commonplace. Arenson—a dry, cynical, bloodless stick of a man—might conceivably have cherished resentment. He might even have feared further injury from a woman he had once—if ancient rumour did not lie—been anxious to marry. Supposing he had poisoned his hostess's food, was there any reasonable excuse for his plying old Petty with questions after the event?

Yes, she decided, Arenson or any one else might have done just that very thing, if the authorities had been to him making embarrassing inquiries. He would be on tenterhooks to find out on what grounds suspicion rested, if the doctor who attended the dead woman had seen anything wrong—oh, any number of things. He might have done it as a blind, pretending entire ignorance of all that had happened. Petty could have been frightened or bribed to say nothing about his visit, though later on—and this would be part of his object—she would come out with it, thus scoring a point in his favour.

It was possible, of course, that the unseen person had been the caretaker of the house; or it might have been one of the servants from the flat below; only, would Petty have been so agitated over questions asked by one of her own kind? It seemed unlikely; still, whatever the case, Diana meant to have the truth of it at once. Uncle Nick, always considerate, had allowed Petty to stay on for the present in what had for so long been her home. She might, however, depart any day, after which it might not be easy to corner her.

Westward they swung along Knightsbridge—and now the huge bulk of the Albert Hall hove in view. As they skirted its flank Diana was struck by another thought. What a good thing Petty had mentioned Uncle Nick's name! Otherwise one might have imagined . . .

"Here, this won't do!" She laughed a little hysterically. "What mad notion shall I be getting next?"

Lights were already glimmering through the haze when they turned into a broad cul-de-sac, the lower end of which was spanned by an opulent-looking brown stone mansion, with an imposing entrance guarded by twin bay-trees. This was the modern house built not twenty years ago by a fraudulent financier whose spectacular trial and conviction had filled the papers for a twelvemonth. Blundell had bought the freehold at auction, turning it into three flats, of which the ground floor one, with absurdly large and lofty rooms, was occupied by himself. The top was let to advantage to a wealthy Spaniard, seldom at home; while in between Rose Somervell had lived, in smug luxury, alone with the servant who for half a lifetime had been her dresser.

Inside was a vast expanse of lounge-hall or lobby, panelled in cedar, with hideous Sèvres vases in niches, and grey carpet a full inch thick. It was all heavily magnificent, the sort of thing Aunt Rose had loved. The door to Blundell's flat lay on the left, and just beyond rose a sweep of wide, shallow stairs. Diana mounted them, and pushed the button beside a second impressive door.

Complete silence. She rang repeatedly, but still no answer came. Petty was not here, evidently. Did it mean that she was gone for good? Down Diana went to the street, and rang the caretaker's bell. A young, plump woman in a green overall appeared, recognised her, and in tribute to her recent bereavement assumed a woeful expression. Pardon the mention of it, but had Miss Lake had any news? As Diana shook her head, she scanned the caretaker's face. It showed only sympathy—so its owner as yet knew nothing about the verdict of poisoning in her former tenant's case. She had been referring solely to the murder of Margaret Fairlamb—which was just as well.

"And to think," said the woman in hushed tones, "that only that same afternoon your poor mother and me was talking together! Asking about my little Alfred she was—if he'd had his tonsils out yet." She paused, overcome by the recollection. "Was it Mrs. Petty you was wanting, miss? She's up there, right enough. I've not seen her go out this day."

"She didn't answer the bell. Are you quite sure she's there?"

"Well—as sure as I can be. She might have popped out just now while I was in the scullery washing up; but I hardly think—" The caretaker stopped, a look of fear in her eyes. "She's been acting a bit queer these past few days," she faltered uncertainly. "I was saying only this noon to my husband as how . . ." Again she stopped. "Suppose I just run up with you and make certain? You see—well, she's turned seventy, hasn't she? You never know, she may have come over faint-like."

Mr. Blundell had a key, so she informed Diana as with ill-concealed anxiety she hurried into the entrance-hall. His chauffeur-butler would be in, if he wasn't, for she'd seen him come in not ten minutes ago. Yes, Mr. Blundell often drove himself. For days at a time Mr. Gaylord wasn't wanted for the car.

As she spoke the caretaker rang the ground-floor bell, which was answered by a big, friendly-faced young man to whom she put a quick question.

"Mrs. Petty?" he repeated, respectfully acknowledging Diana's presence. "No, I've not seen her go out. Want the key? Here you are, then." He took a Yale key from the gigantic, over-varnished oak press which served as a coat cupboard, handed it over, and asked doubtfully, "What's it all about? Anything up?"

"Oh, I expect it's all right! Only the young lady was wanting a word with her, and she couldn't seem to make her hear."

Gaylord hesitated, then followed them upstairs to stand by, big and awkward in his off-duty clothes, while the door was opened. Diana was now feeling strongly apprehensive. Supposing the old woman had succumbed to some seizure, how was she ever to find out what at the moment seemed so vitally important?

With a tremor in her voice, the caretaker called, "Mrs. Petty—are you there?"

Dead silence reigned. Gaylord switched on lights, and the trio entered the drawing-room, spotlessly clean and in order. It was a fine room, a little over-furnished in good antiques, the larger pieces now shrouded in dust-sheets. The walls were painted a greyish-rose, the thick curtains were of brocaded damask, delicate powder-blue in colour. Over the Adam mantel hung a big de Laszlo portrait of Rose Walsh at the age of forty. There was a slightly queer look to everything, owing to the ornaments having all been placed at angles, cata-cornered. The invaders took a brief survey and passed on, Gaylord leading the way and walking softly, his big feet sinking into the thick velvet carpet. The dining-room next—olive-green, dignified, with copies of old Chippendale, and ship-paintings—also copies—on the walls; and now the late owner's bedroom, luxurious, effete. Diana shuddered at sight of the wide, low bed with gilded swans supporting a canopy of rucked, rose taffeta, glanced past it to the dressing-table with its incredible array of engraved and painted bottles, and on to the Empire day-bed, on which lay a rug of summer ermine, folded with the satin lining outside.

The kitchen and pantry likewise were empty. So was the little boudoir-dressing-room adjoining the pale-green bath, and hung with quilted chintz.

"Here! Will you take a look at this?"

It was Gaylord calling, his tone astonished. He was standing in the doorway of Petty's bedroom, whistling between his teeth. Diana joined him, the caretaker close at her side. Together they took stock of the clean, cramped space with its cream-striped wallpaper, white iron bed tidily covered with a coarse counterpane, deal chair, enamelled chest of drawers—and nothing more.

"Well," said the caretaker, "What about it?"

"Don't you see? She's taken her box—and that there cupboard's got nothing in it. She's cleared off, that's certain. I wonder if Mr. Blundell knows?"

The caretaker looked relieved, but flummoxed.

"There, now! I'm glad, anyhow, it's—no worse. But would you 'ave believed it, going off like that with never a word to no one? Very quiet she must've been. Dear, dear. I said she's turned queer. This proves it—don't you think?"

They returned to the kitchen. The caretaker touched the electric cooker.

"Kettle's warm," she announced. "So she's not been long gone. Clock's running, too, and these plates in the rack are still damp. Now where's she got to, and at her age?"

"Nephew in Peckham," declared Gaylord confidently. "Come and fetched her, I expect, on his motor-cycle. You see, she's drawing her pension now; and I heard Mr. Blundell say he was giving her a matter of two quid a week, so she could go up to Sunderland, where she come from—that is, if she was a mind—and not be a burden to her folks."

"Is he doing that?" murmured the woman, awed. "My word, but he's a good man and no mistake! But supposing she's wanted—here?"

There was a self-conscious pause, during which the two recalled Diana's presence. Gaylord cleared his throat and swayed from one foot to the other.

"Oh, I expect she'll stick round London on the off-chance," he said discreetly. "Stands to reason she will, for all she's in such a rare state over being arsked questions she can't answer."

Diana was eyeing the cheap alarm clock which ticked away on the dresser. Gaylord noted her swift glance at her watch and smiled humorously.

"Don't be going by that clock, miss," he advised. "She kept it like that a-purpose, same as most cooks—don't arsk me why. This one's five and twenty minutes fast."

Five and twenty minutes fast! Then it had been fast last Tuesday. Diana's heart stood still as one precious prop was swept from her grasp. Adrian could have been here and still reached the tea-shop by five-thirty. In place of the ten minutes she had assumed, he would have had over half an hour. Suddenly she remembered that he had looked at her strangely when she mentioned what her mother had overheard and had instantly demanded details.

"Tell me," she addressed the waiting pair. "On the Tuesday my mother was here, did either of you see any one go out from this flat? I don't mean Mr. Blundell. Was there any one else?"

Their blank expressions told her that here was no deception. Both shook their heads, exchanging glances. The caretaker remarked that she nearly always knew if some one went in or out of the house. That was what puzzled her about Mrs. Petty. She had been in the whole of Tuesday afternoon.

"And Petty's nephew—do you know his address?"

The caretaker did not. Gaylord, however, had driven the old woman there once, and thought he could describe the locality. The nephew was a corn-chandler, in a small way, living above his shop, which was in a narrow turning off Peckham Rye. He traced a plan on the clean scrubbed table.

"Here's the High Street, miss. That'll be the turning, by a chemist's. The right-hand side it was. Name's Petty, same as hers."

"Thanks so much. I'll try and run along there one day. Well, I suppose I'd better be going."

She picked up her gloves from the dresser, and then stared hard at an object unnoticed till now. It was a clean, folded handkerchief—too good to be Petty's, too large and not fine enough to have belonged to Aunt Rose. With a little laugh she caught it up and slipped it into her bag.

"Mine," she murmured. "Waiting for me to claim it, I expect. Will you turn off the lights?" and she quickly left the flat.

How did one get to Peckham Rye? A policeman advised her to take a train from Victoria, whither she hurried by taxi. Now she was alone, she struck a match and examined the handkerchief. It was a woman's, undoubtedly, and it bore in one corner some initials marked in indelible ink. She thought they were E. and D., with a central one too faded to decipher. About to refold the square of linen again, she stopped and pressed it against her nose. It gave forth the ghost of a pungency at once familiar and distasteful. Some perfumes survive ordinary washing, none better than this, which she despised. It crossed her mind that within the week a blast of this same odour had hit her full in the face. The owner must have been drenched with it—and hand-in-hand with the thought came the recollection of Adrian's bitter observation about a négligée reeking of scent.

"If it is hers," she reflected, "then my theory's knocked to bits. Or—no, maybe it isn't. Why need one assume this handkerchief was left behind on one particular occasion? There may have been plenty of other times."

All at once, in her ear, she heard her mother's musing question: "By the way, did your Aunt Rose ever use chypre?"

Chypre! This was the stuff. The odour of it had been in the kitchen when her mother went in. Moreover, the woman who did use it might have had a motive, albeit mad and mistaken, for committing first one crime then another. Was the notion entirely wild?

CHAPTER TEN

SHE emerged from the Peckham Rye Station in a thoroughfare noisy with trams, lorries, and motor-cycles, found the chemist's shop, and turning the corner, saw the sign: *"G. Petty, Corn and Feed."* Threading her way between sacks of dog biscuits and dusty-smelling oats, she entered a dark, empty shop and rapped on the counter.

A glazed door opened and a youngish man dressed in a baggy brown suit and a clean but ill-fitting collar came out. She asked if he was G. Petty. He nodded and gave her a curious glance.

"I'm Miss Lake, and I'd like to speak to your aunt. I know she's here, because I've just seen her, in there. Will you tell her I'm here?"

G. Petty's expression subtly altered.

"Right you are, miss. She's just having her tea."

He reopened the door and went through. She heard him say, "Now, don't upset yourself, Ma. Nothink to hurt you. Ivy, will you just give an eye to the shop?"

A young woman with coarse, dark hair and a purple knitted jumper came out wiping her mouth. G. Petty whispered to Diana that the old party was not quite herself, what with all the excitement, and would she make allowances?

"Poor old thing! She won't mind me. Why, she's known me all my life."

In spite of this assurance Diana saw the nephew had no intention of allowing a *tête-à-tête*. When the old servant had risen with a quavering smile he took his stand, awkward but stolid, near the small, red glowing stove. His wife called to him reproachfully: "George! Aren't you asking the young lady if she'll have a cup of tea?" Whereupon the omission was repaired with such thoroughness that Diana found herself unable to refuse the proffered hospitality. Strong Indian brew was pressed upon her, Petty with palsied haste handed her Genoa cake tasting strangely of cardboard and soap.

"Well, well!" The old woman prattled breathlessly. "Fancy you coming here, Miss Di! You could 'ave knocked me over with a feather, so you could."

She was a frail, brittle little creature, very respectable in her decent black, her waxed pink skin drawn taut over her sharp face-bones, her scalp glistening frostily through her sparse white hairs. On a chair lay her hat, with a knot of battered roses at the side—so she had but lately arrived. She still indeed wore her coat, shabby, but handsome, the one Rose had given her years ago, but with the baby lamb collar removed; yet, though the room was oven-hot, she was shaking like a leaf.

"Do sit down, Petty, dear. I can see you're tired. Gaylord told me where I'd find you, and I wanted to make sure you were all right. You see, the caretaker seemed surprised you hadn't said good-bye."

Stammering, Petty looked beseechingly at George.

"I told you so, didn't I, Ma?" he remarked. "You see, miss"—to Diana—"Auntie's got all of a dither, what with being by herself and—" He hesitated. "Having the police on to her night and day over this here death. But for the gentleman below looking after her so thoughtful-like she'd have hopped it before now—though I kept telling her not to do nothing silly. 'Twasn't her they was after."

"Oh, Mr. Blundell's bin ever so good!" babbled Petty hastily. "I wouldn't want to worry him, troubled as he is. I—I did write him, didn't I, George?"

"Posted the letter as we come along," confirmed George. "Only she's had enough of Nosey Parkers—not mentioning names, of course." In an undertone he confided: "If I hadn't given in to her and sneaked her off quiet, she'd have gone to bits. Understand?"

Diana nodded, but was not satisfied. Suppose Petty's eagerness to escape unobserved meant the guarding of a secret soon to be wrested from her? Somehow she must get rid of George—but how to accomplish it? Drinking her tea, she encouraged the timorous old creature to ramble on, which she did, mainly about her nephew. Yes, George was like her own son. Many's the time, in the old days, he'd called for her at the theatre. Even as a little nipper he'd said he'd always look after his auntie.

"He will have it, miss, the thing's blown over, like. It's almost a week now, since—" A sudden horrified recollection sprang into her faded eyes. "Oh, Miss Di! And me forgetting your own poor mother! What must you be thinking?"

"Let's not speak of her, Petty. I quite understand. As for the other—well, I'm afraid it hasn't blown over. That's what I wanted to break to you. Mrs. Somervell was poisoned."

"Poi-poisoned?"

Wild-eyed, Petty had sprung up. Her false teeth rattled in her gasping mouth. Darting Diana a glance, George strode firmly to her.

"Easy, now, Ma. It's nothink to do with you. There now! Like me to fetch a drop of brandy?"

"Do," murmured Diana, snatching at the excuse. "She'll be all right with me."

When the door closed behind him, Diana took the gnarled hands in hers with a steady pressure.

"Petty, dear," she said quietly; "don't be frightened, will you? There's something I must ask you while your nephew is out. Only this: What was Miss Dilworth saying to you in the kitchen the afternoon my mother called? I want to know that, and also why you denied any one was there."

One swollen, arthritic hand struggled free to clap itself over an affrighted mouth.

"Oh!" whispered Petty. "So your mother did know?"

It was Elsie! The bluff had worked.

"She did," lied Diana glibly; "and the details of it are terribly important. Oh, it is quite safe! Just trust me, won't you? Now, why did Miss Dilworth come, and what did she want to find out?"

Rocking her frail body, Petty looked this way and that, and finally gave way.

"'Twasn't the only time," she moaned. "Miss Dilworth was on to me from the very day my lady died, trying to worm out I don't rightly know what! Made me swear not to tell. Said as how it might mean trouble for me. Fair frightened me, she did, acting so queer."

"Get you into trouble? And what business was it of hers?"

"Why, none at all, miss." For the first time Petty seemed to take a sensible view and brightened accordingly. "She hated my lady—never took no pains to hide it. Making out I was put upon, hadn't ought to work so hard at my age and all. Her, a working woman like myself!" The old voice trembled with scorn. "And wasn't she in the dining-room 'anging about the very meal my lady was took bad? That she was—and rare vexed my lady was, to be sure!"

Now Petty's tongue was loosened it was not difficult to get the whole story hitherto pent by unreasoning fright. On the given afternoon the secretary had once more slipped upstairs to prod Petty with her mysterious questions. What sort of questions? Oh, all to do with the illness. How soon after lunch had Mrs. Somervell fallen down in a faint? Had she, before she telephoned, mentioned any especial sensation, and if so, how had she described it? Did she vomit? What had there been for lunch? Anything that could have disguised a strange taste? What had the police said on these matters? Oh, Miss Dilworth knew all about the police visits. Not much went on she didn't know.

"Did she go back at once?" interrupted Diana. "Or wait in the passage till my mother had gone?"

"She didn't come in again, miss, but she may have stuck in the passage for a bit, hoping to hear more than I'd told her. 'Twould 'ave bin like her, worried as she was."

"She was worried, you think?"

"Oh, Miss Di, she was fair highsterical! And the way she slid out, quick as a wink, when she heard your mother's voice! I'd bare time to whip up the handkerchief she'd dropped to keep your mother from seeing it. That evening for something to do I rinsed it out and run the iron over it—and there it lays now, on the dresser, waiting for her to come and claim it."

"I see. By the way, Petty, what was there for lunch that Sunday? I suppose there wasn't any food that could have disguised a strong taste?"

"Only the horseradish, miss," answered Petty so promptly that it was plain she had given the matter thorough consideration. "Made with whipped cream, it was, like my lady would have it; but horseradish is hot-flavoured—like nothink else, as you might say. Still, all of us ate it, so how could only her be poisoned?"

"Who served the meal?" asked Diana, waiving the question.

"Mr. Blundell carved, same as always, when he was there. I handed the plates and the vegetables, then the sauce and gravy. It was just the four people; if it 'ad bin more, we'd 'ave had extra help. There was the second helpings, though. Now, how was they managed?" Petty knit her waxen forehead. "Seems as how young Mr. Somervell got up and passed the two sauce-boats himself to—oh!" She broke off with a gasp. "Don't think I mean nothink by that, Miss Di! It's just that I remember him crossing the room and bumping into Miss Dilworth as she turned round quick-like from showing Mr. Blundell her bits of writing. I noticed, because of her going off into fits of giggling."

Diana comforted her distress.

"There's no reason why you should remember anything very clearly. The horseradish may have had nothing to do with it; but one other thing

I'd like to ask. My mother told me Aunt Rose had grown very absent-minded. Did you notice it, too? And when did it begin?"

"She was growing forgetful, and no mistake! Why, she'd give me orders three times over! Sleepy, too. Said it was the dark days setting in. I've seen her doze off at breakfast with her tea half drunk. I used to slip in and make fresh for her; but I can't rightly say when it started. Not long after we come home from France. Yes, about the time Mr. Adrian begun coming—or maybe before. I do know Mr. Blundell spoke to me about it—and he mentioned it again, to the doctor, the evening she died."

"What did the doctor say?"

"Just nodded, like as though he'd expected it. The word he used was auto—auto—"

"Auto-intoxication?"

"That's it. Called it a symptom, and said as how she'd never ought to touch the port. That was the trouble of them cures. She'd come home so 'earty she'd eat and drink whatever she fancied."

The Vichy cure had been in September. Adrian had met Uncle Nick and paid his first call early in October. Better not go too closely into these dates. Indeed, much as she wanted to know, Diana decided not to probe any further into Petty's unreliable memory. Besides, here was the nephew back again, doubtless from the corner pub, with two inches of brandy in a thick tumbler. He, at least, was alert—too much so, for Diana's liking. She rose to go.

"She's quite calm now, Mr. Petty. The little talk has done her good. Here's my telephone number. Let me know if she wants anything, won't you?"

"It's very good of you, Miss."

On the chaff-filled threshold George coughed meaningly.

"I'll tell you what's wrong with her, Miss. It's the hundred quid Mrs. Somervell left her. She cooked that lunch—and cleared away all the scraps. Some party—I'll not say who—has fair put the wind up her. That's why she's come away."

"Poor Petty!" murmured Diana compassionately. "Only a hundred pounds—and to be thrown in such a state! Why, no one, no one in their senses, would ever dream—"

"Now, would they?" interrupted George quickly. "No, I keep telling her it's the big lump of property they'll go for. It's no concern of mine, but when a person that's no blood relation turns up out of the sky and gets left a whole fortune two days before the party drops dead—well, I'll say no more, but I dare say you get my meaning."

She had got it, only too well. George Petty was voicing the opinion of the whole news-reading public. Of what use, she asked herself wretchedly, was her information about an hysterical, infatuated typist? All it proved at present was that Elsie Dilworth knew suspicion of murder had arisen and was in a fever of anxiety lest it point to the man she loved. Only one person—Diana herself—conceived the possibility of the woman's terror springing from a personal cause. Was it worth while trying another bluff?

It was. With bold decision she entered a telephone booth and rang up her godfather's flat. Blundell was not in. She asked for the secretary.

"Miss Dilworth, miss?" Gaylord was brisk, casual. "Miss Dilworth's left."

"Gone home, you mean?"

"No, miss, left off working for the master. Some days ago."

"Oh!" Diana felt startled. "Do you know why she left?"

"Well, miss, we understand it's a sort of breakdown. Nerves, you know—but I can't rightly say."

"But you have her address, I suppose?"

"No, miss, that we haven't. She moved a matter of a few weeks ago, and where she's been since we don't none of us know."

She hung up the receiver and moved slowly to the ticket office. In the train she remembered the two letters from Aunt Rose to her mother, all this time stuck in the back-flap of her bag. She got them out and read them through carefully. As she had expected, they were filled with tittle-tattle, grumblings over minor discomforts, gossip about fellow-visitors at Vichy. The writer had collected a new and delightful notable, one Sir Francis Dugdale, who was by way of being something very important at the Home Office, and she was preening herself over the capture. Such a fascinating man and, it seemed, one of her warmest admirers for years. When she got back, she must give a little luncheon party, have Sir Francis meet Nick. The two could jabber politics and finance to their heart's content. It was the sort of thing Nick most enjoyed. Disappointed, Diana slid the thin sheets back into their envelopes. In all the dead woman's tight firm scrawl, there was no mention of Adrian, indeed nothing whatsoever to shed a glimmer on her problem.

CHAPTER ELEVEN

AT THE end of three days of incredible rush Diana saw her father off to Southampton. Poor Herbert, gaunt, nervous, but very distinguished-looking in the new overcoat she had ordered for him, was now aboard his boat-train, a lost, intimidated child amidst his strange medley of new companions; and she, alone on the foggy Victoria platform, drew her first free breath, and wondered if the total absence of any news was a good sign.

There had been an inquest, briefly reported. From its non-committal character she hoped all danger was past. She suffered to think that Adrian, since the announcement about the poisoning, had kept studiously away from her, but that was her doing, and she must bear it as best she could. He, like herself, was waiting for further developments. It could not now be for long.

As she reached the barrier she saw her godfather, tempestuous, out of breath, shouldering his way past the ticket-collector. He had come to see Daddy off, and was a moment too late.

"Gone!" The bluff, battered features registered disappointment. "Couldn't be helped. I've caught you, anyhow, that's the main thing. Bearing up, are you? That's a good girl. I knew you would."

He patted her arm, looking anxiously into her face.

"I was delayed," he explained. "But I'm in time to drive you home. You're going there, aren't you?"

"Yes, but please don't trouble. I'll just jump into a 'bus."

"Not while my car's here. No, don't argue with me! Come right along. I want to talk to you."

She stopped dead still and met his glancing eyes.

"What is it?" she whispered. "Tell me now."

His only answer was to propel her through the jostling crowd to the Grosvenor Gardens exit, and into the waiting Sunbeam where he tucked a fur rug cosily over her knees, and instructed Gaylord to drive through the Park to Seymour Square.

"Herbert told me yesterday you'd had an offer for the flat," he began. "Going to take it?"

"I have, already. Six guineas was far too good to turn down. But what were you—"

"Sensible girl! Now where'll you go?"

"Oh, I'll find a room somewhere. I've not had time to think of it. All this has come so suddenly, I'm still a bit dazed. Please, Uncle Nick—I must know why you wanted to talk to me. Has anything—happened?"

He took her gloved hand and gave it a series of spasmodic squeezes. His voice when he replied was gruffly kind.

"Yes," he admitted, "but don't take it too much to heart, will you? It may mean just nothing, you know. The fact is, our young friend Adrian was taken in charge, early this morning. I've been trying to bail him out. That's why I'm late."

"Adrian . . . he's been arrested? Oh!"

Now the blow had fallen, she knew that in her secret heart she had always expected it. She felt dizzy and slightly sick.

"Why?" she managed to ask. "Was there any other reason besides— the money?"

"Don't know of any." Blundell said this slowly, his brow deeply furrowed. He did not look at her—an ominous sign, she thought. "My offer of bail was refused. It always is, in these cases, but I had a try all the same."

Uncle Nick had offered bail. Why? She could hardly take this in.

"But does that mean you yourself don't think Adrian did it?"

"May not have been," he mumbled, still avoiding her eyes. "How do you feel about it?"

"Me? That's altogether different. I know he didn't. It's simply impossible." Diana paused, moistened her parched lips and added: "You see, Adrian and I are engaged."

"Engaged? Good God!"

Blundell turned, stared at her, and mopped his forehead with a plaid silk handkerchief.

"When did you get engaged to him?" he demanded, deeply concerned. "Before, or was it after?"

The question grated on her. Too well she understood its drift.

"It was the afternoon I got home from Leeds. My mother knew, but I've said nothing to Daddy, nor to any one else. It seemed better not to mention it."

She fancied he seemed relieved. For a moment he stroked her hand, trying to adjust his ideas to the altered situation.

"Well, well!" he said at last. "This does complicate it a bit, eh? Most naturally—oh, I quite see it!—you and he fixed matters up on the strength of this inheritance. Made a difference to him; but I'm glad you've had the good judgment to keep it dark. Much wiser, all considered. Take an old lawyer's advice: Go on being mum. Just in case, you understand. As I say, it may come to nothing. He'll come up before a magistrate in two days' time. Then we'll know better where we stand. Of course he'll want expert counsel. We must see what's he's doing about it."

"We?" she echoed, puzzled. "You can't mean—?"

She stopped. What did he mean?

Blundell showed slight embarrassment.

"I can't directly offer him advice," he explained awkwardly. "Not in the rather peculiar circumstances. Anything I might suggest must go through you. I would, though, like to do something—find him a good man, see he's well looked after."

"But why?" she asked again. "I'm afraid I don't understand."

"Because—" He hesitated. "I feel in a way—well, responsible. After all, I did play a certain part in bringing those two together. I stood sponsor for the boy. I owe it to him and I owe it to myself to see he has a fair deal from start to finish. I'll tell you what: You and I'll team up, put our heads together. Two heads are better than one, aren't they?"

His last remarks subtly annoyed her. Her godfather, she knew, held the lowest opinion of female intelligence. He expected women to be either mothers and sisters, or purely frivolous ornaments—nothing between; and if he was speaking to her in this manner it was manifestly to soothe and comfort her, exactly as he would have handed a bit of toffee to a child with a hurt finger. Still, his intention was kind. She ought, moreover, to be thankful he was adopting this attitude, which was the last thing she had expected of him. She roused herself to attend to what he was saying—something about her own welfare.

"I'm so sorry. Would you mind repeating that?"

"It was just my promising Herbert to keep an eye on you. I can't do that very well, can I, if you're not fairly close at hand? Well, then, here's the proposition. Just came to me as we were talking. Your Aunt Rose's flat—standing empty till the March quarter. Mine, to do as I like with. What about popping straight into it? My two lazy servants will see you get proper food and attention. Give 'em something to do."

The suggestion, for all its practical advantages, made her shrink. She could not place herself under any further obligations to a man who, despite his manifold good qualities, had always antagonised her.

"It's terribly kind of you," she murmured. "But, no, really I couldn't accept. I shall be all right. I'm used to looking after myself."

"I dare say; but now's different. It may be you and I'll be wanting to hold conferences—over this Adrian business, you know. Now, why not humour your old godfather's notions just this once?"

It was a wistful reproach. He had noticed her coldness to him. After what he had done for her father, he deserved better consideration. Offering bail for Adrian, too, though he must believe him guilty of Rose's death....

"Very well, then," she agreed, feeling ashamed. "If you're sure you want me, I'll come."

"Good work!" He brightened, became business-like. "That's settled then. Will this afternoon be too soon for you? Right—Gaylord will call and fetch you and your belongings, and you can leave Mrs. Todd to wind things up in Seymour Square, as I understand your tenants want to move in at once."

They were nearing the Marble Arch when she spoke again.

"Aconite," she said slowly. "Do you know anything about what it does to people?"

"I do now," he informed her. "I've read up on the stuff. Hold on! Maybe you'd like a look at my old *Medical Jurisprudence* that's been collecting dust for donkeys' years—part of a solicitor's outfit, though not much use to me. Shall I tell Gaylord to turn back?"

"If you're not pressed for time."

He gave an order through the speaking-tube. The big car swerved, skirted the Serpentine, and emerged in Knightsbridge. Three minutes more, and they had entered Blundell's library, leading off from the left of his private door.

In keeping with the rest of the house, the room itself was magnificent. The ceiling, gracefully carved, had been lifted entire from a palazzo in Milan, the bookshelves, flush with the walls and filling two sides, had pilasters of fine decorative value—but there beauty ended, and the present owner's execrable taste carried on. The Turkey carpet was a nightmare of hot reds and nauseous greens, flagrant as only a Turkey carpet can be; brown velour curtains at the deep windows gave an oppressive sombreness on even the brightest day; furniture seemed to have been chosen for sheer size and bulkiness, while each ornament, from the Third Empire Boule clock on the mantelpiece to the inkstand fashioned from an elephant's tooth was an assault to the eye. There was warmth, though, from both central heating and a red-glowing fire, comforting sight after the grey mistiness outside. Diana drew towards it to thaw her stiff hands, her host drew forward a great grandfather's chair covered in brown leather and having moved a footstool under her feet, busied himself at a brass-bound cellarette surmounted by a bronze bust of Napoleon Bonaparte.

"Ever see this?" she heard him say, and as she looked towards him a tinkling music fell on her ear. Blundell had a whisky-tantalus in his hand—and it was playing a fragment of "The Blue Bells of Scotland" till he set it down again. She forced a smile. Aunt Rose would have loved this excruciating toy. She remembered that somewhere there was a cushion that gave a groaning wheeze when you sat on it—as you were sooner or later certain to do.

"Is the book in here?" she inquired. "I really mustn't stay."

Slightly chastened, her godfather returned the tantalus to the cellar-ette, got out other things and, in a moment set at her elbow a glass of brown sherry, and a clumsily-carved cigarette-box.

"Drink that up, it's good stuff. Now for old Taylor's."

Diana did not care for sherry, but she took a cigarette and lit it. The indrawn smoke helped her to relax. After all, what evidence could there be? None—obviously. And how strange that Uncle Nick's arm should be the one she was finding it comforting to lean upon! It was pathetic to see his childish eagerness for her approval. One thing was certain: If she continued to accept his benefactions, she must reconstruct her whole attitude towards him—yes, whatever effort it might cost her. . . .

"Here we are. Now, read for yourself."

A heavy volume lay on her lap. The print was so small it ran together before her eyes, but by dint of concentration she began to gather a few facts. Aconite was a plant, quite a common one, with flowers. Monks-hood it was called. She must have seen it in dozens of gardens, never guessing how every portion of it was highly poisonous. Especially the root which, in its raw state, closely resembled—

"Horseradish?"

The book slid to the floor. Blundell picked it up.

"Quite so," he soothed her. "Now don't get worried. Just let me clean this pipe of mine and I'll read that article through to you."

In a sort of deadened stupor she watched him doing something with a pipe-cleaner he was dipping into a small bottle of clear liquid and running into the stem of a briar-pipe. A sickly, sweetish odour came across to her, reminding her of hospitals.

"Chloroform," Blundell remarked as she wrinkled her nose. "Noth-ing like it for this job. Over in a jiffy. Yes, as a matter of fact we did have horseradish that Sunday, with our roast beef. You may recall how fond of roast beef your poor Aunt Rose was. There! I'll put this up." He crossed to the cellarette, returned with his briar stoked and lighted. "Now then. We can pass over the bit about the active principle—aconitine is it? That's right—used in liniments and so on. Nothing to do with us. Main point about any sort of aconite is, it's undiscoverable in human remains, unless some bit of the actual plant—in this case it was the root—happens to lodge in the organs."

Her cigarette had gone out. She must have lighted another, for here it was, between her fingers; but she did not recall it, so strained was her effort not to miss what was being said.

"Tell me that again. Do you mind?"

She heard him talking very patiently. There was apt to be a good deal of vomiting. Just pure chance whether solid matter remained in the stomach. If none did remain, there was no possible proof of murder having been committed.

"I see." Her brain worked laboriously. "Then it's a gamble?"

"So I'm told. Quite a good gamble. There must have been plenty of times it's turned out all right for the person responsible; but it may, as we've seen, slip up."

Elsie Dilworth could easily have got hold of this book. So, for that matter, could Adrian—though he wouldn't need it, with his medical knowledge. . . .

"You honestly want to hear the rest of this?" She nodded. He balanced his pince-nez on the broken bridge of his nose, hooked its black cord behind his enormous ear, and began:

> "A mistake of this kind led to fatal results in three hours in a case which occurred in Lambeth; and another set of cases occurred at Dingwall, in 1856. Here three persons were poisoned by reason of having had sauce, made with the root of aconite, served at dinner with roast beef in the place of horseradish sauce. They were healthy adults; and all died within three and a half hours. . . ."

Diana rose, stumbled over some cumbersome object, and made blindly for the door.

"I must get out," she mumbled apology. "I'm afraid I can't bear any more."

She must be behaving very stupidly. She realised it from the puzzled, worried look her godfather gave her as, with compunction, he bustled after her.

"Good Lord! I ought to have known better. Want to get home? I'll come with you."

She heard herself voicing a stubborn protest. She would much rather go alone. He did not insist, but saw her to the car, where Gaylord still waited.

"Just tell him when he's to call for you, won't you? I'll have the flat ready. Sure you're all right?"

The cold air restored her balance. What a fool she was to go to pieces like that! No wonder Uncle Nick despised women . . . but what was it he had read to her? It seemed when she tried to review it a hopeless blur, out of which only the word "horseradish" stood clear. No use. She must steel herself and go over it with a calmer mind. Suddenly she realised why she felt so heavy and queer. It was the smell of that chloroform, faint though it had been. Always, from a small child, she had hated it. . . .

"You look a bit done, miss. Hadn't I better give you a hand up the stairs."

"No, no, Gaylord! It's just that I didn't stop for much breakfast."

"Well, it's lunch time now, miss. Turned one o'clock."

Was it? She had supposed it could not be later than eleven. . . .

With a sense of dull fatigue she climbed for the last time the three flights to her beloved home. From to-morrow onward the cheerful rooms at the top of the house would be given over to strangers.

CHAPTER TWELVE

AT A quarter-past five Diana, with the help of Mrs. Todd, stowed her garments into Rose Somervell's huge, scented clothes-cupboard. That dreadful, taffeta-draped bed, those gilded swans! It would feel strange sleeping in it—but what did it matter?

"Humph! What's this?" Mrs. Todd's voice floated grimly to her from the bathroom. "Whole strips of her beautiful lino come loose for want of a few tacks. Your old Mrs. What's-her-name doesn't seem to've kept things as I'd have liked, for all she had the place to herself for so long. My word! The Queen of Sheba couldn't have done herself no better in the way of curtains—and just for a bath! Ripped at the hem, though. More carelessness!"

The speaker emerged and picked up the big bunch of red roses which had just come up with Uncle Nick's card attached. Through steel-rimmed spectacles she surveyed them approvingly.

"Well, I must say! Brighten you up a bit, won't they?" Searching for a suitable vase she continued: "That Mr. Blundell's what you'd call a real, good-hearted man. I said it last Christmas when he sent us in the dozen of champagne, and I say it now. This is a sad break-up, Miss Di, but if it had to be, well, you couldn't have tumbled to nothing better, now could you?"

Diana absently assented. She had kept silent about Adrian's arrest, just as she had done about her engagement. Let Mrs. Todd read the news for herself in the paper she was sure to buy on her way home. She longed to be alone; and then, by sheer perversity, wanted to run after Mrs. Todd and drag her back the instant the door had closed on her comfortable form. Angrily she took herself in hand. This flat wasn't haunted. If she started letting its empty grandeur get on her nerves, where would she be?

Now was the time to tabulate her ideas. She stood before the crackling log fire in the drawing-room, and by way of preliminary studied the life-like portrait of the late occupant, painted when the latter was at her most vivid and arrogant.

"She was good-looking, anyhow," she reflected, thrusting aside the slightly uncanny feeling that the blue, heavy-lidded eyes were meeting her own with sardonic scorn. "Even old and stout she had presence—and charm, of a kind. I suppose she was a good actress. They all rave about her, still; but she did have a selfish nature, and what a wicked tongue! It's quite possible she'd been spreading more stories about old Felix. It's certain she had her knife into Elsie. Was she scheming to get Elsie out of her job? She could have done it—and Elsie may have known she could."

Fear of being ousted from a remunerative post might have provided a sufficient motive for murder. The secretary had easy access to a work dealing largely with poisons; she had shown a highly-suggestive anxiety after the death, and as soon as the post-mortem verdict was announced had left her employment. All Diana's attempts to locate her had failed. At the Bloomsbury boarding-house there was no news of her. Perhaps, though, Uncle Nick knew something. Why not run down now and find out?

Blundell was in, in fact just on the point of coming up to see if she was comfortably installed.

"I've been kicking myself for giving you that nasty turn. You must have thought me an addle-pated old ass!"

"I'm the one to apologise, Uncle Nick. I wanted too, to thank you for the roses. I wish, though, you wouldn't take so much trouble!"

"Trouble? Who have I got to take trouble for if not you?" The three-cornered eyes crinkled with good humour. "I kept her supplied with flowers. If I can't do the same for you, why, it's a pity, that's all. Was there anything you wanted before I buzz off? I'm dining with a client."

"There were several things—but only if you aren't in too great a hurry. Could I, do you think, see a copy of Aunt Rose's will?"

"Oh, Lord, yes—right now. Here you are."

Unlocking a drawer in the heavy mahogany table which occupied the centre of the library, he spread before her a long, folded document. "As you see," he said, "it's quite a simple affair."

So it appeared, for all its redundant legal jargon. There were but few minor bequests, which included ten pounds to an old stage-door-keeper, a set of turquoises and a seed-pearl brooch for herself, and the big portrait and a Sargent drawing of Rose for Uncle Nick. All that remained when the estate was cleared and death-duties paid went to Adrian Somervell, of New York City; but in none of this was Diana interested. She skimmed rapidly and turned to the signatures. First came Rose's, smug, firm, self-assured. Next, the witnesses. She stared hard. They were Herman Gaylord, and Elsie K. Dilworth.

"By the way," she murmured, handing back the paper, "have you the least idea what's become of Miss Dilworth?"

Blundell looked at her, momentarily arrested. Then his forehead wrinkled with whimsical chagrin.

"I wish I knew," he said, with a shake of his big head. "All I had from her, after six years of good service, was a typewritten note telling me she'd all of a sudden crocked up. Not a sign of an address. I can't make it out."

"And you don't know where she went when she left her old boarding-house?"

"I didn't know she had left till I went round to inquire. Regular machine that girl was. She was worth a lot to me. I'd give something to be able to help her, if she's ill. I even wired her sister, up in Lincolnshire, but she's not been heard of in that quarter. It's funny, don't you think?"

Funny? It was more than that. Decidedly odd. . . . "And you don't yet know what began this inquiry?"

"The devil I do! I'd give a cool thousand to find out." As though aware that his explosive irritability required an explanation, he added that it was the underhandedness he resented.

"If any person had doubts, why didn't he come out openly with 'em? You see the position it put me in. I was hampered, and so was the doctor, by not getting here till she was in a state of coma. That concussion, and then the partial paralysis muddled up the real symptoms. You understand what I'm getting at. If a statement was made it should have come from me."

He toyed with his keys, suddenly looking old and weary. With a determined change of subject he spoke of the Sargent drawing, mentioned in the will.

"Beautiful bit of work. Got it hanging over my bed. Look at it whenever you've a mind. It's as she was when she first brought me her affairs to handle. She was playing, I remember, the part of Polly, in *Sunbeams*."

"Uncle Dick," said Diana after a pause; "can you tell me exactly what led up to the making of this will?"

She could see he did not want to comply. In the livid light of the reading-lamp the laughter-creases in his cheeks looked as though they had been left high and dry for all time.

"Why not?" He lowered his body into one of the huge leather chairs and crossed his short thick legs. "Of course you would want to know, wouldn't you? Well, to begin with, she'd often discussed with me how she ought to leave her property. No near relations, didn't take to the idea of charitable institutions—understand?"

"Then she'd never made a will till now?"

"She said not. I've seen nothing amongst her papers to disprove it." He polished his pince-nez and continued: "She seemed lately to dwell more and more on old times. Particularly on the boy, Adrian, I expect because she knew he was in London. She got to brooding, and asked me if I thought Adrian was keeping away from her because of any hard feeling. She was hurt. Not that she fell on his neck when I first brought him round. Oh, no! Why, she made out to be a wee bit huffed. It soon passed over when he took to coming on his own."

The blood mounted to Diana's cheeks.

"But did he? I'm positive he came only when he was invited."

Blundell glanced at her. "Well, well, maybe I'm wrong," he said soothingly. "I got the idea, after he dropped in with a bunch of chrys-anthemums . . . but there, we'll not argue the point. Anyhow, it was the very next morning she rang up to say she wanted to hold a business talk. I went along, and she told me straight out I was to draft a will for her to sign. When I heard who was to get the main bulk of her property I was astonished. I suggested taking time to think it over, while I made just a few inquiries. But would she? Not much. Her mind was made up. She'd known Adrian from a boy, she reminded me. That was enough for her."

"But you did make inquiries?"

"Naturally—and they were quite satisfactory. I got the draft ready myself, to please her. For some reason of her own she was dead against Miss Dilworth knowing anything about her private concerns. I took it up, and she signed it."

One of Diana's questions had been answered. Elsie Dilworth had been ignorant of the contents of the will till the author was dead and buried—or at least there was good reason to suppose this.

"How did Aunt Rose seem when she signed?" Blundell betrayed obvious symptoms of discomfort.

"A trifle nervous," he admitted. "Most ladies are, when it comes to putting their names to legal documents. Gaylord will tell you I joked her a bit, to ease the strain. I've since wondered—no," he corrected hastily; "I'm exaggerating. Hind thoughts don't count, do they?"

"You've wondered if she might have been doing something against her real inclinations?"

"Now, don't you go putting words into my mouth!"

Blundell sprang up, patting her shoulder with the playful condescension she found so galling. "I didn't mean anything of the kind. Whew! I must be off. Oh! I'm forgetting. I'm taking you to see Adrian at ten in the morning. That suit you? The sooner we have a talk with him, the easier we'll both feel."

When he had gone she got down the *Medical Jurisprudence*, firmly resolved to master what she had failed to take in that morning; but she was at first too shaken to read. Why had that admission been retracted? If Uncle Nick meant to spare her, he was going a bad way about it. A devil whispered that the impulse prompting that astonishing will had been not generous but self-seeking, like most others emanating from the same source—a good deed done with an unavowed purpose, though what purpose—

Gaylord had come in to mend the fire, and to remind her that dinner would be coming up at seven-thirty.

"Gaylord," she said casually, "I've just learned that you witnessed Mrs. Somervell's will. How did she strike you at the time? Was she at all nervous?"

From his obvious embarrassment she could see he understood the reason of her question.

"Nervous? Oh, no, miss. I'd never have said that." He examined the smut on his hands. "Very quiet, I thought her. I think she'd a bit of a cold, and had got sleepy with being by the fire. I can see her now as she was when I went up—lying back comfortable in her chair, yawning, and puffing away at her cigarette."

The description was wholly unlike the picture her godfather's words had called up. Perhaps, though, Rose had dissembled her nervousness before the two witnesses.

"Is that all you noticed?"

Gaylord smiled. "Well, not quite, miss. You see, it was like this: Mr. Blundell rang through and said cook and me was to come up. Cook was making pastry, so Miss Dilworth offered to go in her place. Well, then, when the two of us went into the drawing-room upstairs, the old lady—I mean Mrs. Somervell—tossed her head and gave Miss Dilworth ever such a look. You couldn't have helped noticing it."

Diana asked if Gaylord had seen previous signs of coolness towards the secretary. A broader grin answered her.

"Plenty of 'em, miss. It seemed as how Mrs. Somervell never missed a chance of ticking her off good and proper. I think this time Mr. Blundell quite expected her to pass some nasty remark, the way he started in cracking jokes."

"Did either you or Miss Dilworth get any idea of what was in the will?"

"Not me, miss. Miss Dilworth. . . . Well, she did look sort of queer when we came out, but I put it down to her being snubbed, as usual. I remember she snapped out very cross, 'That woman treats me like a dog with the mange!' Maybe I oughtn't to talk like this; but you did ask me, didn't you?"

"I shan't give you away, Gaylord. Thank you."

Dusting his broad hands, he took a step towards the door.

"Was there anything more, miss? Because if not, I'm just going to dodge out for an evening paper."

"Nothing more, Gaylord. I'm going to read here a bit, and then go up."

She heard him quit the flat, and then, after turning over what he had said to little purpose, she went back to the article on aconite. Aconitum napellus. . . . It would have wanted very little of the root, grated and mixed with the horseradish on one particular plate, to do the damage. Which of the four did the mixing? For there were certainly four to be considered—Petty, Arenson, Elsie Dilworth and Uncle Nick himself. Petty? Too faithful and too stupid, oh, by far! and yet there was the nephew, George, who was not stupid at all, and with his undoubted influence might have schemed to get possession of the hundred-pound legacy. His sneaking his aunt away and standing guard over her might mean fear lest the childish old woman give something away. It was worth thinking about.

What a demon of a plant! Within a few minutes would begin that tingling sensation Rose had complained of—first in the lips and tongue, next in the stomach. Later would come numbness and nausea. Sometimes the victim would be unable to stand; always he would find extreme difficulty in articulating. A sense of impending paralysis, blindness, even lockjaw were possible. Coma quickly set in, and in from three to seven hours the sufferer would be dead.

Arenson? A queer, cold fish, an unknown quantity, even to his theatrical colleagues. Once, it was said, he had been in love with Rose, who had flouted him; and then there was the three years' quarrel, recently patched up. Diana would have said Felix was a coward. Still, to kill in this manner called for no great daring or risk. Suppose—

Was Gaylord back already? Some one had come into the flat, using a latch-key. The person seemed to be lingering with but slight movement in the hall. Doing what? The prolonged hesitation struck Diana as odd. She laid down her book, and stole without noise to the half-open door. She glanced out, and drew back.

There, within three yards of her, stock-still and gazing fearfully round, was the departed secretary.

CHAPTER THIRTEEN

ELSIE, back again, and from her furtive manner not anxious to be seen. Her attitude was a listening one, but what had struck Diana still more sharply was her altered, hag-ridden appearance, in grotesque contrast to the jaunty green hat and dangling jade ear-rings she continued to affect. There was no rouge now on her muddy complexion, her hazel-green eyes were red-rimmed and small. Her clothes hung on her gaunt, big-boned frame, and her badly waved hair, once mouse-coloured but recently brightened with henna, straggled in dispirited wisps round her ears and neck.

Feeling sure this room was her objective, Diana held a rapid debate with herself. Should she accost the secretary boldly or hide and watch her? A second cautious peep made her decide on the latter course. The woman's late behaviour and present air of secretiveness vetoed any hope of getting the truth from her by persuasion or bluff. Better find out why she had come, and afterwards—

Not an instant too soon was Diana flattened against the windows with the thick curtains covering her. Indeed, she was not yet sure she was hidden when a swift, surreptitious movement told her Elsie had entered. She heard the key turn, and experienced a slight shudder to think that here she was, locked in with a creature quite possibly mad. Adrian had suggested it, how seriously she did not know; but her momentary nervousness was quickly submerged in intense curiosity, mingled with which was the hope that now she might be on the verge of some vital discovery.

Mad? No! Far too much method here, in spite of the wild, tormented expression of eyes for one second gleaming red with reflected firelight. Without hesitation, the intruder had pulled the green-shaded lamp round so as to focus its rays on the big table, planked down a pair of dark, fleece-lined gloves on the blotting-pad, and from a small attaché-case she carried taken out a bunch of keys. Her movements were business-like, brusque; and though she was on the far side of the table, there was no doubt as to what she was doing. She was opening all the drawers in turn and running with practised thoroughness through their contents. Twice she lifted out a file and pored over it with a strained, desperate sort of eagerness; but throughout she worked so quietly that only an occasional crackle of paper betrayed her occupation. Whatever it was she was looking for, it was not the will, for when she came upon it—the document was clearly visible in the lamplight—she put it back without a glance.

Every drawer had been hauled out and replaced, not before the searcher had thrust her arm into the farthermost recesses and drawn it out again with a gesture of despair. Now she gave up and stood, leaning clinched hands on the table, with her shabby musquash coat flung back to reveal the bony cavities in her neck, and the harsh cone of light throwing her strong features into pitiless relief. Formerly she had been a plain, unnoticeable woman, but scrupulously neat. That was in the days when Diana had known her merely as Uncle Nick's employee, and not thought of her twice. Now she was unkempt, one might almost say unwashed, looking as though she had not slept for nights and been roaming the streets in rain and mud; and yet for a brief interval prior to this last phase, she had indulged in a pathetic coquetry, tricked herself out in garments designed to captivate, saturated herself in chypre! Diana could smell the stale scent now, half-across the room.

With her underlip caught between her irregular teeth Elsie exhaled a sobbing breath. Then, muttering to herself, she began to pad softly about, prying into every receptacle, including the cellarette. Before the expanse of bookshelves she paused, letting her gaze travel over the closely-packed volumes. A few of these she removed, only to stick them back, hopelessly. Her shoulders sagged. She broke into hushed, spasmodic laughter, dreadful to hear, but it did not last long. With another of her lightning movements she turned, swooped upon her gloves and attaché-case, and in a twinkling had quitted the room.

Diana slipped forth to hide behind the door and peep through the crack. She was just in time to see Elsie go into her employer's bedroom, where she remained for a few minutes, only to come out again with the same baffled expression. For a second she hovered in the hall, undecided. Then she plunged her hand into the huge oak cupboard and took from the nail the spare key to the flat above. In another instant she was out of the door and had softly closed it.

Did she mean to extend her search amongst the dead woman's belongings? Diana waited till she felt it was safe to look out, then reopening the door a mere crack saw the tall figure disappearing round the bend of the stairs. The door of the other flat was being unlocked. A shaft of light streamed out of it. Half a minute passed—and then down the invader rushed, so precipitately that Diana barely had time to dart back to the library. Now, if ever, was the moment to speak to Elsie; but while she was considering the wisdom of this a little metallic "ping" announced the return of the spare key to its nail, and immediately the hall door shut. The secretary was gone.

Quick! She must be followed, for only in this way could her present habitation be discovered. She had no intention of being located, that was evident. Probably she had watched in the gloom across the way until she had seen both Blundell and Gaylord go out before she ventured to enter. She might get clean off before Diana could carry out the purpose now uppermost in her mind; but it was worth a try.

Within fifty seconds Diana had made a dash for her coat and hat and was running along the single outlet Queen's Close possessed. Its short length terminated in a broad street leading from the park down towards Kensington Station, so at the junction she paused to scan the distance in both directions. Yes, she could make out the angular form in the musquash coat at the parking-place in front of the Albert Hall. Hurrying, she overtook it just as the traffic was held up and, unnoticed, crossed the road behind it to the opposite bus stop. Elsie boarded a downgoing bus. To the top of it Diana scrambled, and kept a sharp look out at each stopping place.

Along Knightsbridge they trundled, up Park Lane, along the crowded hurly-burly of Oxford Street, then by a devious route to Baker Street Station. There! Elsie was getting out. Three minutes more and, still unaware of pursuit, she was entering a Number Thirty, travelling east. Again Diana kept out of sight by riding on top. They reached the huge, dingy mass of King's Cross Station, rounded the side, and climbed the long slope towards Islington. Now they were in a neighbourhood of slums, with here and there some rather better backwater given over to artists and professional people to whom low rents were an attraction and the surroundings no serious disadvantage. It struck Diana that hereabouts would be as good a place as any in which to lose oneself.

The Number Thirty bus, following tram-lines, stopped opposite a low, walled-in embankment, grass-covered, and with a railing round it. Some sort of reservoir it was, not far from Sadler's Wells Theatre. Here her quarry descended, one of a crowd, and so inconspicuously that she was well away before Diana saw her hurrying figure detach itself from its chance companions. The bus was moving on. She swung off it perilously, just escaped a tram and managed, by extra speed, to lessen the distance between the secretary and herself. On the two went, Elsie with bent head and long, awkward strides, Diana afraid on the one hand that she would be seen, on the other that at any moment the woman she was tracking would vanish into some dark doorway just round a corner. Neither calamity happened. Elsie did not turn, and paused only at a news-and-tobacco shop, coming out at once with a newspaper in her hand.

Now she crossed and entered the bottle-necked opening to a small, dimly-lit square, where low-roofed houses huddled round a railed enclosure of laurels and stunted plane-trees. It was a shabbily-decent place, aloof and superior to the street just quitted. Elsie was already on the far side before Diana, anxious to remain unrecognised, dared overtake her, the result being that when she turned the corner of the iron railings the pavement before her was empty. All the houses facing her were dark; but as she looked a light flared up in the upper front window of one of them. For an instant only, then a blind was drawn down to hide it; but it had given a reliable clue.

With bold resolution she rang a jangling bell—and waited. After a long interval of total silence, two grubby little boys, pottering in their own interests, appeared, as by accident, in the tiny area below. She addressed the larger one.

"Might I see Miss Dilworth?"

The larger boy stared up at her indifferently, took a juicy bite of an apple, and transferred his attention to the apple itself.

"Miss 'Oo?"—lusciously. "No sich lady 'ere."

Elsie, she then thought, might be using another name.

"Never mind," she persisted. "I'm speaking of the lady who has just gone in. I may have got the name wrong, but—"

Another stare, loud champing of apple, and a contemptuous shake of the head.

"We ain't heard nobody come in—'ave we, Ted? I say! Got that bit of string? Then whoopee!"

Up the area steps the roisterers charged and off into the echoing distance. Diana was left to ring, and to hammer on the iron knocker, now in the discouraged belief that the woman within had no intention of answering. There must, she reflected, be a landlady now absent, but sure to return in the course of time. Doggedly she decided to await this event; but thinking it was a mistake to remain here in full view of the upper windows, she made for the other side of the railed garden.

For perhaps five minutes she walked slowly up and down, keeping her eye on the ribbon of light which she was convinced marked Elsie Dilworth's room. A few wayfarers passed her, but not one turned in at the house she was watching. Then a taxi blundered in through the bottle-neck of the square, prowled tentatively round, and halted expectantly beneath the gleam of radiance. Evidently it had been summoned, whether by telephone or by the two small boys there was no saying. In any case, the light above now blacked out, and even as she made haste to skirt the railings she saw Elsie emerge, dressed as before, but laden this time with a heavy suitcase and what looked like a typewriter. Too late to catch the muttered direction given to the driver. The woman she had tried to corner had got into the taxi and was being rattled away.

Gone—and the luggage indicated it was for good and all. Not the least use hoping for another taxi in this trackless waste of what might be Pentonville or Islington, Diana knew not which. The chase had failed, just when success of a sort seemed a matter of patience. All that remained was to take note of the sign dimly visible on the railings—Floyd's Square, and the house just vacated was Number Seventeen. That done, she wended her way back to the thoroughfare and began her long trek homeward.

What had Elsie hoped to find, either in her employer's papers, or in the flat overhead? She had left a handkerchief in the latter place, but it was hardly likely she would return for that, impossible she would search for it amongst business or private files. Almost certainly she had been looking for a document of some kind—but of what kind, and why?

These questions Diana turned over painstakingly when, regaining her new quarters, she sat down to try and eat some of the delicious meal kept hot for her over a spirit-lamp. She was dead tired, but coffee revived her a little, and still more did the cigarette she took from the silver box at her side. They were Aunt Rose's cigarettes, but how mild! Poor darling Mummy had not been much of a smoker, or she would never have thought that her friend could have suffered through indulging in these. What was it she had said on the subject of Rose's excessive smoking? It was in that last letter, still reposing, with the two letters Aunt Rose had written from Vichy, in the back-flap of her handbag. Idly she reached for them—and, with a shock of astonishment, withdrew her hand. The pocket was empty!

CHAPTER FOURTEEN

IN THE car with her godfather next morning she related the whole of her strange adventures. Half-way through Blundell interrupted her, comically perturbed.

"Good God!" He rubbed his chin. "What's that poor woman up to, ransacking my papers? I knew she'd not bothered to return my duplicate bunch of keys—not that I troubled about it. She's honest as the day. And you ran her to earth! Fine! Good work!"

"But she's gone again, this time we don't know where."

"Did she take all her luggage?"

"I couldn't say. I saw two bags. I've written down the address, in case it's of any use. Here it is—17 Floyd's Square. Islington, I suppose; but wait, I've more to tell you."

In another minute her companion was frowning in even greater bewilderment.

"Stole letters from you? Surely not. Why do you think a thing like that?"

"Simply because there's no other explanation. Nothing can fall out of this pocket. See, it fastens with a strap. The three letters—two of them Aunt Rose's to my mother—were there yesterday. I particularly noticed them—and the bag was in my hand or within reach the whole of the day, except just that little time when I was in your library. I left it on that marquetry table by my door."

"But why?" he objected. "What's the sense in it?"

"In her taking my letters? My idea is she saw the lights on and wanted to find out who was there. The quickest and safest way was to look into my bag for a card. There wasn't a card—I never carry one—but the letters would tell her what she wanted to know. Maybe she's a better reason than we think for being so inquisitive. She has been behaving oddly. You admitted it yourself."

"We all noticed it," he muttered. "Were those letters anything you wanted especially to keep?"

"Not now. I'd just forgotten to destroy them. Aunt Rose's I did save till I had time to read them. I hoped they might help me; but there was nothing in them except gossip about Vichy and the people she was meeting."

"Humph! Well, whatever Miss Dilworth wanted, it couldn't have been your letters."

"No, because she didn't know I would be there. I hoped you might be able to suggest a reason."

He shook his head. Possibly, he hazarded, she had left something of her own behind, though he still could not understand her secrecy.

"The trouble is, she may come again. I've hung on to the spare key so the servants could use it when they clean up. I can't have you bothered, though. We must put it where Miss Dilworth can't find it, just in case she pays us another visit."

She did not mention to him her rather stupid obsession, due, in part, to what Mrs. Todd had said about the loose linoleum and the ripped curtain hem. Just before getting into bed she herself had noticed whole inches of the taffeta bed valance unsewn at the bottom—a trifling matter if Rose Somervell had been less fussy about the tidiness of her home. It had certainly seemed to her as though an exhaustive search had been conducted all over the flat, and that the searcher might want to continue operations. In the light of day, however, the whole notion crumbled. Her other idea was more substantial, and had better be divulged.

"You probably don't know," she said hesitatingly, "that Miss Dilworth had entirely lost her head over Adrian. Not liking to hurt her feelings, he let her think he couldn't marry any one because he'd no money. That's one important point. The other is, she disliked Aunt Rose."

Blundell turned shrewd eyes on her. For a second she fancied there was pity in them.

"By jove!" He brought his gloved fist down on his knee with a soft thud. "You're thinking Dilworth may have twigged the contents of that will? I shouldn't have supposed . . . but it's a possibility, no doubt of that. Rose always said she was devilish sharp. Warned me against her, in fact."

"You've not forgotten, have you, that she was in the dining-room while the four of you were at lunch?"

"No," he answered slowly. "I'd not lost sight of it; but what about us others? There's Petty, there's Arenson, there's me. Oh, yes, I'm a suspect too. Now try to deny it!"

Diana flushed, feeling sorely tried.

"What I meant was, Adrian knew nothing whatever about this will, but Miss Dilworth did know, having witnessed it. Suppose she did manage to catch sight of a few sentences? She may have imagined that with Aunt Rose out of the way Adrian would have money and be willing to marry her. If she did commit this murder, it would be so easy to understand her questioning Petty as she did, after the death."

"Questioning Petty? Here, that's news! How did you find out?"

She gave him a brief account of her talk with Petty. She saw from his frowning attention that she had made an impression.

"Doesn't that show she was worried sick for fear the body would be exhumed? If you'd seen her last night! Why, she's half out of her wits!"

He did not at once reply. When he spoke it was with an evasiveness which might mean reluctance to accuse his former secretary, or simply disbelief in this theory.

"I wouldn't think too much about any of this," he advised, "till the boy comes up before the magistrate. Maybe he'll go scot-free, then your troubles will be over."

Would they? Not so long as the real criminal remained undiscovered; but she kept her thought to herself, for they had now stopped outside the prison where, pending his examination, Adrian was detained. Pale again and with a smothered feeling, she followed her godfather's short, powerful figure through the doors and into a bare entrance-hall, where a stolid official was dealing as best he could with a slim, excitable girl in a handsome mink coat. Diana looked at her. She had dark, flashing eyes with tears trembling like dew-drops on her long, blackened lashes. She was smart and expensive to her finger-tips, and her accent was American.

"Permit or not permit, miss," the guard was saying detachedly, "the prisoner refuses to see you. Now what's to be done about it?"

"But I will see him!" The visitor stamped her foot, her whole willowy person vibrating with fury. "Look, do you realise who I am? My father's Carter Ackland. You've heard of him, haven't you? Well, then! I'm offering you this—" A five-pound note crackled in her hand. "Just to take me in. Will you do it, or won't you?"

Somehow, with no glaring discourtesy, she was put finally aside.

"Now, sir," said the official to Blundell; "can I do anything for you?"

So this girl was Blanche Ackland! Heiress to millions—lovely too, in an over-finished, metallic way, yet Adrian had refused to see her. Diana, watching her make a sullen retreat, felt a wan triumph, succeeded by the fear that she, also, would be denied. The guard's manner reassured her. It was comforting to be towed in by some one who commanded so much deference as Uncle Nick seemed to do. She could even bear his inevitable jokes.

"We got here a minute too soon, didn't we? Otherwise you'd be five pounds to the good, eh?"

"Ha, ha! Not bad, sir. The same prisoner, is it? Right you are, sir, I'll not keep you a moment."

They were shown into a dingy, overheated room furnished with a table, some wooden-seated chairs, and nothing else. Into it came Adrian, escorted by a warder—and Diana's first thought was that though they had been admitted neither she nor her godfather was welcomed. Adrian was perfectly composed, a shade more abstracted than his wont, but too well she understood the brief glance he gave her before looking away. There was question in it, and certainty of the answer. A hard lump came into her throat and remained there.

"Well, my boy!" Blundell's voice, in trying to be natural, was gruffer than usual. "What have they been doing to you? Come on, give us the whole story."

Adrian looked at him, but did not speak till they had taken seats at the table, Diana and Blundell on one side, the warder at the end. Then he removed his glasses, polished them, and gave a faint shrug.

"As you see," he said uneventfully, "I've been arrested. For murder. That's about all there is to it."

"All! But on what grounds?" demanded the solicitor truculently. "Man, they can't lock you up without reason! What's the evidence!"

Adrian made no attempt to answer the question. After another glance at his two visitors, as though to establish something in his own mind, he remarked that he had been advised to secure counsel.

"Why, I can't imagine." He seemed to be addressing no one in particular. "If they won't believe what I say, what's the good of having a lawyer say it for me?"

How like Adrian! Diana made a despairing gesture, but let Blundell speak for her.

"Utter rot, my boy! Naturally you must have counsel—good counsel, too. Know any legal chaps?"

"No."

Adrian gave the negative without interest or apparent concern.

Blundell blew his nose violently.

"Well, then! Let Di put you into touch with her father's solicitor, and let him arrange matters. It'll be done at once."

"Thanks," returned Adrian indistinctly. "But I'd rather she didn't bother. I'll manage by myself."

"Now, what sheer bilge!" Blundell was growing discomfited, consequently irritable. "See here, don't you realise our one idea is to get you a square deal? Why do you suppose I did my damnedest to bail you out?"

Adrian looked at him again, this time with a slight frown.

"You tried to bail me out?" he repeated slowly. "I didn't know that. I can't quite see your reason, but—thanks again."

"Reason be blowed!" Blundell pushed back his chair, got up, and strode towards the door. "Look," he said, turning. "Maybe if I'm out of the way, Diana can talk some sense into you."

Diana felt intensely grateful for the considerate action, but when the door had banged and she was left with only an indifferent warder to hear, she was as badly tongue-tied as before. Adrian, facing her, might have been a total stranger. Desperate, she made a trivial remark.

"Bobbie Ackland was outside. Why didn't you see her?"

"Why should I see her?"

The warder was looking boredly at his watch. Diana clinched her hands to keep back the tears, and leant forward persuasively.

"Adrian, dear, I'm sorry you weren't pleasanter to Uncle Nick. He's being so decent to us both—and when you think how he felt about her, can't you see what this means?"

His eyes met hers. "Why," he asked, "do you say both of us? You've told him—?"

"I had to. I've let the flat, you see, and Uncle Nick has most kindly insisted on my staying for the present in Aunt Rose's place. He arranged this interview. He's willing to help in every way, and—oh, darling, we may need lots of help! Surely you understand?"

"Of course." He pondered, trying, she thought, to sift out some problem. "As for the matter you mentioned," he resumed, coldly and with even greater constraint, "you and me . . . well, I want you to consider it finished. Washed up. In fact, you've got to look at it like that. I appreciate your coming here, but don't do it again, will you? And I particularly ask you to stay away from the court. Promise?"

"Oh, dear!" Her voice broke. "Why must you be so utterly stupid? Nothing's altered. Nothing! How could it be? This is just some ghastly mistake. You do know I've never, never honestly supposed—"

Once more he was looking at her, and this time what she saw in his eyes sent a cold shock through her.

"Adrian!" she whispered unsteadily. "What is it? I've got to be told!"

CHAPTER FIFTEEN

HE DELIBERATED so long that she began to hope he would answer her question. Then he shook his head.

"It won't do any good," he said quietly. "I want you to keep clear of this whole business. Forget about—everything. Hadn't you better be going?"

She had always known he had this streak of obstinacy in him. It frightened her, but she held her ground.

"Not till I've made you listen. Hasn't it ever occurred to you that you aren't the only person who might have hoped to profit by Aunt Rose's death? Think it over now. Who did you tell me was mad? Loony was the word you used. Now, have you got it?"

"You're dreaming," he said after a long pause.

"Wait till you've heard." Diana talked rapidly in a lowered voice, sketching in the same points she had mentioned to Blundell. "Well, then," she finished triumphantly, "doesn't all this impress you?"

"Ridiculous," he summed it up. "Nothing in it. Can't be."

"Oh, Adrian, how dense you're being! It's got to be proved, naturally, but I can see it, as clearly as anything. She's hiding herself because she's terrified. Her plan went on the rocks."

"Why?" he mused aloud. "Who guessed it wasn't a natural death?"

"How do I know?" Diana spoke impatiently. "The caretaker, maybe. Some distant relation who's keeping himself dark. Listen, I've not done yet. There's something I've not told any one, because it seemed too utterly fantastic, only after last night it looked less so."

Furtively she glanced at the warder. Seeing him engrossed in squeezing a splinter out of his thumb, she resumed with more confidence.

"You see, all along I've felt it was no common thief who killed my mother. I can't believe in this robbery motive. More and more I've come to think she may have been got rid of—oh, how horrible it sounds!— because she had said something that threw Aunt Rose's murderer into a panic. Had you thought of that as a possibility?" She saw him flinch.

"No. I hadn't. I'm sorry you've got that idea."

He had misinterpreted her again.

"Oh, please!" she begged, almost voiceless with misery. "Surely you must see what I'm trying to suggest. Remember what I've just been telling you, about the afternoon Mummy went to that flat. Keep in mind the things she may, without meaning to, have hinted, when she was talking to Uncle Nick—and remember it had to be some one who knew the workings of our street door. Oh, dear, what's the use? I must simply say all this to your lawyer, when you've got one. He'll listen. I'll make him." Every word she uttered was serving to make matters worse. Precious minutes were passing, the warder was looking restlessly at her as a signal for her to go.

More gently Adrian said: "I understand there is a barrister coming round to-day. Also the American Consul-General—though he can't do much. It's no use cabling any of my friends. There's no one I can apply to for help in these hard times. Ladbroke—he's the house-surgeon at the Prince Regent's—has arranged about the lawyer. You've met Ladbroke, I think. Blond chap, terribly decent."

She felt a slight degree of relief.

"Then that part of it's all right. Thank heaven! Oh, darling, they can't possibly do anything to you! How can they?" She made a last wistful appeal, and then, as he remained silent: "Adrian! Haven't you a single thing to say to me before I go?"

They were both on their feet, the table between them. "Only what I've already said: Keep clear of that court." It was like him, she told herself, to want to spare her the pain of seeing him stand before a magistrate, just as it was like him to repudiate the tie of their engagement while he was under a cloud; but these reflections left her unconsoled, her fears the more frightening because of their intangibility.

The ante-room she crossed was empty, but as she left it she came face to face with the blond doctor who had let her in the evening she had called to see Adrian. He eyed her doubtfully, but stopped.

"You're Dr. Ladbroke, aren't you?" She held out her hand. "I'm afraid the other night I didn't recognise you. I'm Diana Lake."

He smiled. She liked his honest blue eyes, now strained and preoccupied. Although not much more than thirty, he had the air of a much older man. Suddenly she was comforted to know that Adrian had one friend on whom he could rely.

"Stupid business, this," he said tentatively. "How does Somervell strike you?"

"Rather odd. I couldn't get anything out of him. What has he told you?"

"Very little, I'm afraid. So far he's said only one thing of any consequence—extremely vague, at that." The house-surgeon glanced over his shoulder and spoke guardedly. "He said that for some reason beyond his comprehension he seems to be the goat."

"Goat!" she echoed, mystified. "What does he mean?"

Round the bend of the corridor Blundell appeared, coming towards them. Ladbroke shrugged, moved a step away, and stopped as Diana beckoned impulsively to him.

"I'd like to talk to you about—what you've just said. Not now, but after the examination. You understand? If things go wrong."

"Exactly." He nodded and gave her his professional card. "I'll come and see you. Just give me a ring."

A moment later in the car, Diana explained who her companion was. Blundell snorted, but seemed pacified.

"I'm glad there's one person he's not trying to shove off," he grumbled. "I'd begun to think he didn't want any help."

"I'm afraid I see why he's taking this attitude. He doesn't think either you or I can possibly believe he's innocent, with that will against him. It's my fault, I suppose. His pride won't let him accept any favours from us."

"Poor lad! Well, it can't be remedied, but it's too bad, all the same."

"Of course he'll be released," she argued. "They can't hold on just a vague suspicion. Can they?"

"Oh, certainly they can't," her godfather muttered, but in such a way that she sensed a dwindling confidence. She bit her lip and said no more.

Later in the day Dr. Ladbroke rang her up to say that the barrister he had introduced had talked with Adrian.

"He's a good chap. His name's Michael Hull. At the moment that's about all I have to tell you."

"Is it?" she demanded, struck by his slightly evasive tone. "I'd far rather know the—worst."

"It's all a bit complicated." The speaker made a lengthy pause. "But rest assured Hull will do a proper job of it. Don't try to see him just yet— and by the way, Somervell sent you a message. I was to remind you not to come to the court."

"I shall most certainly come. You needn't tell him, though."

The afternoon post brought a note from Mrs. Todd. The first sentences dealt her a sickening blow:

"Oh, Miss Di, what a horrible thing this is! Who would have thought it of Mr. Adrian? A wolf in sheep's clothing, so to speak. It's past thinking of, and would have broke your poor mother's heart. It's a true word that money is the root of all evil—but him so nice-spoken, always seeming to think of nothing but his doctoring . . ." It was some time before Diana forced herself to finish the scrawl, the remainder of which made little impression on her. Mrs. Todd was going in daily to the young couple who had taken over the flat, and her comments on their domestic economy were bitter. Although able to afford six guineas a week for rent, the Glovers—decidedly not out of the top drawer—made a terrific fuss about gas, lighting and food.

"One pound of butter's to do us for the week, and only the nasty sort of margarine for cooking. Oh, well, live and learn, as the saying is, but it's a sad come-down for those used to better things."

The complaint brought home to Diana the cataclysmic changes of the past fortnight. Her mother dead, her father soon to be separated from her by half the globe, and now all else that she valued dangling by a thread which at any moment might snap in two. Useless to dwell on these things; but to Diana it did seem as though some unseen, incredibly evil power had singled her out to smite and smite again. There was no understanding it. She must not attempt to understand, but set her teeth and go on.

Two days later she received a surprise call from the Scotland Yard inspector, Headcorn by name, to whom the investigation of her mother's murder had been entrusted. He informed her that the two pieces of jewellery assumed to have constituted the main motive for the attack had been found the previous afternoon in an Amsterdam pawnshop.

"My mother's ring and brooch? Are you sure?"

It was the last news she had expected. Dazedly she felt there must be some mistake.

"Not a doubt of it, Miss Lake. Diamond Sunburst, Tiffany setting, right number of stones; square-cut emerald, answering description. Yes, they've both come to light. A bit of luck the Dutch police happened on them before they were broken up."

"Then it was robbery," she murmured, her eyes blank.

The inspector, a big, slow-moving man with small, serious eyes and a wart on his nose, examined her with interest.

"Had you a different notion about it?" he inquired. "Some idea I've not heard you mention?"

"I—in a way, I may have had," she stammered, all at once seeing how thin and feeble her theory had been. "It's not worth mentioning now, because of course it's quite exploded. I suppose you don't know who pawned the jewellery?"

Her informant shook his head. Only the bare facts had reached the Yard, an hour ago, by telephone.

"I may be running over to Amsterdam myself to put the screws on this pawnbroker. I'm not satisfied he's told all he knows. When I've seen him you'll hear if there's been any result." On his way out he paused to ask if Diana would mind passing the news on to her friend, Mr. Blundell, when she next saw him. "He'll be out now, I expect, but he's particularly requested us to let him hear how we're getting on."

Alone, Diana cursed herself for confiding her moonshine theory to Adrian. To have expressed even a tenuous belief that the two murders hung together had been sufficient to make him in his over-sensitive state take it to himself. The breach between them had widened, and again it was her own impetuous fault.

Still, this discovery need not upset the first half of her idea. Elsie to her mind was the one person likely to have poisoned Rose Somervell, wherefore if to-morrow's result did not set Adrian free her next move was plain.

"But he will be set free," she repeated. "I'm a fool to think anything else. What evidence can there be?"

Twenty-four hours later her question was answered. Before a crowded magistrate's court in West Kensington she saw a pill-box produced and its scarcely-visible contents exhibited. These few minute particles of what had been certified to be grated and dried aconite-root had been found clinging to the inside of a pocket belonging to the coat worn by the prisoner on the day he lunched with the victim. The coat had been taken from the prisoner's wardrobe in his bedroom in Bloomsbury Street.

A formal indictment was read. Adrian Somervell, of New York City, now domiciled in London, was charged with the wilful murder of his former stepmother, Mrs. Rose Somervell, of 6, Queen's Close, London, W. He was committed for trial at the Old Bailey, and he reserved his defence.

CHAPTER SIXTEEN

LATE in the afternoon the world that had crashed about Diana re-formed itself. An impression lost sight of during black, hopeless hours illuminated her brain with all the brilliance of a new discovery. Why, she had her proof! How was it possible she had ever forgotten it? Tears, unshed till now, ran down her cheeks. She brushed her hair into its usual flat waves, dabbed powder on her nose, and telephoned Dr. Ladbroke.

At six o'clock, wrapped in her grey lambskin coat and with her head held high, she was slipping across Knightsbridge into the Park. The house-surgeon was waiting for her, under an inky cedar of Lebanon. He grasped her hand hard, and together they set off into the gloom of an avenue.

"Don't say anything just yet," Diana begged when they had covered fifty yards in silence. "Just let me talk first. I know what you must be thinking. I was, till I began remembering things."

When they reached the fountains she was still speaking. Under the brim of his soft hat the doctor's eyes remained gravely attentive with a look of weighing what she said and suspending judgment.

"Adrian can't act. I'm an actress myself—of sorts—and I know. I tell you, till I broke that news to him no suspicion of any kind had crossed his mind. He'd bought a paper and—so exactly what he does do—never bothered to look at it. Think of it! Why, the news of the exhumation was on all the posters! It was being shouted in the streets. Don't you see, if he'd been guilty, he'd have looked first thing to see who the well-known actress was and find out what was happening."

Diana was appealing to him now. It seemed a tortuous age before his slow answer came.

"That does put rather a different light on it," Ladbroke admitted. "You say the newspaper was folded up exactly as it was when you saw it before? Actually, of course, the thing was on the front page."

"But even so he'd never seen it!" she insisted. "I could read it in his face. There are some things you can't be mistaken about."

"No, I quite agree with you there. I myself find it practically impossible to believe him the sort of coldblooded schemer he'd have to be to—to commit that sort of crime. It was that stuff found on him. I was knocked to bits."

"But you do see my point, don't you?"

"I—God knows I want to. Yes, as a matter of fact, I do."

"Oh, thank God!"

Ladbroke, returning the sudden pressure of her hand on his arm, felt moved with a vast relief. It was a moment before either of them found composure to go on.

"That stuff in his pocket," said Diana scornfully. "Do you imagine if he'd put it there it would ever have been found?"

"I see that point, too, but"—somewhat dryly—"I warn you it's not much of an argument. It can be said—and depend upon it, it will be said—he emptied out the pocket and brushed it, only as he's near-sighted, a bit of it got by him. It clings—and there was only an infinitesimal amount of it, remember. However, it didn't get there by itself. Think he picked it up accidentally on some object he laid down and transferred it to his pocket without noticing?"

"Either that, or some one in the room put it there."

"You meant that?" He gave her a startled glance. "You're right, it could have happened. I imagine he believes it did happen, and that explains his saying he was the goat."

"Certainly."

"There was probably more of it," continued the doctor musingly. "Only in the course of time it got shaken out. Well—any more ideas?"

"Several. Do you by any chance recall a woman who came to see Adrian just before I did that evening you let me in?"

He glanced sidewise at her, hesitating.

"You mean a weird female with ear-rings?"

"Exactly—Elsie Dilworth, my godfather's secretary. I'll tell you about her." Diana proceeded to do so, emphasising the possibility of a double motive. "I believe she was fool enough to hope she could get Adrian, provided he had money. Indeed, it seems entirely plausible—to me—after watching her as I did the other night."

"It takes a bit of believing, doesn't it?" he pointed out. "Assuming you're right in the main fact, why should she plant evidence on him?"

"I've thought of a reason, only just now. Suppose she doubted her ability to get him by fair means but was determined he shouldn't escape her?"

"I'm beginning to grasp it. You mean her aim was to dig the stuff up out of his pocket as by accident and hold it over him like a bludgeon?"

"Why not?" Diana returned calmly. "No amount of denials would have helped him. He'd have been caught, landed—in her clutches for all time. Don't let's forget his is the motive everybody's prepared to believe in. She knew that."

"My God, it would have been a stranglehold and no mistake," admitted Ladbroke, reluctantly admiring. "There's one snag, though. Why didn't she use her hold? At the crucial moment she seems to have thrown up her hand."

"Maybe she weakened. It would be a fiendish thing to do to any one you loved, wouldn't it? Or maybe she meant to do it but never got a chance. Oh, I quite see how difficult any of this will be to prove; but what if it could be shown she had had aconite in her possession?"

"Ah, now you're talking! But I should doubt if there's much hope of proving that with any one concerned."

"We'll have to see, shan't we? Now let me tell you about the other possible suspects. We can't entirely overlook the third guest at lunch—old Felix Arenson."

"Yes. And the other one?" demanded the house-surgeon quickly.

"Oh, the housekeeper's nephew."

"I see." There was a brief silence. "Well, how does he come into it?"

She outlined her tentative idea. George Petty might have got into some difficulty from which only money could rescue him. It was credible to suppose he had induced his gullible old aunt to carry out a plan in his behalf, telling her she would only be drugging her mistress, so that the key to the safe in the bedroom could be got hold of and jewels stolen.

"Petty would swallow any story George told her. She's been frightened out of her life ever since, and so has George. I saw him this morning at the court. Don't you think it suggestive that he should have come in white as a sheet, his face literally streaming with sweat, and that the instant the indictment was pronounced he should beam all over as though a big load were off him?"

"I must say your ideas are very ingenious. What about this man Arenson?"

"I watched him, too—and he showed just the same reactions. He was wedged far back in a corner, his old face so pale his red beak of a nose flamed out like a beacon. He kept wetting his lips with his tongue—till the end. I saw him again outside, very brisk and perky. He was speaking to Dame Charlotte Moon, though she's been his sworn enemy for years. He actually asked for a lift in her car. I could see they were both dying to talk it all over."

Diana stopped, suddenly recalling something else. Why, she wondered, had Dame Charlotte exhibited similar signs of acute nervousness and subsequent relaxation? She saw again the long, sallow horse-face of the tragedy-queen, as it had turned with a worried expression towards the prisoner. She saw the black-gloved hands ceaselessly fumbling with a tortoise-shell lorgnette or clasping and unclasping a huge, ugly reticule; and then, later, that smile of triumphant satisfaction! It had puzzled her vaguely at the time, and so it did now. Dame Charlotte had never cared for Rose. Adrian she could not have known even slightly. . . .

"I beg your pardon! You said something about Mr. Blundell?"

"I only wanted to know how much of this you've told him."

"Very little. It's difficult. You see, he's bound to be biased, however hard he may try to keep an open mind. Mrs. Somervell was, I think, just about the one person he deeply cared about. I believe he's taking a decent attitude mainly to spare my feelings."

"All that matters," said Ladbroke, "is that you give a full account to Michael Hull. He's ready to see you. Shall I arrange an interview for to-morrow morning at ten?"

"The sooner the better. Oh," she sighed, "if you knew how it's helped me to talk this over with you! In the whole of London there's no other person I feel like being frank with. I've been so hopelessly bottled up."

"You needn't be any longer," he told her simply. "Adrian Somervell's my friend. I admire his work. In fact, I consider him little short of a genius in his own line. If anything happens to him—but no, don't let's think it!"

With a strangely-lightened heart, Diana bade him goodbye on the pavement by the Albert Hall, and turned towards Queen's Close.

In front of her door an enormous, oyster-coloured car was standing, with the door open, and a stiff chauffeur beside it. Two well-dressed men were just emerging from the house, and, coming face to face with her as she turned in, ceased their earnest conversation. Both were immaculate, with a look of opulence. The older, heavier-built man, now staring at her with hard, appraising admiration, had a big, florid face suggestive of high-living counteracted by fresh air and Turkish baths. She had seen him before, or else his photograph. In a flash it came to her that he was Lord Limpsfield, Uncle Nick's pet client, of whom Aunt Rose had boasted.

The trim, dapper companion—she noted his waisted overcoat—was dark, with neat features and a sulky mouth cleanly-defined under an abbreviated smudge of a moustache. He, too, seemed familiar-looking, but Diana could not place him. When she turned to close the door she saw the two of them inside the car, with the chauffeur spreading a rug over their knees as obsequiously as though they had been royalty. In another moment the stream-lines of the oyster-coloured car had swept out of the Close.

"So I've set eyes on the great Lord Limpsfield," she reflected indifferently. "I'm not surprised Aunt Rose adored his coming here. I don't suppose there are three such cars as that in the whole of London. It's simply super! She'd never trouble about how he got his first million. Face value was enough for her."

As she passed the entrance to the lower flat she remembered she was expected to dine with her godfather. The prospect appalled her, yet she must, she supposed, go through with it. She entered her own quarters to find that in her absence fresh flowers had arrived. Every vase was filled with them.

"Oh, if only he wouldn't do this!" she lamented. "I know he means it kindly, but how I wish I'd taken one room of my own, no matter how uncomfortable, so I shouldn't have to eat six-course dinners to prove I'm grateful for things I don't want! It's beastly of me to feel this way. I am thankful for this lovely flat, and it's the greatest possible help to have everything done for me and not have to bother. All the same, I've got to hang on to some independence, so I shall simply draw the line at accepting any more favours."

It was a harder resolution to keep than she could at the moment foresee.

CHAPTER SEVENTEEN

THE room was light. It was morning, and here, on the bed-table, was her breakfast, deposited some time ago, as she realised when she came to pour out her tea. How done-up she must have been to sleep like this! She would have gone on sleeping, too, but for this ringing in her ear.

How incredibly stupid of her! It was the telephone, at her side. She picked up the gold-lacquered instrument, heard Colin Ladbroke's voice, and remembered her appointment with the barrister. Ten o'clock it was fixed for, and it was now after nine.

She was making a dash for the nearest taxi-rank when Gaylord came running after her to say that here was Mr. Blundell's car, and he had been told to take her wherever she wanted to go. Now it came back to her. She had been offered the Sunbeam for as long and as often as she might care to use it. Uncle Nick on the whole preferred the runabout— or so he had firmly insisted.

Oh, well, why not? It was late, and she might as well save the taxi fare. She sank into the luxurious seat, instructed Gaylord to drive her to the Inner Temple, and tried as the grey streets flashed past to recapture some details of the interminable evening. Over sole with mushroom sauce and pheasant shot by Lord Limpsfield the previous week-end Uncle Nick had offered her kindly advice, not failing to make plain to her that from now on she must be guided entirely by Adrian's counsel.

"He'll most likely put you on to a reliable private inquiry man, who'll begin snooping round trying to collect evidence against some one of those present. I'll come in for my share in due course. Oh, yes, I shall! For which reason it won't do for me to express any more opinions. I shall have to lie low and mind my manners."

The recollection of such painful jocularities caused her to writhe. They were about all, however, she seemed able to remember with any degree of clearness.

At the Temple she dismissed the car, and climbed two flights of stone stairs to a door bearing a long list of names in black letters. A pasty-faced youth with a pen behind his ear showed her into a room whose shabbiness was relieved by some good Persian rugs and a few old maps framed and hung on the olive-green walls. Presently the door opened and Michael Hull came in.

He was a staid man of forty-odd, with grave, prominent black eyes under spiky brows which gave him the look of a highly-conservative black-beetle. Seating himself across a mahogany table from herself, he swung an eye-glass, and coughed tentatively. At once Diana felt, with a sinking heart, that his attitude was one of extreme pessimism. At the same time he seemed to her wholly conscientious and determined to put up a hard fight for his client.

He asked her a great many searching questions, at first about the late Mrs. Somervell. She answered with perfect candour, emphasising her belief that Adrian had never made the slightest attempt to curry favour with Rose.

"He couldn't. He's too indifferent. Besides, it hadn't ever occurred to him he had anything to gain by it."

"H'm!" The eye-glass continued to swing. "Was Mrs. Somervell aware of your engagement to her stepson?"

Diana coloured as she replied that till more than a week after the death there had been no engagement.

"I see." The unexpressive answer made her supremely uncomfortable. "And now, perhaps you will tell me exactly what you said last evening to Doctor Ladbroke. Don't omit anything."

Diana complied. When she came to her own now-extinct supposition regarding her mother's murder she saw the beetling brows draw together with marked incredulity.

"I quite see how absurd it is now," she apologised, "but I did have some reason for thinking it before. Don't you agree?"

"Well—my opinion is of no consequence." He cleared his throat and leant forward gravely. "Now, Miss Lake, it's as well to grasp at once that we're confronted with a case which to outward seeming is practically cast-iron. There is the strongest kind of a motive, there is opportunity coupled with the requisite medical knowledge, and in addition material evidence of the most damning kind. I'm referring, of course, to the actual poison found in Dr. Somervell's pocket."

"Put like that, it does sound utterly hopeless," returned Diana steadily. "And yet I know, if you don't, that he simply could not have done this murder, or even thought of it. One of the three people I've been telling you about must be guilty. I suppose we must make it four people, if we include my godfather, Mr. Blundell. I've given a possible reason in each of three cases. Surely that's something to go on?"

"Oh, obviously! We must make investigations immediately, as regards motive and the possession of aconite. Now, let me see." He began jotting down notes on a clean sheet of paper. "Mr. Arenson," he murmured, "Mr. Blundell, whom you quite naturally count out—and the housekeeper's nephew. Is that the list?"

"You're leaving out Miss Dilworth, the secretary. Didn't I tell you I considered her by far the most likely suspect?"

With a slight start Michael Hull looked up—and this time with a distinct gleam of pity in his prominent eyes.

"The secretary! Oh-ah! I sincerely ask your pardon, Miss Lake. My fault entirely. The fact is, Miss Dilworth happens to be the individual who first reported a suspicion of foul play."

The room reeled. Elsie, herself? At one stroke Diana saw the secretary transformed from a scheming murderess to a furtive onlooker, taking note of what went on and quietly resolving to act as an instrument of justice. All her calculations were wrecked. Elsie, present in that dining-room. . . . What had she actually witnessed?

It was the first question Diana managed to utter, and the answer brought infinite relief. Miss Dilworth had seen nothing, only made certain shrewd deductions which later on were proved correct to the last detail. She had, it appeared, made her statement to the Home Office under seal of strict secrecy. Quite understandably she did not wish her name to be made public until it was established that murder had been done.

"However," continued Hull, "I found out quite easily exactly what did happen. Here is the Home Office communication, if you care to look at it."

Diana scarcely glanced at the paper handed her. Things were still spinning round.

"But why did she give this information?" she whispered. "What could have been her object?"

"She declared she felt it a public duty."

"Duty! I don't believe it. She did it purely out of revenge."

Hull looked shocked and alarmed.

"Really, my dear Miss Lake!" he protested. "I must beg you most earnestly not to make assertions of that kind. Don't you see how they would inevitably be construed?"

"I don't, I'm afraid."

"It might be assumed that Miss Dilworth was a party to the deed. That after being repulsed by Dr. Somervell she decided to denounce him."

"Oh!" Diana bit her lip. "All the same, I stick to my opinion. She undoubtedly believed Adrian was guilty of murder, but that only proves she knew he was going to inherit Mrs. Somervell's money, which fact she could have learned from the will itself when she witnessed it. As you know, she failed to turn up at either the inquest or the examination. She's hiding—because having done this impulsive thing she's simply sick with remorse."

"We must not draw hasty conclusions," the barrister counselled her. "Possibly she did act on an impulse she has since regretted, but we are not yet justified in going further than that, if as far."

"Was she calm or upset when she saw the Home Office people?" asked Diana pointedly. "Have you spoken to them personally to find out?"

"I have. She was highly agitated."

"I knew it!" declared Diana in triumph. "She's not quite sane."

"Sane or not," retorted Hully dryly, "she was right in her facts, and I was going to add she seems to have given those facts in such a convincing way as to command attention. You may not realise it, but the Home Office receives thousands of such stories. Out of them only a very few are considered worth more than a cursory investigation."

"Did she say the poison would be found in Dr. Somervell's pocket?"

"Oh, no, not that! I'll read you a precis of her statement." Adjusting his eye-glass, Hull read out: "She spoke of the will she had been asked to witness only two days prior to the victim's death. Second, she expressed certainty that the chief beneficiary would be discovered to be, financially speaking, in very low waters."

"There was never any secret about that," interposed Diana. "What else did she say?"

"That the beneficiary had been seeing the victim frequently, was on exceedingly friendly terms with her, and had been a guest at the meal immediately following which the fatal attack began. She also spoke in detail of the victim's symptoms, mentioning in particular the partial paralysis of the lips and tongue, wrongly attributed to stroke. In addition, she called attention to the fact that Mrs. Somervell's own doctor did not attend her, and that the partner who was called in was a total stranger, knowing nothing of her general constitution. Lastly Miss Dilworth gave her own firm belief that death was due to raw aconite root, mixed with the horseradish sauce on the victim's plate at the time a second helping was taken."

Diana leant forward excitedly.

"She actually said it was aconite?" she demanded.

"She did, but her guess is less astonishing than you may think. She explained that she had just read a novel in which a murder committed in this way was minutely described; that after the death she recalled having seen the horseradish sauce, whereupon she questioned the housekeeper very closely, consulted the *Medical Jurisprudence* in Mr. Blundell's library, and put two and two together. Quite accurately, as I need not remark."

"Mr. Hull," said Diana, "you may swallow that story. I don't. If Elsie Dilworth knew what poison had been used, or any poison for that matter, it was because she'd used it herself. I thought for a moment my theory about her was blown to atoms, but it isn't. She committed this murder—and for the very reason I've given—in order to force Adrian Somervell to marry her!"

The barrister looked at her with puzzled interest. Evidently he did not follow her argument. Perhaps, indeed, he fancied her a bit mad. She explained almost impatiently.

"She's a determined woman, Mr. Hull. She put doubts into Petty's mind hoping Mr. Blundell would hear of them and ask for the exhumation himself, but when nothing happened she took matters into her own hands. She meant to place Adrian in danger of arrest, but to get hold of the stuff she'd dropped into his pocket in time to prevent it's being found by the police. He couldn't have been indicted on the will alone, could he?"

"Well—perhaps not," admitted Hull cautiously. "But how do you suggest she failed to forestall the police? It was, if I may say so, a vital slip."

"Adrian was avoiding her," said Diana slowly. "After that Sunday he never saw her at all till she came to the hospital almost grovelling and begged him to—I've got it!" she cried. "That night he had on his new suit!"

"New suit?"

"Of course! And the aconite was in his old one, hanging in his wardrobe. She couldn't tell him about it, for he'd have gone straight home and got rid of the stuff. When she saw the clothes he was wearing her gun was spiked. No wonder she's acting like a mad woman. Who wouldn't, in her place?"

It seemed to her the black eyes held a shade more respect.

"Well, well! This must be gone into. We may possibly be able to find some other occasion when Miss Dilworth tried to get into personal contact with our client, or else to obtain access to his room. She must certainly be located, though I warn you it will at this date be extremely difficult to secure proof of her guilt."

He moved the papers about on his desk, and added that there might be a simpler explanation for the secretary's erratic behaviour.

"She's impetuous, obviously. No doubt hysterical. A woman of her age and habitual restraint frequently does go off the deep end under emotional stress such as she, on your showing, has been subjected to. Isn't it probable she realised her proper course would have been to acquaint Mr. Blundell with her suspicions, and that after her rash act she shrank from facing his very natural displeasure? It would account for her resignation, and—supposing she had left behind some memo-randa or diary she was anxious to retrieve—for her visiting his home when he was not there. You say she also went up to Mrs. Somervell's flat? To see the housekeeper, perhaps. She would not have known the old woman was gone."

"But why did she steal my letters?" objected Diana, unconvinced.

"If you'll forgive my saying so, you may have lost the letters during the course of the day. I don't think I should build too much on that incident."

Diana was silenced, but only partly shaken.

"I dare say you are aware," resumed the barrister, "that Mr. Blundell also requested the Home Office to perform an autopsy?"

"Did he?" The news took her by surprise. "When?"

"Not just at first. I understand it was after inquiries had begun, and following unexpected information given him by"—he hesitated—"well, in fact, your mother. The date was—yes, here it is—the late afternoon of November second."

She nodded. It was not astonishing after all. He had been going on his mission when she met him outside her door and was so struck by his odd manner.

As she had expected, she was strongly advised to keep her engage-ment concealed from every one except the private agent to whom the inquiries were to be entrusted.

"There are cases," Hull explained tactfully, "where a wife or a fiancée may tend to influence a jury in the right direction, but here it may have an undesirable result. We don't want to—to strengthen a motive already—in the public eye—overwhelmingly strong."

The agent he had selected was a man called Mortimer Bream, shrewd, and completely trustworthy. She was to tell him everything and at once. In fact, Hull had taken the liberty of arranging for her to meet Bream in a quiet restaurant, situated in the Strand, at one o'clock. Would that be convenient?

It was nearly one now. Diana left the office, took a restless turn along the Embankment, and walked through Villiers Street to the place of meeting.

CHAPTER EIGHTEEN

THE inquiry agent turned out to be a small, entirely neutral-looking man whose age was as hard to place as the colour of his eyes—a human flatfish, Diana decided, able to fade at will into any sort of background. To her astonishment, he seemed to possess enthusiasm of a dry sort. He was sympathetic, and she opened her heart to him without reserve.

The restaurant, false-beamed in Ye Olde Englyshe style, seemed exclusively given over to clerks and typists from the Law Courts, no one here she was in the least likely to know or see again. She was therefore startled when, towards the end of her recital, she was asked, more by gestures than words, to take a discreet survey of their next-door neighbour and see if she recognised him.

Not too quickly she turned. The solitary luncher was well-screened by a newspaper. On the point of shaking her head, she looked again, and this time noticed that the hand supporting the paper was of a dusky tint, the wrist, slender as a woman's, encircled by a platinoid watch-band and a turquoise-studded bangle. Memory stirred. Once before, not long ago, she had observed this odd coupling of ornaments on a dark skin. She gave a slight nod to her companion, who beckoned the waitress, asked for his check, and without hurry followed her into the Strand.

"What's wrong?" she asked. "Did you think that Indian was listening to us?"

"I'm quite positive he was. More than that, he was just behind you when you came in, and he didn't choose a seat till we'd got our table. It ought to have struck me sooner, but the thing seem too unlikely. Just walk through here and wait for me a second." He showed her a narrow passage leading into the Temple. "I'm going to make sure what he does next."

Presently Mortimer Bream joined her, and they walked on to a lonely bench in Fountain Court.

"He's still there. Maybe he's heard all he wanted. Now, who is he? Do you know?"

"I haven't an idea, except that I saw him quite recently in a place called the Daffodil Tea-Rooms, near the British Museum, with a crowd of other Indians, all, I think, students at the School of Economics. At least, I believe he's the same. If he has two gold teeth then there's no doubt about it."

"Gold teeth? I got a flash of them, when he was grinning at the waitress. Now why should a chap like that want to listen in on your remarks?"

"Don't ask me," said Diana, shrugging. "I can't believe he was doing it. And yet—" She had remembered something else.

"Yet what—?"

"Oh, nothing worth mentioning. It was just that the time I saw him I was with Dr. Somervell. When we went out I noticed—or thought I did—that he seemed interested in us. I couldn't imagine why."

"Well, if you see him again, be sure to tell me. Meanwhile I intend to check up on him at this—did you say the School of Economics? Fancy that, now! I didn't know that institution ran a course for spying. I may be wrong about him, of course. Put him out of your mind, and let's see if I've got my job properly mapped out."

With a stub of pencil he wrote down a few notes in a little book, and read them to her.

"Theatre manager, Felix Arenson: Learn nature of quarrel between him and deceased, query letters in case, discover if his Hampstead garden grows monkshood, and if not, how, when and where he could have got hold of any. That right? I think so. Corn-and-feed man—name of G. Petty?—ditto, with especial attention to disgraceful entanglements. Study auntie. Next, the secretary—whereabouts unknown."

At this point Bream appeared to meditate.

"The Crown," he said, "will be wanting her as a witness. Unfortunately for us, they will probably get her before we do. You see, we don't want to advertise, and the radio's barred to us. The last thing we want is to scare her. In fact, it might be fatal, if we hope to discover anything from her. So we're decidedly hampered," he summed up, tapping his lower teeth with his pencil.

"We've got to find her, Mr. Bream!" Diana spoke urgently. "Do you know what my great fear is now? That she'll commit suicide. It came into my mind the other night when I saw how utterly desperate she looked. For all we know she may already be dead."

"Then her body will be found."

"And if it is, how shall we ever get the truth?"

"Well, well, don't worry. I'll concentrate on her first. These others won't run away."

Reassuringly as he spoke, Diana fancied he was as little convinced of Adrian's innocence as Hull seemed to be. More and more was she realising the tremendous strength of the Crown case and the small chance she had of overthrowing it. Her sole comfort lay in the knowledge that an effort would be made at once. Mortimer Bream was not the sort of man to let grass grow under his feet.

After she had parted from him, she made her way to the big, cheerful Corner House by Charing Cross to order coffee and think matters over. Why on earth should that vulgar Indian youth be concerned with her affairs? She was still incredulous, inclined to think that little Bream's profession had made him over-suspicious. If this Indian crossed her path again, she might believe there was something in him, otherwise she would continue to look on the incident just past as irrelevant.

On the chair beside her lay the noon edition of *The Evening Banner*. She picked it up and read its re-hash of yesterday's court sensation, unable to understand how with news like this to print the paper should devote half its front page to the dull topic of Arterial Highways. Who in a thousand readers cared about Arterial Highways? Yet with one accord all newspapers seemed determined to force them down the public's throat. Popular rags like this went thrice daily into rhapsodies over Improvement and Expansion, breathing patriotism, sounding their slogans with what amounted to religious fervour. Diana herself had grown weary of hearing about the new Minister of Arterial Highways, Sir Norbury Penge, who, with mysterious suddenness had become a household word. Who was he? No one she knew had ever heard of him till the past few months, yet now every day or so one was confronted by his self-righteous, efficient, rather good-looking features, accompanied by captions heralding him as a modern St. George appointed by Providence to free England from the dragon of sloth and backwardness. Here he was now, spread across two entire columns, as smug as—

She frowned hard at the page. Why, Sir Norbury Penge was none other than Lord Limpsfield's companion, seen on her own doorstep last night! So he was one of the big fish come to Uncle Nick's net about whom Aunt Rose had so snobbishly boasted! She remembered now that her mother had mentioned him, though not the fact that he and Lord Limpsfield were friends. Oh, well, it was all totally uninteresting. Now her coffee was drunk, how could she occupy herself? Mr. Bream had told her she might assist by going amongst her theatre acquaintances and trying to pick up ancient gossip. She would do her best, of course, but who in her own circle would know anything of what took place years ago between Rose Somervell and her manager?

Dame Charlotte Moon! The name leaped to her mind, and at the same time she wondered again what secret anxiety could have caused the old actress's strange tension at the court. There would be no harm in paying Dame Charlotte a call. She telephoned from Charing Cross Station, boarded a bus, and within twenty minutes was ushered into a drawing-room of the most stodgy depressingness it was possible for her to imagine.

Dame Charlotte likewise was stodgy and depressing. She was going through her accounts at a repulsive Victorian desk above which loomed a bust of Shakespeare and a whole wall of the signed photographs of dead and gone celebrities, from Sir Henry Irving downward. Her dress was brown, trailing, and covered with fringe. Her small, dull eyes had a far-away expression, and though she greeted Diana with lugubrious kindness, her condescending manner remained preoccupied.

It was easy enough to steer her on to the topic of interest, but nothing came of it. If at any time she had known the details of the Somervell-Arenson breach she refused to be drawn, and in speaking of the murder itself she seemed chiefly at pains to point out that the victim had never been her intimate friend. She had, she admitted, been slightly astonished at being called on to lend her experienced aid over the funeral.

"However," she added with a massive shrug, "a fellow artist—in quite another line, to be sure, one's loyalty to the Profession—one could not well refuse, could one? I did what I could, and I cannot wholly regret it, in spite of this hideous sequel. I even gave up an important committee meeting at the Duchess of Wight's to drive down to Berkshire for the interment, and caught quite a severe chill standing by the grave in a mist of rain; but Mr. Blundell kindly gave me tea at his really most charming cottage, indeed insisted on putting me up for the night. The next day I was well enough to attend the service at St. Martin's, for which I had been fortunate enough to secure my own dear Bishop of Lulcaster and other distinguished men—but you have seen the list, I'm sure. All my doing, of course."

Grimly and with a shudder of distaste, Dame Charlotte spoke of the shock the subsequent discovery had been to her. Mr. Blundell himself could hardly have been more horrified.

"I have felt the deepest pity for him. Poor man, he does not deserve this, after his long, disinterested devotion to Rose Walsh—a friendship some of us may have been prone to misinterpret, for there are many evil-minded people in this city of ours, though I, having seen something of him, hold no such view. He has a kindness of heart which goes far towards making up for any little social lacks; and without a shadow of doubt it was his very warm-heartedness which led him to introduce this young criminal—"

She paused, her eyes turned expectantly towards the door, through which a subdued maidservant was sidling with an envelope on a tray.

"Delivered by district messenger, Madam."

Dame Charlotte seized the envelope with trembling haste, tore it open, and for a second anxiously inspected the contents. As she gazed Diana saw her expression alter to gloating satisfaction. Then smiling and distrait she laid on the table beside her a typed letter and a cheque. She was absolutely purring now with contentment. To the girl watching her there seemed something almost ghoulish in her pleasure.

"Forgive me, my dear," she resumed, and then, with conscious hesitation: "The fact is, I have just received a little windfall, much appreciated in these hard times. Yes, a quick turn-over on the Stock Exchange, due to a friend's kindness—and I very naturally wanted to see at once what it came to. I rejoice to say it is more than I had hoped. It will cover my income-tax, with a bit over for charity."

Which, thought Diana cynically, would begin at home. . . .

"We were saying—?" Dame Charlotte remembered, and with some difficulty hid her smug delight under the mask employed for her celebrated Greek roles. "Ah, yes, to be sure, poor victimised Rose Walsh . . . your godmother, was she? That explains, then, your interest in this crime. But for vile trickery she might have left you some small legacy, poor, motherless child! The wretched creature, Somervell, must have been clever indeed to wind so shrewd a woman round his finger, but rest assured British justice will make short work of him. Come to me again, if you want comfort and advice. I shall always be glad . . . Must you go?"

Unable to support more of this in silence, Diana rose to take her leave; but on her way past the table she could not resist a covert glance at the letter-heading and the cheque, both in plain view. She saw her own present address—6, Queen's Close, and the crabbed signature, Nicholas G. Blundell. In a twinkling certain mysteries became crystal-clear.

Lottie Moon, arch-snob and guardian of domestic virtues, possessed one weakness—playing the market. Hadn't Mummy frequently declared that Lottie always wangled tips from her entire circle of influential connections, be they duchesses or archbishops? Well, then! She must have seen at a glance that the astute Blundell could serve her—and Uncle Nick, awed by her grandeur, had without a doubt been all eagerness to comply. Hence the lofty tolerance towards social short-comings, hence the blind eye to a relationship previously suspect; but these were not the only riddles instantaneously solved.

Moving down in the creaky lift, Diana saw the whole reason for Dame Charlotte's anxiety till the indictment was delivered—for her adamant insistence on Adrian's guilt. It furnished matter for reflection, and for ten minutes or so Diana remained in a muse.

CHAPTER NINETEEN

MORTIMER Bream embarked on his task with the deepest pessimism. If there was anything in Miss Lake's theories—which he regretfully doubted—he did not see the slightest possibility of proving it. No eyewitness had seen the accused drop grated aconite on the victim's plate, but the same truth applied to the other potential suspects. None of the latter was in the least likely to have aconite in his possession now, nor would it be easy to discover when or where the said poison had been obtained.

Aconite—otherwise monkshood—grew all over England, both wild and in gardens. You could dig it up yourself, but you could not buy the raw article anywhere, for the simple reason that neither chemist nor herbalist stocked it. In October there would still have been plenty of it about. You had only to identify the spiky leaves in the absence of the purplish, bell-like flowers—and any person could obtain coloured plates and full information from a library, as Bream himself had just done. Somervell would probably know all about it. The secretary-woman had openly declared her sources of knowledge. Unfortunately it was Somervell who had inherited the victim's money, all but the small pickings.

"Oh, I dare say he's guilty," grumbled Bream. "He'd been seeing a lot of the old lady, and it looks as though he has a way with the opposite sex. It wouldn't be the first time a nice, sensible girl like Miss Lake has been taken in by a scoundrel. After all, what do her beliefs boil down to? Just this—that no man with a murder on his conscience could have shown such total lack of concern for his own safety. Poor girl! I could tell her of cases . . ."

Brilliant men, too. Why, there were classic examples of the most staggering carelessness! What about Professor Webster, of Boston, who had allowed human remains and even a distinctive dental-plate to be discovered in his own laboratory, the place of all others likely to be searched? Webster, ambitious for advancement, had been in a chronic state of financial embarrassment. Somervell might not turn out to be heavily in debt, but he had admitted wanting both further study and marriage—with a bank-balance, on the day of his arrest, amounting to ninety-five pounds, seven shillings and twopence! In the circumstances any jury would think that he had brushed the lining of his pocket, only not thoroughly enough. Altogether matters looked blightingly bad, and on closer scrutiny they might look worse.

And yet, this Indian. . . . Had he followed Miss Lake in by chance or for the purpose of overhearing her conversation? To Bream a vast deal depended on settling this question, and during the few minutes he had left his companion in the passage to the Temple he had done his best to accomplish it.

In the restaurant again, he took a good look at the dark-skinned youth, who lounged at his ease, blowing smoke-rings towards the ceiling. He seemed neither hurried nor worried. Whatever his intention might have been, one would say he now had nothing weighty on his mind. His face seen in profile showed a flattish nose, a sleepy, sloe-black eye with a hint of cunning in the set of it, a sensual mouth, and inky hair plastered back, glistening like a crow's wing. Though broad of shoulder, he had delicate hands; but what chiefly struck Bream was the extreme newness and foppishness of his clothes. All he wore looked just out of the shop—pointed, brown shoes of reversed calf, loud, fawn-coloured tweeds, orange knitted pullover, green striped tie. He looked well-pleased with himself. When a waitress passed he reached amorously for her hand, nothing abashed at the coldness of her glance.

"Packet of Players," said Bream as the girl drew near, and as he spoke he retired behind the cash-desk. "That one of your regulars?"

"Who? Oh, him!" She tossed a scornful head. "No, and what's more he'd better keep clear of our place, unless he's looking for a good box on the ear!"

Only a casual, then.

"Too bad," reflected Bream, disappointed. "There did seem just a faint chance that some one of our line-up wanted to keep close watch on the defence's operations. It would have meant the possibility of a vulnerable spot we ourselves haven't yet seen. Oh, well, I'll know this boy amongst a thousand. That's something."

After bidding Diana good-bye, he made at once for the Bloomsbury Street Boarding-house which had been the prisoner's home, and held a talk with the soft and blowsy landlady. It was clear she had till lately warmly approved of her American guest, who had been prompt of pay, uncritical of board and bed, and, though never exactly a chatty young man, worthy of respect and liking.

"I keep asking myself how ever he could have done it!" she mourned. "It's hard to believe even now when there does seem no doubt of it at all. It puts me in mind of that Frenchman the papers was so full of just after the war. Murdered ever so many poor women just for their savings. What was his name, now?"

"Landru?"

"That's it. Well, then, every one of those girls thought what a nice man he was, didn't they? Not that all of them were girls. It's the old ones that seem to fall hardest for soft soap, as I dare say you've noticed. Yet Dr. Somervell never seemed to me to . . . but there, I suppose I only saw the one side of him. Rose Walsh—why, I remember her, a good thirty years back, when I first came to London! *Meg of Mayfair* I saw her in. Sixty-three, wasn't she? I'd have given her all that and more."

Bream asked if it was true that for a time Dr. Somervell had been rather thick with a woman-guest called Dilworth. The landlady bristled, almost affrontedly.

"Thick!" she snorted. "I'd have said the thickness was all on her side. I'm sure I used to feel quite sorry for the poor boy. If ever a man was run after! Why, she fastened on to him like a leech—and the fixing-up she did to herself, getting that mousy hair of hers permed and dyed! Some days she did look a fair show. She must have been spending all she made on clothes, all for the one purpose—and it never came off—at least," she corrected herself, "not as she wanted."

"Who was Miss Dilworth? Did you know anything about her?"

"Not a blessed thing. In the main she was very stand-offish, never talked about herself. I couldn't even have said how she got her living till after she was gone and a gentleman she was secretary to called round to see if I had her new address—which I hadn't. A very kind sort of man he seemed. He was quite worried about her. Yes, she was a queer mixture. I never could make her out."

Bream inquired if Miss Dilworth ever went into the country? He was told that she did, on Saturday afternoons or Sundays, in good weather, taking her golf clubs, though she never said what golf course she visited.

"I'm telling you, she was that close-mouthed about her doings. You can't surely think she was mixed up in this murder?"

"I have a lot to check up on," explained Bream, "if Dr. Somervell is to put up a good defence."

He next asked if Miss Dilworth had ever paid by cheque, learned that this sometimes was the case, and secured the name and branch of her bank, also the date of her departure—sixteenth of October.

"Early in the morning she popped off. Must have spent the whole night packing, for at a quarter to eight she'd got all her belongings down here ready to load on to a taxi. That's what first showed me something odd had happened—and before breakfast was over I'd heard all about it."

Willingly the speaker launched on an account of what, evidently, had caused lively excitement—and it was amusing to see her wavering between the horror she felt in duty bound to feel towards the doctor, and the indignant sympathy he had recently inspired. She herself had slept through the disturbance, occupying, as she did, a folding-cot in the office; but those above had all been startled by Miss Dilworth's hysterical screams. Miss Walsover—such a nice, bright girl, book-keeping at a library—had been positive murder was being committed. Only old Mr. Lampson, however—he was a chartered accountant, very accurate in his statements—had been an eyewitness.

"Soon after the rumpus began, he came out in his pyjamas to see what it was about—and there was the doctor, dressed, and carrying Miss Dilworth, in a regular Mae West get-up, across the passage to her own room. Kicking and crying she was—and he was red in the face. He put her down inside her door, banged it shut, and turned to find Mr. Lampson standing there. Not one question would he answer. He just banged into his room, and locked himself in."

Bream wished to know if Dr. Somervell drank. The landlady heatedly denied the suggestion. No, she was certain it was nothing of that kind. It was just that he couldn't stick the persecution.

"Though you may guess the stories that got round. It's true for a time he had been going to her room a good bit. She invited him—I've heard her; and in the beginning Miss Walsover made one of the party till, as she says, she felt Miss Dilworth was tired of being chaperoned. Only a little after that we all noticed the doctor was veering off, and Miss Dilworth getting so haggard and desperate-looking you'd have said she was just preparing to chuck herself in the river. Whatever did happen, I for one stick to it she was to blame, for she took the lead, and at her age she'd ought to know better."

Bream was growing more and more depressed. It did not require these ill-veiled hints to make him envisage an all-too-familiar situation. It was true that Miss Dilworth might have had the most urgent of reasons for forcing Somervell into marriage, even though it took a crime to accomplish it; but unluckily the thing cut two ways.

Suppose Somervell, anxious to marry Diana Lake, had suddenly found himself faced with awkward consequences? Money alone hushes up an affair of that kind. Without it all future happiness might be wrecked.

Keeping to his main object, he tried to find out whether Miss Dilworth had written to the doctor and made any attempt to see him. The landlady did not know.

"She said she would call in for any letters that might come for her, and so she did, more than once, though I never saw her. Maybe Kate, the doormaid, can tell you something."

Kate, a wild Irish rose with untidy black eyebrows, declared that during the first week Miss Dilworth had called twice, taken her letters out of the rack, and left immediately. She must have come a third time at the lunch-hour when the door was sometimes left ajar, for some circulars addressed to her disappeared; but it was unlikely she had seen Dr. Somervell, since it was a weekday, and but for Sundays the doctor did not return for lunch. Neither Kate nor her mistress knew Miss Dilworth's writing well enough to say if she had communicated with any one here by post. Definitely she had not telephoned.

None of this was at all satisfactory. In thoughtful mood Bream turned his steps towards the Holborn branch of the Essex and Home Counties Bank to see what he could learn there.

It seemed that for the past eight years Elsie K. Dilworth had kept an account which at no time had been overdrawn. The manager described her as a very reserved, business-like woman who seldom discussed her personal life. The oldest cashier recalled that once, in a rare burst of confidence, she had told him what an extremely good berth she had, and how her employer, unlike former ones, treated all his staff like human beings.

Latterly, though, Miss Dilworth had appeared restless, fed up with life in general, and in a vague way had spoken of making a change. It was about this time that a distinct alteration in her style of dress was remarked.

"When did she last come in?" Bream wanted to know.

He was informed that on the morning of second November Miss Dilworth, looking ill and harassed, had drawn a cheque to self for the unusually large sum of forty pounds. Since then she had not been seen. A Mr. Blundell, for whom she had worked, had called by in his efforts to locate her, but even now, after several weeks, there had been no news. Wherever she was, she was paying cash, for no cheques had been received. Her pass-book was to hand, and this—although by now the manager was rubbing his chin dubiously—the detective was allowed to examine.

Bream noticed that the disbursements, regular and strictly limited till last July, from then onward took a sharp up-curve. All at once Miss Dilworth had spent lavishly, and to judge by the names to which payments had been made all her extravagance had been in the matter of wearing apparel. It was out of the question that a solicitor's secretary could spend like amounts with only her salary to depend on, generous though that salary evidently had been. Had she private means? Bream glanced at the adjacent column, ran back over the preceding pages, and gave a start. Most assuredly this was the case!

At irregular intervals over the past six years sums of varying amount had been deposited. They ranged from eighteen to eighty-seven pounds, eleven shillings. During the first three years they were few in number, but they had increased in size and frequency till the largest and last, paid in on twelfth of October of the present year. To sum it up, Elsie Dilworth had been receiving from a source unspecified anywhere from a hundred and fifty to two hundred a year over and above her stated earnings.

What did it mean?

CHAPTER TWENTY

IT WAS too early to theorise. Deciding that his next step must be a discreet canvassing of Elsie Dilworth's fellow-workers, Bream first assured himself of Nicholas Blundell's absence, and then presented himself at the office, situated in Fetter Lane.

He found two male clerks and a young girl typist, the latter so singularly plain looking that he tended at once to discard a preliminary idea. He spoke with each member of the staff, explaining his reason for tracing Miss Dilworth, and receiving unhelpful answers. No one here had the faintest notion where she had gone, or why she had left her post. Even the senior clerk, who had worked side by side with her for five years, was wholly ignorant of her private life.

"It wasn't just shyness," he declared, scratching his ear with a pen. "It seemed a matter of what you might call a negative personality. Determined, though. Oh, dear, yes! She'd plenty of concentration and obstinacy. You could see it working inside her—but she didn't talk about it. I couldn't tell you who her friends were—if she had any—or what she did in her off-time. I fancy she lived a very solitary life—till lately, that is."

"Then you did notice a change in her?"

"Did we!" The clerk smiled. "Since the middle of last summer. She got all keyed-up, rather—well, skittish, if you understand. In her clothes she was a different woman, but again not a hint as to what was causing it. And then, it ended—like that." He snapped his fingers expressively. "She turned queerish. When? Oh, this autumn. Not all at once, you know. More and more nervy, till without a word of notice or warning off she popped. Just went. I'd never have thought it of her. Reliable as they make 'em, all these years. It seemed as though something in her had cracked under a strain. I'd never connected her with this American who's been charged with Mrs. Somervell's murder. Friends, were they?" he inquired with hopeful inquisitiveness.

"Just boarding-house acquaintances," Bream replied, and led the talk round to the matter of Miss Dilworth's private income. The clerk, Parsons by name, was astonished to learn of any. For several minutes he listened uncomprehendingly, and then he smiled again with a look of indulgent enlightenment.

"I believe I can clear up that little mystery," he said and, opening a drawer in his desk, drew out what Bream saw to be his own pass-book. "Just run through this," he continued. "See these deposits? Forty-three, ten, six on August twenty-eighth, roughly the same on October thirty-first. And there are others, running back over a considerable period. Well, then! Those represent what Mr. Blundell chooses to call bonuses. It's his own little system, to ensure keen interest and a high standard of work. It's unusual, oh, decidedly! You won't find many employers doing a thing of this kind, I dare say; but as he says, it pays him, and that it's right we should share when he happens on a bit of luck. Gifts? Not quite. Perhaps I'd better explain more fully."

Mr. Blundell, he said with loyal pride, was a man of rather remarkable judgment where the stock market was concerned. Through his contacts with big financiers—like Lord Limpsfield, for example—he often got on to good things. When he chanced a flutter on his own account, he would offer to do the same for his employees, assuming all risk of loss.

"Though I can assure you he doesn't often lose," added Parsons triumphantly. "This last bonus marks a quick getting-in-and-out with Verysharp Steel. I'd been doing a big of overtime, and this was my reward. Miss Dilworth, who never minded giving up her Sundays, must have benefited quite a lot in the way I've described. That's my chief reason for thinking she must be clean off her rocker. She won't find another berth equal to what she's had; and yet"—he wrinkled his sallow brow meditatively—"her going was planned. Must have been. Bramshaw—that's the junior clerk—will tell you she left everything absolutely ship-shape."

Bream was beginning to form an unpleasant theory as to the reason for the secretary's disappearance. The withdrawal of forty pounds fitted in with it; but he must not be hasty. He remarked that Mr. Blundell must be not only a kind-hearted but a rather quixotic man. Parsons nodded as he put up his pass-book.

"He's Colonial," he answered, as though accounting for much eccentricity. "What I mean is, he takes a broad, human view of things. A bit unexpected till you get used to him, but always in a good humour. Like a big schoolboy, I always say; and still, in spite of his harmless joking, I believe he can read most people, men and women too, like a book. All except Miss Dilworth," the clerk thoughtfully amended. "Since this happened, I imagine he's all at sea. Her conduct's a sore subject with him. Coming as it did on top of losing an old friend like Mrs. Somervell and then all this ugly business about the death—it was bound to hurt him even more than it would at ordinary times. No doubt he's feeling he deserved better treatment."

"Does he do much business at his home? I understand Miss Dilworth was working at the flat a good deal just before she left."

Parsons replied that certain clients preferred discussion under pleasanter conditions than those offered by the office. Sometimes it was a question of convenience.

"Take Lord Limpsfield—another South African, by the way, and fairly unconventional himself. Well, he always likes doing business over a good dinner and a cigar. During the day he has about a thousand calls on his time. I'd say that in the matter of income-tax alone Mr. Blundell has saved him enormous amounts—all quite properly, of course—just from a thorough knowledge of the tax laws."

As there seemed no more to be gleaned in this quarter, Bream quitted the office, and on his way to Floyd's Square, Islington, took stock of his very meagre results. So far as he could at present see, Elsie Dilworth was an unattractive, repressed woman who had been emotionally bowled over by an unfortunate love-episode. Through revenge or other motives she had given information calculated to ruin Somervell, instantly regretted her rash act, and, foreseeing an arrest, made a stupid effort to save him by suggesting an elopement. In this she had failed, whereupon she had become frightened and made off. Either she wished to avoid giving evidence against Somervell, or, herself guilty, she dreaded personal consequences; or—it was certainly a possibility—she had gone into retirement because she was "in trouble." Three alternatives. Which was the right one?

"Finding her may only complicate the issue," Bream reflected. "And yet I've got to find her. No way out of it."

The tenant of the tiny two-story-and-basement house he now visited proved to be a worn, red-haired woman in the middle thirties, whose name—ascertained from a neighbouring ironmonger—was Mrs. Gladys

Eales. She had one large room to let. It occupied the whole of the upper floor, and when Bream applied for it she gave him a sharply curious glance.

"Well, I never!" she exclaimed. "How things do get about! Whoever told you that room was empty?"

"Then it is available?"

"Well—in a manner of speaking, it isn't. I mean, it's paid for till the end of next week, by the lady who's just left. Some of her things are still in it, so I expect she may be planning to come back. She was ill, you see, and went of a sudden, while I was out the night before last. I found a note with the money. All she said was she was off to the seaside where an old doctor of hers was living, and she wouldn't know till she'd seen him whether she'd be keeping this room on or not. I've not yet had a line from her, so you understand how I'm placed."

"Now I'm here, do you think I might have a look at the room?"

"Well, there's no harm in that," agreed the landlady, slightly hesitant. "I could let you have a definite answer later."

Bream followed her up a flight of narrow, linoleum-covered stairs to an irregularly-shaped room overlooking the dingy square. It contained a divan-bed, a gate-legged table, a chest of drawers, and several chairs, one a large basket one. Two shallow recesses flanked the fireplace, in which was a gas-fire. One was a cupboard, the other was filled by shelves on which stood cups and saucers, a teapot, and, at the bottom, a pile of old newspapers. Opening the cupboard door, Bream saw a few coat-hangers, a pair of metal shoe-trees, and a bag of golf clubs.

"Pity you don't know if the lady's coming back," he murmured. "I could just leave you my address, though, and then when you hear you can drop me a line." He searched his pockets. "I don't seem to have a scrap of paper to write on," he said. "Shall I just tear off a corner of one of these?" And he moved towards the newspapers, the top one of which he saw to be a fortnight old.

"Wait, I'll fetch you something."

Left to himself, Bream lost no time. Swiftly he removed the golf clubs from the bag, and, taking an envelope from his pocket, carefully shook the bag over it. A little dried mud fell out, and this he folded up and placed in his pocket. He was just turning his eye on the worn cabin-trunk in the corner when Mrs. Eales returned. As he scribbled the fictitious name he reserved for similar occasions, he asked if it would be possible to have an answer in ten days.

"I—I really couldn't say." Her manner struck him as perplexed and vaguely embarrassed. "The trouble may be that Mrs. Dixon herself won't know as soon as that. The way she worded her note—I've thrown it away, or I'd show it to you—she might find there was nothing much wrong with her, and again it might mean a long treatment."

Mrs. Dixon! So the secretary was posing as a married woman. His suspicions deepened—and then it occurred to him that it might be a case of a mistaken house number.

No, hardly that, for there were Miss Dilworth's initials—"E.K.D."— plainly stamped on the trunk. He picked a used Remington type-ribbon from the waste-basket and twirled it between his fingers.

"Mrs. Dixon!" he repeated. "Can she be the Mrs. Edith Dixon who does authors' copying? I heard she lived in this direction. Is she a stout, jolly woman with a black Eton crop?"

Mrs. Eales stared.

"Oh, dear no! I can't tell you her first name, but my Mrs. Dixon's as thin as a rake. She stoops, and you couldn't call her jolly. What she does I've never heard her say, but it was owing to feeling so run-down she gave up her last post. That was the second week she was here, and really I don't wonder at it, for in her state she couldn't have carried on any work. I sleep just under here, and I'm sure I was kept awake half the night, what with her roaming round and opening and shutting windows. She'd groan too. Oh, something awful! It was nerves, I think. Did you say black hair? Hers is a sort of red. Touched up, you know."

The various drawers, casually opened, revealed only a few stray pins. With a final wistful glance at the trunk he was preparing to go; Mrs. Eales arrested him with further remarks.

"Neighbours do seem to notice a lot. Why, yesterday, even, I'd another applicant after this room, though how he knew it was empty Heaven alone knows!"

"And what did you tell him?" inquired Bream genially.

"Oh, I made it 'No' straight off, for all he tried to wheedle me into showing it to him. Yes, got his foot wedged in the door, and flourished a brand-new pocket-book just to tempt me. Stuffed full of pound notes it was. And he was dressed up to the nines, as you may say; but I suppose I'm prejudiced against these dark-skinned natives. I just wouldn't like one in the house."

Dark-skinned? Dressed to the nines? A pleasant prickle ran over Bream's face, and his pulse skipped a beat.

CHAPTER TWENTY-ONE

REMEMBERING that London teemed with Indians, Bream subdued his elation. This "native" might not be his Indian at all; but after a little adroit questioning he was convinced it was the same. Mrs. Eales had noticed the gold teeth.

"Maybe," he ventured, "he was acquainted with your Mrs. Dixon, and heard from her that she was going away."

"Not a bit of it!" retorted the landlady contemptuously. "He never mentioned her name, and I don't know why he was so set on having this particular room. He even tried to persuade me to put him up for a day or two while he was hunting another; but as I tell you, there was a look about him I just didn't fancy."

Over a cup of tea in the corner bakery, Bream considered his new fact and tried to fit it into some plausible scheme. Although it gave him definite encouragement he could make nothing of it. Where lay the connection between Elsie Dilworth and the Indian student? Were they in league in some way, and did the Indian fear he was being double-crossed? All he felt sure of was that the latter was anxious to inspect the room to which the secretary might return, and that he had known almost immediately when the room was unoccupied. How had he known? Not from Diana Lake's conversation, for his visit had been paid the day before. It was still hard to think of him as acting in another person's behalf; who would select such a distinctive-looking as well as clumsy amateur for delicate missions? Yet it was even more difficult to conceive of him as a principal. His manner to-day had shown such total lack of concern.

"Principal or agent, there's something in that room he wants to get at—maybe to destroy. Or he thinks there is. Is it in the trunk? It must be. I wonder what his next move will be?"

Cat-burglary, perhaps. There was a rear window on the landing with a short drop to the ground. Come to think of it, he might risk a go at it himself. . . .

Recalling the dirt filched from the golf bag, he took out his envelope and tipped its contents on to a clean plate. Careful examination showed him only a bit of dried grass, no leaves or stems indicative of monks-hood. He sighed, wondering whether Mrs. Eales knew more than she professed, and whether Mrs. Dixon, so-called, would return to lie low and watch the turn of events. It all depended, he thought, on the real reason for her absence. Find that, and it was quite possible the entire problem would be solved. It was odd that already he was dwelling on one suspect to the complete exclusion of the other two.

"Two? Why not three? Why am I paying no attention to this solicitor chap, who was also on the spot, did the carving, in fact, had as good or better an opportunity for poisoning food than any one else? Oh, yes, I'm remembering! He drew up this will; he doesn't benefit one farthing; and as far as we know he and the victim were on splendid terms."

As far as they knew . . .

Pensively Bream wondered if, at any time, Rose Somervell and her solicitor had indulged in warmer relations. There might have been some burdensome, even dangerous, hold over Blundell. Just as well make sure, but for the moment it was a matter which could wait, mainly because the Indian seemed to promise a short cut straight to the heart of things.

"Unfortunately," said the bursar of the School of Economics, "our enrolment of Indians is enormous. I'm afraid I don't recognise the description, but I'll do my best. You've come rather late, and our lectures are over for the day. Just possibly, though, there may be an Indian or two left in the building."

Bream waited in the lobby, and was presently rewarded by the return of the bursar in company with a slender young Indian of well-bred appearance. It was not at all what Bream wanted, for this student, introduced as Mr. Mirza Ahmed, would in all probability hand on a warning to his fellow-countryman. However, the damage was done, and the bursar's next words removed his fears. Mr. Ahmed did know the young man Bream had described, and had his own reasons for wishing to corner him.

"He says Mr. Haji owes him ten pounds, and has been dodging payment for some time. I'll leave the two of you to talk matters over."

When they were alone, Ahmed said with amusement in his dark eyes, "So you're after him too, are you? I wish you luck; but this much I can tell you. Haji's in funds now. Not a doubt of it. Where's he got money from is a mystery, but I'm told he spends it like water."

"So his name is Haji, is it?"

"Abdulmajid Haji—and perhaps you don't need me to tell you he's as slippery as an eel. He borrowed left and right from every one here who was fool enough to lend, and now he's flush he's stopped turning up for lectures. It's possible his father's forked up again, but I doubt it, after the mess he got into."

"I hadn't heard about it. What kind of a mess?"

"Oh, a nasty affair—or might have been." Ahmed hesitated. "Some girl he was running with died in his rooms. It looked for a bit as though Haji might be arrested."

"But he wasn't, I take it?"

"No, it was a natural death. It caused scandal, though, and I expect for his people it was the last straw. Haji's father's a highly respectable government official in Bombay. No, I scarcely see Haji now. I can't tell you his present address, though I could probably get it for you from some of his friends. I suppose you'd like me to try?"

"I would, very much," answered Bream, "provided you can do it without letting him guess I'm after him."

"I'll keep your name out of it," Ahmed promised, and Bream, hoping his ally could be trusted to keep his word, handed him his telephone number.

Returning to Bloomsbury Street, Bream conducted two more interviews, one with Mr. Lampson, just home for dinner, the other with Miss Walsover. Lampson, a bald, brittle man with a prim slit of a mouth, described with almost legal precision what he had witnessed on the night of October fifteenth. There was nothing new in his account. Miss Dilworth, he said, had evidently parted with every vestige of self-control, the doctor was beside himself with suppressed rage and had resolutely declined to discuss the situation.

"Very suitably. Oh, yes, at that period I liked the man, what I knew of him. We sometimes chatted at meals, but he was rather uncommunicative, entirely wrapped up in his work—or so I believed."

Miss Walsover proved to be a shrewd, good-looking young woman, whose sympathies had been wholly with Doctor Somervell. Now, quite naturally, she was shocked and revolted, but she still declared her belief that Miss Dilworth had thrown herself at the doctor's head.

"If certain things did happen," she added, "I assure you they were just a flash in the pan. Once they were over any one could see Dilworth was just repulsive to him."

"And you've not seen her at all since she went away?"

"Not one of us has. I dare say she's some pride left."

Here matters rested, most unsatisfactorily. Bream had failed to discover any attempt on Miss Dilworth's part to get hold of Somervell before the hospital encounter, and his chief fear now was that the more deeply he probed the less desirable facts he would unearth. Again he brooded on the Indian's determination to get into the abandoned room, and his ill-concealed eavesdropping in the restaurant.

"I can't make sense of it," he grumbled. "Is this Haji linked up with Dilworth and afraid she'll blow the gaff to save Somervell's neck? Too thin . . . or is it? Anyhow, I've first got to prove those two are acquainted. Then there's the business of the girl who pegged out in his lodgings. Does she come into it?"

One step at a time, he reminded himself. For this evening he had formed a project, and on its success much of his future movements would depend. Till a late hour, therefore, he tabulated his facts and dates, and then made his way back to Floyd's Square, now silent as the tomb, ill-lighted, eerily damp. There was a passage leading southward from the corner near Mrs. Eales's house. As he had hoped it joined at right angles an alley on which the whole row of cramped gardens backed. Brick walls enclosed it, with inset gates. No light showed except one dim street lamp at the passage end, and a second at the other extremity. In the gloom between he found a gate he could open. He stationed himself just inside and prepared for a tedious and perhaps fruitless vigil.

Presently he was yawning. A distant clock struck two, his legs ached with fatigue, and a thin rain was soaking him to the skin. Then, as he was about to give up, a faint footstep fell on his ear. A late wayfarer was coming along the passage. The sound ceased rather than receded, and a moment later his nerves vibrated as, close at hand, he heard a slight, metallic clang. With extreme caution he peered forth into the alley. By all the powers, he was right! There, by the locked gate of seventeen, Abdulmajid Haji was mounting a dust-bin and grasping the top of the wall for a spring!

Amateur once more shot through the agent's mind. Hadn't the fool wit enough to put on dark clothing? His new, fawn overcoat made a pale splash in the night. He had not even stopped to make certain the partly open gate behind him contained no watcher. However, one tweed-clad leg was just rising aloft when Bream's scorn was transferred to himself. Flower-pots!

Startled by the clatter in the rear, the Indian leapt to earth with terror written on his swarthy face. Bream pinioned him by the collar, and found a small, pearl-handled revolver thrust into the pit of his stomach. In the utter confusion which followed the detective's one thought was that he had got hold of an eel. His own revolver, hurtled from his hand, fell ten feet away, his prey wriggled free, and melted into the darkness. Bream collected his weapon, shouted, and made a frantic dash.

Far along the turnings which descended towards King's Cross the steps hot-footed it, pursued but uncaught. It was a deeply mortified private agent who some ten minutes later approached a young constable calmly pacing his beat and described the attempted burglary.

"Give an eye to the back premises of seventeen, Floyd's Square? Right-o, sir, just as you say; but there won't be another try to-night. Not half there won't!"

Bream bitterly agreed. At home, in his rooms in Great Smith Street, Westminster, he morosely imbibed hot whisky and tried to think how—barring unseen flower-pots—he could have conducted matters to better advantage. It would not have served his purpose to advise the police beforehand that a burglary might be attempted on a certain house. With a policeman patrolling the alley, Haji would have kept away. As it was, it had at least been proved that Haji did want to get into the room.

"Which is all to the good . . . or is it?" The horizon clouded again. "I'm hanged if I know. Suppose this blighter turns out to be not Dilworth's pal, but Somervell's?"

The same dread troubled him next morning when, as he dressed, the telephone rang and a man's voice, with a trace of foreign accent, imparted information.

"What's that?" he barked. "How the hell do you know?"

"From his landlady. You see, I got his address last evening."

For a full minute Bream stood silent, torn with indecision. Then he clamped down the receiver, snatched his bowler hat, and plunged into the street.

CHAPTER TWENTY-TWO

AT HER next meeting with the barrister Diana broached the subject of funds. She was told not to worry about expense.

"Actually," said Hull, "in cases of this kind it is quite usual for a popular newspaper to come forward these days and defray the cost of the defence—counting, of course, on the exclusive rights of the story. I understand such an offer has been made by one of the Sunday papers; but I don't think we need avail ourselves of it. The fact is, only yesterday Mr. Blundell very generously volunteered to guarantee all fees. It's that I wanted to speak to you about."

Uncle Nick? Impossible! Diana stared.

"Why should he do this?" she asked blankly. "He can't believe in Adrian, whatever he may say—or not say, for that's more like it."

"I dined with him informally last evening," replied Hull, swinging his eyeglass tentatively. "He expressed no views, and seemed a little embarrassed about making his offer direct to you. His reason seems to be a sort of payment of old debts. It appears Doctor Somervell's father, Mr. Joseph Somervell, was exceedingly helpful to him in earlier days—put him into the position of legal adviser to Siberex Oil Combine, which meant a big leg-up. He has never forgotten it, and he could not feel happy now if he did not do something for the son. Mr. Blundell realises, as any one must, the urgent importance of retaining a particularly able counsel. What we want is a man with a power of appeal well above the ordinary—Sir Kingsley Baxter, in fact. I've had him in mind. I need hardly tell you what an immense asset Sir Kingsley would be."

Diana knew the reputation of Sir Kingsley Baxter. He occupied an almost unique position. Twenty times she had heard people say that if ever they committed a murder their first act would be to send for Baxter. She had read his speeches, which had struck her as sentimental and sometimes specious; but she was too clear-sighted not to know how vital these qualities were to Adrian's cause. . . . "Only," continued Hull, eyeing her, "a hitch has occurred. Doctor Somervell refuses point-blank to accept any outside aid."

"Oh! He can't refuse. That is, we mustn't let him. Why is he taking this stupid attitude?"

"I took it to be a matter of pride. He's undoubtedly very obstinate. I was hoping a word from you might move him."

"It won't," murmured Diana slowly. "I think I understand, but I've no influence—none."

Adrian believed Uncle Nick was making this offer for her sake. It was of a piece with his recent behaviour. She was filled with despair. A chance like this to be let go when life itself might depend on it? It was unthinkable. She looked at the barrister with defiant resolution.

"I'll accept for him," she declared. "He needn't know what's being done, need he? And if he's acquitted, why, he can pay the fees himself."

"Oh, undoubtedly!" agreed Hull, not meeting her eyes. "I must say I'm infinitely relieved at your decision. All I need tell Doctor Somervell is that we have arranged matters satisfactorily. I'll engage Sir Kingsley at once." His tone implied that in Baxter lay their one hope. Diana sat silent, cogitating. She had already told Mr. Hull her fixed intention of paying the cost of the private agent herself out of the rent-money she was receiving and the sale of her mother's two bits of jewellery, and stipulated that Adrian was to be kept ignorant. She moistened her lips and asked if Mr. Blundell had said anything at all about Elsie Dilworth in connection with the murder.

"He did not. He showed me, however, Miss Dilworth's note announcing her resignation. It merely said that her nerves necessitated a long absence from office work, and that she never expected to find another post so much to her liking. The letter was dated the twenty-eighth of October."

Diana looked sharply across at the speaker. "Why, wasn't that the very same day she called at the Home Office?" she demanded.

Hull, after referring to his notes, confirmed her belief, but declined to see any special significance in the coincidence of dates. Diana, however, could not help feeling that in some way Elsie's sudden departure devolved upon her other action. She decided to speak of it to Bream, whom she had not seen again, and about whose activities she was in the dark; and then, on her way home, she fell to pondering her godfather's latest move.

It was quite true that Joseph Somervell, at that time a millionaire and Aunt Rose's husband, had done a great deal for his wife's solicitor. It was equally true, she thought, that Uncle Nick had deep loyalties; yet it puzzled her to see him risking large sums on the defence of a man he must perforce regard as Rose Somervell's murderer. Unless she was wrong? Possibly she had been, all along. There was always Arenson. Maybe Uncle Nick could not resist making grand gestures. She sighed and gave it up. Whatever the explanation, here she was again taking what was offered simply because she could not do otherwise. It was almost uncanny how at every turn she was being constrained to act in direct defiance of her own wishes. She was caught in a web of kindness it was impossible to break. . . .

"It is—I know it is—just colossal vanity on his part," she concluded, and hated herself for her thought. "Poor man, he craves approval. It's the breath of life to him. Even Mummy knew that, though she'd have cut her tongue out rather than admit it."

Once one held this mainspring of action firmly in mind, numberless other puzzles were explained. For instance, Dame Charlotte. The desire for applause had led to the bestowal of a "tip" in this quarter, and what had been the result? A woman who was a snob and a prig had been changed into a warm partisan. As for the actress herself, she had unquestionably suffered some harrowing moments after she had entrusted her money to Nicholas Blundell. A murder had been committed. Of the will and evidence she knew nothing. What if Blundell and not the stepson had been charged? Oh, it was easy to see why old Lottie came to the Court petrified with terror and went away exulting! Diana asked herself if other people had harboured similar doubts. If so, they could only have been strangers unaware of the facts.

Outside her own door Inspector Headcorn was waiting. Now wholly absorbed in the thought of Adrian's danger, Diana had nearly forgotten that the search for another murderer still continued.

""What is it?" she asked. "Have you got any fresh clues?"

The Scotland Yard man followed her into the drawing-room and stood warming his back by the blazing logs.

"I flew to Amsterdam," he announced slowly. "I've seen enough to convince me that pawnbroker's a fence, for all it's a hard matter to establish. Well, then! How did a fellow like that allow himself to get landed with jewels placarded all over the place as stolen property? There are just two answers. One—which is his story—that he was caught napping; the other, that he had a private reason for letting the stuff be seized."

"But what reason could he have?"

"He might have been paid for that very purpose—paid enough to make it worth his while, by some one who is dead set on ramming that burglary idea down our throats. It may sound mad, but it's easier in a way for me to swallow than the first theory. The broker's an old fox if ever I saw one."

Diana began to tremble. Here, voiced by the most practical and unimaginative man she had ever encountered, was her own rejected belief!

"You mean my mother's handbag was taken solely as a blind?"

"It's possible. Had you thought of it?"

"Till the jewels were found, I had. It seemed too wild to admit. Shall I tell you why I had that idea?"

With gloomy interest he listened to all she had surmised about Elsie Dilworth. When she had done he shook a dubious head. It was virtually certain the secretary had not been to Holland, and it was hardly less likely she had hired an accomplice to go to Amsterdam for her. Such an enterprise would have cost far more than a woman in her position could afford.

"Are you sure of that?" objected Diana. "Don't forget the money in the bag. It was in cash, small notes."

"That's so."

Seeing him ruminate, she inquired if the pawnbroker had given a description of the person who deposited the jewels with him. Headcorn shrugged as he grumbled that there had been too many descriptions.

"All fishy. The old man and his assistant tell different stories, both trying to save their skins. Both swear it was a man, but we can't lay hold of any reliable facts about him." Shifting his position to get a better view of her face the Inspector continued, "Your notion was based on a belief that this secretary overheard your mother, while in this flat, make some alarming statement?"

"That was my chief reason. You see, my mother hadn't an enemy in the world. I don't know all she said that afternoon, but it's certain she spoke to Mr. Blundell—perhaps to the servant as well—about her telephone conversation with Mrs. Somervell. Elsie Dilworth must have been during that time, for if she had tried to leave the flat my mother would have heard her. A guilty conscience might have made her exaggerate what she heard. If she's innocent, why is she hiding herself? And why did she steal those letters out of my bag?"

"Letters!" The Inspector pricked up his ears. "What was in them?"

"Nothing that could possibly matter. She couldn't have come here for them, naturally, but she did take them. Let me remind you again that she knew the workings of our front door in Seymour Square. She knew more or less the time my mother got home from the theatre, and the fact that Mr. Blundell was giving her the emerald ring and sunburst to take away with her. Don't you see how it all fits together? My mother's murder was a sequel to Mrs. Somervell's."

Headcorn, gazing at her, seemed to have fallen into a stupor. As she went eagerly on, racking her brain for forgotten details, he still stared so oddly that she grew uncomfortable.

"She admitted she'd read a novel giving all the facts about aconite-poisoning. I got it from a library. It's called *Murder May Lie*. Afterwards she consulted Taylor's *Medical Jurisprudence*, in Mr. Blundell's library."

"As a lawyer, he would have a copy of that," murmured the Inspector, moving towards the door. "Wait here," he ordered. "I'm going to make a test. When I call out, speak a few sentences in your ordinary tone of voice."

Opening out of the kitchen passage were two cupboards and a lavatory. In each of these Headcorn stationed himself to listen, and on his return reported that in all three places he could hear perfectly what was said, provided the doors were left ajar. He went back again and was still absent when a ring at the bell sent Diana flying to the door to find the visitor she had been longing to see—Mortimer Bream.

"Oh! At last!" she burst out. "Well, have you found out anything? Quick! Tell me!"

"It's rather disappointing," said the agent dejectedly. "I'd hoped for better results. I'm still hard at it, but I can't say much more than that."

Her heart sank like a leaden weight.

"Where's Elsie Dilworth?" she faltered. "Surely you've located her?"

"Not yet. Oh, she'll be found—that is, if she hasn't done herself in. The pity is it'll be the Crown that finds her, which means we'll lose our chance of taking her by surprise. I warned you she'd be wanted as a witness. They're keener than ever to nab her on account of her non-appearance at the inquest, and they've the advantage of being free to employ Scotland Yard and the B.B.C. I see you've the radio. Been listening to the announcements?"

"No. Why should I?" she answered dully.

He glanced at his watch. "They're due now. Mind if I switch on?"

Crossing to the handsome lacquered cabinet, he turned a knob, and at once the announcer's voice, well-lubricated and flavoured with an Oxford accent, rolled forth. It completed the news items, took breath, and began again to say that information was still being sought concerning Elsie K. Dilworth, formerly of Bloomsbury Street, W.C.1. A detailed description followed, ending with the request that any one possessing knowledge should communicate it forthwith to the British Broadcasting Company.

"That was the third time of asking," remarked Bream, switching off the instrument. "There's just one thing in our favour, which you may have noticed. No mention was made of Floyd's Square. I assume the authorities have got the same hope as ourselves—that she may slide back there to cover."

As these words were spoken the Inspector reappeared, and cast a cold, questioning glance at the new arrival. Diana made the two men known to one another, and sensing the diffidence on both sides, gave way to a sudden impulse.

"Why can't we make an open council of it?" she appealed to them. "If there's even a chance of these two inquiries hanging together, shouldn't we save a lot of time and bother by putting all our cards on the table?"

Immediately she realised her blunder. It was true that demure amusement flickered behind the private agent's lashes, but in the Inspector's ponderous bearing she saw only disapproval. Not one syllable was uttered. Presently, while she reddened with mortification, she found the subject pointedly turned.

"There's a door at the bottom of the linen cupboard," declared Headcorn, addressing himself exclusively to her. "Know where it leads?"

"Door?" Diana frowned at him, puzzled. "Oh, that! It's locked, isn't it? And bolted. No, I've never troubled to inquire. This is a converted house. Evidently a bit was cut off when the flats were made. If you're interested Mr. Blundell's servants might be able to tell you about it."

"James Ryman's house, wasn't it?" said Headcorn pondering. "Sold at auction some ten years ago, if I remember rightly. Well, I dare say it's of no consequence."

So saying, the Inspector turned and, with no leave-taking word, lumbered from the flat. Bream gave a chuckle.

"My company's done it," he declared. "Don't you realise I'm not permitted to consult with the regular Force, and that a Yard man can't possibly besmirch his dignity by holding truck with an outsider like myself? It's simply not done."

"How childish! Well, there's nothing to stop me telling you what he and I have been discussing. It's Elsie Dilworth again. I've been making him see that quite possibly she may be guilty of this murder and my mother's as well. He's just admitted the money and jewels may have been taken to put the police on a false scent."

"Oh?" The agent eyed her alertly. "And his reasons?"

Rapidly she outlined what Headcorn had told her. Bream gave close attention, made no comment, and on his side recounted the history of his own investigations.

"If the truth of Arenson's quarrel with Mrs. Somervell was ever known," he said, "it's forgotten long ago. He once proposed marriage to her—or so she boasted—but there was never anything between them. The general idea is he took offence at some remark of hers. The lady seems to have done a deal of talking, not always wisely."

"I could have told you that," murmured Diana dispiritedly.

"On the other hand," continued Bream, pensively regarding the portrait of the actress over the mantelpiece, "though Arenson's personal sheet may be unspotted, he must have got quite hardened to criticism over his business dealings. It's unlikely he'd want to remove a woman who cast aspersions on a contract, besides which for the latter period the two were on splendid terms. Now for the Peckham Rye couple, aunt and nephew. More wash-outs, I'm afraid."

George Petty, it appeared, was revealing himself an estimable young man, with neither debts nor entanglements. The old woman's queer behaviour seemed adequately explained by the combined influence of the Home Office inquisitors and the secretary who, between them, had struck terror to her timorous soul.

"I'm assuming, I hope rightly, that, in view of the rapid and violent action of the aconite, the stuff used was fresh. It loses potency once it's dried, and the aconite root I've tested shrivels rather quickly. Well, then, I've failed to discover, that any of our suspects had any monkshood growing on his premises. All the Pettys grow is geraniums and aspidistra in pots, the Floyd's Square garden is bare as a bone, and Arenson has a crazy pavement with only a harmless border. If one of these people made a quick dive into the country during the week preceding the murder, I can't prove it."

"But you can't disprove it, either, I suppose?"

"That's it," he assented ruefully. "Still, Arenson was putting on a new musical show, as you know, and seems to have been steadily on the job. George Petty's motorcycle was out of commission, and while it was being repaired he spent his days rebuilding a fowl-house, while his wife minded shop. His aunt never stirred from this flat. Dilworth was working overtime, didn't even take her usual Saturday afternoon off. The same, incidentally, applies to Mr. Blundell."

Bream made this last statement so casually that Diana did not quickly register its significance. Tardily she glanced at him.

"So you've checked up on him, too, have you?"

"No objection, I hope?" The agent looked apologetic. "I know he's not a suspect in the ordinary way, but I'd be making a bad job of it to leave him out entirely." Not waiting for her reply, he hurried on. "Now I'll come to the one factor which promises hope. You remember that young Indian we saw at lunch? Well, he's been after Dilworth's room. Acting on a hunch, I lay in wait in the alley at the back, and at two in the morning saw him trying to climb over the wall. He slid through my fingers. Now the latest bulletin is—"

Bream broke off. His eyes and Diana's, which had widened with excitement, turned abruptly on the door leading to the dining-room. There stood Inspector Headcorn, once more in their midst!

CHAPTER TWENTY-THREE

ON TAKING his abrupt leave of Diana's flat, Headcorn paused a moment on the landing, then, descending the stairs, rang Blundell's bell.

"Master in?" he inquired of Gaylord, who, recognising him from previous visits, met him with a smile.

"Just, Inspector. I'll tell him you've come."

There was no need, for Blundell, still wearing his overcoat, bustled forward to grasp the officer's hand.

"Well, Inspector! Any further news from Holland?"

"Nothing worth mentioning. I've been saying that to Miss Lake, and I thought you'd want to hear it too, seeing you've felt so much concern over the Fairlamb case."

The solicitor, his face fallen into heavier lines, nodded.

"The Lakes are among my oldest friends," he said. "That girl up there has come in for more than her share of trouble. I don't mind admitting I'm disappointed over your lack of news. Knowing those jewels had turned up I expected a speedy arrest. A drink, now you're here? No? Then let me offer you a cigar. Sit down, let's have the details."

"They don't amount to much." The Inspector spoke absently, and although declining the hospitality, showed no hurry to depart. "By the way," he said, "I've been poking about upstairs to test an idea I've got. Oh, not very relevant, I'm afraid! It was to satisfy Miss Lake. I noticed what seems to be a blind door, and was curious about it. Any particular reason for not walling it up?"

"You mean the door in the linen cupboard?" Blundell's three-cornered eyes lit with enjoyment as over a secret joke. "Come with me, I'll show you something worth seeing."

Propelling the Inspector into the library he brought him face to face with the long expanse of sunken bookcases. "Look," he ordered, watching him. "Got the answer?"

"Can't say I have," was the stodgy reply. "What is it?"

"Here, then!" Laying hold of the middle section of shelves the owner tugged briskly, and with the utmost ease the whole section slid towards him on concealed castors. "How's that for a tidy bit of mechanism, eh? Go through, see what's behind."

Insinuating his bulk through the eighteen-inch space, Headcorn saw an arched door set flush with the wall. It slid sidewise at his touch, and disclosed a dim cavity within which ascended a flight of curving stairs. Blundell, following, switched on light which, flooding the stuffy corridor, revealed walls exquisitely panelled in fragrant cedar and a grey carpet soft and thick. Blundell waved a proud arm. He might have been a conjurer producing a rabbit from a hat.

"There you are! Those stairs lead direct to the door you noticed. No use to me, but as Mrs. Somervell said—and I always trusted her judgment in matters of this kind—it was almost a sacrilege to rip out anything so neat and so handsome. Take a look at that panelling. Lifted straight out of an Italian palace, same as what's been used in the outer halls. Oh, Ryman knew how to spend! It landed him behind bars, eh? Yet this place didn't fetch the fifth part of what it must have cost when it came under the hammer, else I shouldn't have bought it."

"These lower rooms were Ryman's own private ones, I take it?" asked Headcorn, fingering the smooth cedar with a touch of awe.

"They were—and up above he's supposed to have kept a sort of harem. Be that as it may, it was his fancy, when he'd worked late, to slip up this concealed way. Whew! Nice bit of dust collected in here. Hold on till I fetch a duster, or you'll be smothered."

Along, Headcorn mounted the stairs, recalling as he did so various Aladdin-like tales of the ruined financier's extravagance. There had been one single dinner where each woman-guest was presented with a diamond bangle, the men with dressing-cases each costing a hundred pounds—all of which had been drained out of widows, toiling clerks, downtrodden school-mistresses. . . .

"Is this upper exit nailed up?" he called out.

"Only fastened from both sides," Blundell's voice floated up to him. "Mutual protection, as Mrs. Somervell used to say. I had the bolts put on."

There was little furring of dust on the woodwork. The carpet underfoot seemed cleaner than might have been expected. Headcorn studied the strong steel rods affixed to the door at top and bottom, felt their surfaces, removed the key protruding towards him and rubbed it between his fingers. He was holding his hand to his nostrils when Blundell came spryly round the curve below him, holding a yellow duster.

"Mind if I open this up?" the Inspector greeted him. "Before I came down to you I took the liberty of undoing the lock and bolts from the other side."

Blundell's face fell boyishly.

"Oh! So you expected something of the kind?"

"Not stairs. I thought it would be box-rooms or what not. Well, thanks for showing it to me. I must tell my wife about it. She has a passion for secret passages, priests' holes, and so on."

"These stairs aren't exactly secret. I've shown them off a hundred times to my friends. That door may stick. . . . No? Might have done, after so long a time. I don't believe I've had it open this twelvemonth . . . not since the Duke of Duxborough, who'd lost heavily through Ryman, was here getting me to trim down his super-tax. Going to take the short cut, are you?"

Headcorn paused in the doorway, peering into the lavender-smelling darkness beyond.

"I may as well, don't you think? I've left a bag behind, and I'd like to apologise for barging off without a word just now. Good-evening, sir. I promise to keep you informed if anything crops up."

"Do, Inspector. And just see to those inside bolts, won't you?"

As they shook hands, the Inspector thought that his host looked worn, worried, yet driven on to further exertions by an unconquerable nervous energy. He gave forth an impression of boundless vitality and power, and that despite the yellowed tinge of ageing features. What a span of shoulder, what depth of chest—and the arms like oak boughs! Short though he was, the confined space seemed crowded with him.

The door closed. In the inky darkness of the cupboard Headcorn heard the key turn, the other pair of bolts shoot into place. He performed his half of the fastening up, sniffed again at his fingers, and, putting on the light, gazed meditatively at the snowy piles of linen. What he sought was not here, but in the second cupboard, amongst cleaning materials, he found it—a chemist's bottle with a greasy label and an inch of amber-hued liquid inside. . . .

He reached the drawing-room just in time to catch a few words spoken by his unofficial rival. With his attention riveted by new matters, he was puzzled to think why Miss Lake and Bream were staring as at a ghost.

"How on earth did you get in?" Diana demanded. "I heard you shut the front door."

Headcorn blinked, comprehended, and, smiling, explained the phenomenon.

"Another staircase? Funny! I've never heard of it. Or have I?" The girl knit her brow. "I was away at school when this house was taken over," she added thoughtfully. "I suppose that explains it. I never even came here much till this flat was lent me. My mother knew, undoubtedly. Were you wondering if Elsie Dilworth used those stairs?"

"In a general way," returned the Inspector guardedly, and with a side-glance at the third of the party. "Not that it gets us anywhere. I advise you, though, to keep that door bolted as it is now. If Miss Dilworth did want to come in here again—well, you never know, do you?"

He hesitated, glanced again at Bream, and with some awkwardness made his adieux. This time he did not return.

On quitting the house, Bream found his Scotland Yard acquaintance indeterminately loitering at the nearest corner.

"Not gone, Inspector?" he greeted him in some surprise.

Without speaking, Headcorn fitted his stride to Bream's shorter one and accompanied him to the Albert Hall. His air was one of reluctant but dogged purpose. One would have said he had something to say, but found it supremely difficult to bring forth. Full of quiet enjoyment, Bream let the battle continue. At last with obvious effort the words came out.

"Going to eat?"

"I sometimes do about now," answered the agent tranquilly. "And you?"

Again professional pride and burning curiosity waged war.

"The fact is," remarked Headcorn grudgingly, "there is just a possibility that your line of investigation and mine may have points of contact. If that's so, it occurred to me we might mutually benefit by—by getting together. Oh, quite unofficially," he muttered. "No obligation or prejudice on either side, you understand. As we both want food, what do you say to our sharing a meal?"

"Well done, old boy!" Bream silently applauded. "Strained your braces a bit, but never mind that." Aloud he acquiesced as uneventfully as though no extraordinary proposal had been made; and so it was that some ten minutes later the two faced each other across a steak and sizzling chips, presided over by an out-size bottle of Bass.

"You've something concrete in mind, perhaps," ventured the freelance, betraying no sign of his secret triumph.

"Actually," replied Headcorn, now entirely human, "it was the Indian I heard you mention as I came back into the room. You did say Indian, I think?"

Bream hid an excited thrill. Was it possible a link existed between the two murders hitherto regarded as wholly separate, and that it was embodied in the ex-student who for more than a week had been leading him up the garden path?

"I did, Inspector. An Indian from Bombay, name of Haji, enrolled at the School of Economics. May I inquire why he interests you?"

"Simply this." Headcorn glanced about the quiet restaurant and sank his voice to a low rumble. "The pawnbroker's assistant, now sacked and in a Dutch jail, caught one glimpse of the man who, he declares, brought the jewellery into the shop. Yes, the two articles taken from Miss Fairlamb's body. In notable distinction from his employer, he swears this man was an Indian—young, flashily dressed, and with two prominent gold teeth."

CHAPTER TWENTY-FOUR

THE news stunned. Bream stared hard, uncertain whether to be pleased or the reverse.

The Inspector asked, "Does that description tally with your man?"

"It does. There can't be two of 'em. How is it you've not collared him?"

"Obstacles," said the Inspector tersely. "In main a general conspiracy to discredit this statement since it was given out by a man since charged with robbing the till. I myself took little stock of it till I caught your remark. I was inclined to share the Dutch police's view that the assistant wanted to revenge himself by representing his employer as a rogue—which undoubtedly is the case. The old man's excuse for not recognising the jewels was that he'd broken his spectacles and couldn't see properly. That went also for his uncertainty as to the chap's appearance. Still, his word was given preference, and while they were chasing various men our Indian slipped away. Haji, you said? That ought to prove a substantial help."

"Abdulmajid Haji when he's at home," pronounced Bream woodenly. "And a fat lot of good may it do you. He booked passage for Bombay last Wednesday. I got word of it too late to do anything except hike down to Tilbury. I was just in time to see the boat steam out."

"No matter," broke in Headcorn eagerly. "Wednesday last? Boat called at Marseilles. Did you wireless the captain?"

"I did. And here's the reply."

From his pocket Bream fished up a Marconigram. Headcorn seized it, and read:

"Abdulmajid Haji went ashore before sailing failed to return luggage aboard but no passenger."

Across the two tall glasses of ale the two exchanged cheated glances.

"So you see," said Bream dryly, "we have a second queer character vanishing at the very moment he's shown himself queer."

"Vanishing?" Headcorn hurled the word at him. "On this island? No fear! Two days, and I'll have him locked up."

"Great!" murmured the private agent. "With the Yard on the job we can expect some action."

"Sarcasm, eh? Call it an empty boast?"

"Not at all. I was only thinking that this secretary woman still seems to be holding out on you. I happened too, to be running my eye over the rather formidable list of missing persons for the past year and realising just how easy this disappearing act must be. At the same time, you people have all the facilities when it comes to drawing a drag-net. I'm only too glad to count on your assistance, for I don't mind telling you unless we can lay hands on this Indian and Elsie Dilworth my accused won't stand a dog's chance."

Headcorn, preoccupied, turned a slow eye on him. It reminded Bream of a mechanical eye worked on a swivel, the dull glaze of which fascinated but chilled.

"And when they're found?" came the shrewd query. "Think it will help? Only if one of them confesses—which you can hardly expect. We may find in one or both a link to connect these two crimes, but that's not saying Somervell isn't guilty. Yes, on both counts. Dilworth may well have tipped him off with what she overheard. Had you thought of that?"

"Dilworth? When it was she supplied the information?"

"Information be damned! We don't know what private row may have changed her attitude towards Somervell. As for this Haji, I can think of several ways in which he and Somervell may have been in league. Haji may have an excellent reason for disappearing. Will he want to be named as an accessory?"

Bream strongly disliked the way the conversation was tending. Uneasily, he thought of his unsuccessful efforts to uncover the mess Haji had been involved in over the girl's death in his rooms, of his fear lest Somervell, a doctor, might be implicated in it. Haji's pointed notice of Somervell in the tea-shop suggested an acquaintance the American was unwilling to admit in his fiancée's presence. The Yard, he well knew, would not share his scruples.

"Blundell's secretary," pursued the Inspector relentlessly, "may be a menace to both Somervell and Haji. Put her in the witness-box and who knows what she'll spill? Maybe it's Haji she's terrified into hiding. As a matter of fact, she may be dead."

"There seems to be about a million 'maybes' in each of these cases," retorted Bream stoically. "We can only stick to our separate lines and hope for the best."

"With this difference," put in the older man. "Your business is to overthrow the charge against Somervell. Mine's to locate Miss Fairlamb's murderer, whoever he may be; but if we clash?"

"You mean shall I regret this purely informal discussion? Never, Inspector! If the worst happens, I suppose Somervell would as soon swing for two murders as one. They'll have to prove the existing charge first before the other, hinging on it, can be preferred against him. Don't lose sight of that."

The eye swivelled again. It seemed to say that Bream was optimistic indeed if he doubted Somervell's conviction.

"You believe in him, do you? Don't tell me it's not in Somervell's nature to commit cold-blooded murder. That's an old one."

"I know little about Dr. Somervell's nature," declared Bream with dignity. "I'm basing my belief on small points which, I admit, aren't likely to convince a jury. For instance, it will be assumed that Somervell induced the victim to make a will in his favour. If he did that, was it common sense to kill her off within two days of the said will being executed? Why didn't he allow a discreet interval to elapse?"

"While he waited," objected Headcorn, "she might have destroyed the will. The chances are she would have done, if it went counter to her wishes and she got courage to consult her solicitor. Besides, death by aconite was likely to be set down to natural causes. The person using it would have known that. If doubt did arise, there was only a remote chance of solid residue remaining in the system, the tendency being for the violent vomiting and diarrhoea to eliminate every trace. I can suggest, in addition, a potent reason for haste—pressing need of funds. Whatever the delay in securing the entire inheritance, the legatee could have obtained at once an advance."

"I've not discovered any pressing need."

"There may have been one, all the same. But your next point?"

"The absence of proof that Somervell knew a will had been drawn up."

"And have you contrary proof? No, I thought not. The victim may have conveyed the information to him when she issued the invitation to that Sunday lunch."

"You consider it likely?" Bream retorted. "I don't."

"She was an old woman and a vain one," said his companion coolly. "I could tell you dozens of cases where women like her have kept prospective legatees dancing attendance on them simply by jiggling a will before their eyes. Then there's blackmail. . . ."

"Blackmail? How do you account for her getting the will executed by her own legal adviser and personal friend? Wouldn't a man like Blundell have scented blackmail as a terrier does a rat? He'd even have spotted the least nervousness on her part. No, if Rose Somervell dreaded any exposure, she'd have called in a strange lawyer, or, better still, bought a regulation form and done the thing without assistance."

Headcorn grunted, and Bream warmed to his subject. "To my mind, that constitutes the strongest argument in Somervell's favour. Blundell's no fool. He's an exceedingly sharp lawyer, employed by such people as the Duke of Duxborough, Lord Limpsfield, and our new ministerial prodigy, Sir Norbury Penge. He was, moreover, deeply attached to Mrs. Somervell."

"How deeply?"

"Ah, you've got that private staircase on your mind! No?"—as Headcorn brushed the suggestion aside. "Well, then, as far as I can find out about the relationship, they were more like brother and sister than the other thing. Thicker than thieves. I'd like to think differently, but I can't."

"So you have tried to upset the platonic theory?"

"Naturally. Blundell is suspect. He could have done the deed, and planted the aconite on Somervell afterwards. But why? I'm hanged if I can see. There was no sign of even a disagreement between him and the victim. She was jealous, but of whom? Why, the secretary—as ill-favoured a woman as you'd meet in a day's walk. One look at the females Blundell employs would tell you he's not much of a lady's man. Another thing. At one time it seems that Mrs. Somervell intended leaving her money to him. If she changed her mind, it was only because she realised the absurdity of it. He must have far more than she left."

"Did she actually make a will in Blundell's favour?" asked Headcorn, taking from his pocket a well-seasoned briar and carefully stoking it.

"Apparently not. I mention it merely to show that Blundell, if he wanted to inherit her small fortune, would surely have tried to dissuade her from the course she finally took. His influence with her was undoubtedly strong. I agree with Miss Lake that he must have been more or less complaisant, or the will in question would never have been made."

"I hear she struck various persons as slightly befogged, just at the last. Know anything about it?"

"I've talked with her own doctor, Sir Eustace Milford. He declares when he last met her, at some reception soon after her Vichy cure, she was at the top of her form. The condition you refer to—absent-mindedness, coupled with a tendency to doze off after meals—may have had to do with overeating and sedentary habits. It's fairly certain she didn't drug, and no one even faintly suggested her incompetence to make a will."

Headcorn bestirred himself, and motioned to the waitress.

"Well, well, we'd better cook up our joint description of the Indian, and call it a day. I'm taking a taxi to the Yard. Shall I drop you?"

At Great Smith Street they parted, Bream well pleased to think that in exchange for unimportant confidences he was to receive valuable aid toward the trapping of Haji. The Inspector, on the small remnant of the drive, performed for the third time the act of putting his fingers against his nose and snuffing hard.

"Cloves," he mused. "Stuff used for toothache. Even machine oil can't kill the smell. Her bottle. Was it she who oiled those bolts and the lock? In that close atmosphere it was the first thing that struck me—oil of cloves . . ."

Entering the block of dingy dark buildings, he reported at once to his chief, apprising him of the turn matters had taken, and laying on the desk his detailed description of Abdulmajid Haji. The big man read it through, raised his brows, and without a word handed Headcorn a paper on which was written a single line. The Inspector scanned it, jumped, and smothered an oath.

"Good God, sir! When did this come through?"

"An hour ago, by telephone. It is certainly your Indian. As you see, he's been found in a ditch near Tilbury, with a pearl-handled ladies' revolver in his hand, and his brains blown all over the place."

CHAPTER TWENTY-FIVE

IN THE morning paper Diana read the short paragraph dealing with the suicide of the young Indian, Abdulmajid Haji. Knowing nothing as yet of his connection with the Amsterdam pawnbroker, her first thought was that Bream would be badly hit by the news. For her part, she could not see in what way the dead man was important. Even his attempt to enter the house in Floyd's Square need not, to her thinking, bear any relation to Elsie Dilworth, while his presence in the restaurant seemed only a rather surprising coincidence.

By the evening, the press had got hold of a plausible reason for the suicide. Some months ago a German girl, Frieda Klapp, had been taken ill in Haji's rooms and had died, screaming out that Haji had poisoned her. Owing to tales spread by other occupants of the house, an inquest was ordered, and although natural death was the verdict, Abdulmajid was said to have brooded over the suspicion under which he had rested, chiefly because of the trouble is caused with his family in Bombay. After living as best he could on borrowed money, he had finally been ordered home. He had bought his ticket—it was found on him—but having deposited his luggage in his cabin had come ashore and failed to return. His landlady stated that on leaving he had seemed gravely upset, perhaps at the prospect of facing parental wrath.

For something to do, Diana visited *The Times* newspaper office, and in the back files looked up the inquest reports on Frieda Klapp. They told her little. The girl, then living with Haji, had fallen ill with what appeared to be ptomaine poisoning. Haji had administered mustard and water as an emetic, and a dose of castor oil, in spite of which remedies she had sunk rapidly into coma, dying just as the doctor reached her side. Only her drunken accusations had led to her body being examined, and nothing whatever was found to suggest foul play. Diana shook a despondent head, and unenlightened returned to Queen's Close, to find Inspector Headcorn once more on her doorstep.

"You spoke the other day," he began, "about Miss Dilworth's looking for something in this flat. You've looked too, I take it?"

"Of course. What else have I to occupy me?" She spread her hands apart with a gesture of despair. "I don't suppose there's a corner of this place I haven't explored. I imagined it would be some kind of paper, just because I saw her going through Mr. Blundell's files. I've even thought it might be a written confession she wanted to get back, though that's ridiculous, isn't it?"

He did not answer. Slowly glancing about, he asked if she minded his making a search, and, scarcely waiting for her eager consent, began prowling round, pulling out drawers, tapping walls, measuring spaces with a pocket foot-rule. She watched him, at one moment thinking he had some definite idea in mind, at the next convinced he was as hopelessly at sea as herself. His painstaking search took over an hour, and at the end when he picked up his hat and stood looking at her, what she saw in his plodding face bewildered her, then threw her into panic.

It was pity.

All at once she understood. The Inspector did believe Elsie Dilworth implicated in both murders, but only as an accessory, a spy who, having played her part, had suffered an emotional revulsion, turned informant, and then, terrified lest something damaging to her had been left behind, had completely lost her nerve and made off. In his view Adrian was the principal, not only in Rose's death but in her mother's as well. Her mother's! No wonder he was sorry for her. Even Scotland Yard inspectors have hearts.

After all, to expect a different opinion had been imbecile folly. Every one but herself had seen clearly the crushing weight of evidence arraigned against Adrian, and believing him guilty of one crime led by logical steps to this second, monstrous belief, for which she alone was responsible. In giving Headcorn all that gratuitous information about Elsie she had started him off on a new and unforeseen track. He might quickly see his mistake; but would he? Not if any uncertainty was found in Adrian's movements after she left him that Tuesday night in the Strand. A taxi would have taken him to Seymour Square well in advance of her slow-moving bus. He, no less than Elsie, knew about the automatic buttons, the time her mother was due back from the theatre. Elsie could have told him the fact of the jewels having been presented to Margaret, though that was unimportant. Any murderer, on the chance, would have taken the handbag, regardless of what it might or might not contain.

The thought of her almost complete isolation suddenly struck her. This luxurious flat might as well have been an island remote in the South Seas. Although daily she was receiving kind notes and offers of hospitality from friends, to all these her answer had been the same—that she was going away for a few months to recover from the shock of her mother's death. Thus quite deliberately had she cut herself off from every former tie; and now she realised the reason. It was because if any one guessed her connection with Adrian she would have to face what she had just seen in Inspector Headcorn's eyes. Not even to her father could she write with any freedom, so that Herbert Lake remained ignorant of how a certain matter touched herself. Apart from Michael Hull, the two detectives, and Colin Ladbroke, she had contact with no person save the man whose generosity surrounded her like a smothering cloak. With him increasingly she suffered from constraint.

All these crimson and mauve tulips, expensive, out of season! The bottle of port, sent up to-day because she was growing so pale. . . . Why must he? And last night, when against her will she had dined with him, why had he thought it necessary to try to divert her, showing off his pet staircase, as though she were an ailing child? It occurred to her she might have taken some interest in that exhibit if Aunt Rose's death had been more mysterious. As it was, having to exclaim over it only irritated her. Uncle Nick's watchful eyes had held pity—the pity of superior knowledge, like the Inspector's. . . .

As generally happened now when mental anguish became unbearable she reached mechanically for a cigarette. She had never smoked much before, but here she was at it most of the time, simply because after a few cigarettes she managed to attain a species of numbed and deadened calm. This enforced idleness—the trial creeping on her by inches and nothing being accomplished was driving her mad. She understood for the first time why people smoked opium. . . .

Colin Ladbroke peered into a darkened hall. In the doorway Diana blinked at him hazily.

"Did I wake you? I was about to go away, but I thought I'd just ring once more."

"Was I asleep? I didn't realise it. Do come in. I'll make some tea."

"Not for me, thanks. It's six o'clock. You'll have had yours long ago. Oh, well, if you insist."

She seemed not to take in what he was saying. He followed her into the kitchen, and noticed that used tea-things stood on the table. She was filling the kettle, taking rather a long time over it.

"Look out! You're getting splashed."

He took the kettle from her hand. It was brimming over. She laughed deprecatingly when he emptied the silver teapot of its cold leaves, but made only vague efforts to help.

"Go and sit down," he bade her. "I'll see to this. You're still half asleep, aren't you?"

She wandered out obediently but with so dazed an air that he frowned after her, puzzled. When he carried the fresh tea into the smoky drawing-room he saw she had tidied her rumpled hair and powdered her nose. Women did these things automatically, he reflected, and recalled a young girl brought into the casualty ward of whom it was said that her first action, on being drawn from under a bus, was to reach for her vanity-case.

"How stupid of me! Did I really let you make tea? No, I'll mend the fire. Have you any news about—him?"

Even as she asked the question she yawned heavily.

"A little, through Hull, of course. Nothing much, I'm afraid. He's putting in his time assembling his material for the monograph he's been preparing. That's like him, isn't it? You know he was much annoyed over not dissecting the pituitary tumour that came in just before his arrest. He hated like hell to miss it."

"Oh, Colin! At a time like this?"

"Hull says he has practically nothing to say on the subject of the evidence. No doubt of it, he's argued in circles till he's all tied up. He sees how futile it is to prove his story, so he's saving his breath."

Diana sat on the low stool before the fire, for long moments not speaking. At last she drank the tea Ladbroke had poured out and winced as at some delayed pain.

"He must hold some opinion," she said. "About who did this, I mean. It's inhuman not to. Isn't it?"

The doctor hesitated. "I'm sure he does hold an opinion which he feels it's useless to mention. It's what he meant when he said that the harder he reasoned the less sense it made."

"Does he suspect Elsie, and thinks his suspicion can never be proved?"

"He's never said so. I tell you, from the first he's refused to commit himself." Colin stared down at the rug. "He keeps repeating he's sewn up in a bag, and that soon we'll all know it."

"I suppose he would think that, seeing it was Elsie who got him arrested. Or does he mean something different?"

Ladbroke shrugged, but did not reply. His blue eyes were now fixed on the display of tulips. Diana watched him, and all at once leant forward.

"Colin!" she whispered. "I think I understand. I've had that feeling too, and somehow it's mixed up with Adrian's not being frank with me. Now I want the truth. Is it connected with my being, in a way, under Uncle Nick's protection? Is it? Is it?"

"He's never said so."

She sprang to her feet.

"Oh, why didn't I guess? It is that! Here, I'll leave this flat, take a room on my own. I came here only to save money, thinking I could at least help pay for the private detective. He doesn't know that, I hope? Hull hasn't let him guess?"

"Naturally not." Ladbroke looked troubled. "See here, Diana, don't do anything stupid, will you? Take every scrap of help you can get, no matter who offers it. Besides, if you cleared out now, mightn't it be a tactical error?"

A wordless message passed between them. Diana caught her lower lip between her teeth and choked down an hysterical laugh.

"It can't be!" she argued, as though to some spoken statement. "Why should Uncle Nick—? Oh, don't think I haven't thought of all this! I can't find one ghost of a reason, not one. It just doesn't make sense." She gasped slightly, finding she had repeated Adrian's own words. Defiantly she continued: "It doesn't—does it? What would have been the object?"

"If you don't know of any, I'm certain I don't either."

"There can't have been an object. She couldn't have wanted to use a hold over him, even supposing she had one—which I'm positive she hadn't. Almost her dying words, to my mother, were full of admiration and affection for him. You see?"

"Adrian sees. That's why he holds his tongue. No, it's no good, unless we can show a strong, convincing motive—and even that of itself won't release Adrian. Not while we've that will staring us in the face."

"You're right, it wouldn't. Colin, we must think! Harder than ever. About Elsie. About Felix Arenson. About that Indian who's shot himself. You know about that, I suppose? Oh, yes, I wrote you! That's why you've come. I suppose little Mr. Bream considers that the Indian's being dead dishes that line of inquiry. Why are you staring at me?"

"Nothing." He laid a firm hand on her arm. "Diana," he said quietly, "if you're not sleeping or anything, promise me not to take any sort of sedative without consulting me first. Understand?"

"Sedative? I've never taken one in my life. What a dear you are, worrying about me like this! You mustn't."

"How are you sleeping, then?"

"Oddly enough, quite well. I'm astonished, but I can't quarrel with it."

"That's the stuff. I'm glad."

When he had left her, she wondered a little at his solicitude and his relief over her answer. She must have been behaving rather strangely a moment ago. It was the helpless irony of Adrian's suspecting not Elsie but Uncle Nick. Uncle Nick, who was the means of obtaining Sir Kingsley Baxter for Adrian's defence. Why, if any power could save the situation, it was—

Who now? A sharp, stabbing ring at the bell—an imperious ring it sounded—sent her nerves quivering afresh. She went to the door, opened it, and stared dumbfounded at the slim, fur-clad figure whose immense black eyes, rayed round with spiky lashes, stared back at her. The visitor wasted not an instant.

"Are you Diana Lake?" she demanded, hard, swift, and with an American accent. "I guess there's been some mistake. I've got a letter evidently intended for you. I found out where you were from a lawyer called Hull. Here, take it. Blanche Ackland's my name—not that it matters. Good-bye."

She turned, ran quickly down the stairs. Diana was left with a whiff of Chanel scent in her nostrils and in her hand a plain white envelope bearing the typed inscription: *Miss Ackland, Ritz Hotel, London, W.1.* At the lower corner was the word *Private*.

Mistake? Too late to ask an explanation. The lower street doors had slammed, a car outside was whirring. Diana drew forth from the envelope already slit across the top a typed enclosure, saw the signature below, and stared again.

Elsie Dilworth! Writing to her? No, to Blanche Ackland. Or was this some stupid hoax?

CHAPTER TWENTY-SIX

The letter was post-marked Guildford, and dated the previous day. It ran:

"DEAR MISS ACKLAND,—If Adrian Somervell still means anything to you, doubtless you will welcome any slight assistance towards clearing him. Mind, I promise nothing; but if you will play fair and not give me away I will do what I can. I am running great risk to see you at all, even in trusting you not to let this letter pass into other hands. If you care to take advantage of my offer, I shall be at the bookstall at Holborn Station to-morrow evening at eight sharp, wearing a brown coat and hat, and carrying a copy of *Home and Beauty*. Don't speak to me; buy a ticket to Finsbury Park, and follow till I stop. Pin a white gardenia to your coat so I shall know you.

"Yours faithfully,
"ELSIE K. DILWORTH."

Diana's heart beat suffocatingly. At first, no glimmer of understanding reached her, and then, in a blinding flash, she comprehended, as Blanche Ackland herself must have done. Elsie had been labouring under the delusion that Blanche was the girl Adrian was engaged to marry! If Adrian had mentioned no name—and he was hardly likely to, in his anxiety to cut short that repulsive scene at the hospital—then the error was natural enough. Diana knew that all autumn Bobbie Ackland had been constantly ringing Adrian up. How she had learned about her rival was a mystery. She had behaved most decently—not that one could pause now to think of gratitude, or even to weigh the precise meaning of this letter. To-morrow evening! It meant this evening. Eight sharp? Seven-thirty was striking—and there were miles to be covered.

Frantically Diana jammed on her hat, found an artificial gardenia, and tearing it from its spray stabbed it with a pin to her grey lambskin coat. She thought of Bream. He ought to be told, though she must make him promise not to interfere and spoil things. She dialled his number, found him out, and left word for him to ring her when he returned. Then, her brain whirling, she ran from the house and fell into a taxi.

In spite of maddening traffic-jams it lacked two minutes to eight when she alighted at the Kingsway entrance to the Holborn Station. No one stood near the bookstall. She took her ticket from a slot machine, and wandered back to pore over the magazines, keeping a weather eye out for women in brown clothing. Men and women bustled by, two girls bought evening papers, but still no sign of Elsie. The clock-hands jerked forward to five past. Maybe in place of a heaven-sent lifeline, that letter was a joke. Some mischief-maker . . . but who knowing Elsie Dilworth's handwriting was likely to do so wanton and pointless a thing? No, if Elsie failed to turn up, it must mean that on sober reflection she had seen the impossibility of helping Adrian without ruining herself. . . .

"*Home and Beauty*, please."

The words made her jump. Minutes ago, she had glanced at a stooped, gaunt, bespectacled female of uncertain age, and dismissed her as out of the question. Her coat and battered headgear were certainly brown, but her hair, black, streaked with grey, and cut short as a man's! Still, she had asked for a copy of *Home and Beauty*, and she had it now, tucked under her lean arm as, without a flicker in Diana's direction, she hurried determinedly for the moving stairs. Diana darted after her, was held up by the punching of her ticket, and set foot on the down-gliding flight to see her quarry near the bottom with numerous fellow-travellers between.

Was it Elsie? In a train full of strap-hangers she tried hard to get a better view of the woman's face, but out-spread newspapers screened her vision. So far she had detected scarcely a hint of resemblance, and only the gay magazine deterred her from getting out at the first stop and going back.

Finsbury Park. A wholesale exodus, and again a near thing to keep in sight of the bent, brown form before it melted into the jostling crowd. At street-level it boarded a tram, Diana scrambling into a seat six rows behind.

Southward—or eastward—they jolted, and now, when the black hair became visible, it was possible to see it was dyed. Maybe the grey streaks were powder. With this idea Diana hoped again, but the woman, even when she got out, kept her face turned away, never looking round to see if she was followed. Down one dark turning and up another the two wayfarers moved rapidly, till the neighbourhood grew familiar. They were approaching the bottleneck of Floyd's Square, marked by the bright bake-shop on the corner. It was Elsie—and an Elsie unaware that her former refuge was now unsafe.

Across the mangy laurels Diana saw her go straight to No. 17, and disappear. No, there she was again, coming up the area-way. Now she was opening the door. Would it be left open after she had gone inside? Open it was when Diana reached it—just a mere crack; and at this sure confirmation came a qualm of fear. So easily might this be a trap; yet she walked into the stuffy darkness, and hesitating saw a light flare up at the head of the cramped stairs. Up she went, on the left saw the plain bed-sitting-room Bream had described, and in the centre of it, under an electric bulb, a figure no longer stooping, but upright, tense, expectant.

Elsie—but how changed! Small wonder she had escaped identification. But what had happened now? The face behind the disfiguring spectacles had grown ominously rigid. With a swift gesture Elsie tore off spectacles and hat, stared, gaped and goggled at her visitor with every sign of stupefaction.

"You?" she mouthed huskily. "*You*—?"

Diana grasped it. Elsie had expected Blanche Ackland. Those dark lenses must have blinded her.

"You were wrong." Diana spoke collectedly. "I'm engaged to Dr. Somervell—not Miss Ackland. She brought your letter to me. What have you got to tell me?"

Speechless, Elsie backed away from her. She moistened her lips and a furtive gleam crept into her red-rimmed eyes. Clearly she was staggered; and it darted into Diana's mind that this had been no attempt to help, but something quite opposite. Elsie had meant to lure her rival here to commit violence on her person. It would not take her long to transfer her hatred to another object; but thinking this, Diana remained cool. If she was at Elsie's mercy, so, in a way, was Elsie at hers.

"Miss Lake!" The ex-secretary rubbed lean fingers over her throat, still staring as though hypnotised. "Your mother," she muttered, and then, brusquely: "Where are you living now?" she demanded.

"Why pretend?" retorted Diana. "You know where I'm living. You went there the night I arrived—and you took three letters out of my bag. I was watching you from Mr. Blundell's door. But you sent for me. Why?"

The effect of her words was curious. Elsie gulped, made a farther retreat, and after more glances partly frightened, partly inattentive, went to the hearth and touched a match to the gas fire. She crouched low, warming her hands. Then, as if some deferred message had reached her brain, she jerked irritably over her shoulder: "Letters? Nonsense! I've touched nothing of yours—and it wasn't you I sent for, so you can go away. I've nothing to say—not really. I must have been dotty."

Diana stood her ground.

"You did have something to say. You're only upset because I'm not the girl you expected. Please go on. I'm waiting."

Elsie rocked her body, moaning strangely. With the baffled feeling of talking to deaf ears, Diana persisted, in veiled language trying to convey her meaning.

"You've made a hideous muddle, haven't you? You're suffering torments now—and you know there'll be no peace for you till you've told the truth. Do let's make a beginning. Was it the will you witnessed that made you bring this charge against Adrian?"

To her horror, Elsie began to laugh. Spasmodic, hysterical laughter it was, chilling her blood. Suddenly, the raucous cackles ceased. Elsie got up and came to the other side of the gate-legged table, on which stood a typewriter. From her menacing expression Diana realised fully, as she had not done before, how she was alone in this house with a creature who had killed and might kill again; and still, somehow, she felt no fear.

"Who knows you've met me? Don't lie! Whom have you told?"

"No one. I swear it. If that's your reason—"

"No one?" The eyes narrowed with cunning distrust. "If you expect anything from me, I've got to make sure."

"I'm not lying. Do believe me."

Elsie wavered, searching her face. Then she shook her head.

"No! I've made one bloomer. That's enough. I tell you, I don't know why I wrote that letter. How can I prove Adrian Somervell's not guilty? Maybe he is."

"You know he's innocent," said Diana, iron-hard. "I shan't leave this room till you've given me your statement."

"My statement!" The laughter started anew and changed to a sob. "And who'll believe me? The very best I can do is to keep out of sight. Put the police on to me, or . . . oh, God, the awfulness, either way! Why am I such a despicable coward?"

The woollen scarf muffling her throat had slipped. With a shudder, Diana saw a gash, freshly-healed, straight across the windpipe—a horrible sight.

"Coward or not," said Diana more gently, "can you stand by and see a man hanged for a crime he didn't commit? Oh, please listen!"—for Elsie had begun a distracted ramble about the room. "Will your life be worth living if that happens?"

Elsie turned on her fiercely.

"Get this into your mind!" she lashed out. "It's one thing to dread what may happen, quite another when you know it *will* happen and nothing you can do will stop it. If I speak, I'm done for. Now, will you go?"

"And Adrian? Is his life less valuable than yours?"

"Be quiet! Let me think. . . ."

Diana held her breath. Elsie went to the window, lifted the cheap cretonne curtain, and peered furtively out. When she turned, her face was an enigma.

"I'll risk it," she said quietly. "But not here. The woman I'm staying with may be home any minute. We'll walk, and I'll tell you my part in this—for what it's worth. That's my proposal. You can take it or leave it. Understand?"

Brisk, business-like, she adjusted her hat and spectacles, tightened her scarf. The alteration of mood was so astonishing that Diana's suspicions flared again.

"Hurry! I may change my mind, you know." A rough hand pushed Diana towards the door. "The passage light's broken. I'll turn this one off when you're down. Oh, so you don't trust me! That's funny, that is. . . . Oh, well, then, I'll go first."

Out went the light, and in inky darkness Diana heard a grim laugh as her companion passed her on the narrow stairs. The door below opened, letting in cold air. Diana moved with Elsie outside; but Elsie was muttering about the gas fire.

"Not be a second," she said, "I'd better put it off." She turned back— and Diana received a violent shove which sent her slithering into the street. Behind her the door banged.

So it had been a trick, after all!

CHAPTER TWENTY-SEVEN

BEATING on the door and getting no response Diana felt her last uncertainty vanish, along with the hope she had been foolish enough to entertain. Never for one moment had Elsie meant to part with any information. Tormented she might be, but her one concern was shielding herself. She had very cleverly hit on a ruse to get rid of her troublesome guest, that was all.

"And I've let myself be taken in!" raged the girl on the doorstep. "I, who ought to have known better. Whatever plan she had in mind, she had to alter it when she set eyes on me. Why, I don't know. Maybe because I'm no bird of passage like Bobbie Ackland. If my body were found in this house. . . . What on earth is she up to now?"

The click-click of a typewriter had reached her ears. Inside these walls the hunted woman was hard at work. Concocting some new devilry? The sounds followed Diana as she walked away, reluctant to quit the square, yet at a total loss what move to make. The tale of the landlady's return was probably fiction. To telephone Scotland Yard meant deserting this spot, and during even a brief absence Elsie might make off. The only plan she could think of was to obtain help from one of these houses.

She tried the house next door. No one came. She hammered on the iron knocker, and after five minutes found her summons answered by an old man, deaf, or befuddled with drink, she could not tell which. The house beyond bore a "To Let" sign. The corner one produced a sleepy slavey, who eyed her with dark suspicion. There was no telephone, she said, her people were at the pictures, and after the two burglaries the square had had during the last fortnight she was taking no chances with strangers. For the third time a door was shut in Diana's face.

The houses opposite looked slightly more prosperous. Diana was crossing towards them when a faint noise behind her brought her heart into her mouth. Turning, she was just in time to see Elsie emerge from Number Seventeen and stride rapidly in the direction of the passage at the other end of the row. She was carrying some bulky object. It was too dark to see what it was.

After her disappearing figure Diana raced at full speed. By the time she reached the passage Elsie had passed the transverse alley and taken one of the two forks which led at the lower end into separate streets. By bad luck Diana chose the wrong fork first, and when she had doubled back to try the other Elsie was gone. For five minutes she continued her search, but it was no use, she was forced to give up. The night's adventure finished in mid-air.

From the nearest telephone booth she rang up the Yard. Inspector Headcorn was not in, so she left a message putting him in possession of the latest facts. This done she went home, consoled by one thing only, the knowledge that Elsie was alive.

She arrived to find her own telephone ringing like mad. As she expected, the voice over the wire was Bream's. A startled exclamation greeted her first words, and following it came a volley of questions.

"So you think it was a booby-trap set for the other girl and you walked into it?"

"I'm bound to think it," answered Diana bitterly. "I think, too, that seeing me instead of Miss Ackland took the wind out of her sails."

"Tell me exactly what happened. Don't miss out anything."

Diana did so.

"And I can tell you this," she finished, "that woman's more frightened than she was before. Her whole manner showed it. Doesn't that look as though I've been right about her all along? She's guilty, Mr. Bream! Now I've seen her I haven't a doubt of it."

There was a non-committal grunt and a short silence.

"And so she's done another bunk?"

"She has. I couldn't see very well, because it was dark, and the railings were between, but she had something with her that looked like a bag."

Another silence. Then:

"I'll hike along up there now, just in case your Yard friend steals a march on me. I must get at that landlady. Bit of double-crossing there, I fancy." The speaker paused, and took a subtly altered tone as he asked: "See here, whom else have you told about this?"

"No one. I've not had a chance."

"Then take a tip from me and keep quiet about it. Don't mention it till I give you leave. Understand?" She gave her promise and rang off. As she undressed she went over the puzzling events in her mind, trying to grasp their whole meaning, and wondering if she would have been wiser to take different tactics with Elsie. Vaguely she felt she had been given a valuable opportunity and muffed it, but looking back she did not see how she could have behaved otherwise. At the time, she had been banking on the remorse which, even now, she found it hard to believe was not a real, actuating force in Elsie's conduct. The impression of having witnessed a terrible conflict was still strong upon her. She could swear that in Elsie she had seen her own wretchedness mirrored, with the addition of self-torture and personal fear. Why else had Elsie called herself a coward?

It was perhaps an hour after her return that she heard a car stop below and the house doors open and close. Blundell was back from the public dinner he had been attending. At once she felt impelled to go down and tell him of her experiences, but with one foot out of bed she remembered Bream's injunction. Uncle Nick would have a more urgent reason than most to want Elsie cornered and cross-examined in the witness-stand. It might mean saving him a cool thousand at least in counsel's fees if her part in this came out; but Uncle Nick by blundering in now might wreak havoc. No doubt that was Bream's idea in cautioning her to keep quiet. Best wait till morning and see if any further development had occurred.

Very early she was wakened by sounds outside. Springing to the window she saw the big car, with Gaylord driving, and Blundell getting into it with a look of agitated purpose. Even as she speculated on the meaning of this the telephone rang, and snatching off the receiver she heard a strange male voice.

"Is that Miss Diana Lake?" it asked gruffly. "Living at Number Six, Queen's Close, Kensington? Right! I'm speaking from King's Cross Station. There's a parcel waiting for you at the luggage office. It will be delivered to you in person if you come along with proper means of identification. The claim ticket's left with the station-master. If you've got such a thing as a passport, better bring it with you."

What could it mean? With trembling haste Diana got into her clothes, and not stopping for breakfast took a taxi to King's Cross. She found the station-master, who, satisfied that she was indeed Miss Lake, handed over a slip of paper. Three minutes later she was holding a heavy, flat paper parcel tied with string and sealed with big blobs of red wax. On it was her name and address, typed, and, also typed, at the lower corner, were the underscored words: "PRIVATE. OPEN WHEN ALONE."

Instantly, with a wild fluttering of her pulse, she knew that only Elsie could have sent her this parcel. She began to see reason in the busy click of keys which had followed her into the night and afterwards filled her restless dreams. The Ladies' Cloak-room offered seclusion. Into it she hurried, turned her back on the attendant who was putting out clean towels, and laying her burden on the window-sill broke open the seals. Inside the wrappings was a cardboard box, on top of which lay a letter, again typed, and without signature. She tore it open and read:

"I had to get rid of you. To the other girl I might have spoken, but not to you. In the first place, you would not have believed me; in the second . . ."

Here several words were heavily inked out.

"Be that as it may, see what you can make of the enclosed, which is all I have to go on, so help me God, and whether I'm right or wrong it's worthless in my hands. I'm out of it. I'm going now where neither you nor the police can find me to drag me back. One thing more. If you'll be guided by me—which you won't—you'll show this only to the lawyers and any others who are dealing with the case."

Without the least notion of what to expect, Diana ripped off the lid of the box, stared down, and grew limp with disappointment. Old newspapers! Nothing more. One after another she turned them over. Copies of the *Evening Banner* and other, mostly popular sheets, with dates running back for perhaps eight weeks, comprised the whole contents. A cursory glance showed her not one marked passage. Once again she saw herself cheated.

Yet why had the sender taken such elaborate precautions? Surely Elsie must be in earnest if she stayed her second flight long enough to perform this task? In earnest—or else mad. Insanity would account for everything. Anyhow, by now the woman was far away, lost as she knew so well how to lose herself. But for that red scar on her throat, one would say—

"But no! That's not her intention. I simply can't believe she'd have the courage to take her life, not after last night. She must be found. This time she shan't escape."

Bundling up the parcel, Diana went straight to the Temple. Michael Hull had not arrived, and when after twenty minutes he did appear she was too engrossed in her own thoughts to notice he was disturbed in his manner. In his private office she poured out her story.

"And these newspapers are all she's given me. While I've waited for you I've studied them line by line, and if there's anything in them I've not found it. What do you make of it?"

Now the odd expression in Hull's eyes struck her. Was this pity again?

"I'm sorry you had to wait," was the slow response. "I was detained by another item of news. Apparently you don't know yet that during the night Number Seventeen Floyd's Square was broken into by the police. Elsie Dilworth was found in her bedroom, which was sealed up and filled with gas. She was stone dead—by her own hand."

CHAPTER TWENTY-EIGHT

"Suicide? I don't—that is, I can't—believe it."

Diana's throat was parched. She had to swallow to get the hoarseness out of her voice.

"She was alone in the house," said Hull. "It was certainly suicide."

"What else was found?" she whispered. "Any note, any—" She could not utter the word confession, but her companion understood.

"Nothing. What you have there is all the light we seem likely to have on the event."

Diana smoothed the letter she had crumpled in her hand. She was thinking that once before in this same room she had seen a door slam in her face, as surely as the real door had done last night. Now again it had happened, and this time there would be no reopening it. She pointed to the two sentences: *I'm out of it. I'm going now where neither you nor the police can find me to haul me back.*

"Then that was what she meant?" she asked dryly.

Hull read the whole letter through, made cautious sounds. Before he had finished, power to reason flowed back into Diana's numbed brain.

"It's—queer. If she really had the intention of killing herself, why not hand me these papers instead of getting me off the premises and writing me a letter? Did you hear me say she'd tried once to cut her throat? She was too cowardly to finish the job. Doesn't that all go to prove—"

She broke off, turning towards the door, which had suddenly been opened by a clerk. It seemed that Mr. Bream was in the outer office. Hull nodded and said, "Show him in."

The little agent, paler than usual, looked subdued and thoughtful. Diana met him with a swift, "Was it suicide? Are you sure?"—but his reply was roundabout. Beginning with his own arrival at Floyd's Square, he described how he had found Inspector Headcorn and a sergeant already there, pounding at the door.

"We began to think the place was empty. Then we smelled gas. The window up there didn't fit tight enough to keep it all in. We borrowed a ladder and got inside the front bedroom, though the gas was enough to knock you over. Full on—and she was lying, in a brown cloth coat, close up against the gas fire, her head in a sort of cowl made of wrapping-paper. She'd been dead a good half-hour—maybe longer."

Diana watched him with horror in her eyes, seeing the picture vividly. Hull inquired if there had been any evidence of a previous struggle.

"None, and no marks of any kind on the body, except the healed wound on the throat Miss Lake noticed. There was a typewriter on the table. She hadn't packed her bags, and there was no food about. We examined all her belongings, but didn't find anything to rouse a moment's query."

"And the owner of the house?"

"Still away. The milkman told us she'd taken her boy and gone to Dulwich for a couple of days." Bream paused, glanced at Diana, and continued: "We got Mr. Blundell up to make a formal identification. He declares he hardly knew her, what with her hair cut short and dyed black, and her general starved appearance. It seemed a decided shock to him. He found in her purse two of his keys on a ring—the ones she'd hung on to—and a latchkey to the house, though we don't know, naturally, how she came by it. There's a good bit to nose out, but I don't imagine it will alter after the doctor's verdict."

The barrister gestured towards the pile of newspapers on his desk.

"I'd better tell you what took the victim out last night," he said, and gave a brief résumé of Diana's latest experience.

"What!" exploded Bream, his pale eyes blazing. "Here, let me look!"

He pounced upon the papers, thumbed them over. "Humph!" he muttered disappointedly. "Seems the same lot I saw in her room the one other time I was there. They *are* the same—with a few additions. Anything in 'em?"

"It's a bit premature to say positively. Oh, I say! Miss Lake!" Hull started up with concern. "Here, let me get you some brandy!"

With a shaky laugh she warded him off.

"I'm all right, thanks. I suppose it's this shock, and the fact that I've had no breakfast."

"I'll send out for coffee. Meanwhile, there's a couch in the file-room through there. Bream, will you look after her? And when she's feeling better you and she might have a thorough go at these papers. I'll study them later." Coffee, quickly fetched, steadied Diana's nerves, and in company with Bream she set to work, once more feverishly determined to wrest some secret from what, to outward seeming, was simply and solely a batch of out-of-date print. In the midst of the task she stopped to ply the agent again with questions.

"You see, it's the stone wall, just as it was before. Every chink closed up. First we had that Indian, now it's Elsie. Two suicides. I suppose there's no chance of proving anything different?"

"If there is, I don't know where to look for it—though I may tell you Headcorn's every bit as anxious as we are to upset the suicide theory. I left him going over that house with a magnifying glass, but it didn't seem very promising. No sign of a forced entrance, no odd fingerprints, no—" He left the sentence unfinished and, holding up a page of newspaper, examined it against the light.

"What are you looking for?" she asked curiously.

"Pin-pricks. There aren't any. Now for the dates. Maybe we'll get a clue from them."

He noted down the dates of issue on a bit of paper, which he compared with the rough calendar composed in connection with the Somervell case.

"November first is the starting-point. Let's see. . . . Mrs. Somervell was buried on October twenty-fifth, Dilworth informed the Home Office and left her employment on the twenty-eighth, and three days later began collecting papers. By November twelfth she'd accumulated a dozen—ten evening journals, two Sundays; and since then she'd added fourteen more. We may assume that before the first of November she was not interested in this newspaper game, despite the fact that already she'd busied herself over Mrs. Somervell's death, and—if your idea is right—

taken her first step towards getting Somervell into her power. Now what started her on this tack?"

Consulting his calendar again, he remarked that Adrian's interview with Blundell on the subject of his inheritance took place at the Fetter Lane office on October the twenty-ninth.

"And the letter Blundell wrote him must have been dictated the day before. October the twenty-eighth was the date of two other occurrences—"

"I know," interrupted Diana. "Elsie saw the Home Office people, and sent in her resignation. Well?"

"Now maybe we're getting something!" cried Bream excitedly. "If we can discover what time of day that letter was dictated—that is whether it was before the lunch-hour when she paid her visit or afterwards—but surely you see what I mean?"

"I'm afraid I don't, quite."

"Why!" began the agent, and then, his vivacity ebbing, checked himself. "No," he resumed, rubbing his chin. "Perhaps I'd better work on it a bit before explaining. It's just an idea that may fizzle out. Let's have another squint at that letter she enclosed with this rubbish."

Carrying the dead woman's message to the window, he examined the obliterated words with a pocket magnifying glass.

"Crossed out with 'x's,' then inked on top of that. . . . Here, how's this? 'In the first place you would not have believed me; in the second, the mere fact of your knowing where I am would sign my death-warrant.' I'm not certain that's correct, and I mean to have the sentence submitted to a test; but I can almost swear to the three words *fact*, *where* and *warrant*."

Diana gripped the arms of her chair. "Does that sound as though she meant to commit suicide?" she whispered. "To me it's more like the confession we hoped for—or something very close to it."

"Is it?" he queried dubiously. "It could mean just the same obsession of fear she seems to have been labouring under all along—possibly an unreasoning obsession. Dilworth may have been the victim of persecution mania. I fully expect the coroner's jury to return a verdict of Suicide while of Unsound Mind, and with more sincerity than is usual." He pointed with annoyance to the newspapers. "I ask you, what is there in all these to give any sane person the jitters?"

Diana was too sick at heart to make any reply. She, too, saw the sound sense in the view just expressed. It was with dull surprise, therefore, that she heard her companion say that all the same it would be their wisest course to keep the newspapers locked in Mr. Hull's safe, and to speak of them to no one.

"No one," he repeated with emphasis. "And that applies equally to what happened last night. Inspector Headcorn and I have agreed we want for the present to keep certain things strictly amongst ourselves, and away from the Press people. Understand?"

Did she? For a single instant what she saw—or fancied she saw—in the agent's eyes sent a feeling strangely akin to an electric shock through her body. It echoed her reaction of yesterday when she had talked with Colin Ladbroke about Adrian's queer attitude towards his own predicament. When she was by herself her breath came jerkily, and for some time she remained staring down at the litter of meaningless print, almost oblivious of her surroundings.

CHAPTER TWENTY-NINE

BLUNDELL was not yet in his office when Bream reached there, but a telephone message from him had suspended all work while the staff conferred in awed voices over their late associate's death. Resolving to tackle one point before attempting to solve the whole exasperating riddle of Elsie Dilworth's behaviour, Bream put concrete questions, with results inconclusive but stimulating. He learned that Blundell dictated his letters in the morning, but that he sometimes had an additional one to give later in the day. No one remembered just what had happened in this respect on October twenty-eighth, though the young girl typist did recall that Miss Dilworth, who for several days had seemed "very queer," had, at about three in the afternoon, come over sick and faint.

"I was in the ladies' room on the landing, filling the kettle for tea. She came in looking ever such a bad colour. Maybe it was a liver attack, as she said; but I remember thinking it seemed more like—well, some sort of shock she'd had."

"Have you any idea what was responsible?"

"No, and I might have been wrong. I do know Mr. Blundell begged her to go home and rest, only she wouldn't hear of it. Yes, that was her last day at the office. Next morning she didn't turn up."

"Do you know what she had been doing just before she felt faint? Dictating letters, typing correspondence?"

"That I can't say. I'd been out to buy stamps. Look, here's Mr. Blundell just coming in. Maybe he can tell you."

Bream turned and saw the solicitor, looking weary and preoccupied, just entering the door. Already, in the early morning, the two had met in

Floyd's Square, and Blundell now gave an understanding nod as though he had half expected to find inquiries going on in this quarter. Inviting his visitor into a small, untidy private office, and sinking heavily into an old-fashioned swivel chair, he asked at once if Bream had reached any conclusion.

"I'll put it more plainly," he said, surveying the agent with keen attention. "No good mincing matters, is there? Are you completely satisfied this affair is what it appears? In three words, is it suicide?"

Bream returned his scrutiny without flinching. If he was taken aback he did not show it.

"I don't see quite how we can make it anything else," he answered frankly. "Do you?"

Blundell tapped meditatively on the desk in front of him, but said nothing. After a moment he roused to ask if any member of his staff had been able to throw light on the matter.

"No, none," said Bream. "I'm glad to have a word with you, because you may be able to help me over one small question. As you may realise, the possibility of Miss Dilworth having poisoned Mrs. Somervell is somewhat intensified by what has just happened, for which reason I'm hoping desperately to get some line on her last day in your employ. You see why, of course?"

"Not quite. What day was it, by the by?"

"October twenty-eighth. It was on that date she saw the Home Office officials and I believe—but correct me if I'm mistaken—on the same date your communication acquainting Dr. Somervell with his inheritance was sent. I suppose Miss Dilworth took down that letter?"

"She must have done. You were thinking—?"

"I'd like to know if you can recall what time of day it was when you dictated the letter. Only if Miss Dilworth took it, otherwise it's unimportant."

The shaggy brows knit over the three-cornered eyes. Either Blundell did not entirely grasp the purport of the question, or he was searching his memory very hard. Suddenly he brightened.

"I've got it!" he exclaimed with triumph. "She took that letter with the others about eleven in the morning. Know why I'm sure of it? Because—" As he spoke he drew towards him a black-bound diary, fluttered the pages, and laid it out for Bream to see. "There you are, October twenty-eighth. See those appointments? They cover the whole time from lunch onward. I was chock-a-block just then, filling in income-tax forms for half my clients. Besides, wasn't that the day the poor woman felt so seedy? It was. I was trying to spare her. Well, there's your answer. Anything more?"

"Just this: I'd been hearing about her being attacked with faintness or whatever it was, and was wondering, to be perfectly candid, if I could connect it up with what she learned about the will. While you were dictating the Somervell letter, did she display any emotion?"

Again the lawyer cogitated, his thick, short legs thrust out before him.

"I remember she gave me rather a startled glance," he said. "Possibly she turned a bit paler than usual. I see your drift now. From the bottom of my heart I wish I could say something more definite."

Bream rose, and fingering his bowler turned back to ask if he might be allowed to see a copy of Mrs. Somervell's will.

"Just to make sure what, if anything, the witnesses were able to see," he explained. "You'll appreciate why."

"Naturally. Well, I've the original here in my safe." The document, folded crosswise in three sections, consisted of four pages, the last of which revealed nothing but the tail end of a sentence and the various signatures. Instantly Bream saw that Elsie Dilworth could not have gleaned any information from the sheet revealed to her.

"Did you happen to notice," he inquired, "whether when signing her name the will was folded so that the other sheets were invisible?"

"They were when the will was handed to her. After that I'm less sure what happened. It's a question I've bothered about a hundred times. Brutal as it sounds, if we could save young Somervell by loading that crime on to an unfortunate woman who's out of harm's way, it would be only common sense to do it."

Bream left him, and took cautious stock of his impressions. He was now almost convinced that the letter to Somervell was dictated not as Blundell said, but shortly before three in the afternoon. Already he had ascertained that Blundell was alone at that time, the first of his clients not arriving till three-thirty.

"That letter was the shock," he decided. "And yet I have to admit it's quite on the cards she didn't feel actually sick till some hours later, which vitiates my whole argument. If it took immediate effect, then it was entirely due to her having shot her bolt, as it were, before knowing the terms of the will. Is it so, or not?"

There was simply no determining. Such a belief, once proved, would shift the kaleidoscope into a new and startling pattern. Picture the emotional state of a woman who, unwittingly, has sprung a trap on the man she loves!

"But it's sewn up at both ends. Only one person in that office knows when that dictation occurred, and if he's lying about it no human power can call his bluff. Is there any way left to tear a hole in this suicide theory?"

Just one. If it could be shown that Elsie on going to King's Cross had taken a bag with her, then one could be sure at that time she intended not to take her life, but to quit London. He hurried to King's Cross to find that the night officials were not due to come on duty till late afternoon. Forced to wait for his information, he returned to Floyd's Square to be met by a disgruntled inspector just taking his departure. No fresh discoveries had been made. He drew Headcorn aside and offered a tactfully-worded bit of advice.

"Inspector, you won't think it out of place of me if I mention that Miss Lake has something more to tell you? It may concern you as well as myself. And while on the subject, might I suggest you conduct your interview with her away from her flat?"

The big man's eyes showed there was no necessity for plainer speech.

"Thanks," was the laconic response. "I'll get her along to the chief's office."

So it was that Diana, for the first time, saw the interior of Scotland Yard, a place far less awe-inspiring than she had imagined. She recounted her tale about the newspapers to an audience composed of a keen-eyed Assistant Commissioner and Inspector Headcorn, was questioned closely, but could not make out what effect she had produced. However, she was once more warned to preserve complete silence over certain incidents, and left with a feeling of dizzy hope interwoven with incredulous horror.

Could it be that three investigations, at first view separate, were all tending towards one and the same conclusion? An insane, grotesque conclusion—or so, till now, she would confidently have believed. These men must know the futility of finding a motive. A thousand times she had assured herself there was none, or if a motive existed it was undiscoverable; and yet there seemed to be something, unguessed by others, which Elsie, suicidal victim, had suspected! Did that something explain a terror which led her to take her life rather than cower in hiding?

"No, that's utter nonsense! If so, she'd have told me straight out what that something was . . . unless, to be sure, she did mean to follow up those newspapers by some guide, some . . . Did she? Did she?"

If so, she had decided against it—*or another person had decided for her.* Which!

It was a vicious circle. Elsie's death was not murder, it was self-inflicted. Headcorn was convinced of it, albeit—if she had rightly read his manner—against his will. Her terrible but precious idea was squashed at birth.

Diana was right. The Inspector would have liked to pick a flaw in last night's appearances. His failure to do so had thrown him into so morose a mood that his chief, quietly observing him, put a pointed question.

"Exactly what do we know about this solicitor, Blundell?"

Headcorn spoke uninterruptedly for three minutes. The Assistant Commissioner gave ear, shrugged, and remarked that it sounded good enough.

"He stands to lose a considerable sum of money if Somervell's convicted," declared the Inspector, and suddenly stopped.

"Which fact won't prevent your investigating his movements on given dates. Am I right?"

"If you approve, sir. After all this time it'll be pure luck if we get anything. With the Fairlamb murder I've done a thorough combing. If this cursed Indian hadn't cropped up and formed a link—"

Again his chief had to egg him on.

"Think you can make anything of this Indian?" he asked shrewdly.

"I doubt it, sir. All very well to question his suicide, but establishing a different reason of death's another pair of shoes. You've seen the photograph of the revolver found on the body? Covered with smudges, and those smudges overlaid with his own fingerprints, correctly placed. Smudges may mean handling with gloves on. He'd a pair of new calfskin gloves in his pocket; but are they our answer?"

"Go on," encouraged his chief. "What other thing's bothering you?"

"His passport—missing, and not found in his luggage aboard the boat. If he shot himself, what's become of it? That passport, sir, must have been stamped by the Dutch official when he crossed to Holland. You can well see why I'm not satisfied."

"That's the stuff, Inspector," the Assistant Commissioner commended. "Keep slogging. Don't let this private chap you've mentioned get in ahead of you."

"Not if I can help it, sir."

Headcorn grinned appreciatively, but sobered directly he had quitted the Presence. It was not that he feared being forestalled in the matter of discoveries, but the knowledge of the difficulties looming in front of him. For one thing he had now to tackle personal employees who had shown themselves singularly loyal to their master. Could he devise traps to catch them?

"I'm much afraid," he reflected, "I'm going to find the path blocked at the very first turning."

CHAPTER THIRTY

LINGERING behind with the sergeant left in charge of the derelict house, Bream fell heir to a titbit of news volunteered by a woman-resident from across the square. Shortly before ten the previous night this woman had noticed a taxi standing before Number Seventeen, with the driver at the house door, ringing the bell and pounding with the knocker. Obtaining no response, the man had at last driven away.

This taxi Bream, without difficulty, traced to the King's Cross rank. It had been ordered in person by a woman easily identifiable as Elsie Dilworth, who had asked that herself and her luggage be collected in half an hour's time. Now it was no longer necessary to inquire about the bag. With a thrill of triumph Bream realised that his tentative suspicion had been correct. Elsie, on leaving the house, had no immediate intention of suicide.. On the contrary, she meant to quit London, planning merely to come back and get together all her belongings. So far, so good; but then came the paradox. There had been no flight. Instead, one was faced with the fact that inside half an hour she had turned on the gas and already succumbed to unconsciousness!

What had caused the swift alteration of plan? Or had it been altered for her? The sergeant still doggedly stuck to it that nothing had been found to upset the original belief. Bream toured the square in hope of hearing that some loiterer had been seen outside Number Seventeen, but his luck was out. Apart from the testimony of the cab he learned nothing, nor did the dismayed return of Mrs. Eales, at nightfall, assist save in one minor direction. He now understood how, in the landlady's absence, Elsie had got possession of the latchkey.

"So it's you, sir!" Mrs. Eales faltered nervously. "Are you connected with the police?"

Bream explained his position, and somewhat sternly inquired why he had not been informed of certain matters. The woman excused herself for her failure to write to him, coming out with a meagre story which neither he nor the sergeant saw reason to disbelieve.

"You see, Mrs. Dixon—or wasn't she Mrs. Dixon? I'm sure after reading about it in the evening paper I've been too upset to know what to think! Anyhow, she sent me two pounds, and said she wanted to keep the room on. By registered post, it was, from some place in Surrey—Redhill, was it?—I've got the letter in my bag, but there was no address in it. I meant to let you know, only my mother being down with pleurisy I've had so much to worry me. I rushed off to her, you know. That's why I was gone when—"

"Never mind that. Did you expect Miss Dilworth back?"

"Just as I was leaving—yes. I'd a card from her to say she might be coming to town the next evening, and in case I had to be out would I put the key in the usual place? Well, I did—so that's how she got in."

"Better show us where you put it," said the sergeant, with a glance at Bream.

Mrs. Eales led the way to the tiny area and pointed to a crack between two worn flagstones.

"I see," murmured Bream, glancing over his shoulder into the dusk of the square. "I suppose you pretty often hid the key there?"

"I've had to, what with no maid and having to dodge in and out."

"Of course. And now may we see the two communications you received from Miss Dilworth?"

Mrs. Eales produced them, and when Bream had noted down the postmarks and dates the sergeant took them over.

Bream toyed briefly with the idea of the key having been taken from its hiding-place and used before Elsie's arrival. It could easily have been put back for her to find, only this would mean the intruder must have remained concealed in the house during Elsie's interview with Diana Lake. Was there any objection to this theory? The overhearing of that interview might have settled the secretary's doom; but Bream decided against it. Why, if it were so, had Elsie been allowed to go out on a problematic mission? If she had suddenly been deemed dangerous, the obvious course was to put an end to her then and there, the first moment she was alone.

"Oh, what's the use?" the agent pulled himself up. "She wasn't doped, stunned or throttled. She died from the effects of gas. Will any jury believe some individual whose presence can't be proved stood over her with a revolver and forced her to gas herself? Not much—and I'm dashed if I can see how else it could have been contrived."

As he quitted the house he was struck by the particularly dense shadow the plane tree opposite cast over the entire front. Some one might have got in unobserved, he argued, and setting aside all idea of foul play turned his attention to a different solution. Suppose his hypothetical intruder entered to find the victim already dead, but having left some written statement incriminating to himself? Such a statement could have been taken and destroyed without leaving anything behind to reveal the fact.

"But can that be proved any more than the other notion? No! As matters stand, there won't be an autopsy or even a remand for further inquiry. If I'm any judge, we've reached another dead-end."

His prophecy was correct, although actually the inquest was delayed for three whole days in order that Inspector Headcorn could push investigations to their uttermost point. Diana Lake's account, now made public, substantially helped towards the verdict foreseen by all concerned—that of Suicide while of Unsound Mind. An hysterical imagination, played upon by remorse and dread of personal consequences, had led to mental derangement. The woman had first played with the thought of further disappearance, then abandoned it in favour of death.

Would the strong emphasis laid on insanity weaken the charge against Somervell? Bream saw it could not, for whatever the victim's mental condition at the last she had at that crucial moment put her finger unerringly on the spot. It would never now be known whether or not it was she who placed the aconite in Somervell's pocket, nor if her futile, frantic efforts to "atone" had sprung from a guilty conscience. By her final act she had drawn a curtain over one entire phase of the puzzle; thinking which, Bream left the quietly conducted coroner's inquest in a tornado of helpless rage.

"Blast her to hell!" he swore. "Alive she was a pest. Dead she's fastened her talons on Somervell, and will drag him down with her!"

Nothing for it now but to work again on the activities for a short while suspended, the foremost being his attempt to check the late Haji's movements over a given period. He found half a dozen Indian students who had been the boy's intimates, but although a carefree, joyous lot they tended when their dead friend was mentioned to shut up like clams. The question: "Did they consider that Haji had sufficient reason for taking his life?" met with a sphinx-like: "Maybe. His father was a hard man— very hard." Only Mr. Mirza Ahmed continued to shrug and to repeat his belief that Abdul flush of money—as certainly was the case—would have been quite content with his existence. Where that money had come from was a puzzle. Haji Senior, on being cabled, declared that he had ordered his son home three months ago. Abdul might have been spending his passage money in the meantime, but that did not explain how he came by more passage money when he required it. No further cheques had been passed through his bank.

The death of Frieda Klapp proved another hard nut to crack. The house in Red Lion Street where the event had happened was now demolished and being replaced by an office-building. The landlady, when traced, could not—or would not—add anything to the published account; the lodgers, mostly foreign, seemed impossible to locate. Armed with a list of their names, Bream wrote letters, some of which were returned, while none, as yet, had been answered. He was reduced to inserting appeals for information in the personal columns of the newspapers, and this he did in regard to Elsie Dilworth as well. So far, nothing had come of them.

One other matter he might have investigated, but, certain that Headcorn would cover it, he left it alone. Every spare moment at his disposal he devoted to an exasperated study of the newspapers lodged in Michael Hull's safe. Despite the fact that the barrister, Headcorn, Diana and even Sir Kingsley Baxter himself, were engaged in the same unprofitable pursuit, he went back to it again and again, searching every inch of the barren print, not excluding the advertisements. Cynically he came to conclude that the coroner's verdict had not erred. Elsie Dilworth had been mad—and here was the last, clinching proof.

Inspector Headcorn, meantime, was doing precisely what Bream supposed—that is to say, striving to establish beyond a doubt the whereabouts of Nicholas Blundell on the night of November first. If he could find the hour between eleven and midnight suitably occupied he would clear his mind at once of one tentative theory regarding Margaret Fairlamb's murder. A slight haziness about that hour would not, it was true, enable him to make out a case; but still it would encourage him to press further.

Interviewing the solicitor's two servants, he was told, once the date was recalled to their minds, that their master on the stated evening had dined at home, in the company of two of his most distinguished clients—Lord Limpsfield and Sir Norbury Penge, neither of whom had left till about one o'clock. Gaylord remembered this well, for the gentlemen had dismissed their cars, and at the time of their departure he had called them a taxi. During the evening it was quite impossible for Mr. Blundell to have quitted the flat. Gaylord, in the kitchen and with the door open, would have been sure to hear, and so would the cook, who was a very light sleeper. The outer door closed softly, but the door of the flat itself was—as Headcorn himself proved—a fair treat for banging.

The cook was not detained. With Gaylord the Inspector spent a longer time, hoping to give the conversation a friendly tone by attention to side issues. Already he had roused antagonism, but the butler-chauffeur became slightly mollified when asked if the clients just named dined here often.

"Not together," was his answer. "I believe this was the first time since his lordship introduced Sir Norbury to Mr. Blundell. That would be about a twelvemonth ago, when Sir Norbury had just got his title."

"I suppose a fair amount of business is conducted in the flat?"

"Oh, yes, sir. Some of these busy gentlemen seem to prefer it. Come to that, they wouldn't find better whisky and cigars, not even in Buckingham Palace—and they get away with a lot too."

Headcorn remarked that Mr. Blundell seemed a most hospitable man.

"There's nothing small about him," replied Gaylord, "nor underhand," he added with meaning. "I've worked for him four years, and I ought to know."

Now to secure confirmation; but first Headcorn took measures calculated to reveal any concerted attempt to support Blundell's alibi. He arranged that while he called on Lord Limpsfield his colleague, Inspector Baynes, should do the same with Sir Norbury Penge. Each officer was to put his questions in a certain way, after which they would compare results. It seemed doubtful if the two visits could be made to coincide in point of time. Actually, they did do so admirably well, in each case the official card ensuring its bearer prompt attention.

The newspaper proprietor was seen at his palatial residence in Belgrave Square. Headcorn was ushered into a handsome but business-like office, where a beautiful blonde secretary was taking dictation.

"You may leave us, Miss Gale," said Lord Limpsfield, whereupon, with a curious but patronising glance from lashes heavy with mascara, the vision withdrew, and Headcorn for the first time found himself face to face with the man who, from having begun life as a Natal farmhand, had climbed by his own efforts to the eminence of a power in the British Empire. He noted the brisk but affable gesture so often commented upon in the press, the keen alertness of the blue eyes set in the broad, rubicund face, and recalled the peer's well-advertised qualities of swift appraisal, courtesy to the Law, and ruthlessness in displeasure.

"Well, Inspector!" The plain man's voice, with its sub-flavour of Colonial drawl, addressed him heartily. "And what can I do for you? Smoke?" A big hand, immaculate, but not over-manicured, pushed forward a box of Coronas. "No? Duty call, I see! Well"—with a comfortable laugh—"shoot it over."

Now it was that Headcorn grew aware of what a less highly trained observer might easily have missed—a faint watchfulness, hardening the pleasant face into a mask. Without appearing to do so, he took in every movement of his host, who, lounging back in his chair, surveyed him through spirals of smoke. Purposely he heightened the suspense by a short delay, then proceeded to state his business after the manner planned.

"A mere detail of routine, sir, which I dare say you'll be able to settle for me in a few sentences. I should like very much to know what you happened to be doing on the evening of November first, with especial regard to the hour between eleven and twelve. Could you tell me where you spent that time, and with whom?"

Lord Limpsfield's gaze, never stirring from the speaker's face, had grown cold and steely, like an iceberg in midocean. Very deliberately the cigar was removed from his lips and tapped against a Lalique ash-tray. To Headcorn it seemed as if the brain which was said to keep tab of a hundred diverse enterprises just as a master juggler rotates a dozen plates without letting one fall, was reviewing in lightning succession every eventuality the question involved before committing itself to an answer.

Was this delay made in hope of further explanation? If so, the hesitating peer was doomed to disappointment. Headcorn waited. He was determined to wait, if necessary, all day, rather than add one word to his polite but terse demand. Inside he was asking himself with one of his rare spasms of skin-prickling if, at last, he had struck ore.

And then Lord Limpsfield spoke.

CHAPTER THIRTY-ONE

"November first?" The peer drew towards him a morocco-bound diary. "In one moment I'll answer your questions."

Silence while he searched and, having found what he wanted, stared hard at the entry. Then, his whole manner noticeably relaxed, he passed the book across the mahogany table for his visitor to examine.

"That's simple," he said, with a smile. "I was dining with my legal adviser, Nicholas Blundell, at his flat in Kensington. It comes back to me now. Between eleven and twelve, you said? I was sitting in his library, deep in an interesting discussion. Didn't come away till—oh, quite one o'clock."

Limpsfield was now entirely at his ease. In place of the metallic glint, his eyes held humorous curiosity.

"Does that statement clear me?" he asked. "And, if so, may I inquire of what charge? I'd rather like to know what regulation I may have been infringing. I may want to take steps."

Headcorn also smiled as he handed the diary back.

"So you were dining with Mr. Blundell. I suppose he remained with you the whole evening without break?"

"Certainly he did. See here, Inspector, what's it all about?" The magnate's expression was frankly bewildered. "What's old Blundell been up to? Exceeding speed limits? He's quite capable of it."

Although the tone implied that all this was a great joke, Headcorn read the undercurrent thoughts as plainly as though they had been uttered. Limpsfield was asking himself, What's wrong about November first? Has something got by me?

"Oh, it's quite on the level," continued the peer, still with puzzled expression. "If you doubt my word, consult the other guest who was present at the time. Sir Norbury Penge. Oh, yes—" in reply to the Inspector's raised brows. "He's Blundell's client too—through my recommendation, as it happens. Penge is a busy man these days. Whizzing about all over the country, hard to nail down. As Blundell had a little business to talk over with each of us, he conceived the notion of inviting us together for old times' sake. I was much interested to hear the latest details of Penge's development scheme, straight from the horse's mouth, so to speak. Well?" He paused expectantly.

"Am I wrong," ventured the Inspector, "or was Sir Norbury once in your lordship's employ?"

"He was," assented Limpsfield. "I'd like to be conceited and call him my discovery. Bright lad, Penge. Best advertising manager the *Banner*'s ever had—which is saying a mouthful. A loss to me when he moved up the ladder, but it's been gratifying to find him sponsoring an improvement plan which has such excellent news value. The swings and the roundabouts, eh?"

Again he paused and, with pretended lightness, returned to the matter in hand.

"Now then, Inspector! You've heard my answer, which I'll swear to if need be—though I can't imagine it'll be necessary. Can't you give me some inkling of what you're after?"

However, Headcorn was moving towards the door. With a gesture intended to soften his evasion, he said, "It amounts to just nothing, sir, now I've had your assurance on the point. I'll have to do my duty and get Sir Norbury's statement, of course. In fact, I'll move on to him now;

but you can take it from me, it's a wash-out, and we may leave it at that. Many thanks. I'll not take up any more of your valuable time!"

So saying, he quitted the room, taking with him the strong impression of a man trying to sift out a problem.

"He's stumped," thought Headcorn. "But not for long. He's only got to turn up a few back files of his own papers to see exactly what I'm after—and then what? Now we'll hear if Sir Norbury is telling a like story."

Soon afterwards, in a cubby-hole office at New Scotland Yard, he was listening to Inspector Baynes's account of a visit astonishingly similar to his own.

"I put the thing as you advised," said Baynes. "Sir Norbury declares most positively that Blundell never left the premises for the whole of that evening. Says he may have quitted the actual room for a few minutes, but that was all. I'll take my oath he was telling me the truth."

"Just how did he behave when you first entered his office?" asked Headcorn tentatively.

"In the very beginning," answered Baynes slowly, "before I said anything at all, he seemed acutely attentive. When I asked my question about what he had been doing on the stated date, he stared very hard at me in what you might call a stilled fashion. Would startled be too strong a word for it? I'm not sure. He's got good control of his features, but I noticed he started to fiddle with his tie—which, incidentally, is about as perfect a creation as you'll see in a walk down Piccadilly. One hand was doing this while the other laid hold of his diary. Then I saw him change. He went on staring, first at the entry, then at me, but in a different way—all at sea, wondering what the hell I was after. Relieved, I thought—though I may have been wrong."

Headcorn nodded. "Anything more?" he prompted.

"Yes, decidedly. When I declined to put him wise to my object, those coal-black eyes of his smouldered. Suspicion, resentment, all mixed up together. He turned curt, with more than a touch of arrogance. I'll lay a fiver he pushes straight off to Blundell to get the explanation. You're prepared for that?"

"Oh, quite! But you're sure he didn't already know?"

"He knew nothing. His mind was a total blank. If he ruffled up, I'd say it was because he doesn't mean to have his precious reputation smirched by having any one even remotely connected with himself running foul of the law. He's a young man who takes himself very seriously. Not surprising, either. It's a big job he's stepped into, and he's naturally anxious to toe the mark."

"Apart from all this, how did he strike you? Live wire, straight-forward chap?"

"Both—with a flavour of the young Mussolini. Good looking and knows it, maybe a spot self-conscious, but plenty of magnetism too. I got a whiff of his charm when his man-secretary showed in a deputation of Town Councillors from some potty little hole up north. Military back, hard handshake, white teeth to the fore under that little black wire-brush of a moustache he cultivates. All good stuff—the sort that gets votes."

"Now for one other point. Any one ring him up while you were with him?"

"Not a soul—and I strung my session out as long as possible, in anticipation of a call. Here are the times—twelve-three to twelve-nine."

"Then you arrived one minute before I left Belgrave Square," remarked Headcorn pensively. "That's odd, in a way . . ."

He had fully expected that the moment his back was turned the newspaper proprietor would have got in touch with Sir Norbury, if not to prepare him for the coming visitation then to find out if the other knew why Scotland Yard was interested in the solicitor who occupied a responsible position towards the two of them. Did the non-perform-ance of this act mean that both men anticipated these inquiries and had arranged in advance not to communicate?

"Nothing of the sort," was the Inspector's prompt veto. "I'll swear Baynes and I sprung a couple of complete surprises, which makes it all the stranger for Limpsfield, believing I was on my way to Penge, not to discuss the matter before I got to him. I'd have done it. So would most men. Why the devil didn't he?"

He was more deeply puzzled when, a day later, the men he had stationed at certain telephone exchanges reported an entire absence of calls between the peer and the knight, while those instructed to tail Lord Limpsfield and Sir Norbury declared their respective quarries had not come in contact.

Was this indifference? Headcorn would have said so, but for the reac-tions witnessed by him and his colleague. As it was, though still firmly convinced there had been no conspiracy to uphold Blundell's alibi, nor even the least fore-knowledge that an alibi might be sought, he found this refusal to communicate extremely provocative. Making certain the two friends had not quarrelled, he began to play with the idea that both were being overcautious, and to conclude that their twin-apprehension must spring from a common source. Still, as that source had manifestly no connection with Blundell, he was forced to shelve it as unrelated to his own particular problem. He had got his answer. Two witnesses, whose names alone carried weight, had independently proved Blundell incapable of being Margaret Fairlamb's murderer—and this they had done not only by their statements, but by their involuntary emotions. Of the second crime, then, Blundell stood completely exonerated. If the two murders did hang together, it followed automatically that Blundell was cleared of the first murder as well.

"Unless, in the Fairlamb case, he used the Indian as his instrument. If he did, all I can say is it's well-nigh impossible to prove." Headcorn gave a regretful sigh. "Oh, well! I dare say I was on the wrong track. I might have guessed it, seeing the entire lack of apparent motive in the Somervell affair. And yet, there's this blasted Haji impinging on both cases! What are we to make of that? Let him go without a murmur?"

It seemed to him improbable that Haji's sole function had been to plant the jewels on the Amsterdam pawnbroker. Then there was the riddle of the rogue's being in funds, despite the fact that his father had cut down on him with the utmost severity. He had tried to keep tab on Diana Lake's activities on the prisoner's behalf; at the same time he had made an attempt to get into Elsie Dilworth's room. These actions proved a keen interest in both crimes, or else that Haji had been hired to attend to certain jobs which the principal dared not handle in person. As the Somervell murder came first and could not benefit Haji, the natural conclusion was that he was being employed. By whom, if not by Blundell?

The answer leaped into his mind: "Somervell!" Why not? Or possibly it was the secretary, herself hoping to profit by trapping Somervell into marriage, and anxious to secure some person totally behind the scenes to obtain poison for her and, later, to perform other services.

There was nothing for it but to map out a course of action which would include a thorough checking of the prisoner's movements during the crucial hour on the night of November first. In the midst of this the birth of a new idea drew him back to reconsider the circumstances of Frieda Klapp's sudden decease. It had struck him that while a verdict of "Natural death" was all very well, this same verdict had been given on Rose Somervell till her body was examined, and that even then it was by pure chance the particles of aconite had not been eliminated. He interviewed the police-surgeon who had performed the autopsy on Klapp. What he learned made him ask still more searching questions, but that was all.

It was just, he thought, one more unprovable business. God, he was sick of it! Wasn't there one thing in any of these cases for a detective to get hold of?

Some time had elapsed before he again called on Diana. He found her looking pinched and white, her grey eyes heavy and encircled, her usually smooth hair clinging in moist rings to her forehead. The air of the flat was over-hot, over-scented from the flowers which filled quite an incredible number of vases. He noticed, too, how disordered everything was—furniture pulled about, pictures awry, even the rugs displaced. Over all hung a bluish haze of cigarette smoke.

Diana stared at him in a dazed fashion, brushed her hair back as though she were removing invisible cobwebs, and whispered, "So it's you. . . . What—what have you to tell me this time?"

Certain that her question referred to one matter alone, he put his answer as briefly as possible. It seemed a full minute before her mind grasped its significance. She turned still whiter, clutched at an over-thrown chair, and gazed past him into space.

"So he was in his library the whole of that evening," she muttered. "No doubt of that, I suppose?"

"Lord Limpsfield and Sir Norbury Penge both vouch for it—as well as his servants. I'm afraid there's no chance of upsetting testimony like this."

A curious expression flared in her eyes, died down immediately. He saw her trying with the fortitude which from the first had commanded his admiration to readjust herself to this latest, most devastating blow. Days ago he had guessed that she bore her godfather no love, only conscientious gratitude for favours she dared not forego; that she had sacrificed her independence for one object—Somervell. Now he asked himself if Somervell was worthy of it, or if the verdict for which he was heading was only his just deserts. The removal of Blundell from the list of possible suspects left but a poor choice of alternatives.

Tactfully he righted the chair, at the webbing of which her fingers were blindly picking.

"At it again?" he inquired in a pitying tone. "Here, let me help you to put the place to rights. You won't find anything. All you're doing is to wear yourself out."

CHAPTER THIRTY-TWO

"I KNOW. Still, Elsie was searching for something—or wasn't she? I suppose even that's not certain. Still, she did take the letters from my bag." With utter weariness Diana began straightening the hearth-rug. "Oh, she denied it, of course; but then she denied everything.

"Half the time I'm at Mr. Hull's office, going over those newspapers. I dream of them at night. The other half, I'm doing this."

Headcorn understood, for all he saw, more clearly than she, the futility of hunting for they knew not what in places long ago searched and found barren.

"Maybe," she continued, looking vaguely round, "it was removed before I came here. No, that's stupid, I suppose." She reddened a little with embarrassment. "I'll have to get that notion quite out of my head," she said apologetically. "It was a horrible one—in the circumstances."

Less horrible, though, than the idea which, very soon now, was bound to force itself on her mind. No need to tell her how, through Hull, he had learned that the prisoner, on his own statement, had walked about the city streets for two hours on the night of Margaret Fairlamb's murder, meeting no one he knew, making no encounters which could remove a doubt certain, at this period, to arise. The trial was close upon them—a matter of days. That she was thinking of it now was all-apparent from the fixed look she bestowed on a silver-framed calendar she had just restored to its place. With sympathy he watched her hand move mechanically towards a box of cigarettes. He struck a match for her, and as he did so noticed an ash-tray overflowing with charred stumps.

"By the way," he said musingly, "is it true that Mrs. Somervell was a fairly constant smoker?"

"I believe so, but it didn't do her any harm. I found some of her cigarettes here when I came. They were especial Virginians, quite mild."

Her thoughts strayed. In short, jerky sentences she told him about her session that morning with Sir Kingsley Baxter.

"It was rather odd. I know what a marvellous man he is, but why did he pay so little attention to what I wanted to tell him? Almost I'd have said he refused to be interested. Are all big barristers like that?"

Headcorn, suppressing his own reflection, explained gently that they were apt, in these cases, to leave all details to their juniors.

"Sir Kingsley's business is to plead—and he's a wizard at the job. You're in the greatest luck to have him on your side."

After the Inspector had gone she made one more stupendous effort to think; but it was like lashing a spent horse to rouse her brain to any action. Somewhere, she kept repeating, there must be a chink through which daylight would stream if only she could locate it, widen it ever so slightly. In the earlier stages there had been—or seemed to be—several such chinks. One by one she had seen them close up, till now thick darkness pressed in on her. The last had been Uncle Nick. The irony of it! Yes, even him she had suspected. She began to laugh, and was still laughing, painfully, when she felt something burning her fingers. It was her cigarette. As she dropped the smouldering end, she became aware that the telephone was ringing hard. . . .

"Hallo?"

All she heard was a buzzing sound. Presently the operator's voice informed her crisply that the person making the call had grown discouraged and rung off.

"But why? The bell had only just begun to ring. I tell you, I was quite close, so I know."

"If you will replace your receiver," came the robot accents, "you will probably be called again."

She hung up, but no further summons broke the stillness; her head felt as if wrapped in cotton wool, and she realised nothing whatever save a dull longing for sleep.

From now till the trial her days slid by in a sort of timeless nightmare. Christmas had passed and she would have forgotten it entirely but for carol singers under her window, and a magnificent dressing-bag from Uncle Nick. Even the suffering she had grown used to was curiously numbed, like physical pain making itself felt through partial anaesthesia. She ate, she slept, she made pointless excursions on foot, or in the car always kept at her disposal. Elsie's worthless legacy was constantly before her eyes, columns of blurred print even when, scarcely knowing what she did, she roamed the flat which had been Rose's, staring vacantly at some innocent bit of furniture, or pausing for long moments before the late owner's portrait. Once something unaccountable happened. She came to from a sort of waking doze to find herself in Petty's bedroom, kneeling in front of the one gas-fire the flat contained. Panic seized her. Trembling, cold with sweat, she fled from the room, but for the rest of that day the vision of a brass tap remained static in the centre of her brain, and at intervals afterwards back it crept with horrid enticement.

And then, like a reef suddenly looming out of a fog, the trial was upon her.

Blundell, with whom she had dined the evening before proceedings opened, begged her to keep away from the Court.

"I shan't be able to sit with you, you know. I'm being called as a witness. Besides, I don't quite like the look of you just lately. You've been pluckier than most, but the strain's been rather too much."

"I must go," she said stubbornly. "And I shan't have to sit alone. Doctor Ladbroke will be with me."

"Ladbroke?" Her godfather wrinkled his leathery brow. "Who's he? Oh, I remember! Adrian's hospital friend. Well, as you think best. Now, don't be downhearted," he urged. "Drink up that champagne. It's my especial brand, ordered up for you. Let me tell you, there's no saying what arguments a fellow like Baxter may have up his sleeve." And he fell to relating, one after another, the K.C.'s famous defences.

Diana was only half-listening. Vivid in her memory was the black rage Uncle Nick had shown on first hearing that Rose Somervell had been poisoned. She could see now the swelling veins at his temples, the eyes glazed with animal hate. All that venom had, she believed, been directed towards one definite object. What strange miracle had transformed the crouching lion into a lamb willing to be shorn that the man under arrest should have his chance of escape? The mystery of it continued to elude her. Again she was forced to repeat that in some curious way she had always misjudged her godfather, that it was her misfortune to feel none of the affection his sterling qualities ought to inspire.

Back in the library, she felt her eyes and thoughts drawn with a perverse fascination towards the section of bookcase which covered the hidden stairs. Even now she could not debar herself from speculation as to what could have happened on the evening her mother was killed. These stairs connecting with the upper flat would have offered the owner such an easy means of exit from the house—yes, and of re-entry, too. They might have served another purpose too, at an earlier date. Heaven knows she had considered every conceivable role the stairs could have filled, only to be met in each case by the insuperable barrier of Lord Limpsfield and the Minister of Arterial Highways. Those two had been there, talking with their host till long past the critical period. Inspector Headcorn was convinced they had supported an alibi without knowing what was required of them—in other words, the final test of truth-speaking.

She shook herself free of her stupid fancies. Her godfather was looking at her again, keenly, but with commiseration. She apologised confusedly for her inattention to what he was saying and begged to be excused.

"Quite right," he agreed. "Get a good night's rest. Pity my little private way's locked from your side. You could have saved yourself the extra steps."

He had guessed, then, some portion of her thoughts. How much more did he suspect? At any rate, he could hardly be unaware that inquiries had been made of his servants, whatever his two clients might have said to him. Unreasonably she was thankful that upper door was fastened. For one instant she had a terrifying vision of herself trapped, like a mouse, in the cedar-scented, stuffy darkness behind those rows of calf-bound books. . . .

"What's this? Feeling a bit faint?"

A hairy, short-fingered hand—it made her think of a lion's paw—was laid kindly on her arm, while three-cornered eyes, crinkled round with anxious furrows, peered solicitously into her face. Though she had meant to go, she was still rooted to her chair. Involuntarily she shrank from the paternal touch and, getting up, moved towards the door.

"No, no. I'm absolutely all right. . . . Please don't come with me. This room's got rather close, that's all."

"It's my beastly cigar." As he spoke, he ground out a Corona only one-third smoked. "What an old ass I am! A spot of brandy? Look, I've poured it out for you. There! That'll pull you round."

Rather than argue she drank from the huge goblet she found pressed into her hand. The queer lassitude left her to return again when, shut in her own quarters, she managed somehow to undress and to drag herself into bed.

By some strange mercy which had protected her during these weeks of strain, on this night of all others she slept like a log.

CHAPTER THIRTY-THREE

Fog, seeping into the Old Bailey, hung like a dingy transparency over black gowns and coarse grey wigs. It misted the yellow light-globes, quivered in wreaths over the packed rows of spectators, and blurred the twelve faces of the jury now turned, as one, on the witness undergoing cross-examination.

The witness was Nicholas Godfrey Blundell, solicitor. Strangers saw in the box a man slightly past middle age, more vigorous than most men in their twenties, and with a manner blunt, frank, and obliging. The anxious furrows graven on his forehead bespoke an earnest desire for accuracy and fairness; the semi-circular creases framing his wide mouth seemed ready for smiles at the least slackening of the tension. He looked a man who had suffered keenly but without parade or secret rancour; a man hurt and puzzled by influences beyond his control. There might be an open impulsiveness about him which the average Englishman would find it hard to understand, yet so compelling was his earnestness, so genuine his good nature, that those watching him felt inclined to condone his slight crudities.

Very different was the counsel conducting the cross-examination. Sir Kingsley Baxter, tall, angular, and calculating even in his suavity, gave an impression of altogether a more sophisticated type. He was polished, not bluff. There was a sharp edge to him, and a nervous brilliance soon to be more apparent than now, when every faculty was bent on eliciting facts concerning Rose Somervell's illness which might throw an altered light on events as set forth by the prosecution. How he could accomplish this no one so much as dimly imagined; yet the feeling grew that there might be more in this case than had hitherto appeared.

Sir Kingsley, proceeding: In regard to your late secretary, Elsie Dilworth, Mr. Blundell. Was it a habit of hers to consult you at unsuitable times?

Blundell: Well—occasionally. She believed business always came first.

Sir Kingsley: On this occasion was the matter important? Or, better, could it have waited till your return to your own flat?

Blundell: I suppose the idea was she didn't want to wait. It was Sunday, remember.

Sir Kingsley: Was it your suggestion or hers that she work on Sunday?

Blundell: She volunteered to come for the morning. She did that now and again when we were in a bit of a jam.

Sir Kingsley: So she volunteered to come. . . . Can you positively state it did not strike you as unusual for her to intrude on Mrs. Somervell's luncheon-party?

Blundell (hesitating): I *was* a trifle surprised.

Sir Kingsley: Oh, you were surprised! Now, Mr. Blundell, can you say if Miss Dilworth had previous knowledge that the accused would be lunching with Mrs. Somervell?

Blundell: That I don't know. She may have learned of it from chatting with Mrs. Somervell's housekeeper.

A murmur ran through the court. Diana felt a shiver of excitement, which Colin Ladbroke, beside her, seemed to share.

Sir Kingsley: Exactly when did Miss Dilworth come into the dining-room?

Blundell: Midway through the meal. I remember I was at the side-table, carving a second helping of beef for Mrs. Somervell. Miss Dilworth stood by me, showing me the shorthand she couldn't read.

Sir Kingsley: Had she often any difficulty deciphering her notes?

Blundell: Very seldom. Around that date she was getting nervous. These notes were all of a muddle.

Sir Kingsley: And what conclusion did you draw from that?

Blundell: That she wanted a long holiday. I made up my mind to see she got one.

Sir Kingsley: It did not occur to you she might have muddled her notes on purpose?

Blundell (after pause): No—not at the time.

Sir Kingsley: Have you thought of that explanation since?

Blundell: In a way. It would be unlike Miss Dilworth's character as I know it, but she had certainly changed.

Sir Kingsley: Could you have said then what was responsible for her nervous condition? I'll make it more definite. Had you any idea of her being the victim of an unfortunate love-affair?

Blundell: Absolutely none. I never connected love-affairs with my secretary.

Sir Kingsley: Not even when for some time she had worn quite different clothes? Adopted what two witnesses have described as a gay style of dress, coupled with the use of lipstick, rouge and other accessories?

Blundell (scratching his chin): I did wonder a bit. I can't say I failed to notice it.

Here a ripple of amusement had to be checked by the judge.

Sir Kingsley: Did you at no time connect her altered appearance with a close association with the accused?

Blundell (frank smile): I never knew of any association. At most I'd have said they were acquaintances, owing to living in the same house.

Sir Kingsley now asked how long Miss Dilworth had remained in consultation over the notes. Blundell replied that it was long enough for the hostess to show distinct annoyance. Miss Dilworth had seemed unaccountably dense.

Sir Kingsley: Mr. Blundell, an incident occurred when your secretary quitted the room. I want to hear your account of it.

Blundell: On her way out, she knocked against the accused, who had got up to fetch the gravy and horseradish sauce from the sideboard.

Sir Kingsley: One moment, Mr. Blundell. Had you by that time served Mrs. Somervell's plate?

Blundell: As far as I can recollect, I had handed it to the housekeeper, who had put it before her mistress.

Sir Kingsley: You are not perfectly certain of this?

Blundell: No, because I was carving more beef. I looked round when I heard a sort of cry from Miss Dilworth, who then went off into a fit of giggles. I saw her trying to wipe the gravy off where it had splashed over Doctor Somervell's coat. She was using her handkerchief. He told her not to bother, but she insisted on repairing the damage she'd done.

Fully ten minutes of questions revolved about the points just covered. More clearly than ever Diana saw how simple it would have been for Elsie, while her employer studied the notes, to deposit a small portion of the grated aconite in what remained of the sauce on Rose's plate. Just as easily could she have contrived the accident which would have enabled her to sift a few grains of the poison into Adrian's pocket. Unfortunately Petty and Felix Arenson had already described the foregoing incidents, and from neither version could anything definite be deduced. The fact that the coat itself, produced in court, did actually show a faint grease stain down the two fronts tended to weaken the defence's argument.

Blundell could not recall noticing if Elsie made any move towards the plate he was serving, nor could he say if any appreciable amount of sauce was left on the plate.

Sir Kingsley: Assuming there was a small residue of the sauce, do you think you would have noticed if a little grated or shredded aconite was placed on the same spot it would have caught your eye?

Blundell: I doubt it. I used my glasses for looking at the shorthand, but took 'em off again to go back to the carving.

Sir Kingsley: I shall demonstrate that aconite is so much the same colour of horseradish as to mingle with it indistinguishably. Now, then! Was Mrs. Somervell wearing glasses?

Blundell: No! She never put 'em on in company. Wore 'em only when she was by herself, or with an old friend, like me.

Sir Kingsley: But she did require glasses?

Blundell: Couldn't read without 'em. It was the looks she objected to.

Colin Ladbroke scribbled a note on the back of an envelope. Diana saw the action, but let it pass, so wholly was she taken up by the next set of questions, dealing with the will. To her disappointment nothing new came out of them. Soon her godfather withdrew from the stand, to be replaced by Petty, trembling, gasping like a fish.

The matter of glasses was again touched upon. Petty averred that her late mistress, like most persons of her age, had grown extremely long-sighted, but she confirmed Blundell's statement about the reluctance to wear glasses except under necessity. Very adroitly Sir Kingsley capitalised this fact; but, unluckily for the defence, the probability that the victim would not have seen a foreign substance on her plate before covering it over with a fresh helping of sauce could not counterbalance what was definitely known—namely, that the sauce was handed her by the accused.

The prosecution had shown that aconite dropped into the ladle would have mingled with the sauce already there and been deposited with the first spoonful taken from it. In this way the victim would have received the full measure of the dose, while those who came after her got none.

In short, all Baxter succeeded in doing was to bring forward an alternative theory with rather less to support it than the one previously postulated. Whether he could persuade the jury that the accused lacked all knowledge of the will in his favour remained to be seen. It was evident, now, what he intended doing. Not only did he mean to show Adrian ignorant of the will, but Elsie informed. At the same time he was planning to suggest a motive in Elsie's case—a tricky and delicate business.

Incredulously the audience heard him build up his structure. Elsie, in her statement to the Home Office, had been uncannily right in several respects. She had been accurate in declaring that the victim had just made a will bequeathing the bulk of her property to a man in financially low waters; accurate about the poison employed, and the manner of its administration. According to one witness—Petty—Elsie had been present in the room while the orders to the butcher and greengrocer had been telephoned. Later she had asked point-blank questions as to what guests were expected for the Sunday lunch. On top of these facts came her strange behaviour, all indicating emotional turmoil. The hospital incident was recounted, with fresh detail. Undoubtedly, having shot her bolt, Elsie had regretted it, and striven desperately to induce the accused to get away before arrest.

Round the court ran the admiring whisper, "He may do it yet." Diana herself caught the infection. Sir Kingsley had hit on the one possible means of raising doubt in the jury's minds, and then feeding it by placing the secretary in the limelight and fixing attention on her hysterical actions.

The first day closed on a note of definite hope.

Other whispers had arisen, but as yet were confined mainly to proletarian circles. However, Diana herself, on the second day, felt a growing resentment as she became aware of the idea subtly being instilled into the jury's minds. Was she wrong, or did she sense a drop in temperature? She saw the new sort of glances the jurymen directed at the prisoner in the dock, understood, and at the noon adjournment vented her hot anger to Colin. He bade her be patient.

"After all," he said, "Baxter's got to show Somervell as a victim. How can he do that without furnishing some convincing excuse?"

"Do you mean there's no other course but to let people think there was an affair between Adrian and Elsie? There wasn't. You know that as well as I do. Look at the way he's handling all these witnesses from the boarding-house! Oh, Colin, has he got to do it?"

"Baxter knows what he's about," was the answer, to her mind unsatisfactorily evasive. "You may be sure he sees exactly what he's up against."

Oh, well, was her bitter reflection, what did it matter that false belief was fostered if only Adrian was acquitted? Adrian himself must by now be past caring; and yet, when she next saw him, she wondered if this were so. He was still composed. His brown eyes behind their lenses continued to rest on each witness with unobtrusive detachment, one might almost call it scientific interest; but on his lean cheekbones had appeared the dull splashes of red which to her meant mortification. She recalled how little, at any time, he had pled in his own defence. Realising the futility of protesting against the predicament in which he found himself, he had chosen a dignified silence. Now he was forced to listen to hints he could not deny with any hope of belief—hints on the acceptance of which his very life depended. Diana could guess why Sir Kingsley had not been eager to hear her version of things. It might have interfered with his scheme.

George Petty had been wiped out of the picture. Felix Arenson proved a nervous, unhelpful witness, and Blundell's two servants gave aid in only one direction—to show that Elsie Dilworth had bitterly disliked the victim. Once in the cook's hearing she had spoken of Mrs. Somervell as a "damned, stingy old bitch," and hoped she would "choke herself to death on that brandy she was forever tippling." Laughter had to be suppressed over this, the only, reference to Rose's fondness for drink. Admittedly the actress was a woman who did herself well, but it was not suggested she drank to excess, or that the indulgence affected her shrewd business judgment. Only in the matter of the will had she displayed impulsiveness, and even then she had taken her solicitor's advice.

There was neither proof nor disproof that the victim had informed the accused of the will by which he benefited. If she wrote him a note, that note no longer existed; if she declared her intention on the afternoon he took tea with her and was invited to lunch, the fact was undiscoverable. In like manner total mystery surrounded the problem of when and how the aconite had been obtained—and so two minute but important flaws, emerging to view, heightened the tension. Baxter had scored two points, both of which he undoubtedly would use to the utmost advantage.

Adrian's own testimony irritated by its meagreness. Diana would have been shocked at any attempt on his part to save himself at the expense of an Elsie now dead, but the flat repetitions of "I don't remember," and

"I'm afraid I didn't notice," made her ready to sob with despair. Colin kept a tight grip on her arm.

"Don't you see," he muttered, "that's his best possible defence? It's typical of him not to have noticed what didn't concern him."

Perhaps; but then the jury had been pumped full of counter-suggestions. The accused to them was a quiet but unscrupulous Don Juan; and what of the victim's initial antagonism towards him, with its sudden veering to partiality, mental states affirmed by her own solicitor? Unexplained they must indicate either seduction by designing charm, or threats of exposure. No middle course existed.

On the third day the defending counsel delivered his appeal. It was a masterly effort, combining skilled argument with forensic legerdemain. It dazzled; it hypnotised; it demolished with hammer blows every insecure premiss raised against it. From a simple and moving word-picture of the earnest student of medicine and brain surgery, Sir Kingsley passed to a hypothetical reconstruction of the crime which, if accepted, would exonerate the accused of both knowledge and blame. The court sat entranced as proofs of the dead secretary's infatuation were cited, the linked chain of unbalanced actions terminating in suicide held up commiseratingly yet in such a manner as to show how Elsie Dilworth and only she could with malice aforethought have planned and executed the murder. Why her intricate plan had miscarried was developed convincingly. Just possibly too convincingly—for it was at this point the catastrophe occurred.

Somewhere, from the foggy rear of the gallery, a woman's voice cried: "Shame!"

Few saw the interrupter as she was hurried out, weeping, but the one word, hurled into the spokes of oratory, had the force of an exploding shell. Listeners rubbed their eyes. Hundreds recalled that Elsie Dilworth—a working girl, perhaps herself a victim—had, when all was said, performed her duty as a citizen by passing on her suspicions to the authorities. Some might think she had shown great courage, foreseeing, as she must have done, an agony of mind which in the end was to make her take her own life. In a reflux of moral indignation they asked themselves what truth was contained in this rigmarole woven about a poor creature powerless to ward off slander.

Sir Kingsley continued, but to a public no longer his to sway. Cold scepticism had descended over the court long before the judge, with merciless logic, laid bare what emotionalism had so nearly concealed. The jury were instructed that in a case where evidence was of necessity circumstantial motive must be accorded full value. It was their task to decide which motive, as set forth by fact, carried the greater weight.

The jury filed out. Colin drew Diana outside, and procured her strong tea, which she forced down, though it sickened her. She clung to his arm.

"Colin! They must see he couldn't have done it. What do you think?"

"They ought to. Baxter did a good job of it—on the whole. Blast that idiot woman!"

There was only twenty minutes to wait. Back the jury came, and the foreman, a carpenter with a soured expression, was addressed by the judge. In a firm Cockney-flavoured voice he gave the verdict of Guilty. It was over. The judge reached for the square of material which custom calls the Black Cap, spread it over his wig, and pronounced the death sentence.

CHAPTER THIRTY-FOUR

MORTIMER Bream managed a word with Diana as, blanched and unseeing, she was shepherded into her godfather's car. She turned and looked through him.

"Yes," she whispered. "Keep on. We mustn't stop—yet."

A moment later a touch on the detective's arm roused him from meditation. He recognised the house-surgeon from the Prince Regent Hospital.

"I hear there'll be an appeal. Think it will help?"

"You heard the evidence. I don't imagine it will be differently construed."

"I did hear the evidence," Ladbroke said, in an emphatic undertone. "Come along to the corner pub. I'd like to talk with you."

Presently, in a quiet corner of the bar, the doctor drew from his pocket an envelope scribbled over with notes.

"As to the victim's eyesight," he began. "It seems most unlikely she could have read the will she signed without putting on her glasses; yet the chauffeur-butler was never asked whether at the time she wore them or not."

Bream considered the point and shrugged despondently.

"Blundell may have read the will to her. We can inquire."

"I've done it," said Ladbroke. "A moment ago. The fellow, who hadn't a notion what I was after, says if she'd been wearing glasses he'd have noticed it, because it would have been the first time he'd seen her with them on. So we may take it she didn't run through that document herself. Now, one thing more. Apropos of Mrs. Somervell's hard-boiled character,

Miss Lake let fall an observation which impressed me immensely. She said that she didn't imagine Mrs. Somervell honestly trusted any man living—*except Nicholas Blundell*. Get the connection?"

The ghost of a gleam shone in the agent's chameleon-like eyes.

"You mean the victim might, simply on trust, have signed something without personal knowledge of what it was?"

"Exactly."

"I see . . . but what if she did? She'd have known it was a will, because of the two witnesses. Besides, there *is* the will, with one living witness to vouch for his own signature and for hers. Doesn't Blundell's helping her to will her property to some one other than himself guarantee there was no tricky business afoot?"

"Does it?" the house-surgeon muttered. "I'm not so sure. What I do see is that the fact you mention knocks any theory I may want to concoct straight to blazes."

"Then you have got a theory?"

"None a jury would waste two minutes over. There were odd things, though. Why, at the Home Office, did that secretary avoid all specific mention of names?"

"Why did she do anything as she did do it?" demanded Bream cynically. "Loony, that's all."

"With a clear line on her motives," objected Colin, "we might think her extraordinarily sane. Suppose, at a venture, she intended her statements to incriminate not Somervell but another person? Some one to whom she was under obligations, some one who, if mud was stirred up to no satisfactory purpose, would turn into a formidable enemy?"

Bream nodded with understanding. "Blundell," he said softly. "I may tell you I've had my eye on him for some time, and with more reason than you may think." Lowering his voice to a whisper he related what he had learned of Elsie's fit of sickness and his private but unprovable deductions. "I still believe it more than probable she was bowled over by shock the moment she took down that letter to Somervell and discovered she'd set a trap for the wrong man. It would explain several puzzles, but I'll have to point out one serious objection to it. That expression she used in making her deposition—you remember the wording? 'Financially low waters.' If that cap fits Blundell, I can't see it. The man's perfectly solvent, solid as Gibraltar, no troublesome creditors. It's true for a time he was living on an overdraft—"

"What!"

"No need to say 'What,'" retorted the detective calmly. "I could tell you others who do that, if their investments happen to be paying big dividends. It releases capital, nets larger returns. Just depends on the difference between the bank rate of interest and the percentage earned elsewhere. This overdraft was cleared off about the date of the exhumation. I grant you it might have looked peculiar if Blundell had fallen heir to Mrs. Somervell's money; but he didn't touch a penny of it, so what conclusions can we draw?"

Ladbroke was eyeing him thoughtfully.

"How much have you found out about his private affairs?" he asked.

"Not all the ins and outs. That's too tall an order by far; but quite sufficient to show the woman must have been hopelessly barmy if she imagined he was on the rocks."

"I hope you can nose out a bit more. And this overdraft—just when did you say it was cleared off?"

Bream thumbed the pages of a shabby notebook.

"Here we are. Bank manager's statement—very snootily given. The third of November. . . . What's up? Has that rung a bell?"

"No . . . no." Ladbroke had risen restlessly. "I'm afraid it hasn't, but—here's my card. If you get on to anything, no matter what, will you promise to let me know on the dot?"

In the taxi seized outside the door Colin studied the notes jotted down during the trial. Under "glasses" he read "stingy old bitch." One matter could be settled at once. Besides, he could not bear the idea of Diana all alone, or—what was worse—with that unspeakable—

He stopped. Was this family friend a hypocrite and blackguard? The man had secured Somervell the finest counsel money could purchase. He had done other acts for Diana, for her spineless father, all denoting kindliness of the most substantial sort. His position was unassailable—and Adrian, from the first, had known it.

"Still—we'll just see . . ."

He found Diana in the dusk of the drawing-room. She was shivering, though she still wore her lambskin coat and the fire on the hearth sent out a welcome heat. Gripping her icy hands hard in his, he put a blunt question. She stared blankly and then broke into a little cracked laugh.

"Oh, yes," she answered him. "I did say that. How clever of you to remember!"

She might have been referring to something in the remote past.

"You meant it?" Colin was trying to rivet her attention. "You and your mother both took it for granted Mrs. Somervell intended leaving all she had to Mr. Blundell?"

"We were mistaken," she said lifelessly. "There was never an actual will. If you're thinking that some—unpleasantness between them made her change her mind, that's out of the question. There was nothing of the sort."

"So I conclude," he agreed dryly. "No, that wasn't quite my idea. I was merely wondering what would have happened to an earlier will, supposing there had been one. She'd have destroyed it?"

"I imagine so. Anyhow, no will was found."

"Your godmother was stingy," he went on. "Oh, no need to mince words! Would a generous woman have left an old servant who'd slaved for her thirty years the paltry sum of a hundred pounds? I'm remembering other things, too—how she sponged on her solicitor friend, used his car to save keeping one herself, let him provide her with trips abroad, in fact got all she could out of him—oh, you told me! Maybe, all along, she led him to expect that at her death her entire property would come to him. No, I'm not hunting for a motive for getting rid of her. Not now. I'm only trying to reconcile your belief with what did happen. I'm thinking that one destroys a will only if one knows its contents to be null and void by the terms of a later one. That without this knowledge there'd be no reason for destroying it."

"Is this a conundrum? Oh, Colin, don't! I can't bear any more."

"Diana, forgive me! You've got to bear it. Here, let me fetch you a drink of sorts. We can both do with a stiff whisky."

He found whisky and a siphon in the dining-room, stood over her while she drank, and at the first sign of relaxation began anew.

"This flat was searched," he said slowly. "You say by the secretary."

"You heard Petty's evidence. Elsie did it."

"Have you ever thought why? Mayn't she in the first place have taken her cue from another person who, directly after the death, started doing that very thing?"

Her hand shook as she set down her tumbler.

"Mr. Blundell?" she whispered, frowning. "He did, of course, go through all Aunt Rose's papers. It was his duty as executor. Why should Elsie see anything queer about that?"

"She wouldn't, unless, already believing there was some hocus-pocus about the will, she surprised him searching in out-of-the-way places.

Say under a mattress, behind drawers—that sort of thing. One act like that would have been enough to confirm a suspicion previously born."

Diana's grey eyes had begun to show reawakened life. He could see her effort to adjust her mind to this new aspect of things, but it was short-lived. She covered her face and turned from him.

"Even if you were right," she muttered, "there's nothing here now. Every possibility of it has been drained dry."

"Elsie didn't think so," he reminded her. "Up till the night you took possession. Else what brought her here again?"

She considered this briefly.

"That's so," she assented. "But she'd been away several days. If there had been any chance of my finding a stray will, should I have been invited to take up my residence in the flat?"

"Yes, if Blundell was positive there was nothing to be discovered. He'd have satisfied himself, depend on it; but that's not saying he'd either found and destroyed a paper or simply given up trying. Maybe he'd come to believe no such will ever existed. Mrs. Somervell might have been fooling him—and fooling your mother. So she may have done; and again, she may have spoken the truth. See here—do you know of anything taken from here before you arrived?"

She thought for a moment.

"Yes. The Sargent drawing of Aunt Rose. It's hanging in his bedroom."

"Is it? Good! Now we can prove if my idea's correct. When Blundell's out, I want to examine that drawing. See if the board and nails at the back look as if they'd been tampered with recently. Can you manage it soon?"

"I'll do it now," she said. "Oh, yes, he drove back to discuss the appeal with Mr. Hull. I'll say I want to borrow one of his legal books. Will you wait for me?"

At the door he suddenly thought of another faint possibility. The private staircase she had told him about—had she examined the interior of that?

"No? Well, I'd rather like to look it over myself. Oh, not for any very definite reason! Could you unbolt the other side of the top door without being seen?"

"I'll try," she promised, and disappeared down the broad stairs.

In five minutes she was back, both actions accomplished with ease. The cook had left her alone, she had manipulated the section of bookshelves without difficulty, also slipped into the bedroom. There was slightly less uselessness in her air as she said that the drawing had been removed and put back into its frame.

"I'm sure of it. The paper's cut round with a knife, the nails fell out when I took it down. But to hide a will in a picture-frame! It's too utterly silly."

"Don't let that bother you," Colin said with satisfaction. "I'm certain nothing of the sort was done. It's only that a person who'd exhausted all the likely places would turn to the unlikely ones, that is, if he was determined the paper, will or not, shouldn't fall into the wrong hands. Now for those stairs. Let's be as quiet as we can."

There was nothing concealed under the carpet, nor did any of the panels appear to be movable. If there had been, Blundell, as owner, would have known of it.

"If the professional detectives haven't seen anything wrong about this place, I don't know why I should," declared Colin, brushing dust from his knees. "At the same time, one wonders if and when these stairs were used. You still feel convinced there was no intrigue between those two old people?"

"I can't think there ever was. Oh, Aunt Rose had lovers in her day, but not Uncle Nick. I'd say in that way he didn't attract her. What are you looking at?"

"This lock. It's been oiled. By which party? And the oil smells of—yes, it's cloves. Now it would be interesting to see if—"

He was back in the upper flat, doing exactly what Inspector Headcorn had done, that is searching the shelves in the adjacent cupboard for a bottle containing oil of cloves. Nothing of the kind was discoverable.

"Another job for you," he said. "See if in Blundell's place you can locate any lubricating oil that smells like this." He held the key under her nose, then replaced it in the lock. "Try the bathroom—his. I don't know if it'll be much use. Hallo! Your bell's ringing. Slip out of this quick. You can attend to the bolts another time."

A florist's boy stood on the outer landing with a long white box. It contained red roses, with stems a yard in length. Diana touched them with a gesture of repulsion. The envelope attached she did not trouble to open.

"Colin," she said, "how can any of these things help us? You know, as I do, nothing we may find now will reverse this judgment."

It was damnably true. All he could do was to return her gaze in contrite misery.

"That's beastly of me," she murmured. "You're right, we must keep trying—till the last gasp. Thank you for coming."

"You ought to have some one with you," he declared with brusque energy. "Look, can't you get hold of some woman friend who—"

"Plenty—but I'd hate it. No, Colin, don't worry over me. Only see me often. Now go."

CHAPTER THIRTY-FIVE

DOGGEDLY little Bream returned to what he regarded as a hopeless task. He had not required Dr. Ladbroke's comments to strengthen certain latent suspicions, but the crux of the matter remained as before. In only one respect had his opinions altered. He was beginning to wonder if, after all, the newspapers in Hull's safe were not the rubbish he had first imagined.

It had come about through noticing that, oddly enough, the issues of earliest date were a trifle fresher-looking than the later ones. It might mean merely that these had not been exposed to sunlight and dust; but drawing a long bow he inquired at the news-stand closest to Floyd's Square and made an interesting discovery. A woman answering Elsie's description had, on the first of November, ordered back numbers of papers the dates of which, recorded in the news-seller's book, ranged from early September to late October, and in each instance coincided with those of the fresher copies. So, while not furnishing proof that Elsie had been totally sane, it did suggest a method in her madness.

The question arose, why were these particular dates selected? The reply amazed him. The woman had asked for those issues which had contained most information on the Penge Scheme for Arterial Expansion! Her excuse had been that she owned a bit of land adjoining a Yorkshire town, and was anxious to learn if her locality was likely to benefit by one of the projected highways.

A blind? A few inquiries assured Bream that it was. Elsie came from Lincolnshire. If she owned land in Yorkshire or elsewhere, her sister, long estranged from her, knew nothing of it, nor did her fellow-workers. Bream went at the newspapers again, and saw how each edition featured the Penge Plan. It formed, indeed, the one common factor of any import-ance, and if he had discounted the fact before it was only because his eye, like all eyes, had grown so accustomed to Arterial Expansion blazoned over front pages that in a way he no longer saw it at all.

As he re-read every word a number of dissociated ideas began to rub elbows. Blundell was legal adviser to both Penge, author of the Plan, and Limpsfield, proprietor of most of these papers. Most? He ran through them swiftly. No, all of them. Was that accidental? Certainly, now he thought of it, the Limpsfield Press had of all others been most vociferous in advertising this scheme which, as he owned no property, had never interested him. But agreeing the Limpsfield papers had been deliberately chosen, where did Blundell come in? If the solicitor had wangled possession of Rose Somervell's money in order to sink it in a remunerative investment, it would have been quite another pair of shoes. As it was—

Suddenly Bream recalled that Penge and Limpsfield had been the two clients who upheld Blundell's alibi on the night Margaret Fairlamb was murdered. He had heard about it from Diana, and knew the Yard was fully satisfied that no collusion had prompted the separate statements. The incident served only to draw the three men together in another way. Not a damaging way, either. On the contrary, by making it certain the second crime could not be laid at Blundell's door, it had furnished the strongest argument against his being guilty of the first. All the same, it would be well to learn of the interviews at first-hand. Considering the issues at stake, Inspector Headcorn would not, he felt sure, deny him detailed information.

What he did hear when, after some delay he got in touch with the Inspector, was a fuller version than had been given to Diana. The new items, however irrelevant, were oddly intriguing.

"Oh, yes, both those notables cheered up mightily the minute they knew it was their solicitor and not themselves I was inquiring about," said Headcorn dryly. "It didn't concern me to ask why, and I dare say I'd have got the same reaction with a number of other prominent people."

"But you're convinced, are you, they weren't shielding Blundell? They were with him the whole of that evening?"

"I'll take my oath on it."

Bream then asked if—unofficially, of course—the Inspector could tell him anything about the Penge Plan.

"All above board, is it? No shady business, no profiteering?"

Headcorn replied confidently that under the present regulations there was small chance for profiteering. He had heard much discussion, some of it adverse, regarding the huge improvement scheme, but no suggestion of wangling for private gain.

"Nowadays every foot of commandeered land has its price properly fixed. You won't see it rising to any fancy figures."

Bream stifled a sigh. It was the wrong tack again. He took the opportunity to sound Headcorn on the almost-abandoned Fairlamb inquiry, which he perceived was a sore topic.

"You still think our dark-skinned friend had some connection with it?" he asked.

"Must have done," grumbled the other. "Though in what capacity has got me beat."

No more could be drawn from him, but his very silence showed Bream that the Yard, like himself, was ardently desirous of uncovering the hidden places in the dead Indian's career. On the spot he resolved to let Elsie Dilworth go and risk one more throw on Haji's former house-mates. His advertisement had been appearing for some days without evoking a single reply. He reworded it, offered a tempting reward, and held his breath to see what might happen.

The following evening he received two communications—not in answer to his Indian appeal, but prompted by the appeal for information touching Elsie's migratory movements. One was from the manageress of a Trust House Hotel in Little Harben, Dorset, the other from an inn called The Haymakers, situated near a small village in Wiltshire. At each of these places a woman now believed to have been Elsie Dilworth had stayed for two nights, under different names. Expecting nothing worth while from the venture, Bream secured a car and set off to interview his two informants.

In each case the woman—once posing as Mrs. Edith Dixon, once as Mrs. Brown—had undoubtedly been Elsie. The handwriting in the two registers settled it; but at the Wiltshire inn he learned nothing of value, and at Little Harben he was turning away disappointed when a final remark made him pause. It seemed that the brother of the manageress had been talking at the desk when the new arrival broke into the conver-sation, and roused amusement by her excited manner.

"You could see she was queer," the stout functionary continued. "Her, a perfect stranger, getting all worked up over—what do you think? Why, just a few acres of bad farming-land my brother practically gave away a couple of years back!"

"Farming-land?"

"Yes—and the questions she fired at him! Who bought it, what price he got, where the land was situated—oh, no end of things!"

"And where was it situated?" Bream wanted to know.

"Oh, to the north a bit, just where they're cutting one of the new motor highways. That's what my brother was grumbling about—his selling at such a low figure to some scatter-brained poultry-farmer that when he was about to go under sold again for—well, we don't know what he got, but it must have been a good ten times what he gave."

Highways again! Mad or sane, Elsie Dilworth had been genuinely concerned over the Penge Plan. With what object?

Bream drove round the town—unimpressive, not even a market-centre, yet now preening itself on the four beautiful "arteries" run straight as a ruler through straggling outskirts and carrying with them the promise of "ribbon-development." He made the acquaintance of the disgruntled brother, learned that the lucky poultry-farmer had departed for places unknown, and from other sources collected an assortment of facts which sent him back to London deeply pondering, but no whit the wiser on points that mattered. He determined to locate, if possible, this A. J. Barstone, who from a failure in fowls had done an excellent land-deal and shaken the dust of Little Harben from his feet; but he feared that with this, as with all his inquiries, he would go far afield without striking one cross-line of evidence.

He had by now a vague working theory. The difficulty of it lay not only in the shortness of time at his disposal, but in the ultimate probability—he would have said certainty—that after all his efforts the vital aspects of his case would remain untouched. When the Appeal was heard and dismissed, only the fact that he was still being detained, kept him from admitting he was beaten. Like a distracted terrier he was running here and there on his divergent trails, unable to follow any single one for long, when a letter reached him from Northumberland. He read it, held sceptical debate with himself, and after five minutes' moody wobbling, tossed a half-crown. It came down heads.

It was settled. He despatched a wire by telephone, and within the hour was in a third-class carriage, speeding towards the northern border.

CHAPTER THIRTY-SIX

As THE execution approached, Blundell earnestly begged Diana to get away from London. Her health, he could see, was suffering. She could accomplish nothing by staying on here and leading a hermit's life. He strongly advised her to join her father, who all this time had never once guessed how the outcome of the murder trial was affecting her, but who, in every letter, urged her to come to Hollywood.

"Not now," was all she would say, and at last the subject was closed.

She had, it was true, a vague intention of quitting this flat for some obscure place of her own, where she could live on the remittances Herbert was sending. If she had as yet made no move it was because, now all hope was gone, a leaden inertia kept her rooted to the spot. The date of January 17th loomed ahead, red danger-signal in a fog. Towards it she was being drawn, but for long periods, even worse than before the trial, her faculties seemed submerged in a sort of wretched coma, wherein sensation was mercifully deadened. That, she supposed, was what happened when agony reached a certain point. She would wake one day to find herself old and maimed. It was no good thinking of that future time now.

In the state just described she sat, one evening, by the drawing-room fire, dimly thankful that her godfather was dining out, and that she could be left alone. Gaylord had removed her dinner-tray, and left the smaller tray with her coffee on the needlework stool before her. Later on, perhaps, Colin Ladbroke would drop in. He had the habit of doing that when his work permitted him; but he seldom came before nine, and it was now only eight. He would have nothing to tell her. Almost she regretted the effort she would be obliged to make to manufacture conversation.

A coal clinked on to the hearth. In the distance of the cold night taxis honked and a bus rumbled its way along the Park. Round her were soft colours, beautiful textures, flowers as usual continually renewed; but through the smoke of her cigarette she saw, not the room she had grown to loathe, but the harsh outlines of a condemned cell, with a trapped man sitting motionless on a camp-bed.

Into the picture melted another—Elsie, gaunt and huddled, her head covered in a paper-cowl and thrust close to the unlit gas. That faded, giving place to a roadside ditch, where lay an Indian boy, shot through the heart, one dark hand clutching a pearl-handled revolver. . . .

Her mother, now. Those kind eyes up-staring, that pathetic head, with its loosened russet braids, propped against the stair. . . .

She could sit still no longer. As she had done countless times before, she sprang up and began an aimless prowl, in one room and out another, lighting a fresh cigarette when the old one burnt her fingers. Dullness descended. A slight swimming in her head made her steady herself by whatever bit of furniture was nearest, but if she noticed it at all it was to accept it as a symptom of nervous collapse. . . .

How she came to be lying on the floor of the bedroom defied comprehension. She woke to the fact—though "woke" seemed the wrong word for one whose eyes had been wide open all along—through smelling singed wool, and becoming conscious of a hurt place on her temple, as though in falling she had struck her head. Had she fallen? Evidently—which must mean she had fainted. Very odd, for she had not the faintest recollection of feeling really faint.

Nor could she recall turning on the lights; but the two lamps were on, shining softly down on her through their large-fluted shades. She did not feel ill, only lazy and reluctant to move. Indifferently she lay, watching a tiny column of smoke soaring from the carpet, and only tardily realised it came from a long, completely charred ash which had been her cigarette. Even then it did not at once occur to her to pick up the stump, or to wonder how long she had been unconscious. The first question to stir her comfortably-blank mind was why her head appeared to be enclosed in a sort of box, oblong and three-sided.

Blinking, she saw that the box-thing was simply the central space of the Queen Anne desk, which was built on the "knee-hole" plan. It stood against the wall opposite the bed, and as she lay on her back she was looking up at the underside of the top which formed a bridge between two tiers of drawers. Inertly she continued to gaze, her eyes glued to a minute triangle of white paper—part of a dealer's tag, she supposed—affixed to the rough wood just where the left pedestal joined on to it. For a long time she studied this white tag. Or was it a tag? At last, idly, she raised her hand and touched it, to discover that it moved, but would not come away. Then she saw why. It was the protruding corner of a larger sheet which had somehow got tightly wedged between the immovable top and the column of drawers.

Through her partly-dormant brain shot a sky-rocket idea. She scrambled to her feet, fetched a nail-file, and, squeezing back under the desk, began prodding at the triangular bit. She managed to draw it out another inch, but no more. She had guessed, though, just how it had come to be in its present position. It had been crowded out at the back of an overfilled drawer, doubled over against the wall behind, and then insinuated into the horizontal crack plainly visible from the rear. Every one of these drawers had been pulled out during her search. The top drawers were roofed with deal, so that this paper, whatever it was, had remained concealed, stuck as it was between the layer of deal and the walnut top covering the whole.

And the top would not come off! Well, then, she must smash it. She was in the act of sweeping the blotter and various accessories to the floor when the bell rang, and Colin walked in, to find her with feverish red spots in her cheeks and grey eyes glittering.

"What's up?" he demanded. "Here—have you got a temperature?"

Shaking back her hair, she dragged him into the bedroom and showed him what she wanted done.

"I'd never have known anything was there if I hadn't tumbled over and—"

"Tumbled over! You mean you fainted?"

"Oh, what does it matter?" Impatiently she shook off his hand. "We must break this open—quick! Shall I fetch a coal-hammer?"

"Hold on." He transferred his eyes to the desk. "My mother's got one of these bits of furniture. If I'm not mistaken. . . . Look!"

Under his manipulation the top had come loose. He lifted it up, and Diana pounced upon a dusty folder, in part printed, the rest filled in with writing she recognised. Breathlessly they studied it. Colin whipped over the first page, stared at the group of signatures at the end and gave a low whistle.

"A will," he murmured. "There was one, after all. You see what it says?"

Diana had seen. Rose Somervell, four years previous, had bequeathed the bulk of her property to her friend and legal adviser, Nicholas Godfrey Blundell.

"It doesn't change things, you know."

They were seated side by side on the rose-covered bed, under the fringed canopy, discussing their find.

"Doesn't it?" Her face fell. "But you said—"

"I thought there might be something of the kind. What I mean is, the new will cancels it. I'll show this to Hull, naturally; and it does raise questions. Only you mustn't build any hopes."

"Never mind that now." She brushed aside his objections. "Let's think this out. You say she drew up this will herself?"

"Evidently. You buy these forms at a stationer's. Know who the witnesses are?"

"I've never heard of either. I'd say Eliza Tompkins was a charwoman, and Henry Patterson some trades-person."

"Which means she kept this to herself. Or does it? If Blundell knew nothing about a will with these terms, he couldn't well hunt for it, could he? No—wait! How's this? She may have told him she'd made such a will, but never showed it to him."

Thinking it over, Diana declared that this was exactly the sort of thing Rose might have done.

"She was cunning, you know. That would explain his trying so desperately to find the document among her papers; only not finding it, he would conclude she'd invented a mythical will for the simple purpose of keeping him her slave. We don't actually know, though, if he did try to find it. Besides . . . oh, dear!" She put her hands distracted to her head. "I'm more hopelessly muddled than before. What's wrong that I can't think properly?"

"How about some coffee?" he suggested. "Shall I make it?"

"Coffee!" She moved into the drawing-room. "There was some just now. I don't remember drinking it. If I didn't—Heavens! What a mess! Did I do that?"

Following, he found her gazing blankly down at a tray which was a brown lake of coffee—stone cold. A glance told him what had happened. She had poured her cup full and gone on pouring. The overflow filled the tray to the brim and had dripped in a pool on the rug.

"Colin! That's queer. Am I losing my mind?"

He looked at her.

"There's some left in the pot," he said quietly. "I'll heat it up in a jiffy."

He returned from the kitchen to find her still staring at the drenched traycloth.

"That's funny," she whispered. "Do you know, I seem to be doing the same sort of things she did. Rose Somervell. It's just come back to me how Adrian said that once he saw her pour tea in a cup already full. And a moment ago I found my cigarette burning a hole in the carpet. She did that—when she fell down in that attack. Do you see? That's the burnt place, there."

She gave an uncertain laugh, but her eyes held a serious question. Without answering, he put firm fingers on her pulse, glancing, as he did so, round the room.

"Drink your coffee," he said, and when she had taken the cup he handed her stood gazing first at the hearth, then at the ash-tray beside the tray. On the small table at his elbow was a box which had contained a hundred cigarettes, the same brand as his own. About a dozen remained. He waited till she had turned away, then sniffed at the box and set it down again.

"Have you always smoked as much as you're doing now?" he asked. "Maybe it's that."

"How can it be? I have been going it rather hard. She did, too. Inspector Headcorn asked me about it, I remember; but I told him what mild tobacco it was."

"Who buys these for you? Or do you buy them yourself?"

"Of course I buy them. Why, what on earth—"

She stopped, stared at him and came a step closer. "What do you mean?" she demanded.

"Nothing. Tell me more about the fainting. What were you doing, and how long were you unconscious?"

As best she could she described her sensations.

"It's all so silly. I can't believe I did lose consciousness, and yet . . . how long was it? I don't know. Long enough for half a cigarette to burn out. What's the time now?"

"Ten minutes past ten."

"Is it?" she exclaimed, astonished. "Surely not! It was eight when I sat here. It doesn't seem possible." Suddenly she thought of the will. "Oh, let's not bother about me! I'm all right now, and you ought to be getting along to Mr. Hull's. Oh, Colin, don't you think we may, at last, have got something worth while?"

"I'm afraid not." His face was white and drawn as he set down his cup. "Fetch me the paper, will you? No, it's all too tenuous. Still, we'll see what Hull makes of it."

She disappeared into the bedroom. Very deftly Colin shovelled the loose dozen cigarettes into his coat pocket, and replaced them by similar ones taken from his own packet.

"Cut down the smoking a bit," he advised when she rejoined him. "Get out all you can, and whatever you do keep quiet about this." He tapped the will before depositing it in his note-case. "Now, then! Shall you get off to bed?"

"Yes, though I'm wide awake now. If Hull does have any new idea about things, will you promise to ring me up, no matter how late it is?"

"I promise," he said gravely—absently, she thought, as though his mind were occupied with other questions. "But don't expect much, will you?"

CHAPTER THIRTY-SEVEN

As soon as Diana was alone she plunged her face into cold water, drank what remained of the coffee, and strained every nerve to see in what way her discovery might affect matters. Her brain was alert, but her thoughts jumped about like puppets on wires. Involuntarily her hand strayed towards the cigarette-box, hovered, withdrew. No, on the bare chance that these queer lapses came from over-smoking she must break the habit, whatever it cost her.

Rose, she decided, might have let her former will remain undestroyed for a simple and obvious reason—namely, that it had mysteriously disappeared; but if she had never intended to destroy it? Would that mean she did not know that a later document had rendered it invalid? Dull-witted she had been towards the last. How lightly this had been touched upon during the trial! It seemed as though no one on either side had remotely questioned her sanity. Why? Because the solicitor who prepared her last will and testament, himself not benefiting, knew her intimately. It was true that others considered her sane—Petty, Gaylord, Mrs. Ransome, Blundell's cook; but the great point was Blundell's word for it. It occurred to Diana that just here might lie a stupendous fallacy, unperceived, impossible to prove. Rose might have been sane in the ordinary use of the term and still in a condition so unlike her usual shrewd self that she might have signed a second will without realising it. Certainly she had never mentioned the will to any one apart from Blundell. Her friend Margaret had assumed she meant to tell her about it later on, but that interpretation of a cryptic remark had come after the incident was revealed.

Had this wildly improbable thing really happened? Colin might say it was useless to consider it now since the truth could never be known. All the same, Diana did consider it, again and again forcing her mind back to the salient points. Could Nicholas Blundell have schemed to have forty thousand pounds willed away from himself? It sounded fantastic. If so, he could have had but one reason: To safeguard himself completely, in the event of trouble, from all breath of suspicion.

Yes, that was excellent logic; but it left the core untouched. One still had to provide Blundell with a motive for removing Rose, and what motive could there be? The threadbare question! It must be a strong motive, overwhelming, in fact, since it entailed the sacrifice of so much substantial gain. Jealousy? Latent madness? Fear of exposure? Diana reviewed them all, dwelling longest on the last and, as before, vetoing it simply because Rose's own attitude gave it the lie. With her last conscious breath Rose had voiced only affectionate, admiring friendship for Blundell. If a wish to injure him had lurked in her lazy, self-centred mind, Margaret would inevitably have guessed it. Such a notion was unthinkable—and no other was left.

At last, feeling that her brain was only snarling itself into fresh knots, Diana undressed, got into bed, and lay staring up at the dark ceiling and waiting for Colin to telephone her. Twelve struck, then one. It was shortly after this that, still wide awake, she heard a powerful car stop under her window, and men's voices floating up. Subdued voices they were. Only her vivid wakefulness made it possible to catch them, and to identify her godfather's gruff tones amongst the confused rumble. She slid out of bed, parted the thick taffeta curtains, and looked out.

By the pavement, frostily gleaming, stood Lord Limpsfield's magnificent, oyster-coloured car. From it three figures had alighted, and were mounting the shallow steps.

A sharp, late-risen moon shone full on them. The largest man spoke to the chauffeur, who climbed back into his seat and drove off. Even from this angle she recognised Lord Limpsfield himself. Blundell, of course, was the one now opening the door; and the third? He looked up and around, nervously—a dapper, bare-headed man with hard black eyes and a close black moustache. He was the Minister of Arterial Highways, Sir Norbury Penge. The trio went inside and the door closed quietly.

Blundell had probably been dining with these clients in some place where private talk was difficult, therefore he had invited them home for a drink and a chat. To do so at this late hour seemed to argue a closer connection than Diana had hitherto conceived; but it was not that or the question of what they meant to talk about in privacy which set going another train of thought. She was recalling that Limpsfield and Penge were the witnesses who had confirmed Blundell's presence in his flat throughout a certain evening, and that on their word and theirs alone—if one discounted Gaylord—rested a most vital alibi. Inspector Headcorn was fully satisfied they had spoken in good faith; but was this so? Suddenly Diana wondered if even Headcorn and his fellow-inspector could have been taken in by skilful acting. Limpsfield and Penge might have some urgent reason of their own to keep their solicitor clear of scandal. Their statements might have been pre-arranged. They might even have foreseen the elaborate precautions Scotland Yard would take in the attempt to snare them.

It was the wildest conjecture. Considering who these two men were, what they represented, Diana at a less abnormal time would have scoffed at it. Now she queried everything. She would have given her soul to listen in on the conversation going on below in the desperate hope that a chance word might reveal collusion. She even toyed with the idea of getting dressed and going downstairs on an invented pretext; but any open move would defeat her purpose. Oh, she groaned, if only she had not locked and bolted the door of the inside stairs! At the foot, behind the bookcases, would have been the ideal—

Had she locked that door?

With a shiver she remembered. No, she had forgotten to do it! Days ago it was, after her unavailing search for the oil-bottle Colin had wanted her to find. Gaylord had been about, and she had been obliged to leave the locking up till another time. Blundell, of course, might have been in there and noticed the door was unfastened. If so, he would have turned the key, incidentally making some astute deductions which he had kept to himself. The blood singing in her temples, she slipped on her dressing-gown and mules and crept along to the linen-cupboard.

The door was not locked! With infinite caution, she edged through, and in thick darkness, feeling her way, crept to the bottom of the little, narrow stairway. There, crouched low, she strained her ears. A low mumble penetrated to her, but she could distinguish no words. She must open the lower door—a grave risk. She felt for the steel knob, turned it, taking an age in the process. Now the door was open a mere crack, through which, high up, a dim glow entered from the tiny space at the top of the bookshelves. A whiff of cigar smoke wafted to her nostrils. She waited, holding her breath.

At first she heard nothing but a crisp rattle of papers. Soon, however, a voice she knew instantly for that of Sir Norbury Penge spoke in dictatorial, waspish tones.

"That man of yours on the premises again?" it asked.

"Gaylord? Oh, no! I got rid of both him and my cook for the entire night. You see, I remembered your nerves."

It was Blundell speaking. He sounded easy, reassuring, but subtly different from his usual self.

"I'm thundering glad to hear it," returned the Minister, mollified, but still petulant. "What with your giving evidence in murder trials, having to furnish alibis and what not. . . . Oh, sorry, old man!" It was a grumbled apology. "That got you, did it? No offence! I was forgetting both those poor women were your friends. What struck me was the devilish bad luck, just now, to have police inspectors poking into your affairs. You never know what they're up to, once they start nosing round. Sure you've left no memoranda lying loose?"

Diana, huddled in darkness, felt a strange mingling of disappointment and electrified excitement. These visitors did not connect their solicitor with murder, therefore her main hope was blasted; but some other matter was afoot which must be kept secret. She put her ear to the crack and heard Lord Limpsfield's rich voice saying in accents of reproof:

"Come, come, Norbury! Blundell's no fool to go leaving memoranda about. Every scrap of paper stays in his strong-box at the bank, except when he fetches it out for us to look over. Isn't that so, Blundell?"

"Certain sure," soothed Blundell. "And back it goes first thing next morning. Nick's taking no chances. Now, then! Here's the list of our newest holdings—Wolverhampton and North Riding districts, likewise Hertfordshire. Complete with alleged developments. Like to run through 'em?"

"Thanks." There was a gurgling noise as Sir Norbury drained his glass. "Let's have the map. . . . I say. Limp!" His tone changed. "What price that letter in *The Daily Beam* complaining about public funds squandered on unwanted highways? Your leader made hash of it, but the *Beam*'s got a million circulation. We don't want the Labour crowd giving tongue, do we?"

"They won't." The peer laughed comfortably. "Future stuff of that sort will go down the drain. I've fixed Peterson. Handed him a nice block of shares in Wyckhampton Improvements, Ltd., over lunch to-day. Don't you fret yourself about a Labour organ with me controlling four-fifths of its advertising support. The beauty of teamwork, what?"

The voice purred on contentedly, thickened by a cigar:

"H'm . . . a pretty turnover. We've a fortune now, on paper. Three fortunes, I should say, and it'll mount higher, and go on mounting. Oh, God, yes, this is only the start! Nick, old son, my compliments on the spade-work. You must have done a long bit of burrowing before you brought us into things."

"Six years it took me," was the proud boast. "Buying here, there, up and down the country. All on my own. I turned out my pockets."

"And a few others, no doubt?" The sly dig came from Sir Norbury. "Big opportunity, nursing estates. I trust your books are squared?"

"To a farthing. Here, you're not drinking. Port, or whisky?"

The momentary silence was broken by the faint tinkling of music. It was "The Bluebells of Scotland," rippling forth placidly as the trick whisky tantalus was lifted. Strange, silly sounds! Sir Norbury jerked out an irritable: "Christ!" followed by a grudging laugh.

"I'd like to smash that bottle. It is whisky, is it? Good. The port you keep sent me home all wonky after our last evening session. You complained about it, too, Limp—or am I wrong?"

"What's that? Oh, the port. Something balled me out. I oughtn't to touch port. Look, I'll read over the items, you check 'em. That'll save time."

Then came a long drone of figures, coupled with names of towns, options, concessions, all unintelligible to Diana, who nevertheless was fast gathering two facts—first, that she was listening to the innermost working of the great Penge Plan; second, that the enterprise was a gigantic fraud, conceived by her godfather, and operated by him in conjunction with his two companions. The revelation made her gasp; but she could not yet see that it impinged on her problem. What chiefly interested her was the casual reference to the port, suggesting as it did a faint doubt as to the guests' condition on a given occasion. How, though, could she know if "the last evening session" had taken place on November first? It might have been on another date—and, furthermore, the speakers themselves betrayed a total lack of suspicion towards their host. Later remarks confirmed this. Business concluded, the talk turned on the Somervell crime.

"Nasty mess, that," Lord Limpsfield commented. "When that secretary woman made off I was in the devil of a stew. Penge had the right idea. We were both afraid she'd twigged something. That was one false alarm. The other was the question in our minds: Who benefited by the lady's death?" He chuckled reminiscently. "A nice pickle if it had been you, Blundell. What about it, eh?"

"Me?" The solicitor conveyed mild astonishment. "Oh, no chance of that! I was attached to Mrs. Somervell. She thought something of me; but there was small point in her leaving me money. In a manner of speaking, the boot was on the other foot."

"First and last," declared the Minister of Arterial Highways in a sour tone, "I was cursing you to blazes. My man of business present at the very meal his hostess is poisoned! And that's not all. When they did land that young swine, why the hell did you go staking him to the best counsel in England? He might have got off. How would that have looked for you?"

"Decent gestures do no harm," pronounced Lord Limpsfield largely. "You're a good fellow, Nick, and with the jackpot you'll haul in over this show you'll never miss an odd thousand, will you? No, no, I always say vindictiveness don't pay! Look at Ryman. Would he be doing his stretch if he hadn't rounded on the smaller fry?" A chair creaked as he rose. "Oh, well, it's all turned out nicely, though I still think it was a stroke of luck to have the secretary out of the way before the trial began. Do you know, I've had to turn down a Sunday story headed:—'The Mystery Woman—Victim or Accomplice?' That'll show you. What's your theory about her?"

"I've no theory," said Blundell, and his voice shook with some unclassifiable emotion. "All I say is I was properly taken in by the pair of 'em, him and her—blast their skins!"

There were sympathetic throat-clearings which struck a final blow to Diana's hopes. That these three men were associates in an illegal venture meant nothing. She was left exactly where she had been an hour or more ago, too wretched now to attend closely to the coming remarks.

"Ryman," mused Sir Norbury. "Fifteen years was his dose. We'll get the same if this deal ever springs a leak. What'll you do with the papers overnight, Blundell?"

"Put 'em in my private safe—where no burglar'll get his hands on 'em," Blundell said with a touch of his schoolboy satisfaction. "Want to see me do it? Then come along."

The safe, similar to the one in Rose's bedroom, was let into the wall behind his bed, as Diana had discovered. She waited, therefore, for the mingled footsteps to die away before shifting her cramped muscles; but noticing that the sounds seemed to halt within the library she raised her head from her knees to listen again. To her horror the crack of light over the bookshelves was swiftly widening. Good God, they were coming in here!

There was no time to think. Springing up, she fled, banged her head against some sharp obstruction in midair, reeled dizzily and missed the stairs. At the same instant the ceiling-globe burst into glare, a startled oath sounded behind her, and turning she met a shower of loose papers. In the briefest possible moment she got a nightmare impression of blanched faces peering in, of a square hole yawning where solid wall had been, and of a squat figure surging past to block her exit. That figure was Blundell's, but by a fantasy of terror it seemed to her no man, but a lion, lowering, ready to attack. An old lion—turned man-killer. . . .

"You're at it, too, are you?"

Half-suffocated, he had spoken these words straight into her face. Instantaneously her vision cleared. Triumphant with understanding, she met the pale, blazing eyes so close to her own and made her announcement.

"Now I see what happened," she said steadily. "She heard what I heard, so you killed her. My mother, too. You murdered them both, to keep them quiet."

CHAPTER THIRTY-EIGHT

A DEAD silence ensued. Diana remained flattened against the panels beside the open safe, her blue dressing-gown clutched across her chest. Blundell still blocked the stairs, while the lower exit was filled by the white shirt-fronts and rigid faces of Lord Limpsfield and Sir Norbury Penge. The eyes of the latter pair were directed not at Diana, not at their host, but at some indefinite point between. Blundell watched them narrowly, but with a pretence of not doing so. His choked breathing came more naturally, the swollen veins at his temples resumed normal size. At last he spoke, tentatively, as it were, throwing out a feeler.

"She's unstrung. Most understandable. Suppose we get her in there, and see how we stand."

Neither guest answered, but with one accord, slightly hesitating, they moved back into the room. Immediately Blundell shot his right hand into the safe, slid some object into his pocket, and touching Diana's arm jerked his big head towards the doorway.

"Come," he said, and smiled.

She knew then that she would have to obey. Marshalled from the rear she moved into the smoke-wreathed library, where a red fire burned on the hearth and a strong reading-lamp cast a cone of light on the central table.

"Sit down, won't you?"

She did so, on an ugly carved chair backed against the bookcases, and drew her dressing-gown over her knees. Again pregnant silence. The two guests glanced furtively at her, then down at the Turkey carpet. She saw that Lord Limpsfield's face-muscles twitched, while his rubicund colour was mottled in patches. The younger man's sallowness showed a sickly, greenish tinge, his throat moved spasmodically, and one well-manicured hand fidgeted with his careful bow tie.

Presently Lord Limpsfield said raspingly:

"It's a pity you never told us about that communication with the upper floors."

Blundell shrugged, his leathery cheeks still creased in their travesty smile; but he made no reply. Sir Norbury jerked at him:

"This girl—who is she?"

"The daughter of an old friend. I must apologise for her. The fact is," he paused, moistening his lips, "she's Somervell's fiancée."

"Somervell's . . . but her name?"

The three-cornered eyes flickered a glance at the questioner.

"Lake," was the mumbled reply.

The two men started violently, then their faces became stone masks, behind which Diana believed she could read every reaction. Both Limpsfield and Penge had heard Blundell's incautious outburst to her, and her accusation. Now they knew who she was they were, without doubt, recalling many things, foremost of which was that in the conference just past no attempt had been made to moderate voices. Almost literally Diana could see them putting two and two together and weighing the result. Within three minutes they were realising that their colleague was an assassin, and that whatever his crimes he must be shielded. A moment ago the trapped girl had been saying to herself that it was impossible anything could happen to her. Here she was in a house close-built against other houses, in the heart of a handsome, prosperous district—not alone with a murderer, but in the company of two influential, prominent citizens, each of high standing, each with a reputation to protect. Now she saw the sickening fallacy of her argument. In the very fact of there being reputations to protect lay the absurdity of her expecting the least mercy.

She was doomed.

It did not astonish her, therefore, when Lord Limpsfield let a considering eye travel upward as far as her chin, only to veer away. He was more terrified than she. When he drew in a long breath and slowly expelled it she read his meaning. There would be no good bargaining with her. Talk was waste of time.

"Well," he said with dry pointedness, "and the next move?"

"Take the papers," answered Blundell softly. "You'll find them scattered on the floor, in there. Go home. I'll handle this."

"You can manage?"

"Oh, easily!" The solicitor paused, adding in a lower tone: "Haven't I managed well enough so far? I promise you there won't be another—accident."

For the one and only time during this strange scene Limpsfield stared straight into the opposite pair of eyes. As if what he saw convinced him he tightened his lips and motioned curtly to the third confederate.

"Penge, get the documents."

The Minister of Arterial Highways feebly shook his head. Diana thought he was going to be sick. He contrived to pour himself a full tumbler of whisky, the tantalus playing its snatch of a tune till he set it down. When he drank, his teeth clattered against the glass. Limpsfield let him be, strode heavily behind the bookcases, and returned with a burden of papers which he fitted into the brief-case Blundell held ready for him. No one looked at his neighbour. Diana, hemmed in their midst, might have been a chess-pawn for all the notice taken of her; and yet the unobtrusive approach of Blundell showed her that the least move on her part would be instantly dealt with. She was at liberty to scream—once. Should she try it? She remembered that it was about two in the morning, that the caretakers, sleeping in the rear of the basement, would not be likely to hear, or if they did would listen for the sound to be repeated and then turn over, not giving it another thought. It was wiser, she decided, to wait, on the remote chance of something occurring.

"Stiffen up, Penge!" Lord Limpsfield jogged the Minister's arm. "Look alive, now. We're going."

Sir Norbury lurched towards the hall. His companion followed stodgily, not looking behind. The flat door banged, and as the reverberation shook the standard-lamp another noise became audible. From afar off it sounded, the faint, clear trilling of a telephone. Hers, or was it next door? Colin, perhaps. . . .

She sat listening. Blundell, close by her, did the same, one eye cocked aloft. For a minute or longer the ringing continued, then stopped. If it was Colin, he had given up trying to get her. Now he would wait till morning, by which time she would be dead. She found she could view her end with remarkable detachment, speculating on the method to be used, and hoping it would be so inexpertly brought about that it would be recognised as murder. In that case, although she had made a botch of things, Adrian might yet be saved. When she saw Blundell remove the heavy service revolver from his pocket and heft it thoughtfully, she spoke at last.

"You won't shoot me," she said. "You might get rid of my body, but what about the blood?"

He smiled at her.

"It's been done before," he replied, "with a clear verdict of suicide. Why should they question it in your case?"

In a flash she saw the Indian lying shot in a ditch. It was true, if her fingers were found closed round a revolver, no matter whose, if she had access to it, there would be little argument. Blundell would ring up the police, give details of her state of mind. If any one had reason for suicide, it was herself. . . .

"Still, it's not my choice," said her godfather amicably. "I'll make use of it only if you force me. Don't move, now, will you?"

Transferring the revolver to his left hand he walked crabwise, keeping his eyes on her, towards the brass-bound cellarette. On the far side of it he stooped over, still watching her, and removed something—she could not see what—from its interior. When he came back all she noticed was a small bulge in the right-hand pocket of his dinner coat, and a clumsily-carved teak-wood box which she knew usually stood on the table. This he extended to her, open.

"Have a cigarette?"

She refused.

"No?" He raised his odious brows till the furrows of yellowed skin ran into his low-growing mane, the creases in his cheeks deepened, and he began to chuckle. "Perhaps it's as well. I will, though."

He selected a cigar from his case, lit it, and drawing forward an arm-chair, lowered his thick body into it and leant forward, his knees almost touching hers, his eyes gloating over her with a sort of troll-like enjoyment infinitely revolting.

"Now, then, before doing anything hasty," he said, "let's clear up a few wrong notions, shall we? For a start, you think you've got the best of old Nick, don't you? If you were free, that is. You believe you'd only have to walk out of here, tell the first policeman I poisoned Rose Somervell and sandbagged your mother, and have a warrant out for my arrest. Not much!"

With arrogant contempt he spat out a bit of tobacco leaf and with his cigar more firmly clamped, continued.

"The truth is, you don't know anything, you couldn't prove anything, not if you swore on a stack of Bibles. I tell you this: Nothing can be proved against Nick Blundell—not in that line it can't. If I'm sending you out, it's for a different reason—the same reason I sent *her* out, and the other three. To-morrow morning, when you're found, Nick'll be as safe as houses. The execution will go forward per schedule, and not a human soul will ever know you were fool enough to spring a trap on me, except those two who've just gone out, and they won't split! No bloody fear!" He laughed till it was necessary to wipe the moisture from his eyes. "Not even when I tell them the little joke I played on 'em a short time back. They won't think it's funny, but they'll keep their mouths shut. Wouldn't be healthy not to. Well, then, that's one little matter disposed of. Now for the second."

He leant forward still closer, so that the smoke of his cigar puffed nauseously in his victim's white face. Some of his repulsive ease had gone. His old face had sharpened, there was a gleam in his three-cornered eyes Diana had never seen in them before.

"Rose," he said gruffly. "You're thinking she meant to hold this business over my head, blackmail me, or put me in quod. Nothing like it! You're miles out. Rose wouldn't have harmed a hair of my head. I wouldn't have harmed her, if she'd not been the woman she was. I want you to get this straight, so listen. It happened like this . . ."

CHAPTER THIRTY-NINE

IN THE sterilising room of the Prince Regent Hospital a cluster of night-nurses were drinking tea and trying on fancy headgear for the coming Benefit Ball when the street doors swung open violently and the house-surgeon strode in. A dark-eyed damsel settled the diamond tiara in which she was to wreck hearts as Catherine the Great, giggled provocatively, and called out to him:

"Oh, doctor! Did you run into your friend?"

"Friend? What friend?"

Annoyed, Colin frowned at the siren through clouds of steam. She pouted prettily and patted her permanent waves.

"How do I know? He just went out. I thought you might have met him in the tunnel." She giggled again. "Name of Herring, or Brill—or maybe it was Kipper."

"Not Bream?" the doctor fired at her.

"Shouldn't wonder. It was something fishy."

With an irritable snort Colin demanded if the caller had left a message. "Or have you forgotten that, too?"

"Only that he'd just got back to town and—my word, we are in a wax!" This last sotto voce, as the doctor glared, dived into the big lift, and clanged the doors. "Who's given him the bird, I'd like to know? Look, girls! Do I carry a snake, or—no, I'm wrong, that was Cleo. Whose bell is that? I knew it! Back to the grind," and sadly she exchanged the gems of an empress for a very stiff, starched cap.

Colin, on the topmost floor, burst without ceremony into a brilliantly-lit room where a dusty-haired man sat hunched over a microscope. Amongst the litter of test tubes and slides he planked down a packet of cigarettes.

"I've a job for you, Pilcher. Chuck that, and hump yourself!"

"No smoking," murmured the dusty-haired man. "It fogs the lens—and less row, while you're about it. Can't you see I'm counting?"

"I said 'Hump yourself' not 'Help yourself.' These gaspers are for analysis. I've a notion they're doped. Do look lively!"

With great deliberation the worker wrote some numerals on a pad, wiped his spectacles, and glanced indifferently at the packet.

"Gaspers? Too cheap a line. Nothing in it. Get yourself a drink—there's a bottle in the stink-cupboard—and clear off. These slides must be done by morning or there'll be a hell of a row. Eighteen, nineteen. . . ."

Colin leant over and spoke straight into the analyst's face.

"Do you want to save Somervell from hanging? Yes, save him. That's what I said. Answer me that!"

"Somervell?" Pilcher blinked, perturbed, and shook his shock of hair. "No go, old boy. Somervell didn't dope. What's the idea?"

"Get busy with these and I'll tell you. How long will it take?"

"M-m-m. . . . Useless. And I was hoping for bed one of these nights. Well, come back in a couple of hours. That do you?"

"It'll have to. Here, wait! Give me three of those fags. I'm going to smoke 'em—yes, smoke was the word—and when I've finished I want you to ask me to write my name on this envelope. Oh, and make me tell you how many notes you've written on that pad. That's all. Got it?"

"How many—? See here, are you thinking—?"

"Never mind what I'm thinking. Just you do as I say."

Colin placed one of his three cigarettes between his lips and lit it. The other two, together with his matches and fountain-pen, he laid on the table, then seated himself and inhaled deeply. Pilcher resignedly polished his microscope lens and proceeded with his peering. From time to time he paused to jot down a figure, or to fit in a new slide.

Soon Colin felt an agreeable drowsiness steal over him. Slight though it was, it was sufficient to make him regard his frantic rush that evening as a maudlin waste of energy. Comfortably he eyed the clock on the wall. In an hour, he reflected, Hull would be back from his barristers' dinner. Yes, Hull would be at home, and could give his opinion on this will. Hull would be home. . . .

He yawned, noticed his cigarette was all but ended, and lit a second from the stump.

"Ladbroke! What ho! Were you napping?"

Colin jerked forward in his chair, rubbed his eyes, and after an appreciable interval replied testily: "Napping? My hat! I'm smo—" He glanced at his right hand, sat musing another long moment, and muttered: "No, I've smoked the lot. Unless you pinched one?"

For answer Pilcher pointed to three stumps on the floor.

"I've called you three times," he said.

"You're a liar. I heard you—once."

"Have it your own way. Is this writing yours?"

Colin stared at the signature held before him. It was his own.

"Now, then," resumed Pilcher, "how many time did I put down a note?"

"Oh, I kept count! Three times since I sat down."

Pilcher showed him nine entries, ringed round to separate them from the rest. Colin looked, remained seated, and presently began rubbing his hands together. His skin was very dry. Slowly he got up, went to the mantel where a small mirror hung, and studied his pupils.

"Slight dilation." He counted his pulse. "John," he said, yawning heavily, "I rather believe I'm right. You've heard of this before, haven't you?"

Pilcher nodded.

"I've not come across it, though. You still want the analysis?"

"Obviously. God knows where it'll get us. Maybe nowhere, but . . . Hell! I must get into the air. What's the time now?"

"Ten to twelve."

"Is it? That's hard to believe, but—yes, you're right. I'll be back later."

He descended unsteadily to the basement, found some lukewarm tea which had the one virtue of strength, and by means of it cleared his head sufficiently to venture forth.

Reaching Pelham Crescent, South Kensington, he found Michael Hull just in and waiting for him. As he had expected, the sight of Rose Somervell's former will roused little enthusiasm.

"It's evidence of nothing," said the barrister wearily. "Even if we knew for certain that the beneficiary was aware of its existence, don't you see it would still be worthless?"

"Suppose we could suggest that the victim in signing the second will was in total ignorance of what manner of document it was? That she died under the delusion that this will held good?"

Hull's eyebrows beetled incredulously.

"Impossible! How could such a suggestion carry weight?"

"I'll show you," said Colin, and related all he knew and suspected with regard to the cigarettes. "If the test comes out as I anticipate," he went on, "it will provide us with the very type of explanation we want. It may even give us a solution for another puzzle. Yes," as Hull put on his glasses and stared at him, "I'm referring to a certain alibi, supported by two well-known men. Oh, I don't say we can prove it! I'm only hoping to demonstrate scientifically that the thing could have been done."

Hull rose and walked about the comfortable study, his pale skin lined with worry. He stopped to demand how Diana Lake could have been drugged with cigarettes of her own purchasing.

"Once the brand was known it would only be a matter of opportunity to remove as many as one chose and substitute doped ones which would look and smell the same. The object in Diana's case? I can't see that it concerns us, if we can definitely show—"

The bell rang. Colin looked interrogatively at his host.

"Bream," murmured the barrister. "There was a message saying he'd call."

Bream it was. He looked tired, but strangely keyed-up, also relieved to see Colin.

"I don't know if my news will do any damage," he began, "but here it is for what it's worth. You remember the S.O.S. messages I was inserting in the Agony columns? I got one answer—of all places, from the Northumberland County jail. It came from the resident physician, and said that a prisoner in the infirmary had a statement to make. I went north to see him, and when I found him a wreck from morphia—he'd been jugged for stealing a doctor's bag—I was prepared to discount all I got from him. Here, Dr. Ladbroke, is where you can help me. Does the name Woodford mean anything to you?"

"Woodford?" Colin frowned. "You don't mean an assistant the Prince Regent sacked last September for pinching drugs?"

"Then you do know him! What more can you tell me?"

"He worked in our research department, and handled supplies—a sharp chap, very obliging, but he went to bits through doping. We didn't bring a charge, just let him go."

"That tallies," said Bream. "Now, listen: Woodford says that in August he carried some reports round to Dr. Somervell, who was laid up at his boarding-house with a bronchial cold. That sitting by the bed was a woman who during the few minutes he stopped to chat made some reference to the man she worked for—a solicitor. Follow me? Well, it so happened that Woodford that same morning had been very urgently asked to supply the name of a competent lawyer. He noted down this one's address, and passed it on to the applicant."

"Who was—?" demanded Colin, as Bream paused.

"A pub acquaintance of Woodford's. Abdulmajid Haji, whose girl had just died accusing him of having done her in, and who was in the hell of a stew for fear of arrest."

Hull's eyeglass clattered to his shirt-front. Colin's white face grew more intent.

"Go on! And then?"

"Haji begged Woodford to arrange an interview for him with Nicholas Blundell. Woodford did so, although Blundell was not over-eager, as criminal affairs were not in his line. I repeat, Woodford arranged an interview, but he doesn't know, or says he doesn't, if it actually took place. Haji swore not, and after the inquest, which exonerated him, he gave

Woodford a wide berth. A month later, Woodford, in trouble himself, appealed to Haji for a loan to enable him to leave town. Haji refused, declaring he was broke; but the next day he came round, handed Woodford ten pounds, and Woodford cleared out."

The two listeners looked at each other, then at Bream.

"Just my thought," said the agent. "A lad who's stranded, borrowing from all and sundry, suddenly turns generous to the tune of ten quid—why? Not on his own account. He'd nothing to fear. Was he deputed to help his friend out of town because that friend represented the sole link between himself and some one who as early as September strongly objected to having his name brought up in connection with a case of suspected poisoning? I can't prove it—but I believe it was."

In the same breath the barrister and the doctor demanded details of the Frieda Klapp inquest. Bream read from his notebook.

"Directly, her death was due to heart failure—which, in turn, was set down to acute gastro-enteritis, from a cause which did not appear. Maybe it was the tinned salmon she had on her own admission—Haji's word for it—eaten at her last meal, though the salmon could not be traced, since she had not said where she had it. The doses administered to her had emptied her digestive organs of pretty well all contents. Don't lose sight of that. It's important."

"Anything more?" inquired Colin keenly.

"Stomach-lining showed extreme hyperaemia, modified since death—also, a slight brown staining. Some mucous was present. The membrane of the duodenum was likewise inflamed, with a few dark patches which had become mortified. Heart flaccid, brain healthy—"

"Why don't you say it? If aconite had been found, we should have an exact replica of the Somervell report. Am I right?"

"To a T. Taken all in all," said Bream shrewdly, "we may call it a most unsatisfactory verdict, but one which could not possibly be upset."

Colin asked if Woodford had furnished any further details.

"He did," replied Bream quietly, "though I suspect what I got was a well-edited version. He's acquainted with the term 'accessory before the fact,' and is consequently in a mortal funk. Still, as you said of him, he's an obliging chap."

CHAPTER FORTY

WHEN exchanges were complete, ultimate proof—or the hope of it—still seemed unobtainable. Even granting a reprieve could be secured, the path might remain blocked. Bream, nevertheless, went with Colin to the hospital to hear the analyst's report on the cigarettes. Colin scanned it with triumph.

"It's what I expected. You see, don't you, how the trick was played?"

Bream did see; but the past was past. As he pointed out, it would still be putting forward what was hardest to believe in—that Blundell hoodwinked a woman into willing money not to him, but away from him.

"Not but what I can think of a reason for his doing that identical thing. It's simply that I see no chance of bringing it home to him—none. I doubt if the Yard itself . . . and yet, that's an idea. . . ."

"You mean get the Yard to take an interest?"

"I don't know if I can. This dope might work it. Yes, Headcorn would see how it might affect the alibi in the Fairlamb case. You'll let me borrow this report? Thanks. And will you speak to Miss Lake at once about our plan for catching Blundell red-handed over the smokes? I think I'll do well to keep behind scenes."

When Bream had gone Pilcher made a communication which sent Colin whirling excitedly on him.

"What! You'll swear to that?"

"No. It's my impression; but we may be able to turn up the bill. Leave it to me," and shouldering on a disreputable overcoat he prepared to seek a well-earned rest.

"It would provide us with a strong link in the chain," thought Colin. "And God knows we need strong links." About to leave the building, he remembered his promise to Diana, but wondered if he ought to disturb her as late as this for news which might only lead to more disappointment. Then he recalled that she had been deprived to-night of her usual soporific, and drunk additional coffee. Quite likely she was waiting now, on tenterhooks, for his call. He turned to the telephone and gave her number.

Five whole minutes passed before he hung up, and during that time he had heard her bell ringing steadily. It seemed extraordinary that with an extension beside her bed she could sleep through the noise. He stood debating with himself, vaguely uneasy. Then he strode firmly out. There could be no danger. She would not dream of letting Blundell know about the will she had found, while she herself remained ignorant of having been doped. He would stop worrying, and push off to bed.

A sensible decision, considering it was just two o'clock, and he must be breakfasting at eight; yet in the street his steps lagged and halted, as though an invisible leash were straining in the opposite direction. Twice he stopped, twice went on again in the direction of his flat in Gordon Square. A lone taxi prowled past him. He let it go, and then, as its red tail-light rounded the corner, he sprinted after it, shouting like a lunatic.

"Queen's Close, Kensington," he panted. "Drive like hell. . . ."

Number Six was dark from basement to mansard. Now he stood on the stone steps listening intently and hearing no sound he felt so foolish he was of half a mind to go away again. Nothing could be wrong. The bedroom window was open, the curtains behind it fluttering in the cold breeze. Diana was sleeping very soundly, that was all. It would be cruel to wake her; but he pressed his finger on the button still marked "Somervell" and kept it there.

Each moment he expected Diana's face to appear at the window above, but all remained as before. Suddenly his heart began to thump. He rang the caretakers' bell, and after long waiting saw a muffled form at the area door. A man's voice, clogged with sleep and resentment, demanded his business. He explained—and even to his own ears the words sounded asinine. The man grunted with disapproval, disappeared, and was replaced by his wife, who, shivering in a raincoat, seemed to share his view.

"I can't see any call to disturb the young lady, sir—except it's important. Why, it's gone two! I couldn't, if I was a mind to, not having no key. Not any more I haven't."

"It is important!" urged Colin. "If she can't hear a telephone that rings in her ear, don't you see what it may mean? Look here!" He leant over the railings. "If anything's happened, I'll hold you responsible. Does that move you, or must I fetch a policeman?"

The woman stared, shuffled reluctantly up the steps.

"I suppose we'll have to wake poor Mr. Blundell," she grumbled. "But you must deal with him, for I won't. His cook's got a spare key. There!" she pushed the Blundell button. "Now, sir, I'll leave you to it." And she scuttled back to her basement.

It was the last thing Colin had wanted, yet now the bell was rung his worst fear was that no one was in to answer it. He rang again—long, persistent peals, keeping his eye glued to the upper windows. It seemed to him that the entire house was untenanted—and a sickness attacked the pit of his stomach; but suddenly, without warning sound, a puff of warm air blew against his legs. He started, lowered his eyes, and saw that the big door had opened on darkness so dense that it took him a second to discern the thick-set figure, clad in trousers and dressing-gown, blocking the gap.

"Who's there?" It was the gruff, kindly drawl once heard in the witness-stand, and again at the close of the trial. "Doctor Ladbroke? Why, so it is!"

Colin stepped quickly inside, but before he could explain, the solicitor switched on fights and apologised for seeming rather fuddled. His man was away, and the fact was he himself had just waked up.

"It took me a bit of time to get on some clothes. I trust you've not had the deuce of a wait? Come along in,"—and he led the way hospitably towards the door of his flat, where no light showed.

"I was worried about Miss Lake," said Colin, "or I shouldn't have knocked you up at this time of night. We both know the state of mind she's in. When I rang up and got no answer—"

"Mind the step up," interrupted Blundell, turning on his own hall lights. "That's quite all right, it's no hardship, not in the least. Now, then, what's this you're telling me? You rang up and . . . In here, doctor, where it's warmer."

Against his will, Colin found himself being shepherded into a lofty, book-lined room stale with tobacco smoke. A few coals still glowed red. Blundell stirred them fussily, keeping up a garrulous patter.

"Don't mind if I seem a bit slow on the up-take. Fact is, I hadn't very long dropped off, after a visitation from some clients who stayed till all hours. Beastly cold you must be. Let me offer you something to thaw you. Ah, here's the whisky—and a clean glass, by luck. Don't jump, now," he chuckled as a tinkling tune played a few bars. "Scotch, you see—very appropriate, eh? Say when."

"It's the key to her flat I'm after," said Colin, declining the drink. "You've got one, I understand. If I could just run up and make sure—"

"Key? Oh, to be sure, Diana's spare key!" Blundell scratched his head. "Certainly, there's an idea . . . if I can lay hands on it. Yes, my servants keep one. Unfortunately, they're both off duty to-night, and I don't quite know . . . Think there's any need? What I mean is, if the poor child's sleeping, is it a good thing to wake her, maybe give her a fright into the bargain?"

"My fear is she's not there at all," said Colin distinctly. "It seemed to me impossible she could sleep through all that ringing."

It struck him that Blundell's denseness was slightly exaggerated. This long pause, the vague alarm in his face, first irritated then roused his suspicions. Was he being put off for some definite purpose?

"Not there? Surely you don't think that!" The solicitor tinkered again with the fire, laid aside the poker, and squinted up at his visitor in troubled fashion. "See here, doctor," he demanded bluntly, "I've not seen her since this morning. She was all right then. Have you talked with her since?"

"Yes, and I felt uneasy," lied Colin. "That's why I'm here now. If you could just get me that key?"

"Good Lord! You don't imagine—?"

"I don't want to imagine, Mr. Blundell. Suppose we look it up there, that's all."

For the first time the solicitor's face turned full towards him. One hairy hand fondled a chin on which Colin now noticed a fiery red scratch. Razor cut? Too jagged. With a shiver, Colin wondered if the owner was trying to conceal it. That dressing-gown too, so closely bundled about the neck. . . .

"By jove, yes! That would set both our minds at rest, wouldn't it? You'll think me doddering—but the fact is, what you say is rather upsetting. You're the doctor, though. Ha, ha! Obviously we must make certain, or we'll both go on stewing, eh? I'll have a hunt now for that key. It can't be far." Blundell reached a carved box from the far end of the big table and flung it open carelessly. "Smoke, doctor?"

There was a similar box under Colin's eye. Inwardly alert, Colin noted the two compartments exhibited for his choice—fat Turkish, common Virginias like his own—and selected one of the latter. Blundell tendered a match, watched solicitously till the tip glowed, and with a cheery, "I'll not be two ticks," bustled from the room.

Instantly Colin started to extinguish his gasper; but in the act he paused, examining the moist end narrowly. His breath came short and sharp, his eyes roamed the room from the hideous carpet to the bookshelves and back in a circle. At the same time an odour which all along he had absently noticed caused him to sniff the air.

So faint, scarcely perceptible through the heavy cigar smoke—yet, God, how familiar! He studied the cigarette again, stuck it in his pocket and stole very softly out.

On tiptoe he followed a short passage to a doorway brightly illuminated from within, halted, and gazed in upon a white-tiled kitchen. Two yards distant, his broad back turned, Blundell was standing, motionless. Waiting—for what?

"Shall I help you hunt, Mr. Blundell?"

The solicitor wheeled suddenly and with a brief flash of startled annoyance quickly suppressed. The fronts of his dressing-gown fell apart disclosing two inches of stiff shirt front and a black bow tie.

"What's that? Oh, I've found it!" Covered to the chin again, Blundell displayed a Yale key. "It was hanging on the dresser; but I keep asking myself if we aren't being idiots. Tell me, doctor, what gave you this notion? Was it something she—"

"Thank you."

Colin snatched the key and tore from the flat. At the top of the stairs he unlocked Diana's door, clicked on the lights, and the next moment was peering in on a bed tumbled but empty. Wasting not a second, he dashed to the dressing-room, then on to the bath. Empty again—and likewise the clothes cupboard. As he plunged back into the drawing-room Blundell met him.

"What's up? You don't mean she's not in her room?" Without answering Colin pushed past him to the dining-room, and on to the small kitchen, the pantry, the passage cupboards, all alike deserted, with not the slightest trace of disorder. Vague thoughts surged in his mind. He would call a policeman, have Blundell's flat searched; but as he formed this tentative resolution his eye fell on one door yet unopened. The maid's room, unused since Petty's departure. Blundell appeared, anxiously prowling. With one accord the two sniffed at an odour totally unlike the one Colin had scented below. It crept nauseously, to the nostrils—coming from this room?—

"Gas!"

Colin scarcely heard the dry whisper, "Is it locked?" But the same thought sickened him as he tried the knob. It yielded—and into reeking gloom he hurled himself towards a form lying prone before an unlit gas fixture. Two seconds more and out he staggered, heavily laden, lungs bursting.

"Air!" he coughed. "Throw open every window! Wide!"

He laid Diana on her own bed, swept the curtains apart to let in a draught, and without pause began frantic efforts at artificial respiration. The face upturned was paper-white under the tousled blackness of hair, every inch of the body clammily cold. He worked with sweat pouring into his eyes, cursing under his breath.

"Unconscious?" a voice beside him muttered quaveringly.

"Dead," snapped Colin, but suspended his labours long enough to note a swift contraction in the other's pupils.

"Oh, my God!"

To the worker's ears the cry held an infinitude of relief and—triumph.

CHAPTER FORTY-ONE

BREAM reached Queen's Close to find lights blazing but no one in sight till he entered the upper flat.

"Not quite," the house-surgeon answered his frightened question. "I told him she was gone, and so she was, practically speaking. You've fetched the strychnine?"

Bream produced a parcel and in a whisper asked where Blundell was now. Engrossed with the injection, Colin shook an indifferent head.

"I sent him to boil water while I rang you. He was so long I had to go for it myself—and he was slumped in a chair, as though he'd had a stroke. I left him there."

"What's the answer?" inquired the agent significantly.

"Not suicide," was the stern reply. "But if she does die, I don't dream of proving it. God, if I'd had help! He's been given ample opportunity to get rid of certain articles, also to change out of his dress-shirt; but I saw it, he hadn't been to bed. Look to the coffee on the stove. I'll be wanting it—with any luck."

The kitchen was empty, the coffee unpercolated, for the simple reason that the electric current was not on. Grimly Bream set it going, then inspected the maid's room, which still stank noisomely of gas, but of nothing else. Practice makes perfect, he reflected, as he locked the door and pocketed the key.

He found the doctor tensely awaiting the result of the strychnine. Informed about the coffee Colin nodded.

"It's things like that which clinch matters—for you and me. I'll show you another." And pulling Bream into the drawing-room he displayed an empty cigarette-box. "You see? I left it with twenty of my own in it. Thinking they were the doped ones, he took 'em off—and hearing my ring, he dumped the lot into his especial box. I know, because he offered me one—and, by the grace of God, I noticed this."

He produced from his pocket a half-smoked cigarette with a V-shaped snag at the unlit end.

"I did that," he explained, "with my nail, tearing open the packet. Take charge of it, will you?"

"Sharp work! He hoped, I take it, to get you mildly fuddled so he could detain you longer than you realised?"

"Exactly. The gas must be given time to finish her. He nearly managed it. It's more than likely she won't recover."

In silence they regained the bedside. If life still lingered in the unconscious girl, Bream could detect no sign of it. Answering his unspoken thought, Colin muttered jerkily:

"If she dies, it'll be all up with Somervell. Oh, we can start a hue and cry, but you know, as I do, it will come to nothing. Just one more human sacrifice, to cover up—what?"

Bream slipped softly back to the drawing-room and put through a call to Scotland Yard.

Diana did not die. Six hours later she opened her eyes, half-recognised Colin, and had to be firmly restrained from attempting to speak. Her weakness was so great she drifted off immediately, to wake at midday. This time memory began to revive, and with a terrible fear in her eyes she tried to sit up.

"It's all right," Colin soothed her; "plenty of time, you know. Yes, I mean that," he added, for he realised what thought was in her mind. "To-day's only Thursday. Now, then, it's too soon to talk, but if you wanted to ask me something?"

"Has he been caught?" she whispered, her voice a rough croak he had to stoop to hear.

A great surge of joy swept through Colin's fatigued body.

"Then he—Blundell—can be arrested?" he asked tensely.

She pondered this in bewildered anxiety, her eyes straying up at the rose canopy of the bed.

"I—don't know," faltered the hoarse voice. "How did I get here? I was down below—in his library."

He saw that she had no knowledge whatever of the gas which had so nearly caused her death. Stroking her hand, he leant over her, his tired eyes burning into hers.

"Tell me only this. Was it chloroform?" he demanded.

"Yes. But how—?"

"I smelt it. Quiet, now, or you'll be sick. I want you to sleep some more. Later on we'll have it all out."

She must not suspect that her story might be successfully countered by the one her godfather had had ample time to concoct. The fact was, Blundell was still the incalculable quantity—at large, aware that his victim still clung to life, at any moment likely to be back with his hypocritical solicitude, his disarming appearance of a man broken by shock. Till a statement was obtained he could not be placed under restraint. In the meantime, he was a potential danger, for which reason Colin had refused to allow another physician on the scene, or a nurse. Strangers might be bribed or hoodwinked into giving information. Diana must be safeguarded from all interference. Colin, holding the fort alone, had agreed with Bream on a policy, in pursuance of which he now waited till his charge had fallen into a doze, then shut the bedroom door quietly and made a telephone call from the drawing-room.

"Get in here as inconspicuously as you can," he was saying, when a slight sound in the passage made him alter his tone, and without perceptible break continue, "Oxygen. . . . Yes, and as quick as you can; though it's hardly any use. She'll just go out. They seldom rally in these cases."

He replaced the receiver, stepped briskly into the hall, and saw Blundell making quietly for Diana's door. Firmly he placed his hand on the thick-set arm.

"Don't go in, sir. I've asked a colleague to come round. You'd like that, wouldn't you?"

"I heard what you said," replied Blundell, with working features. "There's been no change?"

"None. It's only a matter of time, I'm afraid. You'd like to see her?" And he opened the door.

Blundell peered in at the motionless quilt above which a deathly-white cheek could be seen. His lips moved uncertainly, he bowed his big head, and with a gesture of clumsy dignity, thanked Colin and withdrew. When the lower flat door had closed, Colin went back to the telephone, finished his interrupted communication, and returned to sit beside the bed.

At nine that evening Diana was given tea. Her pulse was approaching its normal beat, and she now insisted on being heard. Colin called softly to Bream and Inspector Headcorn, who were playing double patience in the drawing-room; they entered quietly, notebooks in hand, and took seats.

"This must be short and sweet, you know," Colin warned them in an undertone. "Just the bare facts, understand?" To Bream he whispered: "Both those entrances fastened? Chain on the front door, bolt drawn on the other?"

Bream assured him that the two doors had been seen to. The cupboard one was locked and bolted this morning when he examined it.

"I don't suppose it's been tampered with since?"

"Oh, no! He's had no opportunity. We may as well begin."

The curtains had been drawn, the one rose-shaded lamp on the bed-table shed a softening light over the four sharpened faces. Diana, wrapped in a white shawl—her dressing-gown had been got rid of because of its reek—lay with her head propped against two lace-edged pillows. Ill though she looked and was, she was steady and collected. Her sunken grey eyes held what had long been absent from them—positive hope. Colin felt her pulse again and spoke to her gently.

"Suppose," he said, "you begin with going to bed last night. Tell us why you got up."

She drew a quivering breath.

"I heard a car outside. His voice—and two others. It was about one o'clock. I looked down from that window, and just below I saw . . . oh, my God!"

She gasped and stiffened, staring straight ahead past the broad shoulders of the Inspector. The three men faced round. Framed in the dressing-room door, against the dusk of egg-blue walls, Nicholas Blundell faced the company, a service revolver levelled at the speaker's forehead. Amidst a torrent of oaths two shots thundered, the top of Diana's head seemed to burst, and for her it was as though a black curtain blotted out demoniac turmoil.

Some one's foot caught the lamp cord. The alabaster vase which formed the stand fell to the floor with the crack of a splintered bulb. In darkness, thick with acrid fumes, a struggle had begun, three men against an unseen beast of the jungle. Headcorn reeled from a blow like that of a heavyweight boxer. A third shot grazed Bream in the thigh, and simultaneously Colin felt a left punch of staggering force glide off his temple as he made futile grabs at empty space. Blundell, solicitor-at-law, was a maniac, obsessed with but one desire—to sell his freedom at the highest possible price.

Colin flicked the wall-button, and as other lights flared on looked in agony towards the bed. With a sigh of thanksgiving he saw that Diana had collapsed only from shock, though the two neat holes drilled in the padded head-board level with her hair showed the narrowness of her escape. Two more shots remained undischarged. Headcorn, amidst the wreckage of a Sheraton chair, grappled with his assailant, whose right hand still brandished the revolver. Neither was gaining the least head-way. The Inspector panted from the blows rained on chest and head, and blood poured from a cut above his eye. Bream was nowhere to be seen. Stooping, Colin dragged the lamp-plug from its wall-socket, and firmly grasping the alabaster stand aimed a mighty blow at the solicitor's hairy knuckles, which just eluded him. As he took aim again a fourth bullet ploughed the ceiling, and though he had dodged in time, the other fist, planted powerfully in his solar plexus, sent him drunkenly against the bed, too dazed to know whose fingers twitched the lamp from his hold.

"That's done it!"

It was Bream's voice, shrill with triumph. Blinking, Colin beheld the private agent just taking a third deft turn with the lamp-flex round two thrashing legs. He lent a hand in the capture, no easy job even now. Ten seconds more, and Inspector Headcorn sat astride the heaving chest, wiped sweat and blood from his eyes, and gasped in the formal phrase-ology of his profession:

"Nicholas Godfrey Blundell, I arrest you in the name of the law—for criminal assault and attempted murder—and it is my duty to warn you that anything you say will be used in evidence!"

CHAPTER FORTY-TWO

"Odd, in a way, how so much of this affair started right here in the Prince Regent's Hospital."

Saying this, Colin Ladbroke ran a critical eye over the green-walled private room which was Diana's temporary abode, gave a keener glance to the array of bottles on the mantel, and smiled at his patient, who was regarding him in mystification.

"Do you mean because Adrian worked here?" she asked curiously.

"Oh, Lord, no! Haven't I developed that feature of it? Never mind. I'll tack it on to our coming symposium. Yes, it began here—and here it will end quite soon now, for I hear our company just getting out of the lift. What's wrong?" as a sudden flutter agitated the neat bedclothes. "Lost something?"

"My powder-puff, silly! Don't you dare open that door till I've found it."

"I see." He nodded dryly. "Feeling pretty bucked with yourself, aren't you?"

Not entirely, as it happened. Adrian on the threshold brought back painfully the memory of the rift which, during her tribulations, she had scarcely troubled about. In a crucial moment she had doubted him. He had been hurt in a vital spot, and however much he might pretend, the wound unwittingly dealt him might never be quite healed. Her first glimpse of him, she felt, would be the test, thinking which she tried to subdue the sudden, nervous tremor of her heart, which on the least provocation, now, behaved in a tiresome fashion.

The host was welcoming his three self-conscious guests.

"Well, well! Are we all met? Flock in, and sit where you can."

In tramped Inspector Headcorn, a patch over his eye, but looking preternaturally smart in a tight blue serge suit with a carnation in his button-hole. On his heels came Mortimer Bream, natty, but unnoticeable as the grey linoleum on the floor. Behind these two, hanging back a little with detached diffidence, appeared Adrian, newly released from the condemned cell.

His face had sharpened, and he had lost most of his nut-brown tan, but otherwise he seemed exactly the same as before, quiet, a shade preoccupied, his brown eyes thoughtful behind his spectacles, a muscle in his cheek twitching sensitively. Diana hardly dared look at him. The hand she gave him was cold, and she was quick to notice he did not retain it beyond a single, brief pressure. A leaden lump came in her throat, her eyes misted over; and then, as he turned away she saw what somehow might be the omen she was seeking. He was wearing his dark-red tie. . . .

"Drinks, drinks!" carolled Colin, aware of the awkward tension, if not of its cause. "Here, jail-bird, shove some ice into this shaker while I do a spot of uncorking. Inspector, what's on your mind? You're looking dashed portentous."

Clearing his throat rumblingly, Headcorn asked if Miss Lake had been informed of the latest sensation.

"Not yet. I was leaving it for you. Oh, you can spill it now! She's well equal to this particular shock."

"Shock?" echoed Diana, trembling in spite of herself. "Oh! What is it now?"

"No need to brace yourself," said the Inspector, with a comforting glance. "At noon yesterday, directly your recovery had been announced in the papers, the Minister of Arterial Highways, Sir Norbury Penge, put a bullet through his brain."

The full history of events was not yet compiled. Minor phases of it might remain apocryphal; but the following version, pieced together from various sources and supplemented by later discoveries, may be taken as a fairly accurate one:

Rose Somervell, for some weeks prior to her death, had believed that her devoted Nick was hiding from her a matter of importance, and that this matter involved Nick's friendship with Lord Limpsfield and Sir

Norbury Penge, who had begun to pay frequent visits to the flat below hers, but whom she was never asked to meet. She pried and wheedled, but was put off in the most unsatisfactory, and, to her, humiliating fashion. She made guesses, and sometimes her stabs came perilously near the mark. Finally, from Vichy, whither she had been packed to get her out of the way, she wrote glibly of her acquaintance with the one man to whom the least mention of her suspicions would have proved fatal—Sir Francis Dugdale, secretary to the Home Secretary, and—by the devil's own luck—Limpsfield's bitterest political opponent. As yet, be it understood, she knew nothing. Well, then, she must continue to know nothing. Future conferences, hitherto so safely conducted in Blundell's library, must, on her return, be transferred elsewhere. Rose, with her monkeyish fondness for meddling, must be given no leeway.

Here we must digress to the Indian, Haji. Herbert Woodford, then employed at the Prince Regent's Hospital, Gower Street, had in his statement declared that the student, during public-house chats, had confided his acute worry over the girl, Frieda Klapp. She was being run by Haji for disreputable purposes, and now she was not only holding out on him, but sucking him dry under threat of writing his strict father in Bombay a full account of the situation. The talks between Woodford and the harassed Indian turned upon the removal of troublesome persons with least risk of exposure, and Woodford jokingly paraded the medical knowledge he had picked up at his post. Aconite was advocated. Easy to obtain, equally easy to administer in food, it could kill in an apparently natural manner, and—more important—would defy detection in human remains provided no immediate examination was made. Woodford fetched along a specimen of the cultivated plant to show what it was like, explaining that the wild variety was far more deadly. Haji, though admitting he had seen monkshood growing in India, professed ignorance of its properties. He asked many questions, and was obligingly answered.

Woodford made another interesting communication. By experiment he had learned to impregnate smoking tobacco with scopolomin, and following a demonstration he agreed to supply his friend with a quantity of the drug, filched from the hospital stores. At this point matters rested, till, out of the blue, Frieda Klapp died, with her last conscious gasp screaming that her Indian protector had poisoned her. She was heard, gossip buzzed, and an order was given for an inquest.

Haji had carefully given his victim the emetic and dose of oil which could reasonably be counted on to eliminate from her system all solid matter; but faced with an inquiry, he went to pieces and frantically sought legal advice. Woodford obtained the name of Nicholas Blundell, who, before consenting to help Haji, exacted a complete confession. The demoralised Indian made a clean breast of his crime, not omitting to mention the drugged cigarettes which for days before death had kept Frieda in a state of quiescent torpor. The effect of the scopolomin was to soothe her and made her forget from moment to moment impressions just received. She was too lethargic to write the letter she was threatening to write, and if she noticed the bitter ingredient in her curry she forgot it directly. If she had not soon afterwards felt too ill to continue smoking she would not have uttered her strident accusations, the result of a general suspicion lurking in her brain.

Abdulmajid babbled—and Blundell listened, shrewdly concluding there was probably little cause for panic, so long as the post-mortem was delayed long enough for the putrefactive elements in the body to neutralise the poisonous principle. Whether or not he pulled wires to ensure this delay cannot positively be known, but as the August Bank Holiday with its suspension of activity occurred just then, the chances are he sat tight and let matters take a normal course. What concerned him personally was that he had been presented gratis with a safe, practically-tested method of death-dealing, to keep up his sleeve and use if and when occasion should require, and, in addition, he had got absolute power over an unscrupulous youth, whom he might, if he so desired, employ as a tool. Advising Haji against allowing the drug to be found in his possession, he took over the latter's supply of scopolomin and kept it, first learning exactly how the stuff had been used. Already, no doubt, he realised that under certain circumstances drugged tobacco might serve him to advantage. To prevent Haji from slipping away from him, he made generous advances of cash—and, ever cautious, he saw to it that Woodford, the go-between, was given the wherewithal to quit London. He may not, thus early, have been definitely plotting what presently became a necessity. He did, however, foresee that Woodford could, in possible circumstances, represent an embarrassment.

We now come to Rose Somervell's return from France. By chance, or design, it took place a day sooner than expected, and Blundell was not warned. Travelling with Petty by the late boat-train Rose reached Queen's Close at eleven at night, saw Limpsfield's car before the door, and instantly thought of the secret which was being kept from her. Very likely at this period the inner staircase was freely used by both parties. At all events, it was open now, and into it, like a naughty child, the old actress promptly slipped to see what she could overhear. Just as she had anticipated, a three-cornered conference was in progress. Half-gloating, half-angry, she managed to glean quite enough to make her wait till the clients—clients, forsooth!—had departed so that she could flaunt her triumph in Nick's face, and haul him over the coals for his shabby treatment of her.

Rose's moral fibres were not shocked. Possibly she did not fully grasp what the conspiracy meant, or how, if so much as a breath of it got abroad, its three principals would each be ruined. What she did see was that Nick, her trusted crony, had hit on a marvellous road to wealth, and not let her profit by it. Safe Consols—bah! She would show him—and forthwith she did, telling him straight out that unless he lifted her capital from his humdrum, small-paying investments and put it into the glittering Penge scheme she would appeal to Lord Limpsfield himself and demand her share of the spoils. She would have done this—Blundell did not doubt it—and if denied participation she would grumble loudly to every one she knew, not excluding her new lion, Sir Francis Dugdale, whom she proposed to invite for dinner the moment he was at home. However, she could not be permitted to enter into the scheme, for the truth was that, satisfied or disgruntled, *Rose Somervell simply could not hold her tongue.* Shrewd in some ways, she was notoriously stupid in this. She gossiped, she prattled. There never had been any trusting her, and since she had grown a constant brandy-tippler any prudence she might once have possessed was gone beyond recall. It was a fact Blundell had to face. As to his feelings, nothing need now be said. Suffice it to state, the situation was desperate. Rose must be suppressed, the only question being how?

Blundell realised he must make no hasty move, purely because of the will Rose had made—or told him she had made—in his favour. Once the forty-odd thousand pounds would have been extremely desirable. Now, with a huge fortune at stake and a life-ambition dangling precariously, he regarded it merely as an obstacle to be cleared from his path. Unless that damnable document were destroyed or rescinded, suspicion, if a slip should occur, would inevitably point to himself. He thought of the scopolomin and saw a way out of his difficulty. By drugging Rose's cigarettes he could with impunity make a thorough search for the will. He experimented, tried the cigarettes on himself, and kept Rose supplied with them. Promptly she began to doze off at odd moments; but although he hunted high and low the will was not to be found. Did it mean no such will existed, or that it was hidden where he would never discover it? He did not know, and he dared not inquire. He therefore boldly decided to guard against a will turning up after the death by seeing Rose's money bequeathed to some one else, thus cancelling any previous disposition of property and, in the event of complications, providing a scape-goat on whom suspicion would conveniently fall. He thought of Joe Somervell's impecunious son, at present in London. Who would suit his purpose better than Adrian, of whom Rose had once been mildly fond? Only on the off-chance would harm come to him. If all went well, the young man would merely gather in a welcome windfall.

The legal brain worked quickly. Rose's interference and threats had been jokingly dealt with her feathers smoothed by the assurance that all along she had been intended to benefit by the scheme once developments justified it. She was made to see that if a word of the venture got out the high prices Penge was paying for land would be so cut down that profits would be conspicuously lessened. Her greed could appreciate this argument. Solemnly she promised to whisper no syllable—and she did do her best, though there was reason to fear that the very next evening she let slip a mysterious hint or so to her friend, Margaret Fairlamb, over a glass of brandy. It was her last meeting with Margaret—her last with any one outside the household, except Adrian Somervell, who, within a few days, was forcibly brought to her notice. By this time she was placidly subjugated to the scopolomin. Like a sleek cat, she browsed and forgot, undisturbed by the plot to rob her of her life.

She drowsily resented Nick's impetuous presentation of her former stepson, whom she did not at all care to see. However, vanity woke when reason slumbered; she was flattered by what she considered a tribute to her still-potent charms, and inclined to encourage Adrian's visits. Blundell arranged everything—the theatre party, the week-end at his cottage, even the call at tea-time just before the will was to be signed. It was he who wrote the note of invitation, wording it in such a way that the recipient need not answer it. It was not hard to imitate Rose's handwriting so that it would pass muster with a man who had not seen it for ten years. He knew that the note would not be preserved, and that if Adrian did come Rose would believe he came of his own accord. Rose herself gave the verbal invitation to Sunday lunch, Blundell having suggested it.

On the Friday before the appointed day Blundell brought Rose what he represented to be a transfer of stock, the first step towards her sharing in the new venture. She had signed many transfers, none of which she ever troubled to read. Without putting on her glasses she complacently signed her name; and she was so well drugged after a long succession of cigarettes as to retain no memory of there having been two witnesses in the room instead of the customary one. It is true her anger flared up for a second when her befogged eye rested on the secretary, but what did that matter, since she made no remark on the nature of the paper being witnessed? The next moment she had forgotten Elsie Dilworth, forgotten Gaylord, forgotten all she had been doing. The will had been duly signed, and was now in Blundell's pocket.

The actual murder requires little mention. Blundell obtained his small parcel of grated aconite-root from Haji, who went into the country to obtain a fresh plant. Haji, completely in the solicitor's power and dependent on his bounty, could not well refuse orders. He passed the parcel to Blundell in a lonely spot in the park, and was not once allowed to come near either the Fetter Lane office or the flat. As Blundell himself did the carving he found no difficulty in dropping a little shredded aconite into the remainder of sauce on Rose's plate. The whole thing was simplicity itself—and yet, out of the very convenience of opportunity the secretary, self-invited to the scene, got her first important "hunch!"

Elsie Dilworth, be it understood, was the one unforeseen spoke in Blundell's wheel. We now turn to her part in the affair.

CHAPTER FORTY-THREE

ELSIE Dilworth's reactions may be easily imagined when, having watched Adrian Somervell establishing himself—as she thought—in his stepmother's good graces, she was called on to witness a will presumably in her employer's favour. If Blundell did not benefit by this will, then why had he taken such pains to type the document himself? Why had he passed her by and sent for the less-intelligent cook to act as witness? And why—most significant in retrospect!—had Mrs. Somervell looked so queer and sluggish, as though completely indifferent to what she was signing? To Elsie's mind something was being wangled by trickery. The conclusion she drew was the obvious one—for what man plays a trick not to his own advantage?

There was another reason for her belief. Blundell, excellent master and generous to a fault, had the weakness of the inborn gambler. Usually he was successful, but all gamblers come croppers, and it was no secret from her that for some time past her employer had been living on a banker's overdraft. Elsie had seen him sacrifice large blocks of shares at a loss, and could only suppose some secret drain on his resources. In early November a mortgage on the Queen's Close property was under consideration, and the Berkshire cottage was up for sale, although Blundell spoke of purchasing a more pretentious country place, perhaps to allay doubts as to his financial position. For some time past conferences had been held at the flat. Her services were not required, and no records of business conducted on these occasions ever met her eye. Like Rose, she suspected a private venture; but from her superior knowledge she deduced a failing venture entailing possible bankruptcy and the pressing need of an inheritance which, since the advent of a rival, might easily pass into other hands.

After Mrs. Somervell's sudden death Elsie recalled the horseradish sauce, the will just executed, Blundell carving beef at the sideboard. Horseradish—aconite! Were Rose Somervell's symptoms like those vividly described in the novel she had been reading? They were. The old woman murdered for her money—money which should, would indeed, have been Adrian's, but for a wicked, underhand ruse. All Elsie's pent emotions of anger and vindictiveness rose up and swept her like a tornado. She conveyed her story to the Home Office, protecting herself against the possibility of error by withholding actual names, and begging her name to be kept dark till events proved her surmise correct.

Immediately afterwards Blundell's letter to Adrian, dictated to her, dealt her a staggering blow. Blundell did not benefit by this death. On the contrary, it was Adrian. Was Adrian a murderer? If murder had been committed, then he must be. However, Elsie still loved Adrian with an insane passion which nothing could change. She even saw in this débâcle a chance of claiming him for her own; but, meantime, till murder was proved certain, she tried by more questioning of Petty to assure herself the death had been natural. Lingering in the kitchen passage the afternoon of Mrs. Lake's call she heard about the tingling sensation the victim had mentioned soon after eating. She also heard Blundell suggest handing Mrs. Lake the two pieces of jewellery, and remembered the incident when the news of the second murder reached her ears.

That evening, on seeing the papers, Elsie rushed to the hospital with her mad-sounding proposal of flight. She accurately construed Adrian's outraged manner and fled, appalled by the conviction that she had prepared a trap for an innocent man. Powerless to stop the machinery she herself had set in motion, she now lived in hell. Murder had been done. To repeat verbatim her guarded story at the inquest could only turn against Adrian, whereas to state openly that she had meant to accuse a different person would only incur Blundell's enmity. Blundell, in any case, would soon discover the part she had played and guess her mistaken reasoning. In the murder of Margaret Fairlamb she read both a sequel to the former death and a terrible warning to herself. From now onward Elsie was mortally afraid. There seemed but one course open to her—to resign her post and go into hiding. She promptly did so, but made furtive, desperate attempts to right matters.

Cudgelling her sick brain day and night she evolved a theory as to why, if not for money, Rose Somervell had been killed. By what steps she worked it out cannot be known, but, anyhow, very soon she began buying current and back issues of Limpsfield newspapers, choosing those which especially featured the Penge Plan. On the eve of quitting London, she visited Blundell's flat to search for incriminating data, and the Somervell flat to try once more to discover the former will she believed Blundell had been hoping to unearth. Finding the upper floor occupied, she made off, not, however, taking with her Diana's three letters. This theft will presently be explained.

Elsie's despair on reading that aconite had been discovered in Adrian's clothing may be guessed from her abortive attempt to take her life. She could not bring herself to gash her throat deep enough; and now, recovering some balance, she began her feverish wanderings about the south and west of England, wherever Penge highways were being laid out, trying by hook or crook to place her finger on something fraudulent in the scheme. It is unlikely she dug up one iota of proof. At best she may have collected certain stray facts which she hoped might be turned to account by a qualified detective; and with this in mind she wrote oft to Blanche Ackland, assuming her to be Adrian's fiancée, and proposed a meeting. Coming face to face with Diana Lake instead of the expected American girl gave her a ghastly shock. Diana was Blundell's goddaughter. With her mother dead and her father gone to California, where was she living? The answer confirmed Elsie's worst fear. Diana it was who had taken over Mrs. Somervell's flat. This meant she trusted Blundell and confided in him, therefore to speak freely to her was tantamount to informing Blundell—and once Blundell knew—!

Perhaps all along Elsie instinctively realised her employer's hidden potentialities. Certainly at this moment she had a horrible prevision of her own fate; yet the desire to save Adrian was strong. How could she give Diana any information without signing her own death warrant? Whatever move she made, she was caught. One can now see the reason for her last actions. She may have planned, when at a distance, to post Diana some explanation to supplement the newspapers. As she was prevented from doing anything at all, we may leave the problem of her future intentions and pass to Margaret Fairlamb.

When Blundell learned of Rose's telephone conversation, he was seized with panic. Already he had been worried lest Rose's silly tongue had made some betrayal to Margaret. The latter's embarrassed hesitation convinced him that over the telephone things had been said which, if repeated, would wreck his whole carefully laid scheme. Rose's body was about to be opened. Since he had not been able to subject Rose to the treatment given Frieda Klapp, solid matter might remain in her system. If Adrian were accused of murder, his champion, Margaret, would bring out everything she knew in her efforts to save him. She suspected foul play—he saw it in her slight avoidance of his eye; and he believed she was making shrewd guesses as to what had happened. Unlucky Margaret! She was only trying to spare his feelings by not telling him about Rose's absurd jealousy of his secretary; but Blundell, misreading her evasions, decided on the spot that she must be removed immediately—if possible before she saw the evening papers; at any rate, before she had a chance to discuss the exhumation with any one close to her.

Chatting with her, he roughed out his plan. Having handed over Rose's jewellery and seen the roll of banknotes in her bag, he drove her home and stayed with her till Herbert was gone. The unexpected encounter with Diana, whom he had supposed to be away, shook him badly. Plainly she had not read the news about Rose, but even so he mistrusted what her mother might say to her. Unable to prevent the meeting, he made straight for the Home Office and acquired what merit he could by reporting what the dead woman had said to her friend. He then returned to his flat to receive Lord Limpsfield and Sir Norbury Penge.

During the evening the two guests were supplied with cigars which the host had strongly impregnated with scopolomin. The drug was now going to be put to a dangerous test. At a quarter-past eleven Blundell opened the sliding section of bookshelves, keeping close watch on the men's faces. Neither betrayed the least surprise. He put a few questions, the answers to which assured him he could proceed with safety. He effected his exit by way of the upper flat, the slightly deaf Petty having long been asleep; at some distance along the Park picked up a taxi and within a few minutes was walking from the Marble Arch to Seymour Square. Entering Margaret's house by ringing the Cathcart bell he hid under the staircase to await the actress's return. The rest was simple. The weapon he used was a leaden paperweight contained in a sock, which he afterwards burnt.

He had been absent a little more than half an hour. The moment of his re-entry into his library was nerve-racking, but a glance removed his fears. There sat his guests, stodgily smoking, both prepared in all confidence to swear, if need be, that the third of the party had been with them all the time, or at most had quitted the room for only a moment or so. In other words, they had registered impressions, but not retained them. Gradually they revived to find business discussion still in progress. If later on they should puzzle a bit over their after-dinner somnolence, Blundell knew they could be trusted. The last thing either wanted was that his colleague in a nefarious enterprise should be under any sort of cloud.

Blundell remained slightly uneasy over Herbert Lake and his daughter. He schemed to get them both to Hollywood, and Diana, by her refusal to stir from London, revealed to him her attachment to Adrian. Quite likely she knew nothing, but she was a clever, biased girl who always had been antagonistic towards himself. If she would not go away, then she must be carefully watched, muzzled by bounty, and given no chance to work against him. He must first gain her confidence, and this done he must get her out of her own flat and into Rose's, where he could keep her under his eye. In contriving these things he used the diplomacy of which he had become past master. Knowing that for the present Diana would have very little money and would not feel inclined to resume her stage work, he sought out a young couple recently in Limpsfield's employ and begged them to help him in a little conspiracy. They would like a better home, wouldn't they? Very well, then, they were to offer Miss Lake six guineas a week for her flat, and he would pay two-thirds of the rent on the understanding that Miss Lake was not to know. She was a proud girl, he explained, and would not take help unless it were suitably camouflaged. The young people, most naturally, were delighted to move into a flat so far superior to any they had known. Diana thankfully accepted their offer, and, as has been seen, was persuaded to fall in with her godfather's wishes.

She was now to some extent in Blundell's hands. In the beginning, when she was driven out in the Sunbeam car, her benefactor followed in his two-seater to see where she went. It was he who took the letters she so firmly believed Elsie had stolen. The fact was, Blundell had been bothered about these same letters from the moment he had set eyes on them. It will be recalled that he came with his proposal about Herbert when she was sorting her mother's old correspondence, and that he had seen her slip two letters of Rose's into her bag. If letters are preserved, he argued, there must be a reason. In his library, the morning of Herbert's departure, he calmly abstracted the sheets from the handbag lying on the table, in full sight of Diana—while she smoked. In one letter was a reference to Sir Francis Dugdale; in Margaret's, a hint to show the writer's expectation that he, Blundell, would inherit Rose's money. All three were better burned, and burned they were.

Soon Blundell was satisfied that Diana represented no element of danger; but during the visit to the prison he overheard a disturbing remark. Why had the girl not told him her idea about her mother's murder hinging on the other crime? It struck him she might be playing a deeper game than he had supposed. He resolved to clinch the robbery explanation once and for all, to which end he dispatched his tool, Haji, to Amsterdam, with instructions. A pawnbroker of shady repute was bribed to let the ring and brooch be discovered in his shop. The Dutch police fell on them without delay—and Blundell, his mind at rest on one count, turned to the remaining source of danger—Elsie Dilworth, whose latest London address he now knew.

By this time several mysteries were clear to him. He perceived what no one else had yet realised, that his secretary, labouring under a natural misapprehension, had meant to incriminate not Adrian but himself. He guessed why she was hiding, and understood the purpose of her rummage through his papers—contrived, incidentally, with an extra set of keys she had had duplicated from his own. Somehow, Elsie had got on the track of his secret activities. She was trying now to secure proof, and although she would undoubtedly fail, she would, in the last extremity, raise the sort of hue and cry best calculated to start a governmental investigation. He sent Haji to Floyd's Square to ascertain whether she intended to return to her lodgings, and if her room contained a gas-fire. Haji was to gain occupancy of the room, if only for a short time, and conduct a careful search of whatever Elsie had left behind; but Haji was unsuccessful. He was growing nervous about undertaking further commissions, and Blundell, troubled about the Dutch visa on his passport, agreed to pay his passage back to Bombay on the boat sailing next day, provided Haji would perform two additional services.

The fact was that Blundell felt it vitally important to know precisely what Diana was going to divulge in her first interview with the private detective. He also wanted Haji to break into Mrs. Eales's house from the rear and ransack Elsie's trunk. It is probable that at this point his vision went wild through excess of apprehension; but be that as it may, he made stupid moves, which he was soon to regret. First of all, he did not know that Haji, through Woodford, had come to frequent the tea-rooms which all the Prince Regent's staff patronised and where Diana and Adrian had been accustomed to meet. On the face of it, the Indian seemed to him a perfectly safe individual to employ as a spy, and yet he was spotted by Bream, recognised by Diana, and the clue to his identity quickly seized! That was bad enough, but the midnight venture in the Islington alley was notably worse. The luckless Haji was seen and almost collared by the very detective whose suspicions he had aroused. The report of these things, received at three in the morning, convinced Blundell of a very real peril. At any moment now the business of Frieda Klapp would be dragged to light, the similarity between her death and Rose's remarked upon. It was not enough for Haji to quit the country. A wireless message to the boat would reveal the Dutch visa on the fugitive's passport. Haji himself might easily be terrorised into damaging admissions. To Blundell it was all-apparent that the Indian had served his full term of usefulness and must be eliminated with all speed.

He advised Haji to reach Tilbury by an early train, see his luggage aboard, and come ashore. He, Blundell, would drive down and meet him, to hand over the promised cash payment; but he must make sure of Haji's departure, and not, as he put it, be led up the garden path. The two must not be seen together, therefore they would meet in a lonely lane outside the town. Rather than forgo his remuneration Haji agreed to the arrangement, which, indeed, seemed quite reasonable. The morning was foggy. There was a surprise onslaught, an unequal struggle, and the Indian lay dead in a ditch, shot by his own pearl-handled revolver.

His passport was removed, his dead fingers closed on the weapon, and no marks or prints left behind to show that murder had been committed. Doubt did arise, but like other doubts it led to nothing tangible.

Elsie, meantime, continued to elude capture. Blundell believed now that she meant to keep in seclusion till the trial opened, then claim police protection while she gave evidence. That evidence—what would be its nature? Impossible to say, but enough that it would set going the inquiry which sooner or later would prick the vast bubble of the Penge Scheme. Elsie must go. The verdict must be suicide, for which belief her seemingly erratic behaviour had so luckily paved the way.

The Floyd's Square house became familiar to Blundell during repeated prowlings by day and by night. Once he made use of the hidden latch-key, saw the gas-fire he had hoped to find, also the trunk which, though unimportant of content, argued its owner's intention to return. When Mrs. Eales and her little boy went away, he read the note left for the home-coming tenant, and knew his reward was at hand. Next evening, getting off early from the dinner he was attending, he again entered the dark, empty house, replaced the key in its hiding-place, and in the gloom of the upper room saw the two unpacked bags. So Elsie had arrived and gone out. He waited for her to come in, never dreaming of the meeting between her and Diana, or the fact that at this moment she was depositing a parcel of newspapers at King's Cross.

He heard her letting herself in, and made ready for her. No sooner had her dim form appeared in the doorway than he forced her powerfully against the wall, and with one hand pinioning her two gloved ones, held his pad of chloroform within an inch of her mouth and nostrils. She struggled violently, but was no match for his strength. One stifled scream she gave as the vapour gagged her, and presently—an age it seemed—her convulsive movements ceased. He had gone far enough. No more chloroform must be administered, or signs of it might be detected. He laid her unconscious body on the floor facing the hearth, removed her hat and gloves, and for a second put on the light to inspect her. Not a bruise. He adjusted a cowl of paper round her head, turned the gas full on, and left her to die of asphyxiation.

It was his own idea. Would it serve? Chloroform—which he had not to purchase especially, since he used it to clean his pipes—was so volatile that the small amount he had employed would be swamped in an atmosphere long charged with coal-gas. Ether, on the contrary, would have clung and announced its presence above the other fumes. Much sooner than he had anticipated the room was entered. He had a frightening period till he knew for certain the chloroform odour had escaped detection, indeed, till he learned there would not be an autopsy. Then he relaxed and hugged himself. He had committed four murders, two of them extempore affairs, yet in no instance had he left one shred of evidence traceable to himself. A splendid achievement! Nicholas Blundell, respectable solicitor, was a Napoleon of crime, as of strategy.

His exultation was marred by only a single regret, a bitter one, when we consider his peculiar, though typical, weaknesses. There was no one, no one to whom he could recount his triumphs. To the end his supreme cleverness must go unapplauded. When one of his occasional paroxysms of blind rage allowed him to give himself away to Diana the circumstance must have brought him a glorious relief. Now, at last, he could recount his exploits and do so with utter safety.

CHAPTER FORTY-FOUR

"OILED hinges," mused Inspector Headcorn with the mellow detachment of one whose mental hinges are becoming well lubricated. "I dare say, if the truth were known, the victim had amused herself at that eavesdropping game a time or two before anything came of it. Blundell shouldn't have spirited away that oil bottle so late in the day. It might have meant nearly as bad a slip as neglecting to look to his locks and bolts before holding a board-meeting—eh, Bream?"

"I'm not the one to cast stones at him for that last bit of carelessness," answered the agent ruefully, and as he spoke he laid a gingerly hand on his wounded thigh. "Considering the late hour and the fact that Miss Lake was supposed to be doped he'd better excuse than I had for my little slip."

"Mightn't these affairs have presented us with fewer dead-ends," ventured Colin, refilling glasses, "if, shall we say, some *rapprochement* between the law and the freelance had been possible?"

Bream chuckled.

"The more we got together, the happier we should be. Is that your idea, Inspector?"

Headcorn coughed austerely, then relaxed into a smile as he replied that their one infringement of professional etiquette had been singularly ill-starred.

"So it was," agreed Bream. "And I doubt if the soundest united front could have led us beyond the hypothetical motive each of us could image while sitting in his own arm-chair. Uncovering the Penge fraud wouldn't have proved Blundell guilty of murder—and how long would it have taken us to uncover it? If Blundell ever purchased a foot of land in his own name I've not been able to locate it. He had his men of straw acting for him, and he was protected at all points. No, a non-professional deserves all the kudos in this case." Gallantly he raised his fourth dose of the Ladbroke prescription towards the girl in the bed. "I take pleasure in saying it—and I beg leave to drink to her good health and future happiness!"

"And so say all of us," grunted the Inspector, tilting his glass. "My congratulations, Miss Lake."

Diana blushed warmly and avoided Adrian's eyes—a needless proceeding, as it happened.

"And how much health or future anything should I have had but for you others?" she retorted. "Meddling's not clever. I had a luckier break than my predecessor had, but that's the most you can say."

"One thing's always puzzled me," remarked Colin, measuring more gin into the shaker. "Why didn't Blundell have Mrs. Somervell's body cremated?"

"I'll answer that one," said Diana promptly. "She wanted to be buried in that Berkshire churchyard, under a particular willow-tree. She had her mind set on a pink marble tombstone, with a list of her famous parts inscribed on it. It wouldn't have looked well, would it, to disregard her known wishes?"

"Besides," put in Adrian quietly, "once that rather fuzzy-headed diagnosis was given he'd no reason to suppose the death would be queried."

The others looked at him. It was his first contribution, and he still sat, constrained and with a faint suggestion of aloofness, elbows on knees, eyes for the most part directed at the floor. One would have said that during his time of solitary confinement he had lost the habit of speech.

"What you say brings up another small point," said Colin. "Do you suppose Blundell timed the thing to occur while Mrs. Somervell's own doctor was out of town?"

Adrian had no idea; but Bream gave a knowing nod.

"With no wish to be quoted," confided the latter, "this much I'll tell you. Cross, the partner they called in, is Blundell's G.P.—and when I talked to him, and again at the Old Bailey, I got a very strong impression that in some ways he's indebted to his patient. Now, then, would a man in that position, hoping for further benefits, be anxious to cause inconvenience? Remember, he knew these two were on fairly intimate terms, and he didn't know anything about the disposition of property. My notion is he'd sign a comfortable death certificate and sit tight on any private views he might happen to hold."

Colin whistled.

"Not another one! Blundell seems to have made this a hobby." He turned to Diana. "Didn't you mention something of the kind?"

"But of course," replied Diana calmly. "It was his life policy. He took pains to describe to me exactly how he managed people and got them on his side. As an exhibition of self-conceit it was simply revolting, but it told me much more than he imagined. To my mind it all traces back to the crushing sense of inferiority he's always suffered from—for he has, you know, in spite of his bombast. It's been a life-long handicap. Without it, there'd have been no Penge plan—and no murders."

Colin understood, but as two of his guests looked slightly befogged, he bade Diana repeat the details of the long, self-revelatory harangue she had been forced to endure. Her eyes darkened and her colour came and went as she recalled it.

"He wanted me to know. You see, I was one of the stiff, English snobs who'd always looked down my nose at him." She laughed a little, and continued: "Every one did that, it seems, when he first reached London, years ago, and saw himself regarded as a rough, Colonial outsider. He laid a definite campaign to beat down prejudice. He said the great lesson he'd learned was that every human being had his price—that you had only to discover what his particular weakness was and cater to it in order to disarm him and make him your slave. Money, he declared, would buy whatever a man wanted—respect, position, popularity. It might mean you had to juggle accounts in order to spend, but so long as you spent wisely you'd get it all back with interest."

"So that's it!" exclaimed Bream, remembering his conversation with the head clerk in Fetter Lane. "If he helped a lame dog over a stile it was because that dog would fawn on him afterwards, maybe bite the hand that attacked him. It was a system, then, his placing every one round him under some sort of obligation. Well, I can quite see it paid. The secretary, to be sure, turned out a bad investment, but you can hardly blame him for not foreseeing the complication in her case."

"Of course it paid. He had a whole army of devoted allies; but the great thing was it made him feel himself a super-man, holding the strings, making people dance to his tune, and despising them for it. He told me Lord Limpsfield himself was under his thumb. Sir Norbury Penge was just an attractive lay figure, boosted into the limelight, but controlled from behind scenes. Why, even Sir Kingsley Baxter he regarded as his to command! It's a kind of madness with him. What's the word for it— megalomania?"

"I imagine he guaranteed counsel's fees so he could prevent any newspaper from publishing Doctor Somervell's story," said the agent reflectively.

"Exactly, but wasn't it simply a large edition of the good turn that bought the friendship of Dame Charlotte Moon? Look at that for a stroke of genius! Dame Charlotte's respectability acts like a hypnotic spell."

"Speaking of spells," broke in Colin, "how many of us taxpayers ever thought to inquire who'd created this new Ministry, or the man to fill it? For that matter, wasn't it sheer hypnotism that made the man in the street accept unquestioningly these thousand and one unwanted highways?"

"Hear, hear!" rumbled the Inspector. "The scheme could only have been worked with the press behind it. There's power for you! You've only to print a thing to have half the public believing it. Print it often enough and with big headlines, and the whole population will be willing to bleed and die for its faith."

"Limpsfield, I take it, means to fight to a finish?"

"We'll be grey beards before he gives in," declared Headcorn with conviction. "You'll see, there won't be one scrap of paper brought into court. A blessing for us we'd a spot-charge to prefer against Blundell. Otherwise this young lady's account wouldn't have commanded such immediate respect." With a deeply regretful sigh he stretched and rose from his chair. "Oh, well, I suppose my duties are calling me! Coming my way, Mr. Bream?" When the two detectives had set off together in touching harmony, Colin asked his remaining guest whether, on the fatal Sunday, he had indulged in any of Blundell's tobacco.

"One cigar," answered Adrian. "He pressed it on me after lunch; but I'm never very strong on cigars. I chucked half of it away in the entrance to this building."

"Did it make you sleepy?"

"As hell. I thought it was the food."

"And you weren't wearing an overcoat, were you? That settles it. He planted the stuff on you in the car."

Colin reached the depleted shaker, and tipped a small dividend into Adrian's empty glass. "What told you it was Blundell and not one of the others?" he inquired.

"I don't quite know." Adrian sat as before, but considered the question. "Even now it's a hard thing to analyse the feeling I had about him. He was too friendly, too officious. I kept wanting to shove him off."

"Whole races have been hated for less," commented Colin. "*Timeo Danaos et dona ferentes* puts it rather neatly, I fancy; but did the will business strike you as phoney?"

"What if it did? I couldn't find anything wrong about it. No one could. She was sane, the thing was properly vouched for. It didn't make sense for Blundell to be forcing her money on me, even assuming he could have managed it—which there was no proving. There wasn't a darned thing I could say. So I saved my breath."

He finished with a chary gesture. The silence which fell was singularly awkward for all three.

"Do you know," said Diana hesitatingly, "I got another quite unintentional revelation from him. It showed me his feeling for her. It was a real feeling, you understand. Or don't you?"

Both men looked at her. It was the first time Adrian had done so openly, and his level, steady gaze embarrassed her strangely.

"I'm sure I'm right," she hurried on with an effort. "You see, with all her beastly little faults—maybe because of them—he worshipped her. To him she was and always had been his idea of what Woman should be, far above him, unattainable—for I can still swear she never gave him anything. He didn't expect it; but all those years of unselfish devotion, when he was making himself just a door-mat for her to walk on, he was pathetically hoping to win from her some—some genuine regard. At last he believed he had won it. It might be because she was getting old and receiving less attention, but that didn't spoil his triumph. He believed he had got the one thing his money couldn't buy."

She paused and drew a deep breath.

"And then, with one brutal stroke, she disillusioned him. In the library that night she showed him that all, all she cared about was what he could do for her in a material way. It put him back at the foot of the ladder. He saw himself as just crude, good-natured Nick Blundell, the solicitor she'd found a convenience—and it broke him. After that he took delight in planning to kill her. Killing for its own sake became a joy. I saw it in his eyes while he sat there making ready the chloroform pad that was going to finish off his last victim—me."

Colin saw Adrian remove his spectacles and polish them carefully on his handkerchief. The moment had come, he decided, to relieve this diffident couple of his presence.

"Well, well!" he said, rising. "Fascinating though this is, it's just occurred to me I may have some forty odd patients waiting for me to look in on them. Will you two carry on while I make my rounds?"

As he reached the door Adrian got up and followed him out. Gone—and without a word? With a hard lump in her throat Diana told herself that he could not face being alone with her, and that it was entirely her fault. Yet even so, how preposterous, how unthinkable for him to . . .

The door reopened, and screened by the largest mass of early daffodils she had ever seen in one person's grasp Adrian appeared. He deposited his burden on the bed. The cool blooms covered her like a golden fleece. She gasped and buried her face in them.

"Adrian! How like you! And with me here thinking—thinking—"

She laughed, sobbed, and could not go on.

"Thinking," he repeated woodenly, "that a Godforsaken chump like me would do well to clear out for good and all. Was that your idea?"

She looked up at him, and fear took her again.

"What are you trying to say to me, Adrian?" she faltered. "Whatever it is, get it over. I shan't—mind."

He hesitated.

"You're realising, then, that this darned money may not be mine after all. As it wasn't a voluntary will, I don't suppose the courts will uphold it, if it's contested by the next of kin."

Was that all? He couldn't be so stupid!

"I have thought of it," she answered tentatively. "But why bring it up now?"

"Why? Because it means just this—that I'm in rather a worse hole than I was before all this happened. I tried to set you free when I saw what you'd been let in for. There's a better reason now. I've nothing to offer you. You understand that, don't you?"

She had grown very white. It was his way of telling her what she had long ago guessed.

"Of course, dear," she replied after a moment. "I understood that evening at the hospital; but please don't imagine I blame you; we can't help these things. Better go now."

He did not move.

"Wait a minute. I don't get this." He frowned down on her. "How do you mean, you understood that evening? Understood what?"

She shook her head mutely. Oh, why wouldn't he leave her?

"Actually," she heard him mutter, "things aren't quite hopeless with me. I got a cable this morning about a Baltimore post I can walk straight into; but it's only a start, and after what you've gone through, can I ask you to face any more trials? Not possibly."

Light shone on her. With the corners of her mouth faintly twitching, she answered steadily:

"Perhaps it will be better to call it off. I've agreed, haven't I? Now kiss me good-bye."

Their eyes met, hers inscrutable, his mystified, troubled. Awkwardly he leant over. His lips touched hers, withdrew. A queer spasm of question crossed his face. He kissed her again—and this time the crushed daffodils slithered to the floor as his arms closed roughly round her body.

"But, Adrian," she whispered, "if you don't want me, why—"

"Oh, what the hell?" he silenced her. "We can talk any time . . ."

THE END

Printed in Great Britain
by Amazon

22098225R00136